Dark
ECHO

Also by F. G. Cottam

The House of Lost Souls

Dark ECHO

F. G. Cottam

Thomas Dunne Books
St. Martin's Press
New York

This is a work of fiction. All of the characters, organizations, and events portrayed in this novel are either products of the author's imagination or are used fictitiously.

THOMAS DUNNE BOOKS.
An imprint of St. Martin's Press.

www.thomasdunnebooks.com
www.stmartins.com

Library of Congress Cataloging-in-Publication Data

Cottam, Francis, 1957–
Dark echo / F. G. Cottam. — 1st U.S. ed.
p. cm.
ISBN 978-0-312-54433-1
1. Yachts—Fiction. 2. Psychological fiction. I. Title.
PR6103.O88D37 2010
823'.92—dc22
2010019813

First published in Great Britain by Hodder & Stoughton, an Hachette Livre UK company

First U.S. Edition: August 2010

10 9 8 7 6 5 4 3 2 1

For my lovely sister, Kate

Prologue

Rouen, September 1917

Captain Destain was with Sergeant Boulez on the steps at the western entrance to the cathedral when the mist came in. They were sharing coffee brewed at a stall in one of the warren of streets surrounding the great building. He was adamant that neither man had ever in their lives seen the like of this fog. It funnelled and unfurled through the cramped thoroughfares, obscuring detail and devouring space. Destain described it as roiling and impenetrable, worse than anything he had ever encountered before near the sea, in such ports it had been his experience to visit as Antwerp or Zeebrugge. It was palpable, this fog.

Had his men not been such experienced fighters, he thought some of them might have slipped on their gas masks in panic, believing it a chemical attack launched from long range by the heavy German artillery. But they had not heard the whistle of shells that morning. There had been no bombardment from the German front, forty miles to the east. And as they were shortly to come to learn, it was not gas that was attacking them.

Boulez was a mountain man. He had been born and grown up in a village high in the French Alps, where his father had taught him, hunting with an antique flintlock, the marksmanship for which he was so distinguished in the corps. He had an Alpine appreciation of weather, a mountain man's caution and hard-earned expertise. He described the fog as something similar to the mantle of invisibility that descends sometimes at altitude. It was so sudden and impenetrable that your instinct, caught in it, was to drop on all fours like a frightened animal to the safety and security of the snow powdering the earth. Except that there was no snow on the steps of the cathedral in Rouen in September. And according to Boulez, what differed about this phenomenon of the weather was that it was not the familiar, goose-feather grey of the high Alps. It was black in its swirling origins.

Destain had always maintained to his men that the cathedral was not a fortress. You could garrison a cathedral. But you could not make impregnable a building to which all were welcome by the very nature and purpose of its existence. The rich and the poor, the infant and the elderly, they were indiscriminately invited here to worship. In war even more than in peacetime, the role and symbolism of the cathedral as a place of spiritual solace had itself to be sacrosanct.

Nevertheless, the cathedral was heavily fortified. Destain's men were crack troops, well trained, vigilant. They were at company strength. There were eight men altogether at the western façade, two marksmen atop the Saint-Romain Tower to its right and two up in the Beurre Tower to its left. There were units of three guarding each of the north and south portals and there were a further two sentinels at the entrance to the cathedral vault. All were armed with a carbine and a heavy calibre cavalry pistol issued to them because their fighting might have to be done at close quarters. Each man was equipped with a bayonet and a fighting knife. They were not complacent. And they were contented in their duty. The men had been hand-picked for their piety as well as their prowess in combat. They believed the thing they protected was worth the fighting and, if necessary, the dying for.

But you cannot turn a cathedral into a fortress, as Destain

kept repeating afterwards in his grief and shock, as the gangrene slowly devoured him in his hospital bed. And you should not be expected to fortify such a place against men wearing the uniform of your own allies in battle.

The Americans came grinning through the mist. The defenders of Rouen cathedral and the sacred relic it housed smelled before they saw the Americans. They smelled the cloying sweetness on their breath of the gum the Americans habitually chewed on their marches. This clue to them was all the roiling mist at first allowed. But then, at last, the French defenders saw them.

They came on in their doughboy uniforms with the short coats worn over their britches and their spats and shiny leather boots and their stubby Garand rifles carried at port arms. The mist did not seem to disorient or discomfit them in the slightest. They glided through it and only when they were within whispering distance of the French troops guarding the cathedral did they raise their rifles and begin with deadly nonchalance to squeeze off rounds aimed squarely at their brothers in arms.

The fog had deadened the sound as well as the sight of their approach, Destain said. It muffled the reports of their bullets exploding from the barrels of their weapons when the ambush began and they started to shoot. It deadened the sound of rounds ricocheting off the cathedral's ancient masonry. It did not stop us firing back. The return fire, from the top of the towers in particular, was immediate and deliberate and murderous. The men at the portals quickly redeployed to reinforce their comrades. We established a withering field of fire. We were shooting at shadows, of course, but the very air was alive with the hum and screech of lethal projectiles. Nothing could have lived through such a sustained storm of assault. We fought the men of the fog with a blizzard of steel.

But the mutinous Americans came on. Incredibly, they ambled forward casual, alive. At their centre was a man taller than the rest of them and bare-headed. His white-blond hair picked him out in the wreaths of gloom with the haze of cordite thickening it even further in the firefight. He was a glimpse, a phantom. He was, said Destain, the pale, smiling rumour of a man. Destain took the cavalry pistol from the holster on his belt, aimed carefully and fired a round at the American. One was all he had time for. He pulled the stiff trigger once and felt the crash of recoil jerk through his wrist and forearm.

I had never been surer of a shot in my life. And I could shoot. And at that range, the weapon was always accurate. But I must have missed, he said. I must have missed. Because the American just grinned through the fog and raised his rifle and shot me through the shoulder with an impact that put me breathless and bleeding on my back on the cathedral steps. I began to lose consciousness. Sound, already dampened by the fog, became sluggish and indistinct and dim. A scarlet curtain descended over my sight. And then I smelled the mingling, pungent scents of cologne and Turkish tobacco as someone knelt beside me to whisper in my ear. And I knew it was the American renegade, invulnerable to our weapons, come to gloat. I understood English well enough. Of course I did. I had been listening to it spoken in France through three long years of war.

Not your day, sport, he said.

He used the language of a man who had just beaten a fellow member of his own sporting club in a Sunday bicycle race.

Not your day, old chum.

You'll burn in Hell, I told him. And I thought then he would take the pistol from his belt and finish me for the remark. But he merely laughed. It was a grim and callous sound, mirth echoing from an open crypt. It seemed barely human. It was a sound in utter contrast to the character of his words. Perhaps he was only impersonating a man. He was as unnatural, I think, as the fog that had announced and then delivered him. Last I heard the nailed soles of his boots, slick on the spilled blood of my comrades on the cobbles.

Of course, I knew what he had come there for, Destain said.

And the men at the captain's hospital bedside, the grim deputation from the Vatican watching the infection kill him, lowered their eyes as he and some of them crossed themselves.

And so I knew that he would, indeed, burn in Hell. One day and for ever, I knew that the smiling American would come to know damnation.

Martin

One

It was wholly in character for my father to buy a thing cursed. He didn't give a damn for dubious reputations. He believed in nothing he hadn't seen for himself or could not prove. Price was never a consideration either, I don't think, in determining what he chose to acquire, except when set very high. Then, his rapacious appetite for ownership could make a thing impossible to resist. Rarity tempted him. But he was a man, I think, without superstition and I'm sure, even thinking upon it now, devoid of remorse or even the subtler sentiment of regret. His famous nerve had enabled him to build his fortune. Every day that fortune swaggered and grew, his instinct gained a sort of strength and vindication. He was confident and fearless and his decisions were never reneged upon. Bidding at auction for the wreck of an unlucky boat was nothing to him and winning the auction was nothing short of what he would have expected. But what happened next surprised everyone. Perhaps it even surprised my father. I wish I had asked him. I fear I will not now ever get the opportunity. I don't know, though. When I think about what has happened subsequently, maybe that's actually a blessing.

I inherited neither my father's courage, nor his addiction to risk. And without his visceral need to make money, I have always been unproven in that accomplishment, too. By the age of seven or eight, I knew I was destined to be a disappointment to him. I did not share his reckless energy. I was a dreamy, reflective child. And so the precious hours away from business conquest that he devoted to his only son were understandably frustrating for him. In his time spent with me, he could transmit his will to compete to the arena of competitive games. He did it willingly, with relish and focus. But I never cared about who won our chess matches. He would murder me, across the board, and I would grin in goofy admiration. I can only imagine how it must have galled him.

One day, when I was about eleven or twelve, he took off his jacket after another predictable whitewash over a game of Scrabble or dominoes and rolled his sleeve and planted his bristling forearm from the elbow on the table top. I was looking at the bulging strength and sinew of the limb, wondering afresh at where a business tycoon like my dad acquired the muscle, when he said, 'Give me your hand.'

Dutifully, I clasped his palm. It was hard and calloused and dry. And it was another massacre as he slammed my knuckles against the polished oak. He fixed me with eyes of ageing emerald green and said, 'You've the strength of a butterfly, Martin. And about the commensurate will.' He rose, tiredly for my father, slowly. He took a handkerchief from his shirt pocket and wiped the stain of my weakness from his palm. 'When you can defeat me, you will have earned my respect,' he said. 'And who knows? Perhaps you will have earned your own.'

My father had boxed as a boy. More accurately, he had fought. His had been the sort of childhood poverty that announces itself in shoes with composite cardboard soles and clothing sourced through charity and invigorated through flat-iron steam and repeated darning. His appearance did not wash at the educational establishments his brains and a subsequent scholarship achieved for him. He was duly picked on. He was bullied. Out of necessity, he discovered he was handy with his fists. From being jumped in school lavatories and the dark corridors of dormitories, he progressed to the crested vest and ringside cheers of organised bouts. His old trophies, cheap things of plate nickel, are now priceless treasures, holy relics of his fabled past, taken from their cabinet in the library of our family home and faithfully polished by his housekeeper every day.

When I was twelve years old, he dragged the old priest who had trained him out of his seminary and devout retirement to train me too. Had he wanted a champion pugilist for a son, he could have afforded the greatest boxing trainer who ever lived. He could have got Brendan Ingle from Sheffield or Enzo Calzaghe from Wales. He could have gone to America, lured Angelo Dundee out of Los Angeles or sent to Boston for the Petronelli brothers, for Christ's sake. But though the old man wanted me competing, it was even more imperative to him that I would do so on the same terms as he had. So by virtue of the fact that he was still alive, of course, my own coach had to be Father O'Hanlon.

The priest appeared very old and impossibly grey, cajoled by my father back into his elderly tracksuit. The collar was frayed and the elastic perished at the wrists and ankles. The canvas of his plimsolls was the same parchment grey as his complexion. He looked fraught and reluctant under his threadbare, combed-over hair. I was dutiful on the hook and jab pads, half-hearted on the heavy bag and downright sloppy on the speedball. And at the end of the floorwork he put me through I sat next to Father O'Hanlon on a bench as steam expired off my shoulders through a blanket he'd given me against the cold in the empty gym one Cumbrian night.

A wizened hand clapped me on the shoulder. Its fingers gave the meat of me a squeeze. 'If your old man had possessed a fraction of your talent, son, he'd never have earned a penny on the markets,' O'Hanlon said.

I was intrigued by this claim. 'Why, Father?'

O'Hanlon slapped me on the thigh. 'Because he wouldn't have needed to. Because he'd have earned his fucking fortune in the prize ring.'

But things are never that simple. Life is not the movie we all wish in our most ardent and secret dreams it should turn out to be. I trained hard and scrupulously under O'Hanlon. And beneath his impoverished gym attire, I still hold he was as shrewd and thorough a trainer as any fighter could wish for. Under his fastidious tutelage, I reached the national finals of the ABAs. And, modesty aside, I did it without engaging in wars. I reached the final probably the hottest favourite to take the middleweight title for a decade. My father was ringside that night of course, his arm adorned by his most recent wife. He winked and she glittered at me as the opening bell sounded. And for two rounds everything followed my script as I creamed a switch-hitter from West Ham by the name of Winston Cory.

The haymaker from Cory that broke my nose and dumped me on the canvas on my backside in the third was the first punch I never saw and the last I ever took in an honest fight. I made the count, though. I was back on steady legs at the count of four. I knew already, from all my rounds of sparring with bigger boys, I could take a decent punch. I felt far more indignant than hurt. But I was haemorrhaging blood and they had no choice but to stop the bout. So I'd lost. Cory had won. I turned to my corner, to Father O'Hanlon, who looked at me the way a saviour must look when losing a promising soul to damnation.

In the movie version of this story, I know, of course, what happens next. The old man, unable to endure the taint of loss, shuns entirely his defeated son. He leaves his gorgeous floozie shivering at the kerbside waiting for their limo while he bursts into the winner's dressing room full of bonhomie and boisterous congratulation. He slaps backs and proffers cigars. Manly and magnanimous, he is the life and soul of the sweaty little victory celebration.

But it didn't happen like that in life. In fact, my father came in to me as my corner people struggled to staunch the bleeding and splint my nose. He took off his coat and dabbed at the damage with a towel. Blood from me sprayed and flecked at the starched white of his dress shirt. He did not seem to notice, or mind. His touch was so tender and solicitous that I almost wept at the unexpected intimacy of him there.

'You did your best, son,' he said, rising to go once the bleeding had stopped. 'You did your best. You lost only because he wanted it more.'

It was a truth as plain as it was devastating.

Years later, I heard that my father had subsequently given Winston Cory a job. More accurately, he had given him the sinecure that enabled Cory to train properly when he stepped up to international competition as reigning English champion. He held this fictitious position for a couple of years, apparently. He put the fact on record, thanking my father publicly, in a profile published in *The Times* when he came back from the Olympic Games with the silver medal he won there. But this isn't a story about pugilism. It isn't a story about Winston Cory, who broke my nose in the years before he turned professional and made his name and his not inconsiderable fortune out of it. It's a story about a boat, the man who came to acquire it and his son. It's about other things, too, other considerations and repercussions. But even at the time of writing this, I'm rather less sure about precisely what they might turn out to be. So let's just call it the story of a boat and the man for whom that boat became an obsession.

I think my father's retirement came as a surprise to everyone except himself. When I really consider it, I think it may have come as a surprise even to Dad. From the outside, the announcement was abrupt and shocking. To me, profit and publicity and the power and attendant adulation of his business success had been his rich, boiling lifeblood. So his retirement seemed less the abdication which it was described as, and more a sort of suicide. And his explanations for it had the forlorn style and scant logic of an attendant suicide note.

The only way I can rationalise it is to compare it to when a great champion quits at the top of his game. So Bjorn Borg walks to the courtside, and tosses his racquet on to his bag and peels off his headband, and even as the sweat of spent effort dries on his twenty-six-year-old body, he knows the flames fuelling the fire of his competitive soul have somehow been doused and he's had enough, for ever, of the effort required to triumph. I remember that. I'm thirty-two years old. I was six then, and like many boys of my own age, idololised the great Swede. He lost to the French left-hander Henri Leconte in a nothing tournament and the will to win just perished in him as he walked off the court.

Except that it happened to my dad when he reached the age of fifty-five and he announced to a stunned business press that he was relinquishing all commercial commitments in order to retire and sail a vintage boat. He would sail it to America, he said. He would sail his old schooner eventually around the world. But the Atlantic would provide sufficient challenge, he said, for the maiden voyage.

You have to picture the room. The announcement was made in the gilt and leather banqueting chamber at Stannard Enterprises. My father was flanked by the men hand-picked to sustain and expand the empire. But he was already history, bought out by the same conglomerate of venture capitalists whose advances he had scorned for years. The room seethed with pinstripe and polish and bold silk neckties and testosterone and it buzzed in the pockets of the seated reporters with the incoming email on their BlackBerries. The atmosphere was odd, my father's secretary later told me. And not only because she was the one female present. My father had been generous down the years with business tips for these men, many of those tips lucratively acted upon. They were, Sheila said, like well-dressed beggars summoned one last time to the table of a king traditionally munificent with the scraps from his feast.

Eventually, the fact that he really intended to do as he said sank in. They realised that he wasn't joking. One waggish reporter, perhaps familiar with Magnus Stannard's inexperience as a sailor, suggested Southampton to Cowes might be a more appropriate challenge. Laughter ensued. But the laughter was feeble. And it stopped altogether when my father raked the room with the stony sweep of his gaze.

'So far, I've lived every one of my dreams,' he said into the silence. 'Which is why you're all scribbling notations and I'm sitting here.'

They were stilled.

He smiled. It was his humble, self-deprecating smile. 'Look,' he said, 'if I'm realistic, there's a case for starting on the Norfolk Broads.'

They laughed. They roared with laughter. He had forgiven them.

His eyes brightened and softened under their brows. 'Boys,' he said. 'Boys. Where the hell has the fun ever been, merely in being realistic?'

Sheila told me the hardened business hacks rose as one to give him a standing ovation. It was spontaneous, she said, and fierce and prolonged. And there were tears in the room.

I did not need to ask if my father was among those who shed them.

* * *

The auction where he paid too much for his folly of a wreck was held at the boatyard of Bullen and Clore, just outside Portsmouth, on a cold and misty morning in January. My father requested I attend but, of course, we didn't travel down to Portsmouth together. I drove where he flew. He didn't even ask me to meet him at the heliport, preferring to take a taxi to the sale. When he arrived, without retinue and punctually, I was already there, cold and damp and bored from my tedious vigil on the dock.

Bullen and Clore; to me the name had been suggestive, when I'd first heard it, of a firm of Victorian undertakers. But when I got there, I saw that interring was actually the reverse of what they did. They specialised in salvage. Their business was summoning to an undead state the corpses of the shipping world. They raised and reclaimed sunken craft, or they rescued abandoned boats, or they provided refuge and repair for the terminally damaged and the derelict. In their domain of piers and pilings by the sea, you could hear the sound of great and mysterious chains, moaning at the pull of stupendous tides. Amid the iron hulks and sodden timbers, you could half imagine Isambard Brunel in his stovepipe hat, slipping on leather-shod boots in the ooze in the hours before his catastrophic stroke. The mist that day bled out all light and colour, rendering the scene at Bullen and Clore in the grainy sepia of a bleaker age.

The boat concerned in the sale was in dry dock. And it was a hull, more than it was a boat. I knew from my father's description that she was a two-masted, gaff-rigged schooner. Or she had been, in her prime. Time and neglect had torn the low roof from the area where the living quarters should have risen from the deck. Of the foremast, there was nothing remaining. And a storm had snapped the main mast. Its root rose thickly from the deck, cleaved in splinters about eighteen inches above a two-foot brace of corseting iron, the whole broken column about eight feet proud in total from the point where it emerged. That this damage had been done by elemental violence and not the deliberation of a boat-breaker's chainsaw was somehow a comfort.

My father slapped me on the shoulder. 'Gets to you quickly, doesn't she?' he said. Mist was pearling like dew on the wide shoulders of his coat and his breath already stank richly from the day's inaugural cigar. As usual, though, he was right.

It was the lines of her that did it. Even out of the water, she had this sweep of imperious elegance. The timbers of her hull were stained but sound-looking, apparently intact. Her deck, with its brass rail, was a low-sung hymn to grace. She was so beautifully proportioned that, even as a wreck, she seemed somehow poised and dignified. Maybe it was also that she was redolent of the wealth and glamour of the man who had commissioned and raced her. I knew from reading the literature in the sale catalogue that *Dark Echo* had been Harry Spalding's boat. But really, it was her lines. Even with her brass tarnished and her portholes canted or sunk altogether, you could imagine her under full sail on a glittering sea with the whitewashed walls of Cap d'Antibes or somewhere a brilliant promise under the sun on the horizon. It was quite something to picture that, standing on wet cobblestones in the prevailing gloom of Bullen and Clore's monochrome wharf on a winter day. But even beached and wrecked, even then, suspended above the ooze from ropes and chains, *Dark Echo* seemed to possess the power to summon dreams.

The auction took place in a dismal teak and mahogany room with high windows bleared by fog and rain. The room smelled of damp and turpentine. It felt chillier in there than it had outside. There were only two concessions in the room to modernity. On one wall hung an old and faded Pirelli calendar. According to the calendar, we were enjoying April of 1968. Boy, weren't we just! And there was a telephone on a desk by the auctioneer's podium. It was the old-fashioned kind, though, black and enormous and perhaps fashioned from Bakelite. Even in 1968, this instrument would have been borderline antique. The telephone was manned by a clerk in a cheap suit and plastered-down hair. The auctioneer was old and austere-looking. There were half a dozen people seated in the room, none but my father among them looking anything like someone with the means to be a potential buyer. And there was a boy with a notebook who did not remove his raincoat, whom I took to be from the local newspaper. The *Dark Echo* had little in her history to connect her to Pompey. The keel had been laid in Newport, Rhode Island, in 1916. But late and diminished in her long and sometimes illustrious life, here she had turned up. Bullen and Clore were a local firm. The boy might get a single column on a newspage about it. It might make a decent colour story or a snippet on a diary page. There was no photographer accompanying this cub reporter. Cheaper and more dramatic to use an archive shot of the vessel in splendour under full sail, I supposed.

I was right about the people there. There wasn't a single bid from the floor other than the bids made by my father. And my father did have to bid quite tenaciously, against someone on the telephone who seemed really to want the boat very badly indeed. My father went way above the reserve. But he was nothing if not stubborn, and his pockets were nothing if not deep, and he wanted the boat badly himself and he was not a man accustomed to coming second at anything. So he paid vastly over the odds and, when the gavel came down, turned and gave me a smile much more complex than the familiar smirk of triumph I'd expected to see. There was something odd in the smile I could not readily identify. Now, looking back with the clarity of hindsight, what I think flawed my father's smile that morning was an instinct almost wholly alien to him. I think, now, what cramped that victorious smile was an unfamiliar hint of trepidation.

This was immediately followed by another surprise. 'I'd be grateful if you would drive me to the heliport, Martin,' my father said. I nodded, rose and buttoned my coat, fingered the keys to my car and walked over and waited by the open office door while he granted a few quotes – gracious and witty, I was sure – to the lad from the local rag.

Out over on the dry-dock wall a man was supervising a team with a crane and hawsers, hitching a huge protective tarpaulin over the teak and oak cadaver for which my father had just paid a king's ransom. There, the fog was thickening. There were fifty feet of abyss between the wet cobbles on which the men stood and the bed of the dock, and they moved with deliberation. The man in charge wore a seafarer's cap and a reefer jacket over filthy overalls. The mist rolling off the sea was making a belligerent ghost of him as he barked instructions and pulled on the stub of cigar in his mouth, turning the burning end of it into a faint, fiery smudge of orange. He was unaware of me watching him, I think. When the task was done and his team of men turned away and retreated, enveloped by the grey air, he paused and looked at the still, enormous shape of the craft in its shroud. And he tossed the butt of his smoke over the wall of the dock into the mud far below and he crossed himself, once and deliberately, like a genuflecting Catholic at Mass. It seemed an incongruous thing to do, after the cursing and shouting that had chorused the task just completed. I thought perhaps it was just some obscure nautical tradition of which, like all nautical traditions, I was ignorant. Then he, too, was gone, swallowed by the fog. Bullen, if it wasn't Clore, I thought. Undertakerly reverence from one of the salvage bosses about to benefit from my father's ill-spent wealth. Then my father was at my side, taking my arm, a third surprise, for our walk to where I'd parked the car. Our route took us right past the *Dark Echo* in its vast canvas shroud. But he didn't even look at her. He looked straight ahead, the trepidation increasing to make a pale leer of what he probably thought was still his practised grin of triumph. My father was afraid, my instinct told me. He had taken my arm the way a frightened toddler might for comfort grasp his own father's hand.

By the time I had driven the distance to the heliport the fog had thickened to an extent that made taking off impossible. Even Magnus Stannard could do nothing about the official grounding of all flights.

'I'll drive you, Dad,' I said. I did not want the first day of his retirement proper sullied by any suggestion of defeat. I was a good driver. Even he would accede to that fact.

He looked at the Saab. And he sighed. 'I wish I'd bought you a better car,' he said. 'Remind me to sort you out a Jag or something.'

'I like my car. The Saab's fine,' I said.

'Fine if you're a Swede,' he said, getting back in. 'Fine if you follow the gospel of self-deprecation. Which the Swedes, as Scandinavians, have no recourse but to do.'

'As I remember,' I said, 'you chose the Saab for me.'

He laughed at that. He laughed, easily. We were getting on. I could still fuck it up by ramming someone's bumper in ten yards of soupy visibility on the motorway. But we were getting on, me and my dad. I felt a flush of pleasure. Gripping the wheel, God help me, I felt pride.

We dined together that evening. Suzanne was on a research trip to Dublin so I had nothing planned and no excuses to make to anyone. My father phoned his secretary on the journey back to London to make the necessary excuses to his most recent wife. Maybe a text message was too intimate a form of communication for my father. Maybe it was too modern. Obviously phoning her himself was totally out of the question. The early signs were not looking encouraging and, without taking my attention off the opaque view through the windscreen, I made a bet with myself that she would last no longer than her two immediate predecessors.

'I miss your mother,' my father said a minute later. His voice was weary with the burden of grief it always carried when the subject of Mum came up. 'God, Martin, I miss her so.'

'So do I,' I said, which was the truth. I drove on in silence. But though it was not easy, it was not in any way an awkward silence. It was simply that there was nothing further to be said on the matter. A dozen years on from her death, the loss of my mother felt no less shocking or abject. I could not resent him for words spoken straight from his heart. Nor could I offer a shred of consolation.

His mood improved over dinner. He seemed to recover something of himself after the first few sips of champagne.

'What do you know of Harry Spalding?'

'One of Hemingway's Lost Generation.'

My father frowned. 'What does that mean?'

'I don't know. He was a Dick Diver type, I suppose.'

'Dick Diver was a character from Scott Fitzgerald.'

'I know. But you know what I mean, Dad. He was one of those rich American expats who decorated the Riviera in the 1920s.' I wasn't entirely ignorant on this subject. It was a favourite literary sub-genre of Suzanne's. As if to prove the point, I said, 'There were any number of Harry Spaldings. Rich, feckless, sporting and with light artistic pretentions. Gerald Murphy would have provided the template. They summered in the South of France and wintered at Zermatt. Spalding played polo and won trophies at regattas aboard his celebrated boat.'

'You seem very well informed.'

'It was in the sale catalogue at the auction today.'

'Bullen and Clore are not historians, Martin. They are scavengers, the rag and bone men of the sea. Let me tell you about the real Harry Spalding.'

My father wasn't some tiresome autodidact. He was a scholarship boy who had shone very brightly, taught by the Jesuits at Ampleforth. But he had missed out on university and the consequent intellectual insecurity sometimes made him seem pompous when discussing academic subjects or in the cultural arena. He was inclined to be dogmatic, pious and pedantic. That said, Suzanne reckoned he possessed a first-rate mind and she had better credentials than anyone else I knew to be able to pass accurate judgement. But I had to wait for my lecture on the real Harry Spalding, because a waiter had stolen across the restaurant floor and stood at my father's elbow ready to take our order.

We were dining at the Kundan in Horseferry Road. It is an Anglo-Indian, about as discreet and expensive as a restaurant can get. Its core customers are high-ranking civil servants, senior parliamentary backbenchers and legal staff on hefty Whitehall retainers. My father had been coming here for years. In all that time, I doubt the menu had changed at all. I was reminded again that, for a man who set such store by certainty, the sea voyage he planned seemed wildly cavalier, really out of character. I remembered his expression, then, earlier on in the day, as we'd passed the shrouded boat.

It transpired that Harry Spalding was a hero of the Great War. He had started out as a lieutenant, leading a platoon of the infantry 'doughboys' from the States through the latter stages of the fighting in France and Flanders. Woodrow Wilson was the peace-loving American president who finally committed his country to the conflict. And he really was ardent about peace, dreaming up the League of Nations after the armistice to try to ensure that nothing like the war he embroiled his nation in would ever be repeated.

But the American troops in the field were far more influenced by the philosophy and fighting ethos of Wilson's less pacific predecessor, Theodore Roosevelt. Roosevelt had actually led a cavalry charge in the war against Cuba early in the century. He was belligerent, tough and unhesitating in his belief that, where American interests were concerned, might was always right. Teddy Roosevelt it was who established the huge forts where America's fighting forces learned their tactics and became battle-hardened. It was he who saw to it that the soldiers were properly paid and equipped with the best boots and the warmest blankets and the latest weapons technology.

When the call came in 1917, the Americans had to face veteran German divisions who had held their trench lines through four years of assault and counter-assault. But they were fit and confident and well drilled. They fought with courage and distinction. Even in an army that generally excelled, however, Lieutenant Spalding's exploits became the stuff of legend.

'Eventually, he was promoted to major and asked to lead a hand-picked team of fellow assault fighters,' my father said. 'In many ways, this outfit was the precursor of what today we call Special Forces. Rank was not an issue among these men. Class was not an issue. Spalding's own background was immensely privileged. He was the favoured son of one of the wealthiest families in American banking. But he was chosen on merit for his role in the field. All of them were. He led them.'

'Did they have a name? Did this unit have a designation?'

My father sipped champagne. 'They were called the Jericho Crew.' He reached inside his suit coat, brought out his wallet and took from it a picture he put on the white linen of the table between us. I picked it up and studied it in the subdued lighting of the Kundan interior. There was a candelabra on our table and I pulled it closer. The print was new but the picture, I knew, was ninety years old. The men in it were posed like a football team, half standing in a line behind those kneeling in front of them. All wore their hair brutally shorn. All were white and young. They were a hollow-eyed, savage-looking bunch, armed to the teeth with knives and knuckledusters and revolvers and short-snouted, heavy calibre assault rifles. You could judge the weight of shot by the thickness of the rounds wedged into bandoliers wound across their bodies from the shoulder. They all wore the same weird, infected grin. They looked like men drunk on killing. But I did not think this a verdict on the men in the photograph it would be wise to share with my father. I nodded in what I hoped would pass as a gesture of appreciation. But to me the men assembled in the picture looked like the sort of soldiers who sawed battlefield trophies from the extremities of the dead.

'Which one is Spalding?'

My father's forefinger extended over the print and he tapped a figure.

I should have guessed. Spalding, the well-born hero, was half a head taller than the rest. In those days, prosperity almost always translated into physical height. He was very slender. He was loose-limbed, with long thighs and supple fingers. His grin showed a jaw full of white, perfectly even teeth. He was a startlingly handsome man, when you really scrutinised his features. In conventional terms, his facial appearance was almost flawless. But there was nothing attractive about him at all. He seemed dangerous. You wouldn't want to meet him and, if you did, you wouldn't want to turn your back on him. I rubbed my eyes. Perhaps it was just the wine, drunk after a swift beer, itself swallowed after a long day and a tense, fog-hampered drive. I looked again at Spalding. But the effect was the same. The one word his photograph brought to mind, more than any other, was feral.

'Why the Jericho Crew?'

A shrug. 'Haven't been able to source an explanation for the name. Not a convincing one, at any rate. And the men in the picture have all been dead for far too long to provide it.'

Thank God, I thought.

'Wondered if Suzanne might be able to find that out for me.'

'If she can't, nobody can,' I said. 'She's in Dublin at the moment, digging up fresh revelations for a documentary film about Michael Collins.'

'There's no hurry,' my father said, taking back his picture. 'It's hardly important.'

I studied the wine in my glass.

'She's wasting her time, of course.'

'I'm sorry?'

'The Irish are a loquacious people. There is nothing about Michael Collins that we don't already know.'

Over our aromatic lamb and drily spiced chicken, he took me through the rest of Spalding's short and energetic life. The first significant thing he did in the peace was to survive the Spanish flu epidemic that killed something over half of his comrades on the steamer returning them home from France. In the years after the armistice, he took two six-month-long sabbaticals from the bank to sail his bright new toy. In the autumn of 1922, he could stomach the bank no longer and, to his father's apparent dismay, quit the commercial world altogether. Curiously, far from being cut off in the classic retaliatory manner, his already generous living allowance was increased to the point where he could afford to squander a literal fortune every month. He sailed his boat to Europe, a girlfriend crewing for him until she tired of life on the ocean and jumped ship, apparently jilting him for good, on the quay at Rimini. He gambled at the tables in Monaco, where he won. He berthed the boat for the winter and travelled to Paris, where he played tennis with Ezra Pound, and boxed a few inevitable rounds with Hemingway, and bought on a whim a polo pony he never rode and attended a séance conducted by the English black magician, Aleister Crowley. In the manner of all men quietly traumatised by the carnage of the trenches, he drank too much and spoke too recklessly and could discover no great hope or value or salvation in human life.

And how would he, I wondered on hearing this, inured to the practicalities of life by such fabulous wealth?

Spalding spent a period in the middle 1920s in England. He had put out on a jaunt from Dublin Bay and was forced for refuge to Liverpool by a storm that almost destroyed the *Dark Echo*. He found the climate, and perhaps the northern coolness of the people and their detachment, more congenial to his soul than continental Europe. This was the time of his winning things at Cowes and in other places, the great lines of his boat forming a familiar, celebrated shape against the dappled waters of the Solent.

In Cowes, his exploits on the water were still an awed folk memory among old salts whose grandfathers had piloted or crewed in races for Harry Spalding. They still talked about the way you had to watch out for his evil bull mastiff, Toby, should a chart be required and the aft cabin therefore need to be risked. And they still talked about tips aboard a winning boat so lavish that a man could spend the next six months idle, arse parked on the beach in a Ventnor deckchair.

There was amazement at the memory of the yachtsman Harry Spalding, but there was no fondness. And he had possessed no love for himself, it seemed. For in the cold

December of 1929, he had lain down in a Manhattan hotel with his boat berthed in the thickening ice of New York Harbour a mile and a half away and had put a bullet from his own gun into his right temple. He was thirty-three years old and made a beautiful corpse. Even the NYPD detective called to the scene to investigate said as much, seeing Harry in deathly repose. He looked serene in death. The only mark on him was the small hole left by the bullet and a dark, delicate halo of powder burn around the hole. There was no exit wound. The bullet had apparently lodged in his skull.

Having drunk too much to drive, I left the Saab on its meter and saw my father safely into a Mayfair-bound cab before walking across Lambeth Bridge to the home I shared with Suzanne on the other side of the river. When I got in and had taken off my coat, I looked into her tiny study and switched on the light. The air in her workspace retained the subtlest hint of her scent and I inhaled what there was of it gratefully. There were reference books in a line on the window sill with yellow slips of paper marking crucial passages. The award she had won for her work on a three-part documentary series on the elusive Rudolph Hess sat, a little silver-mounted perspex trophy, on top of her computer monitor. She had Blu-tacked it there, incredibly proud. The sight of it now made me smile. The wall she faced when she worked was a gallery of the gifted and the infamous whose mysteries she had worked hard to unravel. There was Auden and the Kray Brothers, and a pencil sketch of Christopher Marlowe and a sepia studio shot of Dan Leno in costume. Among the collage of pictures on the wall was the famous shot of Michael Collins, thin-lipped and preening in his leather gloves and army uniform as Chief of the Irish Free State, a Parabellum pistol swinging on his hip. I studied him. And the man who did for the Cairo gang in one bloody night of assassination looked a cosy sort of fellow altogether, when I recalled the picture I had seen earlier that evening of the Jericho Crew and their leader, Harry Spalding.

I noticed that the flowers in a vase sharing the sill with her books were dying. I would buy a fresh bunch to greet her return. I switched off the light, shaking my head. The flat felt very quiet and empty in Suzanne's absence from it. I closed the study door softly and went to fetch a glass of water from the kitchen. The spiced food and the beer and wine drunk with it would have made me seek water anyway, so close to bed. But it was my father's request, over dinner, that made me really thirsty now. I felt the dry-mouthed affliction of nervousness, even of fear. And it was my father's proposition at our table in the Kundan that had triggered it. That, and the walk back to the flat. The river had been low under Lambeth Bridge, lapping softly and invisible, what little noise it made distorted by the fog. The fog, almost impenetrable in Portsmouth, had extended its tendrils as far as the capital. There was almost no traffic and curiously no pedestrian traffic at all, though it was not remotely late by London standards. But from the moment my father's taxi drew away, I endured the strange suspicion of being trailed though dissipating mist, all the way over the bridge and to the safe refuge of home.

That night I dreamed that Harry Spalding and Michael Collins met, the encounter in some dim and monochromatic no-man's-land. They were uniformed and they took off their caps and their Sam Browne belts and came together to wrestle. And Collins, the broth of a boy from his father's farm in County Cork, naturally the bigger and stronger man and much the more skilled at grappling, gained the upper hand. And then Spalding's limbs seemed to lengthen and burnish and they blackened like those of some great, bony insect and he crushed and then greedily devoured his opponent, his arms and legs segmented now and chittering foully as he scrabbled away into the darkness from the scene. I awoke, sweating. It had been a horrible dream, all the worse, as nightmares so often are, for being so nonsensical and meaningless.

I got out of bed, went back into Suzanne's study and took the cashmere sweater she had left draped across the back of the chair at her desk. It had been the source of the earlier scent, a mingling of her skin and hair and the perfume she habitually wore. I folded it on to my pillow for comfort but still felt spooked. I sat up and took my mobile from the bedside table and texted Suzanne to call me if she was still awake. I was grateful she was only in Dublin, in the same time zone. Her research work could take her anywhere in the world. In Dublin and London it was only just after midnight.

She called me back straight away.

'What's wrong?'

'Nothing. Have you heard of a man called Harry Spalding?'

There was a silence as I'm sure she flicked through the mental Rolodex in her clever, beautiful head. 'Yes. In Paris in the 1920s he once offered Bricktop a hundred thousand dollars if she would sleep with him.'

I had no idea who or what Bricktop was. A courtesan? An entertainer? 'Bricktop's response?'

Suzanne laughed. 'Something fairly unprintable, I should think.'

'Have you heard of the Jericho Crew?'

There was another silence. This one was less productive. 'No, I haven't. It doesn't sound very salubrious, though, whatever it is. Or was. What's this about, Martin?'

'My father bought the wreck of Spalding's boat today. His yacht. The *Dark Echo*?'

At the other end of the line, I heard Suzanne swallow. 'Well. Your father has never been one for superstition.'

'Why do you say that?'

'I'll tell you when I see you, Martin. I'll tell you all about Bricktop, too.'

'My father intends to have the boat restored, made seaworthy once again. He intends to sail her. He wants to sail her around the world. And he told me tonight he wants me to accompany him.'

She laughed. There was no mirth in the sound. 'I thought your father liked me.'

'He does like you.'

'But he wants to take you away,' she said.

'Which means that he must like me as well.'

I could hear her thinking. 'I'll see you at the weekend,' she said. It was Wednesday. She was due back on the Saturday. 'Take care, Martin.'

She never said that. I thought it was an odd thing for her to say. Take care of what?

I lay on the bed for a while with her sweater a soft, sweet-smelling pillow under my head, but I still could not discover sleep. So I went back to her study and switched on Suzanne's computer. Then, almost without thinking, I reached across and switched on Suzanne's little radio. She had taken her laptop with her and our home computer was old and slow. It was nice to have a diversion while it groaned slowly into life. The radio was tuned to one of the digital stations, bebop and modern jazz and fusion, tunes segueing into one another without the hindrance of some insomnia jockey's coffee-and-ego-fuelled patter to spoil the music.

I tapped my fingers on the desk surface and smiled, remembering the unlikely way in which Suzanne and I had first met. It was far below the streets of Wapping, on an East London Line train. She had simply been a strikingly attractive girl sharing the same carriage until three hoodies burst in and began steaming the most vulnerable-looking passengers.

What happened next was down to Father O'Hanlon, who had passed on the necessary skills, and my father, who had secured for me the tutelage of O'Hanlon.

No one, in that modern London way, was doing anything about the gang. Those not being singled out as victims were just pretending that nothing untoward was going on. There were no screams, no threats, no jarring assaults or violation. It was just a normal London commute, wasn't it? It was just routine as those not being robbed stared at the black glass of the tunnelling train windows and the gang approached the pale, pretty woman clutching a laptop case protectively under her arm. Everything was normal. Or, at least, it was until I got off my seat and approached the gang, hauled them round and knocked the three of them cold.

Suzanne later called it my KOWK (knight on white charger) moment. For her, the moment had been DID (damsel in distress). The acronyms amused her. The roles were amusing, too, so absurdly far removed were they from the balance of our relationship once it properly began.

I was arrested and taken to Wapping police station and charged with assault and bailed in person by my beaming father. Suzanne attended voluntarily, as a witness. Six weeks later, I was summoned back to be told that no charges were going to be pressed.

'The scum you encountered used to be known as the Shadwell Posse,' the detective sergeant I saw there told me in the seclusion of an interview room. 'Ever since your brush with them, we've been calling them the Shadwell Pussies. And I'm delighted to say that the name has caught on.'

Suzanne had dinner with me to celebrate my reprieve. A week later, we were living together.

The computer finally came to life. I did a search for Bricktop. I searched images first, and found only old pictures of a venerable black woman and then shots from the same woman's rather lavish and showy funeral. Then I did another search and, of course, discovered who she was – the legend she had been, the picaresque life she had led and the glittering array of talent she had showcased at her nightclub in Paris in that febrile decade after the Great War. I read about Bricktop and her long legs and lengthy list of admirers. Gangsters and painters and hucksters and writers vied for her favours, and some of the names on the list were legendary. Spalding's wealth couldn't get him to the front of the queue, where the likes of Jack Johnson and Pablo Picasso and Duke Ellington jostled and preened.

How long the song had been playing I don't know, but when my attention to the words on the screen faltered sufficiently for me to become aware of it a shiver of cold spread up my spine as I listened to something old and sonorous and crackling with the vintage speed at which I could hear it revolving on the plinth. I looked at the radio. Suzanne had bought it only recently. It was a very modern little item and the sound leaking out of it seemed horribly incongruous. For a dreadful moment I was listening to Bricktop, her dead voice creaking forth seventy-odd years after the death of her failed suitor, on the very day my father had purchased the possession that suitor prized most greatly. The song ended. For once, I craved a spoken voice. And it came, the presenter crediting the performance I had just heard to Josephine Baker. I felt a surge of relief. Baker had been a Bricktop protégé, of course, even a Bricktop discovery. I'd just learned as much. But the long arm of coincidence was allowed to stretch that far. At least, to my tired mind it was. But it could stretch no further, so I switched off the radio before giving it the chance to.

Back in bed, sleep still proved elusive. I breathed in the warm comfort of Suzanne's improvised cashmere pillow and smiled at the irony of how I was behaving now, compared to my behaviour in the circumstances in which the two of us had met. Was I afraid of the dark? Suzanne believed I was afraid of nothing. I'd given her reason, I suppose, to think it. It was an awfully long way from being the truth. But was I? Afraid of the dark?

I don't honestly think that I was. But I was afraid, I know, even then, of the malignant memory of the American called Harry Spalding.

There was at least some method in my father's madness. Before buying Spalding's boat, he had commissioned a precise estimate of what the craft would cost to restore, refit and make seaworthy. The estimate had been carried out by a boatyard on the Hamble with the best reputation for this kind of work in what was an exact, esoteric and quite exclusive business. The original specification of the boat was very high. Craftsmanship to equal it did still exist. But it was uncommon. And it was bought in the modern age only at great expense. Computer simulation could and had made the design of a modern boat a much cheaper proposition altogether. But restoration was a matter of painstaking artistry done with arcane tools and precious raw materials.

Frank Hadley said his yard could do the job. But he told my father honestly that it would take six months if it were to be done properly and not botched. The timescale suited my dad. Six months would enable him to learn the necessary seamanship to sail the *Dark Echo* competently. The boat would be ready by the beginning of July. It was a benign time on the marine calendar to put out across the Atlantic. Benign and Atlantic were not words I thought sat easily in the same sentence. But everything was relative. July was going to be better than March and a damn sight gentler than October.

Suzanne duly came home. She told me all about Bricktop. She told me what little she knew about Harry Spalding's curious sojourn in the North-West of England. She had done a bit of research about a year earlier into hotels that were reputedly haunted. Spalding had been a celebrated guest at one of these, she remembered. The Palace Hotel in Birkdale, though, had long been demolished. The film never got beyond some preliminary outlines. I was so delighted to see Suzanne, and Spalding seemed such a distasteful subject even on the little I knew about him, that I swiftly lost any curiosity I had possessed, really, to know more. My father, caught up in the immediacies of learning about the sea and the disintegration of his latest marriage, forgot altogether his promise to himself to ask her about that curious name, the Jericho Crew. Later events made me bitterly regret the way his making that request of her was allowed so completely to slip his mind. But in the circumstances, at the time, it was a forgivable lapse.

I signed up for the same courses in seamanship and navigation as my dad. I also joined a yacht club. We had already determined that we would not do the courses together. I suppose we knew enough about one another to know that doing so would have scuppered our intended voyage before departure from dry land. What we needed afloat was competence from one another, not first-hand evidence of its comic opposite. So we did the courses separately and, on top of this, I joined a yacht club in Whitstable where, at least in the volatile winter weather of February, I could sail in safe approximation of ocean-going conditions.

What Suzanne thought about all this, I honestly don't know. I think she thought the rapprochement between myself and my father a good thing. I think she thought six months hence too long a distance away, at least at the outset, to fret unduly over. I suppose she assumed that we would possess at least a basic competence between the two of us when we finally embarked. The *Dark Echo* was a racing schooner, more than capable of covering the distance between

Southampton and New York in three weeks. And when all was said and done, the sea was a great deal safer in the age of satellite phones and sonic distress buoys than it had been eighty years before, in Spalding's Roaring Twenties. She busied herself with research into the groundbreaking documentary series centred on Michael Collins and the Irish struggle for independence. And she kept any reservations she might have had about the venture to herself.

You might wonder where I found the time to indulge in this little jaunt with all the preparation it required and the money that was needed to fund the training. A generous allowance from my father would be any stranger's fair assumption. But it would not be the truth. My dad was always generous with me. But I was always independent, particularly so after my mother's sudden death. At both of the universities I attended, I worked for the college radio station, organising guest interviews and fund-raising drives and on-air competitions and so on. After my eventual graduation, I got a similar job working with a regional station in Kent, only now there was a salary involved. Next, I got a job at a London commercial station. If there was any career plan, it was probably to wind up working in radio programming for the BBC. I've always loved the power and potency of the spoken word and have always preferred radio to television because it frees the listener's imagination somehow in a way that television, with its reliance on pictures and its terror of dead time, can never really replicate.

So there I was, fully intending to evolve over time into some Reithian figure of the twenty-first century. Except that fate intervened when I and a colleague at the London station dreamed up a game-show format we had the wit to copyright. The game became a huge airtime hit. The format translated effortlessly to television. And the game became a hit all over the world. It didn't earn me the sort of wealth my father had generated through business. But it did bring me enough money not to have to worry about where the mortgage payments were coming from for the flat for a couple of years.

I finally gave up full-time work two years ago. Retirement at thirty would, to be honest, have been a depressing prospect. But I had an ambition to write. In the last two years I've written and had published two children's books. Sales have been modest, but they've earned a bit of praise. I like the challenge of writing for enigmatic little people with minds that are difficult to unlock. I can think of little more worthwhile for a writer of fiction than firing the imagination of a child. One not too distant day, I hope that Suzanne and I will have children of our own. Or perhaps, now, better altogether to say that one day I hoped we would. I hoped we would have children of our own. It's only realistic, in the current circumstances, to put everything into the past tense. Harry Spalding's baleful curse has imposed that necessity.

The *Dark Echo*'s reputation as an unlucky boat was vague to all of us. I'd heard something from my father when he'd first mentioned his interest in the vessel, but couldn't even recall exactly what. When I challenged him on it, admittedly not very aggressively, he'd reclined in his club chair and said something about sailors and superstition, and had then gone back to the more compelling business of reviving his dead cigar. Even Suzanne was really no more forthcoming. She had heard of the boat, she said, in connection with some act of violence at some gathering in the late 1930s of casino gamblers off the coast of Cuba. But, gently pressed, she could not remember the name or the nationalities of the people involved, or even the port concerned. 'Maybe that's the curse of the *Dark Echo*,' she said, joking. 'Maybe it afflicts its victims with amnesia and they keep coming back for more.' She pulled a ghoulish face and shook her hair like a banshee.

And incredible though it now seems to me, we both of us laughed.

The first mishap at Frank Hadley's boatyard was mundane enough. The surviving portholes had been carefully removed. Those not beyond restoration were to be bathed in acid to remove the corrosive stains and then brought back by polishing to their original lustre. But first, the shattered fragments of glass needed to be chiselled out of them. Even this job was done fastidiously, though, because the porthole glass, each individual circular pane, would have to be moulded and cut and polished by a craftsman. It was important not to damage the soft brass housing while removing the tough glass chips and shards.

An apprentice glazier cut himself chiselling out porthole glass. Nobody thought anything of it. But the wound became infected. The boy developed a high temperature and was taken to hospital where his condition swiftly worsened. He was admitted. And then he was moved to a critical bed with a vicious case of septicaemia. He was young and strong, a Sunday footballer on the brink of a semi-professional career. But he did not look any kind of athlete when the ventilator was required for him in his hospital bed, his gashed hand a grotesque, swollen thing suspended above a body so stricken with paralysis that it could not breathe for itself.

The boy recovered. The swelling subsided and the infection receded. After a week, he was allowed home. But he did not return to his work on the portholes of the *Dark Echo* in the workshop of a glazier's business subcontracted to Hadley's boatyard. He telephoned his old boss and said that he would never cut glass again. Nor, he swore vehemently, would he ever again allow glass to cut him.

The second accident took place at the boatyard itself and was much more serious. A carpenter was planing a length of replacement deck planking. It was hardwood, of course, high-grade teak sourced at great expense by my publicity-conscious father from a sustainable source. Either the wood hadn't quite been seasoned properly and had retained sufficient moisture to stick under the blade, or there was a knot in the burr that had gone unnoticed. But the carpenter, of course, was using original tools. And fashioning hardwood, however skilled you are and however honed your tools, requires a degree of physical force. Either way, the blade of the plane shattered and a steel splinter pierced the carpenter's eye. It was a nasty injury, an agonising disfiguration that cost him fifty per cent of his sight and would impair his ability to do high-spec work for the rest of his professional life.

So far, so unfortunate. But the third accident, a shocking tragedy, sort of put the seal on things. And this one happened with my father actually present at Frank Hadley's boatyard.

They were pulling the root of the old main mast from its foundation at the centre of the hull, raising it clear of the superstructure through the deck. It was an operation a little akin to removing a rotten tooth. The mast itself was not rotten. But it was broken and beyond repair and had to be replaced. A crane had been positioned to pull the root cleanly out of the boat. Hawsers had been lashed to the mast laterally to keep it steady and stop it swinging dangerously once free of the hull. The last thing that was wanted was for it to become a sort of battering ram, smashing the craft it had so staunchly served for so long.

Somehow one of the hawsers was allowed to slacken and it looped around the arm of one of the men on the deck, severing the limb when it came under tension and tightened again as cleanly as a wire will cut cheese, just above the top of his biceps. Work was stopped immediately, of course. The emergency services were called and first aid was swiftly administered by those present. Frank Hadley was a model employer and two of his people on the scene knew all about first aid and the recovery position. But the man with the severed arm writhed on the deck of my father's boat until he died of shock after four or five terrible, gory minutes.

Work stopped. And it did not restart. My father was paying Frank Hadley very handsomely. And Hadley, a scrupulous employer as I've said, was paying his craftspeople very competitive rates. But nobody wanted to work on the *Dark Echo* after the fatality. Even when Hadley had personally swabbed her deck of the dead rigger's blood, and police accident investigators had put away their biros after taking statements, even after the burial a full eight days later, there was no general desire to return to the project. It was the fourth week in February. All over the South of England, we were enduring record rainfall. There was a pump to keep the dock dry under the *Dark Echo*'s supine shape. She was wearing her shroud again, as if in solemn and dignified mourning for the most recent man to die aboard her. For something told me there had been predecessors – male and female, too – all mourned with the same measured, counterfeit decorum. But perhaps it was just the weather, making me gloomy, turning my own aspect as gloomy as that of the leaking sky.

I sat with my father in Frank Hadley's office. Through the window behind him you could see the tarpaulin bulk of the boat in the rain. His yard was on an estuary, as they tended to be, a deep water channel scoured by a dredger through the silt to give the boats he worked on access to open water. In some senses everything was the same as at Bullen and Clore. There was the same pervasive salt smell and the same faint luminescence about the light, even in heavy cloud, that you only encounter on the coast. There were the briny cobbles and the great tow ropes and chains and mooring rings. And, of course, there was the presence of the *Dark Echo*.

But, in significant ways, everything was in complete contrast to Bullen and Clore. The spacious office was a minimalist tribute to good taste and modernity. A cappuccino machine gurgled softly in the far corner. On the wall to our left, and Hadley's right as he faced us from behind his desk, was a bank of LCD screens. They all showed the same series of images. Computer simulations of the hull of a Norse longship appeared in complex three-dimensional patterns. The whorls and ribs of its geometry, after a few moments of viewing, could have passed for an installation of abstract art.

'We're building a fleet of ships for a feature film,' Hadley explained. 'Well, what the audience will finally see will be a fleet. We'll in fact build only one full and exact seaworthy replica. The rest will be interiors, odd detailed sections and CGI.'

Neither my father nor I offered a comment.

'Still damned expensive.'

Again, neither of us replied to him.

Hadley stared at the simulations for a moment. 'We can't better what their engineers did a thousand years ago. Not with the materials available to them, we can't, for all our microchips and megabytes. Form and function perfectly combined, the longship. It was a staggering feat of design and execution.'

Frank Hadley wore chinos and a pale-blue cotton shirt on a tall and youthfully slender frame. His iron-grey hair was finger-combed back carelessly from a side parting. He had a sparkly look, the twinkle of a ladies' man. In that, he wasn't so dissimilar from my father. But his face lacked the strength of character, the firmness of jaw, the star quality, if you will, that my father's face had always possessed in such apparent depth. In isolation he would have carried a certain male glamour. In the same room as my father, this was outshone. Comparing the two of them was like comparing Peter Lawford to Cary Grant.

My father said, 'An unlucky vessel to a boatbuilder such as yourself is surely as the concept of a haunted house to a modern architect. It isn't just an anachronism. It's worse even than an absurdity. It's an affront. An insult.'

Hadley dragged his eyes away from his bank of screens. But he would not meet my father's gaze. He looked down at his hands, linked on the desk. 'My thoughts on the matter are immaterial, Mr Stannard.'

'Magnus, please,' my father said.

'Magnus, then. My thoughts on the subject of unlucky boats are really neither here nor there if I can't get the men to come through the gate for their shift.'

'Get different men.'

Hadley stood. He turned his back on us and looked out of the window at the view through the rain-bleared window, at the lowering sky and the sullen outline of my father's prize, under its tarpaulin. 'You were here when the fatality occurred, Magnus. You were watching the operation. I cannot find either engineer or accident investigator who can justify or explain to me why there should have been a fraction of slack in that rogue hawser.'

'Rogue,' my father repeated. He said the word in a neutral voice, as thought it were foreign and he was merely trying out the sound of it.

'Yet despite the consistent and enormous tension it was under, it discovered the length and elasticity to loop around a man's arm and severe it.'

'Heavy engineering is dangerous work,' my father said. 'I understand a fund has been established at the yard for the poor fellow.'

'It has.'

'And I will contribute to it,' my father said. 'Generously.'

'You saw his feet thrum on the deck, his dance of death in his own spreading pool of blood.'

'It will be interesting to see how a man of your professional reputation deals with the tabloid press interpretation of this peasant witchcraft revival.'

'Witchcraft,' Hadley said. I think he chuckled. But I could not be sure. 'This is not witchcraft.'

My father said nothing.

'Did you ever think to examine the history of the boat?' Hadley had still not turned back to face us.

'I was familiar with the history of the *Dark Echo* long before I acquired the craft,' my father said. By his standards, his self-control here was extraordinary. Anger was one of his talents. Fury was one of his most potent weapons.

'Where is the log?'

'In a strongbox. All five volumes of it. The log is safe and intact.'

'It's customary for the log to accompany the craft to which it belongs.'

'The log is safe,' my father repeated.

'Then I suggest you read it,' Hadley said.

'I have.'

'And I must insist that you let me read it, too.' Finally, he turned. I had misjudged him. He was much more Martin Sheen than Peter Lawford. He did not quite possess the raw charisma on which my father so heavily traded. But he had weight and substance. He was clearly a man of principle where the well-being of his workforce was concerned. Principle was more important to Frank Hadley than tabloid credibility.

My father stood. 'Is there anything else?'

'The press have yet to deride me as a figure of fun. But

they have not been slow to tag your acquisition an unlucky boat.'

'Cursed, I believe, is the appellation of choice,' my father said.

'Well. I have received a letter from a Jack Peitersen of Newport in Rhode Island, where I know she was constructed. He has offered to come and work on the restoration. His great-grandfather worked on the original construction of the boat, he says.' Hadley opened a desk drawer and took an airmail letter from it. I hadn't known they still existed in the age of cyberspace. 'He says that if we employ him to supervise the work, the restoration will be entirely successful.'

'A crank,' my father said, buttoning his coat, patting his pocket, I knew, for his cigar case. 'An opportunistic blackmail attempt by some freak from New England.'

'Except that I had him checked out,' Hadley said. 'He's not a crank. Not according to his references.'

'Then bring him over, Hadley. I'll bankroll the exercise. But on your name and reputation be it.' He paused. 'I'm going outside for a smoke. Please feel free in my absence, gentlemen, to talk among yourselves.'

Frank Hadley sat back down after my father had closed the door behind him. 'The irony is, Martin, that I greatly like and admire your dad. He is a bully and a prima donna. But as bullying prima donnas go, he's fair-minded and generous.'

'You never referred just now to the boat he has commissioned you to restore and refurbish by its name.'

'No,' he said. 'And God help me, I never will.'

'You really believe the vessel cursed?'

He smiled. 'Haven't been aboard her, have you?'

'No.'

'Despite our setbacks, we've accomplished a lot, physically.

We worked hard on her for six weeks prior to the fatality. She's sound enough for a tour. Perhaps you ought to treat yourself to one. Maybe you could get your father to act as guide.'

'Because you won't put a foot aboard her, will you, Mr Hadley?'

It was the second question I'd posed him that was really no question at all.

He looked at his bank of computer images morphing, bloodless, nothing but geometric elegance in black lines on white screens. 'I just hope that this fellow Peitersen can accomplish what he claims he can, Martin. I pray for that.'

I looked beyond him out of the window. The glass was strong and thick and soundless. But it was rain-lashed. The weather was worsening. The wind was strengthening. I could see it in the ragged flights of gulls failing to find the paths they sought to cleave through the grey, turbulent sky. I could see it in the rising swell out beyond the estuary shallows, where whitecaps curled now in the unsteady, rising rhythm of an oncoming storm. For a moment, I found myself wishing with all my heart that the storm would gather and rise to breach the sea defences of Hadley's boatyard and smash the *Dark Echo* to matchwood at her moorings. It was a momentary thought, but it surprised me with its vehemence and the vindictive pleasure I took at seeing teak splinters, hemp braids and tattered fragments of tarpaulin on the tideline in my mind's eye as the old boat's final remains washed up, innocuous at last, when calm returned.

'You're in awe of your father.'

That made me laugh out loud. 'As are most people.'

'Not Harry Spalding.'

'Who has been dead for better than seventy years. Unless, of course, you believe in witchcraft.'

An impatient smile twitched on Hadley's face. He looked

at me. He held my eyes with his, which were pale blue and slightly bloodshot. 'I've no interest in verbal debate with the son of a lucrative client. I've even less interest in allowing myself to be demeaned. But I've a son of my own about your age. And whatever else, I would implore you to read the log before you embark on any voyage aboard that boat. Don't suggest your father show it to you, Martin. Insist upon it.'

My father came back in a moment later, entering on a silence so awkward it must have seemed palpable. He agreed some expenses and countersigned a few cheques. Hadley rose and shook hands with each of us and we were out and into the gathering storm.

My father accepted a lift to Chichester. I didn't ask what business it was he had there. He had retired from the business of making money and, with his marriage already consigned to the past tense, I imagined Chichester was the location for a romantic encounter. It was a place redolent in my own mind of pretty antique shops and quaint, half-timbered pubs. Its narrow Georgian streets would provide a cosy refuge from the elements. I pictured logs in the grate of a saloon bar, horse brasses glimmering on the wall and brandy burnishing in balloon-shaped glasses as warmth and alcohol and the expensive gift on the table between them kindled a seductive mood. My father was the sort of man who stayed friendly with his ex-mistresses. The arctic aftermath was reserved for those he persuaded up the aisle. The old flames were nurtured and cherished in the belief that one day they might flare again in the heat of rekindled passion.

I reckoned he'd had half a dozen girlfriends in the twelve years since my mother's death. The quantity and the variety inevitably begged questions about his extra-curricular activities prior to it. But they were not questions I felt anywhere near strong enough to face. All I had in the way of a parent, my father was nevertheless sometimes a difficult man to love. The knowledge that he had been a serial cheat during his marriage to Mum would, I think, have meant final estrangement between us. I said earlier I was not a physical coward. And I really don't believe I am. But the thought of being cut adrift from family has frightened me since Mum so abruptly left us. There were questions I simply did not dare ask my father. The answers might lead to consequences I was not brave enough to face.

'I'd like to read the *Dark Echo*'s log,' I said.

'By all means. I'll arrange it after the weekend.'

It was now a Thursday. And it was approaching lunchtime.

Chichester had announced itself in a dripping road sign. It was a city virtually without suburbs. In a moment or two he would get out of the car. 'And I'd like to borrow the swipe key Hadley gave you to the yard. I'll return it to you tomorrow.'

He turned to me. 'What on earth do you want that for?'

'I want a look at the boat.'

My father laughed. 'In weather like this?'

'In precisely this weather. I want to know if Hadley was telling the truth about the extent of the work he says they have accomplished.'

'They have done quite a bit.'

'I'd like to see it for myself.'

'Very well.' He took the swipe key from his pocket. Stubbornness was one of the few traits I think he really admired in me. But then, I'd inherited it from him.

The key wouldn't get me into Hadley's inner sanctum. That did not matter. I had no interest in stealing computer files or tinkering with his cappuccino machine. I felt an urgent need to get aboard the boat and experience for myself the baleful atmosphere I believed he'd hinted at. My earlier desire to see her wrecked suggested I disliked the *Dark Echo* more than she disliked me. But that antipathy was itself a mystery I wanted solved. A surreptitious visit, under cover of the storm, seemed just the thing. Suzanne was back in Dublin on the trail of the Big Feller. And I had no other pressing engagements. I dropped my father, who made his way quickly through the torrent to the shelter of an awning over one of Chichester's narrow pavements. I saw him reach into his overcoat pocket for his mobile phone as he nimbly took the kerb. I was reminded afresh that he neither moved nor looked like a man of fifty-five. But then, nor did he act like one, either. Then, through the rainwashed windscreen, I struggled to find a route to take me back to where I'd come from.

The boatyard looked deserted when I arrived back there at just after two thirty. Even if Hadley had hired a fresh team of craftsmen with every inclination to work on the *Dark Echo*'s restoration, it would hardly have been possible in the prevailing conditions. The wind was whipping in from the Solent in savage, briny gusts somewhere approaching gale force. The rain it brought was incessant and heavy, a driving thrum of water on the roof of the car and the surrounding earth. It danced in deepening puddles, giving the yard a depressed and derelict appearance. In the neat cluster of sheds in the distance to landward, I looked for signs of industry; for the blue brightness of blow torches or the white brilliance of welding rods, flickering through their windows, cleaving the gloom. But there was nothing. There were no signs of life either in the boatsheds on the wharf or at the broad slipway where they launched. I was aware of wind singing through the taut security wire strung between concrete fence posts as I used the key to release the electric gate. It slammed again behind me. I looked over to Hadley's office suite, which occupied the second floor of a smart, pale wooden building a hundred yards to my right. His blinds were down. But there were comforting chinks of warm yellow brightness from within between their slats. He, at least, was at work.

The tarp protecting my father's boat had torn in places in the violence of the day's weather. It was very heavy canvas cloth and was criss-crossed with strengthening seams and thick, reinforced stitching. So there was no chance of it sundering entirely and pulling free of the craft. Or at least, I did not think there was. But in places it had snagged and sheared and torn. Wind whistled through it like a wild jeer. The cloth capered and trembled in the wind. It shook and howled like a living thing, in protest.

I reached the boat soaked. I'd dressed for a meeting rather than a tempest. I paused and looked to my left, out to where the Hamble ran out to the Solent, awed by the anger and scale of the pitching sea. My feet slithered on the big cobbles of the wharf and I understood for the first time the giant solidity and scale of the stonework there, the reason for it. Those walls were defences, ramparts. Their immensity was only a pragmatic measure against the elements they defied.

I slithered towards the *Dark Echo* on treacherous shoe leather, cursing my own ineptitude. I'd proven a dab hand at the maths needed to pass exams in navigation. Yet here I was, in danger of falling thirty-five feet on to the concrete where the keel of our boat lay, only for the want of a pair of rubber-soled shoes. I steadied myself. The tarp roared and flapped incessantly, where it was newly torn, the looming shape of it huge around the bulk of the long hull now I'd got this close. I looked up, wincing through needles of rain. The sky, which had glowered earlier, was now just a scudding roof of gloom over the world. I fingered the small Maglite in my pocket. Thank God I'd had the wit to remember to take that from the Saab's glove compartment before entering the yard. I took it out and shone the thin beam of the torch on to canvas. At least I would have no trouble getting aboard. There was a rent in the heavy fabric right in front of me about eighteen inches long. I switched off the Maglite and clamped it between my teeth and hauled myself through on to the *Dark Echo*'s deck.

My first impression was one of cosiness. I felt the childhood comfort of my camping days as a boy in the Cubs and later as a young teenager in the Scouts. The rain drummed, a nostalgic sound on stiff cloth, but couldn't get to me any more. There was the smell of damp, but I was dry in my snug and musty refuge from the downpour.

Nevertheless, this was business. I used the torch to orientate myself. In doing so, I saw the new timber with which they had expertly patched the deck. It had not been treated and varnished yet, but even in the Maglite's beam I could see that the work had been done with faultless expertise. I ran my fingers over it and could not feel the joins. The specification my father had demanded was astonishingly high. But they had worked to it. I looked down along the smooth lines of the deck for the companionway. It was a dark, rectangular maw leading below. All around me, canvas screamed and shuddered. I smiled. It had been a tonic already to see my father's money well spent rather than cynically squandered.

The steps of the companionway were tricky. I could not hear them creak in the noise of the storm, but could tell from their spongy feel under my feet that they had not yet been replaced. I was descending on old and perished wood and did so gingerly. And there was something else. As I descended into the dark interior of the vessel, I began to feel an irrational instinct of fear and even of incipient panic. The boat roared with the exterior life of the storm and the smell of must strengthened and grew in complexity and character as I continued to descend the short flight to the cabins and galley area. The descent took much longer than it should have. Too many steps, I thought. Too great a distance down, it seemed.

At the bottom of the companionway it was very dark. And there was the complexity of smells. The smells were so strong that I was reluctant to turn on the torch in the blackness for fear of what I might see. I could smell a feral, canine smell, like the hair and spoor of a wild dog, that made my balls shrink and the hair on the nape of my neck prickle and chill. The roar of the storm, the buck and ripple of canvas under assault, had receded. It was quiet down here and so oppressively fearful that I struggled to control my bladder.

'Relax, old chum,' a voice said.

I switched on the torch. There was nothing there. I was in the master cabin. There was nothing to see except the gutted, dripping interior of an old boat undergoing restoration. Except that there was a small brass-bound mirror screwed to the right of the door leading to the smaller cabin beyond. I frowned at the mirror. The Maglite beam played in my shaking hand beneath it. And then I looked at what it reflected.

There was an impression of red leather and purple plush tassled in gold; of cigarette smoke and a man's buttoned boot moving out of sight with the speed of a cobra recoiling. And there was a woman's face – the make-up Jazz Age pale, the hair raven and geometric, the mouth crimson – and the rictus of terror so real and raw in the eyes and drawn-back lips that I bolted before this awful vision had even clarified in my mind. I fled. I pounded up splintering stairs and tore the nails from my fingers scrabbling for a breach in the stiff, unyielding weight of the tarp securing the boat. And when I found one, I scrambled through it. And despite the hurl and havoc of the storm, behind me

I heard laughter, male and laconic. I lay on the quay. I recovered my breath and composure. I stood finally and looked towards Hadley's office for reassurance. But the yellow bars of brightness between his blinds had been extinguished. In Frank Hadley's boatyard, it seemed now that all the lights were out.

At the wheel of the Saab, I saw that my hands were dripping blood from my torn nails. Gradually, my fingertips began to throb and then to sing with pain in the aftermath of the shock of what I'd seen and felt. In my seat, soaked and shivering, I found the presence of mind to fumble on the heater switch. I concentrated on driving. The rain cascaded down the windscreen, making driving difficult in the fierce strength of the shifting gusts once I was back on the exposed open road. I tried not to think about the scene in the cabin. The thing was, it was not the first time I believed I had been in the presence of ghosts. But I believed it was the first time I had been in the presence of spectral malevolence. And my raw nerves and the jumping muscles under my skin told me that the ghost of Harry Spalding was a spirit of pure spite and bottomless hatred. I drove. Eventually, London grew closer. Lambeth approached. I parked the car and wiped the caked blood from my hands with a rag from the boot and, with my clothes still drying on me, walked the short distance to the Windmill pub and ordered a double rum that I drank in a single swallow. But even at home, after a scalding shower, changed into fresh clothes, warm and with the weather diminished to just a feeble drizzle against the windows, it was hours before I felt even remotely safe.

There was no point texting Suzanne for reassurance on this occasion. I lay in our bed and wondered how much to tell the woman I loved about what had happened. Secrets have a way of festering, and sharing my most private thoughts and feelings with her was an important aspect of the intimacy that I knew gave our relationship much of its worth. There were lots of things I did not tell her. But I felt no guilt at keeping the boring and trivial stuff to myself. That was just a way of preventing her from thinking *me* boring and trivial.

What would she make of my experience aboard the boat? Would she think me mad? She would believe it had happened. She would be sympathetic to how shaken the experience had left me. But she was too practical and pragmatic a woman to believe in the supernatural herself. She would rationalise it, somehow. She would see it as the consequence of fatigue and an over-vigorous imagination. Then I remembered what she had said, speaking from Dublin, when I had told her about the auction. She knew already that the *Dark Echo* bore the reputation of an unlucky boat. She had made reference to the fact before the catalogue of apparent accidents at Frank Hadley's yard. I would have to ask her about that. It was important, just as reading the log was important.

The phone rang.

'Hi. What's happening?' asked Suzanne.

'Not a lot.'

'How was your trip to Hampshire?'

'My father's expensively assembled team of craftsmen are sharing a serious case of cold feet.'

'I don't blame them.'

'Why do you say that?' I had not told her about the fatality at Hadley's boatyard. It was one of my boring, trivial omissions.

'I'll tell you when I get back,' she said.

'How's Big Mick?' I'd almost forgotten to ask.

'I honestly don't think I've ever admired a man more.'

'Blimey.'

'Your good self excepted.'

'Of course.'

Sleep came eventually that night. But it was shallow and dream-ridden when it finally arrived.

I met my father at his Mayfair house to give him back the swipe key the following afternoon. I made no mention of what had occurred aboard the *Dark Echo*. I had retreated furtively from Hadley's domain, reasonably sure that no one there had seen me. No one there with a right to be there, no one living, had seen me, at any rate. Harry Spalding had seen me, I felt. And I had heard Harry Spalding. I'd caught only the merest glimpse of him in the snakelike recoil of his reflection. But I had heard him speak in the decades-dead voice he still possessed.

Hearing him was enough. But I did not really want to dwell on that. Nor did I want to think about his companion, the woman I'd seen. My father would have believed none of it, which is why I did not tell him. Events earlier in my life had put paid entirely to his faith in me where matters spiritual were concerned. And for good or bad, Harry Spalding was a spiritual matter. I was already reasonably sure of that.

'You look like hell,' my father said. He didn't. He looked rumpled and sated and smug.

'Find Chichester congenial?'

He ignored the question. He poured me coffee from a silver pot. It always surprised me that he remembered how I took it. He hadn't made the coffee, of course. The pot had been wheeled in on its trolley by his housekeeper.

'Why the *Dark Echo*, Dad? Why that damned boat in particular?'

He smiled. But the smile was entirely for himself. 'My own childhood, Martin, was very different from that which I was able to provide for you.'

This was not promising. I sipped my coffee. I would take solace in the coffee, which was excellent. 'I know that, Dad.'

'Please. Don't interrupt.' He stood and walked over to one of the tall windows. 'My mother, your grandmother, did her best. But they were tough times, unforgiving decades in which to be a working-class widow with an infant child to provide for.' He paused, over by the stately windows of his extravagant home. And he allowed his impoverished and sometimes humiliating childhood to return and haunt him afresh. 'Christmases were particularly grim. I was a bright boy and that tormented my mother. I believe she suffered agonies of guilt over all the things her poverty denied me. They were austere times, of course. But my schoolmates were a privileged lot. The comparisons were inevitable, and the privation stark and obvious and sometimes, I'll admit it, shaming.' He cleared his throat.

'There were junk shops, second-hand shops, pawn shops all over the neighbourhood of Manchester in which we lived then. For people like ourselves these places functioned, in a way, as banks. The shoes you sold them were security against the money they gave you for the shoes until you could afford to buy the shoes back. And the difference between what you received and what you paid was the interest. And the interest was marginal, a compassionate matter, usually, of just a few pennies added to the principal sum.'

He paused again, head bowed, remembering. My father still grieved for his mother almost with the raw pain with which he grieved for mine. And she was in his heart and memory now, I could tell.

'Of course, these shops did sell things. Zinc bathtubs would hang from pegs. There would be racks of second-hand bicycles. And in those days, perhaps surprisingly, most coveted among their stock were books. It would have been 1963. I would have been eleven years old. The wireless meant the BBC and a universe alien to the one I inhabited. Television was vastly beyond my mother's means. But I loved books. I was a religious attendee at the local lending library. I thirsted for knowledge and sensation. And lending libraries were free.'

He turned to me. He was a silhouette at the window. My father, the self-made millionaire, a nimbus of light around his greying head, stood remembering.

'There was an educator in the 1930s. A man named Arthur Mee?'

I shook my head. The name meant nothing.

'Mee compiled a children's encyclopedia. By the time I encountered it, it was already thirty years out of date. But its volumes were packed nevertheless for the child I was with exotic and spellbinding vistas of a world for which I was not just eager, but greedy. There was a picture of a giant redwood in one volume, a tunnel bored through its immense trunk big enough to accommodate a car. In another volume, some brave soul had pictured a brown bear, twelve feet high as it reared up in the posture of a man. There were giant marlin and power station turbines and tidal waves and the electronic microscope and the maelstrom and the Seven Wonders of the Ancient World. And I awoke on Christmas morning at the end of 1963 and my mother had bought me eleven volumes of the set of twelve from a barrow outside a Piccadilly junk shop with the money she'd scrimped and saved for me.'

It was guilt that made him talk like this, that prompted this bathos to which he was inclined. His mother, worn out, had died before he'd made the money that would have made her dotage comfortable.

'Come, Martin.'

I followed him. He led me to the library where he took a key from a bureau drawer and opened a locked display case. Behind its carved-oak and scrolled-glass doors I saw Arthur Mee's encyclopedias on their shelf, his name on their worn, blue cloth spines.

'There are twelve volumes here, Dad.'

Beside me, he nodded. He put his hand on my shoulder. He was providing me with the human touch he needed for comfort at the mention of his mother. 'I sourced the twelfth. It's the same edition, printed in the same year. I wanted the full set, with full integrity.'

I looked up at my father's education in the wider world, his bookbound travels, his dreams and aspirations bound in blue cloth. There wasn't a lot to say.

He reached for a volume, thumbed out a spine. Volume six, it was. He held the spine of the heavy book in the palm of his hand and it fell open. I took a step back and looked at the open pages.

And I saw a picture of Harry Spalding's schooner rounding a buoy in brilliant sunshine on sun-dappled water at an angle dictated by taut sails that seemed to threaten disaster and promise triumph at the same exultant moment.

'*Dark Echo*,' my father said. There was an inset picture on the page of text facing the full plate of the racing boat. It was a grinning Harry Spalding in whites and blazer with a trophy in his grip and his blond hair a halo of gold on his head. He possessed none of the lupine menance of his Jericho Crew snapshot. He looked elegant and boyish and almost bashful at the attention accorded his win. He aped the style and character of the personality people wished him to be, almost to perfection. It was all I could do not to recoil.

'When I saw these pictures, Martin, I swore that I would own and sail this boat. And I do and I will. And nothing will stop me. And I hope to God you have the compassion to indulge an old man's vanity in fulfilling that dream.'

I said nothing.

'Do you?'

'Yes,' I said. I sipped from my cup. The coffee it contained was cold.

I could hear the faint hum in the library of the humidor that kept my father's cigars fresh. In the parking garage twenty feet beneath our feet, some fellow from Cracow or Kiev would be waxing the bodywork of the Bentley and the Aston Martin. But later in the afternoon, his old boxing trophies would be taken from their place of pride and faithfully buffed. And suddenly, I understood my father's retirement. At fifty-five, he had capitulated to the dreams of his childhood. He would indulge and fulfil them now, because he had the time and the means. He would not be deterred, either. He would act on these infantile whims with an iron will.

'Could I see the log today?'

'In what demeanour did you find my boat?'

'Demeanour?'

'Condition. Aspect. Boats have each of them a character, son. Did you find her defiant in the onslaught of yesterday's storm?'

I struggled to remember the boat's specifications. She was 121 feet in length, with a beam of nineteen feet and an eleven-foot draught. She weighed seventy tons. She was a two-masted, gaff-rigged schooner with a total sail area of just over 5,000 square feet. She was the *Dark Echo* and she was haunted by the ghost of her first master. And every bone in my body, every ounce of any instinct for danger I possessed, told me he was a murderous ghost. 'What they've done so far has been punctiliously accomplished, from what I could see,' I said. 'They're using long-length, quarter-sawn teak, caulked with cotton and stopped with black rubber, on her deck.'

'Good. Plugs?'

'I didn't see any. Butt joints are minimal and the planks are fastened from below.'

'Hadley told me the spars are laminated Alaskan spruce.'

'I'd happily take his word for it. It was gloomy yesterday afternoon and dark under her tarpaulin. But they looked very handsome, very well finished. Can I see the log today?'

'Of course you can. But it's more than a day's reading, I think.' He took some keys from a drawer in an antique bureau and tossed them at me. I caught them deftly enough. 'There's a storage facility I use.'

I nodded. I knew about the storage facility. I had been there. It was the place in which he secreted stuff he did not want to part with when a divorce negotiation deteriorated into a tug of war or a smash and grab. My father owned a substantial number of valuable modern paintings mostly picked up in the 1980s and early 90s when the painters had still been students struggling to pay their rent. It was over a decade since I'd seen a single one of them hanging in his house. They were stacked in darkness and secrecy in the storage facility in South Wimbledon. Everything of my mother's was there, too, in a room a person with a morbid turn of mind might term a shrine.

It took me an hour to get to Wimbledon and then another forty-five minutes to travel the half-mile distance to the storage facility car park. When I did finally arrive, I could see what had gridlocked the road. There were two fire tenders, as well as an accident investigation vehicle and a Met police car together blocking half its width. There was foam and surface water all over the road and the fire crews were still damping down. It was odd, because I'd seen no column of smoke nor heard the whoop of sirens waiting impatiently in the crawling column of traffic.

Most of the steel-framed, breeze-block storage buildings looked intact. I felt fairly sure that my father's precious modern art collection and my mother's gathered keepsakes would be undamaged and undisturbed. I knew with the certainty of a sinking heart what had been destroyed by the blaze.

A garrulous fire-fighter confirmed it for me. I asked him what had started the fire.

'A strongbox full of old books was the seat of it,' he said, chewing gum, his face black with soot from the smoke. 'Burned with unbelievable intensity, it did. Wonder the fire didn't spread, but it didn't, thankfully. Took us ages to put it out, though. We've been through two shifts just damping down.'

'Someone used an accelerant?'

He raised an eyebrow and looked down and rocked on his booted feet. 'Not for me to say, mate. Out of order for me to speculate. But paper doesn't burn like that. No way. Not at those temperatures. Not without a bit of encouragement.'

I nodded. I smelled the air. It was acrid, still. Foam from fire hoses gathered as brown and yellow scum in the street gutters, seeking drains. I'd hang about, of course. I'd verify facts with the people who ran the storage facility. I'd wait in a grey afternoon in this dismal bit of South-West London's suburbs and establish facts. But I knew with certainty that it was the *Dark Echo*'s five-volume log that had burned, before I could read it, before Frank Hadley could get his judicious hands on it. The fire had been started in the night, in the small hours, when I'd been enduring my wretched, dream-ridden sleep. I didn't know where it left our restoration schedule with Hadley's yard. I didn't even know how long it would take for them to inventory the damage and break the news of the loss to my father. In fact, only one thing was certain any longer in my mind. I would tell Suzanne. I would tell her everything, the moment she got back from Dublin. I did not believe that a problem shared was a problem halved. I did not believe in any platitudes with regard to this particular matter. But I did think that continued secrecy could be dangerous. And I was too scared at the momentum with which events seemed to be progressing to keep matters any longer to myself.

Three

My father used to say that confession was one of my distinguishing talents. Perhaps, he used to say, the only one. None of his jokes were ever really intended to provoke belly laughs. They were all cracked in the way of scoring points. But he had a point, where this particular crack was concerned. My failed vocation wounded him very deeply. It was what I was alluding to earlier when I said I had exhausted my credit with Dad where matters spiritual are concerned.

At the age of nineteen, I thought I had a vocation for the priesthood. The tug of faith in me felt overwhelmingly powerful and I did not try to resist it. I left university and joined a seminary and began to take instruction. I immersed myself in the piety and self-denial of serving God. It was about as unfashionable a life-choice as it would have been possible then to make. My vocation came calling in the 1990s. A certain sensitivity had become voguish among thinking men, an imperative to get to understand your masculinity and be more open and honest generally with women. It was a fad that would degenerate towards the end of the decade into navel gazing and a sad kind of self-obsession. But just then, sensitivity of a sort was acceptable. What was not, were cassocks and incense. The last time the Catholic clergy were fashionable was probably when Bing Crosby wore a dog collar and gave his speaking voice an Irish lilt in those sentimental Bowery-based Hollywood melodramas of the 1930s. Since then, it had all been downhill for the image of the priest.

My friends were appalled. They reacted as though I had become the victim of a cult. Most of them just dropped me. The couple that didn't tried to save me from the dangerous delusion about to sabotage my life before it had properly begun. My girlfriend of the time interpreted the whole process as a crisis of sexuality. I had discovered that I was gay but did not dare confront either her or myself with the truth. Her weird take on what was going on provoked in me the sin of vanity. Could I have been so hopelessly non-committal in bed with her? I hadn't thought so at all.

My father was delighted. My vocation made sense of everything in me that had confused and dismayed him. It justified my lack of aggression and competitive fire. It made a virtue of my dreamy inclination towards solitude. Best of all, I think, it provided him with grace. The sacrifice of his son to the priesthood was exactly like the medieval buying of indulgences by wealthy men too busy generating profit to find the necessary time for prayer. Only it was more so. My father wasn't ungodly, which was a sort of irony. He believed very devoutly in an omnipotent and sometimes vengeful God. But business life had compromised his chances of redemption and he had been lax in guaranteeing adequate compensations for his sins. In short, he was badly overdrawn at the Bank of the Almighty. My electing for a celibate life of poverty and devotion, in the service of his God, put him right back in the black. I'm guessing in saying that, but I think I'm right. I know my father and the knowing of him has come harshly earned. It's a well-educated guess.

I couldn't have been that unconvincing in bed because Rebecca, my college sweetheart, came to see me.

'Have you never admired a priest?'

She pondered this. 'The one in *The Exorcist*. He was cool. Sort of.'

She had on red lipstick and a clingy dress in black fabric

and she wore a push-up bra. She had sprayed or dabbed her skin with Shalimar perfume. She smelled delicious.

'Father Merrin.'

She shook her head. 'The other one. The young, flawed guy.'

'The whisky priest.'

'Him. He was sort of cool.'

'He didn't really believe.'

'That was what was cool about him.'

She brought with her a bag of provisions.

'This isn't a prison visit, Rebecca.'

'That's why I didn't bake you a cake with a file in it. Why are you smiling?'

'The idea of you baking any sort of cake.'

The bag was filled with temptations assembled to coax me out. She'd brought me an envelope of pictures of the two of us taken on a weekend in Brighton. She'd brought me an assortment of CDs. Van Morrison, Everything But The Girl, Prefab Sprout. Maybe she was just getting rid of them. 'Wimp rock' had always been her description of my taste in music. Most poignantly, she brought my football boots, bound together by their laces. I'd played every Sunday for a scratch team on Regent's Park and would greatly miss that ritual. I was missing it already. The seminary overlooked the sea from its hill on the remote and craggy coast of Northumberland. It was a Jesuit citadel built when Queen Victoria was young. I'd been there six weeks. I missed everything.

Rebecca, perfumed, smelled edible.

'Paddy McAloon trained for the priesthood.'

'Who?'

I gestured at one of the CDs she'd brought me. *Steve McQueen*. 'He's the singer in Prefab Sprout. He writes all their songs.'

'Is that your game plan, Martin? Train for the priesthood and become a rock star?'

The only time I'd ever had a game plan in my life was when I'd formulated one for beating Winston Cory. It had put me on my arse with my nose broken. 'I'm not rock star material.'

'You're far too handsome to be a priest.'

'God might disagree with you.'

She shook her head. There were tears in her eyes. 'I've come all the way to fucking Northumberland,' she said. She started to put the stuff back into her bag. Her pictures. My boots. I hadn't cleaned them properly after my last game and Rebecca hadn't bothered either before bringing them. The familiar Regent's Park football pitch odour of soil and dog shit clung to the studs. She dropped a snapshot on to the floor and snatched it up again and pushed strands of fallen hair away from her face. 'Such a fucking waste.'

I lasted nineteen months. I endured in that time no great crisis of faith. The other novices were bright and amenable and good. Some of them were profoundly good. These privileged few, the rest of us felt privileged to be among. From them, I learned what it was to live in a state of grace. I encountered no closet Nazis and no one who thought the priesthood a secure route to a secret future of child molestation. The black propaganda attached to the organised Church proved to be exactly that in my personal experience. The most sinister crime I came across was an occasional tendency on the part of some of the older instructors to sermonise at length. But there are people in all walks of life that combine a fondness for the sound of their own voices with an inability to say anything original. It's a human, not a Catholic or a religious failing.

Of course, the Jesuits owed their bad reputation to events of four hundred years ago. The torture and burnings of the

Counter-Reformation came a long time prior to ambivalence within the Vatican over Mussolini and Hitler, and the child abuse scandals covered up by dioceses in Chicago and Dublin and a depressing litany of other places. But the Jesuit with whom I came chiefly into contact was probably the holiest man I'd ever met. Monsignor Delaunay was said by some to be distantly related to the great French painter of the same name. He organised occasional retreats at a house owned by the Church in Barmouth on the Welsh coast. The house was Georgian. It was a solid, isolated three-storey building overlooking the bay. To its left, majestic in the Welsh mist clinging to the sea, rose the great edifice of Cader Idris a few miles along the peninsula.

There was rumoured to be a monster in the sea at Barmouth. What lent the story credence was that it had originated with fishermen and not tourists. It did not stop Monsignor Delaunay enjoying his daily constitutional of a mile-long swim. He did not have the gaunt, fastidious look made stereotypical in his order by its grim founder. He was a strapping man with a hammer-thrower's arms and shoulders whose sheer bulk defied the freezing water when he swam in the winter. At night, around a driftwood fire in the library of the house, he would tell his war stories of missions to Africa and South America. I always felt there were things he did not choose to share with his raw and innocent audience. But the tales were spellbinding nevertheless. In Barmouth, within hearing range of Monsignor Delaunay, I could really believe I had a future serving a great, merciful, formidable God. Delaunay had the rare gift of making faith contagious.

What did for me in the end was that I just couldn't endure the cold solitude of celibacy. I craved physical intimacy. Rebecca cavorted in my dreams wearing nothing but a splash of her Guerlain perfume. The last three months were terrible.

I was only nineteen and already facing the second great failure to afflict my life. And this one was wholly my fault. There was no mitigation to be had. I prayed, but doing so only seemed to demonstrate the futility of prayer. I prayed, the demeanour of a martyr concealing the instinct of a rabbit in heat. In such circumstances, I could hardly turn to the traditional source in a seminary of comfort and reassurance. Confession would have been of no help at all to someone so desperate to commit sin. There was no choice but to give up, and pack up and leave.

It's fair to say that my father took this badly. Prior to the call of my false vocation, I'd been doing pretty well on a history and politics degree course at the London School of Economics. But the course was oversubscribed and they couldn't see any way two years on to take me back. Despite my qualifications and past academic record, if a place did become available, there were more deserving cases than mine, apparently, on an existing waiting list. I ended up on a straight history course at the University of Kent at Canterbury. My father was gracious enough to pay my tuition fees and to help make up my grant shortfall which, in fairness to him, constituted practically the entire grant. But he did not really speak to me for about three years, and he chose not to attend my degree congregation. I couldn't much blame him. I'd cost him his chance of an easy passage into Heaven. Even to a man as wealthy as my dad, that was quite a loss to endure.

Rebecca, of course, had long moved on by the time of what everyone still talking to me termed my release. She was dating a property developer from Fulham. I saw them together in a bar in Pimlico about eight months after leaving the seminary. I'd had a bit to drink. I might have picked a fight with him, had he been bigger and taller than he was and therefore an opponent I could goad into a scrap without being labelled afterwards a bully. But hitting him, even drunk, I knew was only marginally less infantile than letting down the tyres of his Porsche. I was hugely to blame for what had happened with Rebecca. She was only slightly to blame. The property developer was not to blame at all. But passing what I assumed was his Porsche, on the way home from that bar, I have to say I was sorely tempted.

Between discarding Rebecca and meeting Suzanne, I did have relationships with women. But they were casual and sometimes callous and always fleeting. Romance and spontaneity are, I think, the biggest casualties of the age of the text and the email. Everything now seems so contingent and circumscribed. There's no place for sincerity when you can so easily avoid the honest call of a human voice. Thank God for the Shadwell Pussies, I used to think. They delivered Suzanne, saved me from solitude and brought me love. That's what I used to think, before I sat her down after her return from Dublin and told her everything that had occurred since my father's purchase of the wreck of the *Dark Echo*.

Her flight from Dublin had been delayed and she got back tired and a bit fraught anyway. She was not making the progress with the Michael Collins research that she had been expected to. Someone superior to her in the programme-making hierarchy had fallen into the trap of reaching conclusions about some aspects of Collins' life and character before the research had vindicated them. It was the classic pitfall in their particular line of work. Everybody did it, but that didn't make it any more acceptable a tendency. It was unreasonable and unfair. It had put extra pressure on Suzanne. She got back to London frustrated and angry.

She stood over by our open sitting-room window and smoked a cigarette while she considered what I had told her. She had been a heavy smoker from a family of smokers when I'd met her. She'd cut down considerably since then. But she still smoked Marlboro Reds. And the smoke drifted from her nostrils in two satisfied plumes when she smoked. She stood there in the chill of the window with her cigarette poised elegantly in her hand beside her pale jaw, thinking. Her black hair was cut into a glossy and precise bob. Her eyes, a brown so burnished they were almost black, glittered in the light from the street below. She was dressed in a black pencil skirt and a white shirt and her hair at its edge was geometrically neat above the white, open collar of the shirt. Not for the first time, I thought she looked like a woman from another time, from an era when the circumstances in which the two of us lived would have been nothing other than scandalous. She wouldn't have cared. That was something else again about her.

Smoke wreathed around her lovely head. You could easily imagine Michael Collins making a play for her at some dinner held to fête him during the London peace negotiations that indirectly caused his death. You could imagine Harry Spalding doing the same at some plush and exclusive tennis or yachting club. He would click across the parquet in his leather heels approaching her. His tread would be light but determined. She would catch the eye of any man. There was a challenge in her, though, that the predators among them might find irresistible.

Eventually, she ground out her cigarette stub in a foil ashtray on the sill and flicked it out of the window. 'I'd heard something about the curse of the *Dark Echo*. More precisely, it might be termed the curse on the *Dark Echo*. I did a bit of preliminary digging after our conversation on the evening of the day of auction.'

'Why did you do that?'

She turned to me. 'I did it because of your father's proposition. Because although you sounded proud and flattered, you also sounded afraid.'

'Something spooked me,' I said. 'Looking at Spalding's

face in the group picture of the Jericho Crew, I felt something so strong it was almost a premonition. Walking home afterwards in the fog across Lambeth Bridge, I felt as though I was being followed.'

She nodded. And she wrapped her arms around herself and shivered. The London night was very quiet outside our open window in the flat. But you could feel the drift of river damp on the air. It was now early March and the air still raw. 'You're a very intuitive man, Martin.'

'No, I'm not.'

'Because you didn't see the punch coming that broke your nose? Or because you wasted a year and a half of your life on a failed vocation?'

'Either example would stand as evidence.'

'How do you think the fire was started that destroyed the vessel's log? Bearing in mind that it burned with such stubborn ferocity, I mean.'

'I don't know, Suzanne. In my mind's eye I see the spectre of Harry Spalding with a Very pistol in his hand. He grins his death's head grin in the darkness in the vault as he pulls the trigger and fires a distress flare into the pile of volumes.'

'But we'll never know. Everything burned, so we'll never know,' she said. And this surprised me.

'I thought you'd laugh out loud, telling you that,' I said.

She rubbed at her shivering arms again with her hands. She closed the window. She always waited a while, like this. She hated the thought of my smelling the burned tobacco on her breath. I didn't mind it, really. I had grown up with the ubiquitous stink of my father's cigars all my young life.

'Something happened to me on my earlier visit to Dublin, Martin. It happened on the Wednesday. It happened on the same day as the auction.'

The *Michael Collins* series producer was a BBC high-flyer called Gerald Smythe. He was an obnoxious and unreasonable bully and he was driving Suzanne very hard, I knew. 'Smythe treat you to one of his bollockings?'

I knew she dreaded the edicts sent her via his BlackBerry. But she shook her head. 'Nothing like that.'

'Then tell me.'

She had been on one of those interminably long Georgian streets on the North side of the Liffey. She had been looking under her umbrella, in the rain, for a particular address. The streets were so long and so straight in that part of the city that you could see their gentle incline as they rose towards the distant smudge of the Dublin Mountains. She could hear rain hiss and gurgle in the gutter on its descent to the drains. The streets to her in this part of the city were indistinguishable from one another. In a sense they were featureless. All the houses looked the same; rain-stained and austere with iron boot cleaners outside imposing doors standing at the top of worn sets of stone steps. They were handsome in their way, the houses. But they were a bleak sight in the flat rainy light, dwellings redolent of a harder, plainer age.

After years of near dereliction, this part of Dublin had finally caught the fraying tail of the Celtic Tiger and was coming up in the world. The owner of the house was a psychiatrist. He had bought it only recently. But he was not there, was away at a symposium, and Suzanne had been entrusted with the key. And the neglect was good news for her. This area had provided Collins with a warren of safe refuges. In the period ninety years ago, after his release from the internment camp at Frongoch in Wales, he had hidden here. And it had been the same. Those same steps would have heard the patter of his rapid boots. His soft rap would have sounded on that very bronze doorknocker.

He had been by then a member of the executive of Sinn Fein and a director of the Irish Volunteers. He was a veteran of the Post Office siege during the failed Easter Rising.

His will and his charisma had singled him out as a natural leader in his time at Frongoch. There, the British Secret Service had been sufficiently impressed to begin the file they would compile on him. She stopped walking. She had found her address. She rummaged in her pocket for the key. She climbed the wet stone steps. In his time of hiding here, Michael Collins had been twenty-seven years old.

She opened the front door and collapsed her umbrella, aware of the slight staleness coming from within and grateful that the new owner had not yet commissioned the refurbishment work to the house that would gut its interior. She closed the door softly behind her and unbuttoned her coat.

The interior of the house was dim and chilly in the dank late morning. The hallway was long and high-ceilinged. Its walls were covered in plain and dingy plaster and its floor was stone, and inlaid with a chipped and worn stucco design. At the end of the hall there were stairs leading both down and up. Suzanne guessed on up. Collins was too wily and too practised a fugitive to trap himself at night in a cellar. He would want to sleep where the crash of army boots ascending stairs would provide him with fair warning. He would want a point of exit to take him to the escape route across the flat terraced roofs.

She climbed the stairs. She had left her umbrella dripping on the cold stone of the entrance hall. But she had kept her coat on. The house was not heated in its owner's absence and she could see her breath exhaled in little puffs as she climbed the steep, uncarpeted staircase. She paused only when she reached a door at the very top of the house. She had discovered the address scrawled on a series of expenses chits that were part of a cache of old Irish Volunteers papers kept in the archive at Dublin Castle. They detailed the cost of food and drink ordered over a period of evenings from Dooley's Hotel around the corner. The name attached to these punctiliously numbered and dated chits was not Collins. It was Browne. But Collins, while strict about expenses, was lavish with aliases. And Suzanne had recognised the careful script learned during his clerical service in London as a youth. It had been him. He had stayed here. He had held meetings here. Plans had been formulated and strategy decided upon that had changed the course of a nation's history.

She opened the door.

The room was furnished with a truckle bed, a wardrobe and a single straight-backed chair. There was a narrow, rectangular window, its small panes drab with dust. The bed was long stripped, its bare springs slightly rusted but still taut against the pull of the angle-iron frame. The floor was of bare boards. She shivered. There was nothing menacing about this small and modest room. She could hear rain patter above her on a skylight. She pulled the chair over and stood on it, the better to examine this. One of the boyos handy with a chisel and a hammer had put it there, she knew. The work was neat enough. But it was not an original feature of the house. The wooden frame had been canted slightly so that rain would not puddle on the pane. There was a catch at one edge of the skylight and, at the opposite edge, there was a sturdy double hinge. A man would need to be able to lift his own weight with his arms to lever himself through there from the height of a chair. But Collins had been young and very strong. No bother, as he would have said himself. No bother at all.

She stepped off the chair and walked over to the wardrobe, smiling to herself. She thought they should photograph as a still image rather than film the room she was in. It was intact and complete. They had the budget to run to one of those docudrama recreations of actors playing Collins and Cathal Brugha, or someone, seated on the made-up bed, plotting atmospherically by lamp or candlelight. And she was sure the psychiatrist who owned the place would tolerate the disruption involved in that process. But a still image would better reflect the simplicity of the places in which Collins rested from his war against the most powerful empire in the world, the places where he hid in temporary refuge from his enemies.

She was smiling because she was sure there would be a mirror. She stepped over to the wardrobe and opened it. It was a narrow item with a single door. It opened on the faintest scent of Bay Rum and mothballs. She saw the space where his overcoat and dapper suit would have hung. She saw the thin brass rail screwed to the inside of the door over which his unknotted tie would have hung and smoothed itself out during the night. And above that, she saw the little mirror in which he would have fussed and preened, indulging the peacock vanity that was so much a part of this complex man's make-up.

Suzanne closed the wardrobe door with her secret smile widening. And she sensed a warmth envelop her in the room, in the quiet. And she did not feel that she was any longer alone in it. It was very sudden, this change in atmosphere. She turned sharply and looked around. Everything was the same. But the temperature in there had risen, she was sure. The room no longer had the same raw, desolate quality of neglect that had characterised it only a moment earlier. It felt entirely different. It felt occupied. She could feel a presence. She could almost smell the warm, amused humanity of the energetic presence watching her there, in repose. She heard a slight creak from the bed as though the weight of someone sitting there shifted and stretched in relaxation.

'Then what happened?' I asked her.

'Nothing happened,' she said. 'The moment passed. The feeling sort of . . . evaporated. But I felt it. I did not imagine it. For a moment, he was there.'

'What time was this? Roughly?'

'I'll tell you exactly. It was twelve fifteen. I looked at my watch. And then I left.'

Twelve fifteen. Just after the auction. She had looked at her watch at the exact moment I had looked at mine at the boatyard of Bullen and Clore on seeing the foreman there cross himself in the presence of my father's prize.

'It was why I was still awake and alert when you sent me that text late in the evening,' she said. 'Nothing remotely like that has ever happened to me before. I was still pondering on the experience. It was inexplicable. But it was real.'

I did not say anything. I did not doubt her, though.

'I want to show you something,' Suzanne said. She went and got her travel bag and put it on the table and unzipped and rummaged in it. She took out a Manila envelope with the flap folded rather than gummed, and opened it. She took out the contents, a Xerox copy of a page of newsprint, folded into four. And she handed it to me. She had attached a Post-it note to the upper left-hand corner of the photocopied document. She was very punctilious about her research, even when it was research she wasn't supposed to be doing. On the Post-it note, she had written *Liverpool Daily Post, August 9, 1927*. I removed that and unfolded the photocopied broadsheet page. It was laid out like a diary rather than a news page. There were three photographs, far too many for a news page of the period, which might carry one picture at most. The relevant article was the most prominent. It had been printed under the heading BOATBUILDER ALL AT SEA.

Distinguished boatbuilder Mr Patrick Boyte, 54, yesterday attended James Street police station to witness the release from custody of his daughter, Jane Elizabeth Boyte, 29. Miss Boyte had been arrested and questioned on a matter neither the Liverpool Constabulary, nor the Boyte family, proved willing to disclose or further discuss. Mr Boyte was at pains, however, to emphasise that his daughter was released without precondition or charge, and that bail was never set and, further, that no charge or charges are pending.

Our reporter attempted to engage Mr Boyte on the happier matter of the successes enjoyed at Cowes last week by Mr Harry Spalding aboard his racing schooner, *Dark Echo*. Regular *Post* readers will recall that the vessel put into the Boyte dock little more than a listing hulk in the aftermath of the great storm of April last. Did Mr Boyte agree that the Cowes victories of last week were testament to the refurbishment work completed in his own yard?

But Mr Boyte would not be drawn. 'I've nothing to say concerning the vessel or her master,' he said.

Would he not wish, through the columns of the *Post,* to extend his congratulations to Mr Spalding?

'I would not,' he said. And with his newly liberated daughter on his arm, he bid our correspondent a curt goodbye.

I read this account twice. There was a tone about it, an underlying sarcasm, more spiteful than I would have thought appropriate to a diary piece. That said, being arrested, when you were a woman of quality, was not a light-hearted occurrence eighty years ago. And the Boytes were of quality, both. Patrick was prosperous-looking. The light in the picture exposed the vivid detail of a sunny late-summer day. Patrick Boyte, bald and sturdy and tall, glowered in tailored broadcloth with a thick gold watch chain worn across his waistcoat, and a waxed collar and silk necktie. The hand not gripping his daughter's carried a hat and a cane. Jane was svelte and groomed with bobbed hair and wearing a light summer coat.

It reminded me of the contemporary reportage about the suffragettes I'd read at university, the tone of the piece. It was characterised by the same wise, condescending mockery as those stories had been. But it had been written two decades too late for Jane's crime to be anything to do with the struggle to win votes for women.

And the Boytes had been set up, the *Post* tipped off. Cameras in those days did not take pictures of this quality without a tripod and careful preparation. The distance had been exactly judged and the bright light metred. Someone in the Liverpool police had helped engineer this public embarrassment. The pair had been ambushed on the station steps. It made me wonder what Jane Boyte had done to provoke such hostility. It made me wonder what she had done to get herself arrested.

But that wasn't what chiefly intrigued me. What really struck me, looking at it, was the image of Jane Boyte herself. She shared her father's deep expression of indignant fury. She was fiercely beautiful. And she looked so similar in her physique and facial features to the woman standing next to me that she and Suzanne could have been sisters. I folded the page back into four and put it on top of its envelope on the table.

'Jane Boyte could have been your twin.'

'There is a resemblance. She's a similar type to me. At least, she appears so in that particular photograph. But that's not the point.'

And neither was the arrest. Patrick Boyte was the point, and what he chose not to say to the reporter from the *Post* about the job he had carried out for Harry Spalding.

'I don't think what you have told me tonight about poor Frank Hadley is happening for the first time,' Suzanne said. 'I think it's all happened before.'

'There's more, isn't there?' I said.

She nodded. 'There's more.'

We went to the pub. It was ten o'clock and, of course,

she was tired from the delayed flight. But we went anyway because Suzanne said that what she wanted to tell me would be better said over a drink. We went to the Windmill around the corner from the flat in Lambeth High Street and found a corner table to the rear of the virtually empty pub. It was fittingly nautical. There were old framed prints on the walls of barques and schooners and tugs from the passed age of the Thames as a working river. Some of them could have been taken as recently as the 1960s. But they all seemed distant and antique, so thoroughly lost in time were they.

His boat had belonged to two illustrious owners after Spalding's death. The first of these was a Boston speculator who became seriously wealthy after being one of the very few men to see the Crash of 1929 coming. Everyone with any brains knew there would be a stock market crash eventually. Most believed it was a self-fulfilling prophecy. But Stephen Waltrow guessed it to the week. His buying of Spalding's boat caused a minor stir on the society pages of the Boston and New York newspapers. Spalding wasn't quite cold in his grave when Waltrow made the purchase. And the Crash itself was what most people assumed had provoked the young man's suicide.

In that, they were very much mistaken, Suzanne said. I sipped from my pint of bitter. There was music playing in the pub. Thankfully, it wasn't Josephine Baker. Billy Paul was lamenting his way through 'Me and Mrs Jones'.

Stephen Waltrow was a twin. As boys, he and his brother had sailed dinghies. Their upbringing had been lower middle class. But they had grown up close to the harbour and their father had been a keen boatman and had taught them to sail when they were still in knickerbockers. They had an aptitude for it. They were skilled, resourceful and hardy. At the age of fourteen, they were embroiled in a yachting tragedy when six dinghies involved in a race around Boston harbour were hit by a squall so sudden and savage that there was no real warning of it. Four of the dinghies had capsized and sunk. Seven boys were drowned. It was a wait of nine anxious hours and darkness had long fallen before the Waltrow boys nursed their battered boat back to the slipway from which they had launched. They were shaken and had lost friends. But with the cold resilience of children, they were back on the water the following weekend.

Kevin Waltrow did not share his twin's business acumen. He became a cop. But when Stephen acquired Spalding's boat, he was only too happy to weekend aboard her when he could. Unlike his bachelor brother, Kevin was married with two young children and his new weekend hobby was the cause of some friction at home. This was especially true when, three months after buying her, Stephen suggested the brothers spend an Easter week sailing *Dark Echo* to Long Island and back.

A donation made by Stephen to the Boston Constabulary Benevolent Fund seems to have been what secured Kevin sufficient holiday time to go along on the trip, Suzanne said. What his wife had to say about it wasn't known. Nothing much was known after the boat set off early on the morning of April 4, 1930 into a clear day and a stiffening onshore breeze from Boston harbour. Certainly nothing was reported, though the vessel was equipped with a high-grade Marconi set. Nothing was known or suspected until she was found eight days later, drifting 150 miles offshore, unmanned and travelling lazily with the current.

She was towed back to New Jersey and impounded and searched. Nothing significant was found aboard her. Of the brothers Waltrow, there was no sign at all. Eventually, a month later, she was towed back to Boston. Here, perhaps because of Stephen's wealth or perhaps because of Kevin's status as one of Boston's finest, she was searched more thoroughly and a primitive forensic examination was carried out.

'Did they find anything?'

Suzanne sipped her drink. 'They found quite a lot of blood. It looked as though the brothers might have been fighting. One of them could have been cut on a gaff or something. Accidents occur on boats all the time. But the boys were of different blood groups. And both types were present in fairly liberal quantities.'

'Anything else?'

She nodded. 'Stephen Waltrow's chequebook. It was in a drawer in a bureau in the master cabin. That, too, was blood-smeared. In black ink, in his own hand, he had scrawled five words on the back of it. One sentence: "To be with the others."'

'Did the mystery create much of a stir?'

'Not really. It occurred at a tumultuous time in American life. The country was short neither of scandal nor sensation. But it was the subject of a sort of probe. That's where I got most of my information.'

The investigator was a man called Ernie Howes. Howes was a former cop and private eye who had turned to psychic investigation in the aftermath of the Great War when the collective grief of desolate parents created a boom for self-styled experts in reaching lost sons beyond the grave. Howes ran a lucrative line in exposing fake mediums. But he also fed the appetites of the gullible by filing news stories with an occult slant of his own whenever he could.

The dinghy tragedy could have meant that the boys were somehow doomed. The twins could be written up as a living and dying example of how it just wasn't possible to cheat fate. Or he could just go with the unlucky boat angle. Spalding's suicide had made national headlines. Stephen Waltrow had been the second millionaire in a year to come to a sticky end as owner of the *Dark Echo*. Surely she was cursed? People liked stories about unlucky boats. For whatever reason, they were apt to believe them, just as they were apt to believe in stories about haunted mansions.

'Which story did he go with?'

'Neither,' Suzanne told me. At our table in the corner of the pub, she was worrying at a thumbnail with her teeth. 'He interviewed Kevin Waltrow's widow and was told about Kevin's increasing moodiness and violence in the home in the weeks leading up to the voyage. And cynically, he approached Kevin's seven-year-old son Michael in search of further lurid detail. I don't believe Boston's finest were too keen on stories about recently deceased officers who beat their wives and heard commanding voices in their heads at night. Ernie Howes woke up in a Boston hotel one morning and discovered a live bullet on the pillow next to his head. This item of ammunition was a soft-point police issue .38 calibre. He took the hint. He never wrote a word about the Waltrows or the *Dark Echo*.'

'How did you find all this out?'

'Believe it or not, the outcome of the story is not entirely tragic. Michael Waltrow and his younger sister Mollie eventually inherited the bulk of their uncle's fortune. Michael is eighty-four now, in full possession of his senses and a distinguished landscape painter living out his last years on Martha's Vineyard. I found his number and telephoned him and spoke to him there. I told him I was researching the *Dark Echo*. He did not ask for what purpose, so I was not obliged to lie.'

'He was happy to speak to you?'

Suzanne shook her head. 'Happy would be entirely the wrong word. But he said he was relieved to be able to speak about it at last. It was he who told me about Howes, an unpleasant, sweaty man who stank of whisky and dime-store cigars, he said.'

'What did he tell you about his father?'

'He said his father became possessed by the Devil. From being a gentle, humorous man, he turned into a volatile monster they all feared and none of the household recognised. The transformation occurred over a few weeks. He was convinced his father murdered his own brother aboard the boat before destroying himself. But he was adamant the Devil was to blame.'

'He didn't blame the boat herself?'

'No. He was a seven-year-old boy from a Boston Catholic family when these events occurred. He thought his father became possessed. Still does.'

'What did he do with the boat?'

'Nothing. Mollie Waltrow inherited the *Dark Echo*. She sat gathering rust, a hulk in dry dock. Mollie sold the boat for salvage the day she reached the age of maturity without ever having put a foot aboard her.'

I sat back in my seat and took this in. I swallowed the dregs of tepid beer from my glass. There was music playing in the bar, but it was indistinct in the fuzziness afflicting my mind after what Suzanne had told me.

'How did you source the story about Patrick Boyte?'

I knew Spalding had stayed at the Palace Hotel in Birkdale after being forced into Liverpool to repair storm damage. I just did a Google search for Spalding, Liverpool and boatyard. That piece came up.'

'You were non-committal when I asked you if you knew anything about *Dark Echo*. You were downright evasive.'

'Don't be angry, Martin. I didn't want to rain on your dad's parade. That's all.'

'Then why come clean now?'

'I love you,' she said. 'I care about you. After what you told me this evening, I didn't feel I had any choice but to tell you what I have.'

'My father must know all this stuff.'

'I suspect so. He'll know some of it, anyway. You said he'd read the log.'

'Two owners, Suzanne. You said there were two owners.'

'And I'll tell you about the second of them. But I badly need a cigarette. Can I tell you at home?'

She recounted the second story in her study after I had poured her a glass of wine. There was a small extractor fan in the window in her study and she switched it on before she sat at her desk and turned to face me. It was the one room in the flat where I suppose she felt she could smoke relatively guilt-free. She had turned on the radio, too, when I returned to the study with the wine. Bebop from a jazz station drowned out the hum of the fan's whirring electric motor.

Gubby Tench was a third-rate playboy who bought the *Dark Echo* in the summer of 1937 when he was thirty-nine years old and fresh, if that's the term, from his second divorce. The fact that he was able to afford the boat proved that he had extricated himself from marriage without going broke. But the vessel was floating by this time in much reduced circumstances. A diesel engine had been fitted to cut down on the cost of crewmen experienced at manipulating sails. Tench was adept enough as a sailor. But when financial circumstances demanded it, the engine meant that he could haul in the sails and manage the craft single-handedly in most sorts of weather.

The boat had lost a lot of its lustre. She had also lost her original name. When Tench became the vessel's master, she had been rechristened *Ace of Clubs*. It was an appropriate choice. Tench was an inveterate, even compulsive gambler. His first voyage took him from Miami, where he bought the boat, to Havana, where he berthed her in the bay to go ashore eager for action in the Cuban capital's many celebrated casinos.

The crossing from Miami took him three days and three nights in a fog other masters in the area described afterwards as pretty near impenetrable. It played havoc with their instruments. It interfered with wireless transmission. Compass readings were inconsistent, inaccurate, useless. It would have been interesting, in the light of subsequent events, to know what was happening to Gubby Tench during this weird period of unnavigable weather. But, of course, the log had been destroyed, so nobody knew or would ever know what he had been up to, what he had been thinking.

'Unless my dad knows,' I said. 'He claims to have read every volume of the log.'

Suzanne smiled and lit another cigarette. She was chain-smoking, well above her self-permitted ration of ten a day. 'I doubt Gubby Tench committed a single line to the log during his voyage,' she said. 'I don't think he was much of a stickler for any sort of seagoing protocol. And I don't get the impression he was much of a diarist.'

He arrived in Havana running a high temperature. Epidemics were common in pre-war Cuba. The floor manager of one of the casinos, supervising the blackjack tables, thought that Gubby Tench looked like a man incubating cholera. He was sweating heavily and his breath was a shallow wheeze. But such diseases were generally confined to the slums and contagion rare among high-rolling American visitors. And this visitor had only just disembarked. Nevertheless, the comment was made later by more than one witness that Tench looked feverish and ill. But it didn't affect his form at the tables. On his first night, he won big. On his second, he won even bigger. On his third evening, drawing a crowd by now, he turned from blackjack to roulette and took on the house, betting consistently on the black, taking close to one hundred thousand dollars in winnings by the time the spell broke at around four thirty in the morning.

'By the time the spell broke?'

'That was what the other gamblers and the table operators said it was like. They said it was as though Tench gambled in a trance. They said it was as though he could not lose.'

'I'm surprised he was permitted to go on winning,' I said. 'I'm surprised he was permitted to go on playing. Weren't all the Cuban casinos of the period owned by the Mafia?'

'Some,' Suzanne said. 'The Cuban dictator, Batista, leased some casinos to the Mafia. The rest were run by his cronies and owned indirectly by him. But they were happy to ride out the odd big win. Nobody ever really beats the house if they keep coming back. And streaks like the one Tench enjoyed have always kept the serious punters coming.'

Except that Gubby Tench did not exactly seem to be enjoying his own run of good fortune. On his fourth evening he was so ill, he was attended to at the roulette table by a doctor. He was running a fever of 105. His blood pressure was off the scale. He was soaked in sweat and breathing in shallow, alarming gasps. His speech was slurred when he spoke, though no one saw him so much as sip from the complimentary drinks lined up at his elbow. He drank only from a glass of iced water and the rocks in it chinked audibly with the tremor in his hand whenever he picked it up to sip from it.

Yet still he won. By the conclusion of his fourth night at the tables, he had accrued enough chips to need a barrow to take them to the cashier. They sat in a gaudy hill of painted ivory in front of him on the baize. And he smiled and took a revolver from the pocket of his tuxedo. And he flicked out the cylinder over the baize and shook out six bullets. He blinked at the people around him through the six circular bores he'd made empty. He winked at a girl waiting tables with his tongue lolling and a look so emptily lascivious that she didn't sleep afterwards for a week. Then he picked up a single bullet and loaded it into a chamber and gave the cylinder a spin. He cocked the hammer and put the barrel to his temple with a grin and pulled the trigger.

'All the other players left the table,' Suzanne said. 'Nobody wanted to get spattered in Tench's gore. But they all stayed to watch. These were very free and easy times in Havana, in the 1930s. And they were all gamblers present. And it was an arresting sight, to see a man take a happy punt on his own life.'

Gubby Tench squeezed the trigger. And the revolver's hammer clicked on an empty chamber. And he blinked and a cloud of disappointment seemed to drift across his dazed features. He fumbled among the bullets on the baize in front of him. In total, he loaded five bullets into the six chambers of the revolver's cylinder. He grinned and gave it a spin and brought the weapon up once more to his temple. Somebody screamed. He squeezed the trigger.

'And the hammer clicked on the one empty chamber,' I said.

Suzanne nodded. 'He did it five times. He did it once for every bullet that the gun possessed. Then he shook out the shells and gathered his chips in a tablecloth from the bar and cashed them as his stunned audience clapped him out of there.'

'He was very lucky.'

'He wasn't lucky at all,' Suzanne said. 'Luck had nothing to do with it. Five to one is lucky. But five to one to the power of five? Nobody beats those odds.'

'The only plausible explanation is that the ammunition in the pistol was dud.'

'It wasn't his pistol. He took it surreptitiously from the shoulder holster of a gangster working a security shift on the floor. He seemed to be capable of conjuring tricks, of any feat of dexterity or sleight of hand or legerdemain. He paid a half a dollar that evening for a ride back to his bunk aboard a tobacco boat working the bay as a water taxi. The pilot said the money was wasted. By that stage they believed he could have walked upon the ocean back to the *Ace of Clubs*.'

Which was, of course, Spalding's *Dark Echo*. It was merely masquerading as another craft.

Gubby Tench did not return the next night to the casinos, or the night after that. After four days, the smell was noticed coming from his anchored boat in the bay. Havana was hot and the corruption of death quick and almost overpowering. Police and militia boarded the vessel, assuming that they would find a dead victim of robbery. And they duly found a corpse. But Tench had not been murdered by thieves. Nobody had been aboard the boat but its master. Or nobody had been aboard, at least, who had left any trace of themselves behind.

Tench had sat at the chart table in the master cabin and put the barrel of a Very pistol in his mouth and pulled the trigger. Dollars and gold and silver ingots and promissory notes and even some casino chips lay before him in a bright hoard on the tabletop. He was still attired in his dress shirt and tuxedo. They were sweat-stained, yellow, the garments stretched over his bloating corpse, the fabric of his shirt pulled to reveal a pale torso in elliptical glimpses of flesh between the buttons. The flare had not gone off when Tench had fired the pistol. But the release of the flare had been of sufficient force to blow off the top of his skull. Skull fragments and bits of brain matter were painted across the ceiling and rear wall of the cabin. It was a death as inexplicable as it was messy. There were, of course, no witnesses. And there was no note to cast light on the suicide's motive. He had sought to destroy everything of himself in an inferno in Havana harbour amid his riches, aboard his little floating domain. He had succeeded only in self-murder of a particularly messy kind.

'It's why I didn't laugh earlier,' Suzanne said, 'when you shared your vision or dream or whatever it was concerning the blaze that destroyed the *Dark Echo* logs. The mention of a distress flare reminded me of the awful fate of Gubby Tench.'

I was silent. There was nothing to say. It was very late, now. Cigarette smoke had crept around the little room despite the efforts of the electric fan, and the air in there felt stale and dead.

'I wonder whether they knew one another,' Suzanne said.

'Who?'

'Spalding. Waltrow. Tench.'

'Where was Gubby Tench from?'

'New Orleans.'

'Then it's unlikely,' I said. 'Boston and New York are fairly far apart. Distances were much greater in those days before regular domestic airline flights. New Orleans is positively remote from both of those places, even now. You could argue that banking and financial speculation are sister occupations. But Tench was a professional gambler. He's not only geographically distant from Spalding and Waltrow. Culturally, he's in a different universe.'

But she wasn't really listening to me. 'They were all three the same age,' she said, 'give or take a year or two. I wonder if they met in the war.' She looked at me and I sensed a complication coming. 'War makes a nonsense of demographics, Martin. It has no respect for barriers of class or culture. I'd very much like to see your father's photograph of the Jericho Crew.'

I did not answer her.

'That's funny.'

'What is?'

Suzanne had turned to the radio. 'They've just played this. They're playing the same song again. They're repeating it.'

I recognised the song myself. It didn't sound like jazz. She had the radio permanently tuned to a jazz station. The song was 'When Love Breaks Down', by Prefab Sprout. The failed priest, Paddy McAloon, was singing it. According to Suzanne, he was reprising it. It did seem strange. But it was a small strangeness, a domestic oddity, after the tale of Gubby Tench. I walked over to the radio and switched it off. 'I think it's time for bed,' I said. I put my arms around Suzanne for the comfort of her. Her hair smelled of smoke and her skin of stale perfume and the recycled air you're obliged to breathe aboard aircraft. But her body was warm and yielding and wonderful against mine. I closed my eyes and thanked God again for her. It was God, not the Shadwell Posse, I believed I had to thank for Suzanne. And I thought I heard a single, plangent chord of McAloon balladry from the radio on its shelf. But I must have imagined that because Suzanne stayed softly pressed against me with her hands linked in the small of my back.

I did not want her going anywhere near the Jericho Crew. They were long dead, as my father had pointed out. But to me they were feral ghosts that could maraud across the decades, given the right encouragement. They were malevolent and restless and waiting in an impatient pack behind their hungry leader. No, the Jericho Crew were best left to history and themselves. All my instincts told me so. I untangled myself from Suzanne and went and brushed my teeth and then got into bed and listened to her shower. We finally fell asleep, thankfully dreamless, wrapped in one another's arms in the Lambeth night.

* * *

I was awoken the following morning by an agitated phone call from my father. I looked at my watch and at Suzanne's sleeping head, her hair raven black on the crumpled white of the pillow. It was just before six thirty.

'Appreciate it if you'd get round here, Martin. Pronto, if you've no engagement more pressing. Bring your under-achieving Scandinavian motor car with you. Once again, we face a day apparently beyond the capabilities of rotorblades.'

Groggily, I opened the curtains a chink. I did not want to awaken Suzanne after her trying day and exhausting evening. The weather was foul, our little glimpse of river grey and turbulent in the wind, the cloud low and the rain splattering on the panes and thrumming on the road outside in big, percussive drops. What a dismal month March was turning out to be.

'What's the problem?'

'Frank Hadley seems to be in the throes of some sort of breakdown.'

I cleared my throat. I still wasn't fully awake. 'I take it you know about the fire, Dad?'

'I know about it. Hadley doesn't. The charred log is not the problem.'

'What is?'

'Just get over here, Martin.' As was his perennial habit, he then hung up on me.

Without telling him anything of what I had experienced for myself or recently learned, I tried on the drive to the Hamble to sow doubts in my father's mind. I told him that it was fair from what we both knew to call the *Dark Echo* accident-prone. Our prospective voyage seemed foolhardy.

He pondered what I'd said without immediate comment. He took out his cigar case, chose a cigar and smoked for a while. I did not get the explosion from him with which he usually blustered his way out of a corner. This was not out of respect for me, I knew. It was because the evidence was compelling and seemed despite his wishes to be mounting all the time.

'A thing is only ever cursed in retrospect,' he said eventually. 'And bad reputation is always a matter more than anything of interpretation. If mountaineers are killed attempting to climb a Himalayan peak, and the attempt fails, the expedition is cursed. They've crossed the yeti, or antagonised the mountain gods, or some other similar nonsense impossible to substantiate or refute. If, by contrast, the attempt to scale the peak is a success, it doesn't much matter what happens to the team on the way down. The expedition is judged a success. The objective was achieved. Nothing was cursed. Do you see my point?'

'Not really.'

'In 1970 an expedition organised by Chris Bonington was successful in climbing the South Face of a Himalayan peak called Annapurna. It was the last great unconquered mountain challenge the roof of the world had to offer. Annapurna had always possessed the reputation of an unlucky mountain. One morning, a thousand feet from the top, the climbers Don Whillans and Doug Scott, leading the ascent, left their tent and achieved the summit. On the way down to base camp, two of the party were killed in separate accidents. Was the expedition cursed? Was the mountain unlucky?'

The road to our destination on the Hamble was clear but the driving hard in atrocious visibility and streaming surface water. 'You tell me, Dad.'

'Bonington was a skilled enough climber in his own right. He climbed the North Face of the Eiger. With Whillans, he shared the first ascent of the Central Pillar of Freney. But his chief talents were as an organiser and a manipulator of the media. Annapurna was not cursed.

The expedition was a triumph, because that's how Bonington was able to present it.'

I wasn't convinced. My father knew I wasn't. 'A boat is a repository of human thought and feeling, Martin. Within its fragile hull, our dreams and aspirations of adventure and achievement can be nurtured. But a boat is also a place where our fears and insecurities can become magnified and distorted to a point that can threaten sanity. I can only tell you that the *Mary Celeste* would not have met that enigmatic and disastrous fate with a Columbus or a Drake at the helm.'

I laughed. I had to. 'You're not Columbus, Dad. You're certainly not Drake. I don't even think you're a Bonington.'

He laughed himself. 'I'm not. Not for a moment, I'm not. I'm no more a mountaineer than the *Dark Echo* is cursed.'

Frank Hadley was waiting for us amid a crowd of his men on the quay when we got to his boatyard. The Solent was a gunmetal hue with white topping its waves and ugly yellow foam billowing at the tideline. Some large creature had been winched by its tail out of the water and was suspended by a loop of hawser from a crane boom over the wet dock adjacent to where the *Dark Echo* lay wrapped and silent and blind. There was a strong smell of blood and secretion. The animal carcass was of a porpoise or a dolphin and it was missing its head. The butchered creature turned on its steel rope slowly in the ferocious wind. It looked like something huge but half-finished, like some clumsy joke played against nature. It was bitterly cold on the dock. But the headless creature lashed from the crane was beyond any kind of feeling.

'Washed up this morning before first light,' Hadley said to my father. He looked gaunt under his wind-whipped hair. I had seen the very same expression he wore, the night before, on the face of Patrick Boyte. 'It's a portent, Mr Stannard. It's an omen as plain as I ever wish to see. I don't need superstitious men to explain it to me. I want your abomination of a boat gone from my yard. I'll reimburse you for any extraneous expenses incurred as a consequence. And I'm happy to compensate you for any delay to the original work timetable.'

My father laughed. He looked incredulous. He looked at the turning corpse of the dead creature. 'Because of this? Because a porpoise is injured by a boat propeller in the busiest stretch of water in the world? What kind of fucking joke is this, Hadley? What kind of fucking witchcraft are we discussing now?'

'It isn't a porpoise, Mr Stannard. It's much too big to be that, you see. And it's a long way from home. It's a species of dolphin only usually found in tropical waters.'

A shiver gripped me. It was nothing to do with the cold. I was thinking of Gubby Tench, his relentless luck and terror, and his boat bobbing in the fog in the Gulf Stream. I looked over towards the shrouded *Dark Echo*. That boat.

'And it wasn't a propeller,' Hadley was saying, in the here and now in the rain on the quay. 'It was a fish did that damage. It was a shark.'

But my father would not look at the dolphin's remains. 'I'll sue you,' he said to Hadley. 'I'll fucking ruin you if you do this.'

But Hadley did not look flustered by my father. He was too disturbed already by the deteriorating pattern of events for that. 'I'll be ruined if I don't,' he said, proving the point. He smiled a bitter smile.

There was the movement of a figure at the edge of my vision and I saw that someone was actually aboard the *Dark Echo*, about to clamber off her wrapped deck on to the quay-side. Whoever it was moved with ease and practised agility between the ropes binding the tarp and leapt lightly down on to the cobbles, rubbing his palms together. He had on canvas trousers, a buttoned-up reefer jacket and a watch cap, and his hair was reddish-blond and unruly under the cap. His skin was ruddy, wind-tanned. His appearance made me realise how pale with apprehension were Frank Hadley's little cluster of helpers.

'Who's that?' my father asked.

'That's Peitersen. From America. And he might be your saviour,' Hadley said. 'And if he can persuade you of what he has in mind, I think he might also turn out to be mine.'

My father treated Peitersen to breakfast at a café a mile or so along the road. His intentions concerning the *Dark Echo* announced to the owner of the boat, Hadley seemed much more relaxed. The cliché about weight and shoulders visibly applied to him as he grew and straightened on his dock. Whatever malign forces he thought ranged against him, he clearly felt mollified once his decision had been voiced publicly. Obviously we would have to wait for a window in the appalling weather before the craft could be towed away. But not another minute's work would be done on her there.

As Peitersen approached and Hadley did the introductions, my father retreated from indignant fury back into his usual mode of old-school courtesy. It was a tactical retreat, rather than a capitulation. He could have ruined Hadley in the courts, of course he could. He could have carried out his threat. But it would have delayed his real purpose and defining mission, which was the restoration and relaunching of the boat. I rocked in the wind on the greasy cobbles paving that stone rampart at the edge of the sea. The smell of brine assaulted my nostrils and cruel mutilation hung from a steel rope in front of my eyes. And I was suddenly aware, for the first time, of the depth of the delusion which had overcome my dad. From what he had said on the road to the Hamble, all the *Dark Echo* really lacked was competent PR. She needed a maritime Chis Bonington to talk up her seagoing strengths and racing achievements and perhaps the aesthetic merits of her design. There was no such thing as an unlucky boat.

There were only the unlucky and sometimes tragic individuals occasionally to be found on board. Busy boatyards were places where accidents would inevitably occur. Storage facilities were sites in which bored security staff would sneak a smoke and leave a burning stub to spark a blaze. Sea mammals did not have the wit to avoid the churning screws of a Wight ferry, particularly when their skewed sonar had sent them hundreds or even thousands of miles off their true course.

Nothing would deter him. Everything was explicable. Faith in his stern and almighty God was the only mystery my father allowed into his life. He was not about to see it challenged now by the fear in others of what he sneered at as witchcraft. He would restore *Dark Echo* at whatever terrible cost she claimed. And he would embark aboard her on his transatlantic voyage. And I would have to go with him, not because I was any longer flattered by the invitation, but because I loved him so much and sensed the slippery, brooding danger and could not let him face it on his own. If I did that, I would lose him, I was sure. I did not want my father confounded by terror and madness. And I did not dare to face the loss of him.

These were my thoughts on the quay at Hadley's boatyard. And they seemed perfectly fitting to the circumstances. The headless dolphin swayed and dripped some viscous stuff on to the cobbles. Out on the Solent a ship's horn sounded, withered and deformed by the wind. Hadley's men were grey and pinched and flapping at the extremities of their clothing under a grey sky. My father, magisterial under his mane of silvery hair, looked doomed. And the boat he had bought brooded like a secret under its ragged canvas wrapping.

But Peitersen entirely changed the mood, once we got to the café. He was buoyant and energetic and focused. His eyes were as bright with enthusiasm as the double row of brass buttons on his pea coat. He had, for want of a better word, a style about him. He talked only in terms of sunny practicalities. We would tow *Dark Echo* aboard a flat-decked, seagoing barge as soon as we could charter the vessel and the tug to pull it, and got our weather window. He had a provisional berth for her already in mind. There was a small boatyard we could lease short-term about five miles along the coast. It was not state of the art, like Hadley's place. It was not resourced to create Viking longships for the directors of epic films. But it possessed all the necessary facilities to make *Dark Echo* seaworthy once again. And, he said, tucking into his full English breakfast, to make her once more proud and beautiful.

Talk like this would, I knew, have no trouble in seducing my father simply because it voiced his most ardent dreams in the kind of phraseology he would have chosen to use himself. But I was unconvinced. I studied Peitersen. He was not so young as his lithe movement had promised from a distance aboard the boat. There were lines around his eyes and a suggestion of scragginess at the neck. His tumbling curls of strawberry-blond hair were youthful enough with his watch cap taken off at the table to eat. And he had a tan that suggested the tropics and took a few years off him as well. But the man I had first thought to be about thirty-five was probably in reality more like fifty years old.

'You don't believe she's an unlucky boat, Mr Peitersen?'

'Jack will do,' he said to me, smiling. His teeth were very white against the unseasonal depth of his tan. 'And no, I don't, son. I think she's a boat has had more than her fair share of unlucky owners. But that's been her misfortune. And her fortunes are about to change.'

I looked at my father. The smile he now wore was broad, almost beatific. Peitersen could play him, alright. And the two of them had only just met.

'How do you explain the dolphin, Jack?'

He looked at me. His eyes were blue-grey and as bright as his grin. He was very alert. I thought that if his hands were as quick as his mind, the restoration of my father's boat would take no time at all.

'I wouldn't presume to,' he said. 'It's arrogant for a man to try to justify the mysteries of the sea. I can tell you that, to my mind, the dead creature signifies nothing beyond itself. I wouldn't speculate on why it swam here or how it perished. I prefer to deal in nails and timber and tar and rope. I can make *Dark Echo* respond to the lightest touch of her tiller. I can squeeze eighteen knots out of her under full sail. I prefer to deal in practicalities rather than to dwell on superstition, son.'

I nodded. I really didn't like him calling me son.

'I don't believe in curses. I stick to what I know.'

'I can see that.'

The grin hadn't left his face. 'How?'

'Because you've eaten every scrap of your eggs and bacon and sausage. But you've left your black pudding intact.'

He looked at his plate. 'You're telling me that stuff's edible, Martin, then I'm obliged to take your word for it. But only because you seem such an honest boy.'

My father slapped the table in a show of mirth. It occurred to me that his optimism was probably the reason he'd made such a success of his life. It seemed unsinkable.

'Don't like him, do you?'

We were in the Saab, on the way back to London.

'He's supercilious. He's patronising. And I think there's more to him than meets the eye.'

'I hope there's more to him than there was to Frank Hadley,' my father said.

The new boatyard was on the other side of Southampton Water, between Calshot and Lepe, just beyond the point and the old Calshot lifeboat station. My father had agreed to pay for Peitersen to stay for the duration at a country hotel in Exbury. The hotel was old but very comfortable, with an excellent restaurant. But Peitersen had said he expected to bed down most nights in the yard. He said with the coming of the spring and warmer evenings, it would be comfortable enough and the most practical way of making sure we did not slip behind the schedule agreed. Of course, such talk was music to my father's ears.

'You know, Martin, you don't have to share this voyage.' His voice was gentle.

'I know.'

'You might not wish to come. Suzanne might not wish you to go. I'd understand totally if you pulled out now. It would give me three months to find someone to help me crew and three months is ample time.'

'I'm coming, Dad. Nothing would stop me.'

'Good,' he said. He reached across and gave my shoulder a squeeze. 'I'm delighted that's how you feel.'

We got our window in the weather the following day. I did not go down to witness the events. It was bright and balmy, helicopter weather, so my services as a chauffeur were not required. Peitersen chartered the tug and a barge he'd put on standby, and the *Dark Echo* was winched aboard the barge and secured there without incident. She was unloaded, again without incident, at the new yard after a short journey over innocent blue water. My father told me over the phone that evening that the conditions had made the turbulent grey weather of the preceding weeks seem like some weird Wagnerian dream. Frank Hadley hadn't been present for the extrication of the vessel from his dock. 'Didn't ask where he was,' my father said. 'Probably busy having his dolphin stuffed.'

'Peitersen?'

'Competence personified. He's a boatman to the soles of his sea boots, Martin. And he has the gift of leadership. Men do as he asks, almost before he has to ask them.'

I nodded, which is a pretty stupid thing to do on the telephone, where only words and vocal expression count. But I did not like Jack Peitersen and did not think that I ever would.

But he was true to what he had said in his airmail letter to Hadley. There were no more gruesome accidents. April brought a prolonged spell of warm spring weather and the small team of craftsmen he assembled made solid progress. There was debate over whether to fit an engine and, if so, what type to fit. I did not participate in this. My father was reluctant to have the boat powered by anything but wind. Peitersen thought it was only a matter of practicality that would have no real impact on the aesthetics of the boat and would make it far easier for inexperienced sailors like my father and myself to get her in and out of harbour without mishap. He said the engine was only one of a number of innovations that would improve the boat's performance without compromising her integrity. The others were a state-of-the-art land to sea communications system, a satellite navigation system and sonar as a precaution to prevent us running aground or tearing the hull on submerged rocks or coral banks. All of these would be battery powered.

My father pondered at length on the merits or otherwise of the engine. It would be an exaggeration to say that he agonised, but not so very much of one. Spalding, the war hero and racing champion, had not required an engine. Peitersen apparently laughed when this point was made and said that if the small clean marine turbines of today had existed then, his great-grandfather would have fitted one to the *Dark Echo* as a matter of course. My dad told me the clincher in eventually agreeing to the engine was that it did not prevent the boat from qualifying for official status as a genuine vintage schooner. But I think the clincher was the weight he accorded Peitersen's opinion, as the man's influence grew as a consequence of his obvious expertise and the impressive progress he was making generally with the boat.

There were two big set-pieces in the restoration my father was very keen for me to attend. These were the fitting of the replacement main mast and the attachment to the foredeck of the capstan, chain and anchor. Both were scheduled to be fitted early in May. My theoretical seamanship was impressive enough by now and I knew my way out of Whitstable and around the Isle of Sheppey on an actual yacht under sail. But I began to believe that I really needed first-hand experience aboard a schooner of similar vintage to the *Dark Echo*. It was a prerequisite if I was going to get aboard my father's boat with any genuine sense of competence.

I did an internet search and found a holiday company that allowed you to masquerade as a nineteenth-century seafarer aboard a variety of restored boats. Theirs were all far more spartan than my father intended the refurbished *Dark Echo* to be. You slept in a hammock and bathed in a barrel of rainwater on the deck, and oil lamps provided the only illumination in the cabins once the sun dipped below the horizon. Even the rations approximated authentic provisions of the period. It was mostly biscuits and beef jerky and dried fruit. You ate fresh only what you could catch on a line. It all sounded very Joseph Conrad. And it sounded exactly the type of immersion in the culture of pure sailing I required.

There was a schooner voyage planned for the end of April. Maybe it wasn't so much Conrad as Erskine Childers, in the detail. The vessel embarked from Rotterdam and journeyed through the North Sea to East Friesland and its belt of islands off the coast of Lower Saxony. It was a dank, windswept, even desolate part of the world. That said, I knew it only from Childers' description in his novel, *The Riddle of the Sands*. We were to anchor off the island of Baltrum and stay there for a couple of nights to enable the birdwatchers among the makeshift crew to indulge their masochistic habit. Then it was back to Rotterdam and a hop along the coast to Antwerp, where the vessel was due a refit. She was called *Andromeda*, and she had originally been registered as a British boat, her keel having been laid on the Clyde in 1878. Winston Churchill had been a mewling toddler. The telephone had not been invented. I was to trust my life in the North Sea to a boat built a full ten years before Jack the Ripper began his short season of atrocities.

It seemed a very good idea. Navigation in the tricky shallows off the string of islands where we were headed was notoriously difficult. The tides were swift and the currents strong. Sudden and overwhelming fogs often descended. And there was the elemental force of the North Sea itself. I would learn a lot.

'Will you bring me something back?' Suzanne said.

'Scurvy, probably,' I said, 'given the diet we'll be living on.'

And she laughed. She did not mind me going. The trip coincided with what would probably be her last Michael Collins-inspired journey to Ireland. The previous week, curiosity had overcome her and she had asked if she could visit the Lepe boatyard and see the *Dark Echo* for herself. We drove down and deliberately surprised Jack Peitersen. I didn't want him having the time to prepare anything phoney in the way of a reception for Suzanne.

He seemed genuinely delighted to see us. Where Suzanne was concerned he was full of a courtly New England charm that bordered on flirtatiousness and that she seemed to enjoy. The wraps were off the *Dark Echo* on a sun-dappled day and her brasses gleamed and her portholes twinkled and dazzled in the brightness. She smelled of freshly planed wood and paint and varnish newly applied. And in the spacious master cabin, there was the rich, rising aroma of wax polish and oiled hide from the luxurious upholstery my father had specified.

She seemed a completely different boat from the one aboard which I had endured my earlier moments of terror. Everything was clean and sound and new. Climbing aboard her in plain daylight, in the company of Suzanne and Peitersen, made the earlier experience seem hallucinatory and unreal. I knew suddenly what my father meant, calling the whole weird interval at Hadley's boatyard Wagnerian. But now the portentous gloom had gone. The steps on the companionway had been replaced. They were firm and well sprung under my feet. And descending them, I felt no fear or trepidation whatsoever. My one anxious glance went to where the mirror had hung on the wall of the master cabin. But there was no sign of it now. I saw Suzanne sneak one or two quizzical looks my way, but any anxiety she may have felt on my behalf was unnecessary. The physical reality of what I was seeing aboard the *Dark Echo*, the bright splendour of her, forced the earlier experience to recede in my mind like a bad dream eventually does.

Since our surprise visit to the Lepe yard, Suzanne and I had barely discussed the matter of my father's voyage. She had asked a couple of questions about Peitersen. I'd responded to the second of these by asking if she fancied him or something. Then I'd had to dodge the book she'd thrown at me. And she hadn't asked again. But it was as though for her, too, the Lepe trip had provided a sort of assurance. We did not talk about it. But the experience, the reality of the refurbished *Dark Echo*, just seemed so wholesomely far removed from the vision of Harry Spalding I'd described to her, endured aboard a canvas shrouded wreck. It seemed even more remote from the lurid mysteries of the brothers Waltrow and the gambler, Gubby Tench. In the aftermath of the Lepe visit, those events seemed far more symptomatic of their morbid and hysterical time in history than of the boat itself.

She had her bag over her shoulder, her coat over her arm. A strand of hair had fallen over her face when she had bent down to pick up her bag. She blew it away with a puff of breath. She stood there – slender, resolute and gorgeous.

'Will it be emotional? Saying goodbye to Michael Collins?'

She smiled, looking at the floor. The smile seemed wistful. 'There's no room in my life for ghosts.'

I crossed the distance between us and embraced her and kissed her goodbye.

'There's no room in either of our lives for ghosts.'

She grazed my cheek with her fingers. 'I love you, Martin.'

'Thank God you do.'

The weather on the Eastern Friesland voyage was dismal. The *Andromeda* stank of fish oil and rotting hemp rope and brine-sodden wood. Her sails were mildew-splotched and she had a stew of ancient filth in her bilges too thick for any pump to remove that made her sluggish in the water even under full sail. She had a tendency to wallow and creaked alarmingly when subjected to the conflicting pressures of wind and current.

There were eight of us aboard, so she was overmanned. I spent a lot of time at first being superfluous to requirements, watching the sea over the ship's rail at the stern for want of anything better or more instructive to do. But it was instructive, watching the waters of the North Sea. They were restless, churning, never still. I'd always considered the sea supine, except in a storm. But that was because I was almost wholly ignorant of it. It was a living element, debating with itself, seemingly in turmoil over what to do with its profound depth and awesome energy. At night it seemed calmer. But the night traffic on the surface of the sea made it dangerous if you were not alert.

Vomit was added to the horrible cocktail of smells about two hours after dawn on the second day out when we hit a heavy squall that brought with it a four-foot swell. We roped in the sails. The boat bucketed through the waves and I could feel the old timbers judder with impact under my feet. I knew it would take a lot more than we were heading into for the *Andromeda* to break up and founder. She'd been built for this weather, and worse. On the other hand, she was a venerable craft. And though authenticity was all very well, she did not seem to have been very well cared for.

The sea was a sullen green colour under a pewter sky. The wind blowing from Arctic Norway was a needling blast that numbed any flesh not covered. The deck was awash with rain and sea spray. I was wearing oilskins over trousers and a sweater woven from oiled wool. My sou'wester flapped, trying to tear itself from my head. And I found myself grinning. I was enjoying this, the being out and exposed to something so elemental. Elsewhere, men were out in this trying to catch fish, or deliver cargos, or rehearse for wars. I had no such responsibility and could just revel in the moment.

I felt a tap on my shoulder and turned. It was Captain Straub, the *Andromeda*'s master. Out of my reverie, I looked around. We were the only two people above the deck. 'I see you've got your sea legs,' he shouted. He grinned at me through his beard, which was grey and waterflecked. He was Dutch and his accent was very strong.

'I think I was born with them, Captain.'

'Then you're lucky,' he said. 'Would you care to take the wheel, Mr Stannard?'

'I'd be delighted, Captain.'

'Just keep her on a straight course.'

Straub probably fancied a smoke or needed a pee or

something. We were too far out from land for me to run her aground and it takes two to orchestrate a collision at sea and the bloke at the wheel of the other vessel would be competent. Nevertheless, I felt a grown-up thrill of accomplishment at being entrusted with the wheel. It meant the boat was in my hands; I was responsible for the other seven souls aboard her. The pleasure I felt brought home to me how little I had actually accomplished in my life. But that realisation did not spoil the pleasure itself. It was hardly a surprise, a revelation. We live in an age of diminished accomplishment. For the moment, I thought that steering a seventy-ton schooner through a storm would do pretty well for me. It was physical work. Despite the gearing between the wheel and the rudder, I could feel the force of the swell and the weight of the boat through my arms. There was a binnacle compass on a column next to the wheel. I wiped droplets of water from its domed glass cover and took a reading. I knew where we were and I knew where we were going.

Land announced itself the following afternoon in ragged grey humps on the grey horizon. Grey, too, were the faces of our birdwatchers, gaunt with retching, glad to get into the rowing boat lowered from the side into the choppy sea, heading for something firm under their feet when we anchored off Baltrum. I watched them go but had volunteered to stay aboard. I would have a cabin to myself. The wilderness of sand and reeds and rare birds where my shipmates were headed offered no real attractions.

Captain Straub stayed aboard, too. That evening, we dined together at his table. He was a resourceful cook. He made a sort of casserole from barley and boiled bacon and shallots. We washed it down with *Weissbier* and afterwards had some truly delicious Dutch cheese and his excellent brandy. It was a long way from weevil-ridden ship's biscuits and salted herring. It was altogether a very civilised route to scurvy.

When we had finished eating, the captain rolled a cigarette from a large pouch of tobacco and sat back in his chair and I looked around me, from where I sat, at his cabin. Hunger and conversation had prevented me from properly examining my surroundings any sooner. Straub's cabin was not as large as my father's aboard the *Dark Echo*. Nor was it anything like so sumptuously well appointed. But the really remarkable thing about it was that there was nothing present in it that could not have come from the late nineteeth century. We had dined by the light of candles. An oil lamp hung from a hook above a small table under the starboard portholes. He had navigation charts rolled on a table where his sextant also reposed. He had a slide rule for his calculations, the ivory from which it had been made yellowing from decades of secretions from human hands. We had taken our depth soundings on approaching the island with a plumb line at the bow. Straub had a berth rather than a hammock and the cabin was warm from a wood-burning fire. It was a cosy enough refuge from the elements. But it seemed out of its time and would have unnerved me had I been there alone and not in company.

Straub stood and put a coffee pot on a paraffin burner on the table under the lamp. He lit the burner with a wooden match. I noticed that the boat was still beneath us. The sea had calmed. I saw that there were tendrils of fog drifting now beyond the glass of the portholes.

'Do you believe in ghosts, Captain?'

He had his back to me still. I saw him stiffen almost imperceptibly and then I heard him chuckle thickly. 'I knew that question was coming. And yet I let it surprise me.' He turned. Straub, too, could have been an artefact from the nineteenth century; a human artefact, with his hewn features and his powerful shoulders and the iron-grey bristle of his beard. He raised his arm and the tip glowed in the gloom of the cabin as he drew heavily on his cigarette. He nodded towards the warming pot. 'We shall wait for our coffee, Mr Stannard. And then I shall tell you a story about a ghost.'

We settled into our chairs with the coffee and the brandy bottle on the table between us. Against the portholes, the fog now pressed in a pale and solid blanket. The boat rested at anchor, entirely still. There was no wind and the sea outside was motionless and silent. He had been captain of the *Andromeda*, he told me, for twelve years. He had been her master for a year when he first saw her phantom.

'We were in the Atlantic Ocean, Mr Stannard. The Americans are, some of them, great and fastidious sailors of yachts. I had a party of five aboard, all of them skilled and hardy.' He chuckled again. 'None of them birdwatchers, I fancy.'

I smiled to encourage him to continue and sipped his strong, good coffee.

'We were about four hundred miles east of Nantucket Island and steering an easterly course, though the location hardly signifies. It was September and darkness had descended an hour since. I was over there,' he gestured towards his chart table, 'calculating our average speed because one of the fellows on board had made a query about it. And I looked up and he was sitting where you are now.'

I had gone cold. The coffee was hot in my cup and the fire still warm in the captain's grate. But I had gone cold under my heavy sweater, with my belly full in that cosy refuge. 'Who was?'

'A man in a brown uniform and a steel helmet with a bandage covering the lower half of his face. I say a man. A boy, really. Fright in his young, tormented eyes. A soldier of eighteen or so with mud on his puttees and a rifle that looked too big for him resting across his lap.'

'What did he do?'

'He didn't do anything. He just looked at me.'

'What did you do?'

'I closed my eyes. When I opened them again, he was gone.'

I felt only relief that Straub's spectre had not been Harry Spalding. There was no reason, of course, why it should have been. But ghosts and logic were not easy companions in my mind and what I felt was relief, pure and unadulterated. Spalding had been a soldier. But Straub's visitor had been innocent. And Spalding had never been that. Straub had seen someone else.

He did all the usual things, he told me, made all the usual excuses for himself. He was tired. He was sleep-deprived. He was suffering from stress and probably slightly drunk. He was too imaginative for his own good.

'The truth was, of course, that I was none of those things.'

'Did you see the ghost again?'

He nodded. 'Very occasionally. And very sporadically. I'd say no more than once a year and sometimes the interval has been as long as eighteen months.'

'And the manner of the sightings?'

'They never differed.'

'So you don't know who he is.'

'About five years ago I did some research into the history of the *Andromeda*. This had nothing to do with the question of my ghost. People come aboard the vessel and ask questions and my knowledge of her history was not as complete as it could and should have been. She's a venerable old lady of the sea, Mr Stannard.' He picked up his brandy glass and took a swallow and then refilled both our glasses and took out his tobacco pouch again. 'She has a colourful past.'

I've met some garrulous storytellers in my time, compulsive

raconteurs. My father is chief among the men I've known enthralled by the sound of their own voices holding an audience. But Captain Straub was not one of them. Sitting at his table in his cabin on that fogbound sea, I felt he was telling me this story not because he wanted to, but because he felt compelled.

'I learned that she was commandeered after one of the enormous, catastrophic Allied offences launched during the latter stages of the Great War. Her home port at that time was Whitstable, on the eastern coast of Kent in England.'

'I know Whitstable.'

'She sailed to Calais. She raced to Calais. But the effort was to prove in vain. The battle casualties she picked up had been gassed. None of them could breathe properly. All of them suffered in agony.' He lit his cigarette and gestured to the portholes. 'On the return voyage a fog descended. It was a thick fog, impenetrable, much like this. I suppose the fog impeded the breathing of those poor wounded boys even further. Not one of the young soldiers survived the trip.'

I nodded. 'How did you know I would ask you about your ghost?'

Captain Straub drained his glass of brandy. It was late, now. Between the two of us, we had almost finished the bottle. I don't think I had ever felt more sober in my life.

'I saw him last night. It was the first time in almost two years. And I think he tried to speak to me.'

I did not know what to say. There was nothing I could say.

'Are you familiar with the cruel and wonderful poem about a gas attack, Mr Stannard? I mean the one by the greatest of all war poets, the Englishman?'

'We all read Wilfred Owen at school.'

'Then you will know it. You will know the line about the froth-corrupted lungs. Last night, as I lay in darkness in my bunk, my ghost tried to use his froth-corrupted lungs to speak to me. As long as God permits me to live, it is not a sound I would wish to hear again.'

'Why the change?'

Straub exhaled smoke and smiled and extended a finger. 'You, Mr Stannard. I have racked my brains and can only think you the reason. It cannot be one of the Baltrum twitchers.'

'I take your point, Captain.'

'My ghost is trying to warn me of something, I think. And I think I am intended to pass the warning on to you.'

I did not say anything. I could quite see why he had drunk with such ponderous deliberation throughout and after our meal. The Dutch coined that kind of courage after all, and he evidently thought he might require it if summoned from his slumbers by a visitor in the night. But when we took a turn around the deck before retiring, his footing seemed as sure as it could have been and he seemed fully alert to every detail and aspect of the anchored boat he commanded.

If his ghost came back, the captain did not mention it to me. But I don't think it did. The fog cleared the following morning and we were rejoined by our maligned but oblivious band of Baltrum twitchers. I hope they got to see lots of rare breeds of birds up very close. I hope they were able to take wonderful photographs. Because the weather worsened on the return leg and with it returned the seasickness. I was sympathetic at seeing their suffering, but it was advantageous for me. A schooner in storm conditions is a real task for two men and though her master was a consummate sailor, there was plenty of opportunity for me to improve on my basic seamanship with the rest of the crew laid up and puking.

I did not disembark at Rotterdam. I'd grown fond of the *Andromeda* by the end of the voyage and wanted to see her into Antwerp and the promise of her refit. I was glad I did.

'Take the wheel, Mr Stannard,' Captain Straub said as we approached the harbour. And I did. And I berthed her very competently in the busy port, in the choppy water.

We shook hands on the quay. I had grown fond of the *Andromeda*'s master, too. 'I think you have seen the last of your ghost,' I said to him. He nodded, slowly. He glanced back at the boat I knew now he loved. She looked tired and anachronistic and tiny amid the tanker and freighter traffic of the bustling harbour. But she would be alright. There was life left in her yet.

'You need to take care, Martin,' Straub said. I had not even known that he was aware of my Christian name. My bag was in my hand. It was time to go. I nodded to acknowledge what he'd said and turned and walked away.

I had not been allowed to use my mobile phone at all on the *Andromeda*. The on-board rules, of course, forbade the use of mobiles. It had stayed in its compartment in my bag, switched off. And, of course, I had not been able to charge it. But there was just enough battery life left to be able to send Suzanne a text telling her roughly what time I would be home that evening. Was she back from Dublin?

Yes, she replied. She would meet me in the Windmill at 8 p.m.

That seemed a bit odd. I'm as partial to the pub as most men, but after a week before the mast, what I really fancied was an evening in front of the television wrapped around Suzanne after a scalding shower, and then an hour or so catching up on the world via the internet.

It wasn't until my flight from Antwerp was airborne that the implications of what had happened between Captain Straub and his ghost began really to resonate seriously with me. Straub had thought the ghost was trying to warn him. He had thought the warning intended for me. Any warning for me from beyond the grave had to concern Harry Spalding.

The link between Spalding and the English soldier was the war in which they had both fought and in which the English boy been mortally wounded. He had died aboard the *Andromeda*. I'd been crewing the *Andromeda* for only a few days when, after more than a decade of spectral silence, the soldier apparition had attempted to speak.

The worst of it was that the whole Harry Spalding business had receded so far in my mind, since the trip to Lepe with Suzanne. The Enid Blyton wholesomeness of an English spring day had conspired with Peitersen's gallantry and the potent glamour of the transformed *Dark Echo* to bury Spalding almost altogether in my memory. But Straub's ghost had brought him back again into the forefront. I could see his feral grin and his frame, poised and limber under the civilised concealment of his clothes. I dozed on the flight and dreamed my father and I were aboard his prize, becalmed in a gaseous mist on a sea of blood.

When I got to the pub, Suzanne was seated where we'd sat on our earlier evening of revelation. She looked pale even by her standards and there were shadows as sullen as bruises under her eyes. She smiled at me but the smile was wan under sharp cheekbones. Her hands were linked and rested in her lap. I sneaked a look at them and saw that the right thumbnail had been bitten almost to the quick. She rose and we kissed, and under my hands she felt insubstantial with weight loss. She had that vacant look you see on catwalk models. It had only been a week. She had shed maybe half a stone in seven days. I put down my bag, went to the bar for a drink and looked at her in the mirror that backed the bar. I wondered if she was about to dump me. She looked listless with trepidation. I knew with a horrible certainty that I was about to be dispensed with.

'How was East Friesland?'

'Never bothered to go ashore. So the riddle of the sands remains exactly that.' I sipped beer. I did not know what to say. It was all about what she needed to announce. But she stayed silent and it was a silence I felt obliged to fill. 'Did you know Erskine Childers and Michael Collins were friends?'

She frowned. Her eyes were on the table. 'I think more colleagues than friends.'

'Really?'

'Collins was pretty insular about his friendships.'

'Meaning?'

'It helped if you were Irish, Catholic, and born in County Cork.'

'They had something in common, though. They were both killed in the Irish Civil War.'

Suzanne said nothing. Her head was bowed.

'Weren't they?'

She looked at me. 'I didn't go to Dublin, Martin. I'm sorry, but I lied to you.'

I sipped beer reflexively. I smiled. I don't know why I smiled. I felt gut-punched. 'Oh?'

'I went to France.'

'He's a Frenchman, is he? He's a fucking Frog. You've gone and got yourself a French boyfriend. Jesus Christ.'

'I went there because of the Jericho Crew.'

She was crying now, blinking back the tears.

'I went there because I was frightened for you.'

I'd felt relief when Captain Straub's ghost had not been Harry Spalding. But that was as nothing to the relief I felt now. Suzanne had not lied to deceive me. She had lied out of concern over whatever danger she thought I was in. Behind my back, she had done some investigating. And she had apparently discovered something troubling and scary. But I knew in my heart that no predicament could be so desolate as Suzanne leaving me. Nothing could be as bad as that. I had just seen it proven to myself in the crushing numbness overcoming me when her departure from my life had seemed an imminent prospect.

'You had better tell me what you've learned,' I said. 'You have learned something, haven't you?' There was music playing in the pub. Billy Paul was lamenting his love for Mrs Jones again. The setting and the song were very familiar. We were sitting at a favourite table in our local. But nothing felt entirely familiar. I could see from her expression how badly Suzanne craved a cigarette. But she did not suggest going home. Instead, she cleared her throat with a cough and began to explain what she had been doing while I'd been playing sailor on the sea.

It was the circumstances of the auction at Bullen and Clore that had intrigued her. I had told her about it, about how my father had paid far too much for the boat. After her research into the Waltrow mystery and the lurid death of Gubby Tench, it had nagged at her. She could not understand why anyone would bid over the telephone for what was no more really than a large item of maritime scrap.

There had been two telephone bidders, not one, she discovered. Bullen and Clore, having assessed the unexpected level of interest in the *Dark Echo*, had invested in the services of a proper auctioneer. He was a fine art and antiques specialist from Chichester. He would have been past retirement age in any regular profession. David Preston was crusty, snobbish, vain and, as Suzanne discovered, wonderfully indiscreet. She visited him in the guise of a collector of Meissen figurines thinking about selling some of her collection off. She yachted, she told him. It was an expensive pastime and her boat required refurbishment for which she needed funds. From there it was a gentle conversational nudge to what he called the 'ghastly' business of the recent boat auction he had conducted at the premises of Bullen and Clore.

It was ghastly because Bullen and Clore were a pair of greedy philistines who operated in a shabby and run-down premises and had paid him his commission tardily. It was unpleasant, because one of the telephone bidders had taken their defeat in the auction very badly. They were a Brussels-based company called Martens and Degrue. They blamed poor communication for their being outbid. Strictly speaking, they had a point. There should have been two telephone lines for two telephone bidders, not one over which both were obliged to compete. Dark threats were muttered in the aftermath of the gavel going down. It was all most acrimonious.

Who was the other bidder? Suzanne asked, as casually as she was able.

A Naples-based firm called Cardoza Associates, she was told. They, too, were unhappy about the circumstances of the auction. But it was David Preston's opinion that the auction at Bullen and Clore had been won by the right party. Magnus Stannard, who was surely long overdue his knighthood, was a real English gentleman with suitably deep pockets and a properly generous regard for the custom of tipping. Martens and Degrue and Cardoza Associates could go to hell as far as David Preston was concerned. Hell was probably where they belonged.

But despite the bravado, Suzanne thought the whole experience had shaken David Preston. She left with the feeling that her conversation with him had been less indiscretion on his part than a sort of catharsis. Whatever threats had been barked at him down the telephone line from Brussels had taken their toll. When she left him, it was four thirty in the afternoon in his showroom and he was on his third quite large gin and tonic. And the alcohol inside him did not yet have the tremor in his drinking hand under control.

An internet search revealed nothing about Martens and

Degrue beyond what she had already assumed she would find. It was a fronting company, basically an alias for an enterprise that was publicity-shy about whatever business it was really up to.

'I had more success with Cardoza Associates,' she told me. 'They bid at auctions all the time, all over the world. Mostly what they buy is religious art.'

'It's a fair hop from religious art to the wreck of a dubious boat,' I said.

She nodded. 'Particularly when you consider the source of their funding. Everything Cardoza Associates successfully bid for is paid for by the Vatican Bank.'

'So you went to France to find out about Martens and Degrue?'

'No,' she said. 'You haven't been listening properly. I told you, I went to France on the trail of Harry Spalding, to find out what I could about the Jericho Crew.'

'A cold trail,' I said.

Suzanne sipped from her drink and smiled. 'You've no idea how cold,' she said.

Spalding's family had been in Rhode Island for generations. They had been among the original settlers of the colony. They were wealthy by the time of Harry's birth. But they were very quiet and discreet. Just about the only club or organisation they belonged to, according to Suzanne's research, was a debating society. Several prominent Rhode Island families belonged to this society. Its character seemed not just exclusive, but to have some sort of dynastic element to it. The builder of Harry's boat, Josiah Peitersen, was among its members.

'There were initiation rites,' Suzanne said. 'There were elaborate rituals. And even in the heyday of the clandestine gathering and the exclusive members' club and the elite sorority in Eastern Seaboard America, which this was, there was an incredible degree of secrecy surrounding this society.'

'It sounds like a cult,' I said. 'What was it called?'

'If it had a name, and I think it almost certainly did, it was kept a very great secret. When it was referred to, it was referred to only as The Membership.'

'Does it still exist?'

She shook her head. 'No. It was destroyed in the time of Prohibition, its premises torn down and gasoline poured over the wreckage to burn it where it lay. Bulldozers trundled in afterwards to eradicate all trace of it from the earth.'

'So it was a drinking club.'

'No, Martin, it was not. The Prohibition legislation was the flimsiest of pretexts for its destruction. There were G-men present. There were also two Jesuit priests. One of them was a powerful exorcist from the Diocese of New York. You said cult just now. I think occult would be truer to history. I think that Harry Spalding's family were Satanists, practitioners of black magic going back perhaps to the time of the New England witch trials and the burnings. The report I read said nothing about sowing the ground with salt in the wake of the bulldozers. But I wouldn't be surprised if they did.'

'So Frank Hadley was right with his talk of witchcraft.'

'Perhaps.'

'There's one good way to find out,' I said. 'We ask Peitersen. He's the self-elected expert on the *Dark Echo*. We ask him what his great-grandfather was up to when he debated with the Spalding clan.'

If Suzanne's smile had been unconvincing earlier, now it was sickly. And her face was as pale as bone. 'We could ask him. But there would be no point. Because Jack Peitersen is not who he says he is. Jack Peitersen does not exist.'

I groaned. 'You'd better tell me what you've learned about Peitersen.'

'I'll get to Peitersen,' she said. 'First, I have to tell you about the Jericho Crew.'

'Can I take it Waltrow and Tench were members?'

'To Harry Spalding, they would have been Second Lieutenant Waltrow and Corporal Tench. And they were in it, alright, Martin. They were in it to the bitter end.'

Five

She had been anything but reassured by the visit to the boat-yard at Lepe. She had been concerned on the way there about how I would react to setting foot once more on the *Dark Echo*. And when we arrived and were greeted, she had thought there was something entirely bogus about Peitersen. It was as though, she said, on the other side of the lobster pot and saltbox Yankee charm, there was nothing really there. His smile, she said, was like a sign saying 'vacant' in a brightly lit motel window. Despite my impression of how they got on, she had disliked him even more violently than I had. But she did not just dislike him on sight. She distrusted Peitersen, too.

In the aftermath of the Lepe trip, she felt an obligation to learn as much as she could about the mystery of the boat to which my father and myself seemed so determined to entrust our lives. Despite her detective skills, which were sharp and well practised, she said that she felt a certain hopelessness in doing so. She said it seemed it was unlikely to matter what she discovered. The scheme had already gained too much momentum for her to be able to arrest events now. The whole ill-advised, dangerous adventure had about it the pre-ordained nature of fate. She also had grave doubts about deceiving me. The Collins work was done and dusted. But I did not know that, did I? She was able to persuade herself with the reasoning that if she found nothing, I need never know about France and the deception. But if she did find something, it might help prevent my father and me sailing into some horrible tragedy. There were all sorts of flaws and contradictions in her logic, Suzanne knew. But after her encounter at the Lepe yard with Peitersen, she felt that she had to act.

She learned about the war service of Waltrow and Tench first from their obituaries and then in more detail from American military records she was able to bring up on computer, using BBC access, still claiming she was looking for information to do with her Michael Collins programme research. Her pretext was the IRA's purchase on the black market of surplus American rifles after the 1918 armistice. It was a trade that increased steadily throughout the Irish Civil War. Nobody questioned this supposed line of enquiry. It sounded plausible enough. Searches in the American military archive for Waltrow, Tench and Spalding brought up some details about the Jericho Crew and the tantalising information that almost ninety years after it had been compiled, the file describing in full their activities in France and Flanders was still classified.

'I learned they had a base,' she told me. 'It wasn't an official base, a barracks or anything like that. It was a barn belonging to a farm about five miles to the rear of the Allied trench system near the village of Béthune in northern France. The land is still agricultural. The original farm still exists. They would gather in this building. If any of them became detached from the main party on a mission, or were left behind or lost, that's the spot they would head for as soon as they could. Water, tinned provisions, fuel and spare clothing, and even weapons and ammunition were kept there.'

'I'm amazed the stuff wasn't all lifted by Allied units passing the barn. Even if they'd had a guard on it, the rations in particular must have been a temptation. Soldiers in wartime are not noted for their honesty over that sort of thing.

Pilfering was rife on the Western Front, even among members of the same company, never mind the same battalion.'

'I don't think the Jericho Crew were the sort of people you stole from,' she said. 'Soldiers may not be terribly honest. But they are extremely superstitious.'

'And you thought the barn might still be there?'

'I thought there was a fair chance. This is rural France we're talking about. Space is not at any great premium there, the way it is in England. There's no urgent requirement for intensive farming. And farmers don't knock any building down without a very good reason for doing so. They tend to be a conservative breed. They don't seek out change for its own sake. I thought there was probably a fair chance the barn was still basically intact. And then I was able to identify it in an aerial photograph. I did that, like I did the preliminary research into Second Lieutenant Waltrow and Corporal Tench, without getting up from my chair in front of the computer at work.'

'What did you find in the barn?'

'I will get to that. First I should tell you about what it was the Jericho Crew did.'

I fetched us fresh drinks from the bar. I was tired after the trip from Antwerp. I was tired and grubby and the docking of the *Andromeda* in the grip of my hands that same morning seemed like a memory growing fond with distance already. Billy Paul's adulterous pleading had been replaced through the bookshelf speakers behind the bar by Marvin Gaye, crooning plaintively about the good dying young. Sometimes the bad died young, too, I thought, fishing for change and examining my reflection in the mirror behind the bar. I thought of my father's photograph of the Jericho Crew, of the look of shared derangement in their lost, youthful faces. I shivered, though it was not cold in the pub. I paid for and picked up our drinks and returned to where Suzanne sat. And she started to explain matters to me.

The Canadians invented the trench raid. They had a vigour and an obstreperousness that probably came from the outdoor lives they lived at home. They were not the factory fodder of industrialised England, used to manning a lathe slavishly in a factory in Birmingham or Leeds for a twelve-hour shift six days a week. They were outdoorsmen and the stalemate of the line forced them into ways of finding physical action to alleviate the tedium. So they invented the trench raid, carried out at night, to boost their morale and satisfy their youthful appetite for killing the enemy.

The weapons used were improvised, medieval almost in their design and the crude viciousness of their intent. They had to be silent. So they were basically variations on the knife and the club and the knuckleduster. They used machetes, daggers, bowie knives. The garrotte was a firm favourite, too, in the art of noiseless killing, but it required a degree of skill that came only from experience in the field. And it took a lot of commitment to choke a man to death.

The raids were daring and successful. They raised morale and did physical damage, and they added greatly to the burden of fear and fatigue faced by the men occupying the enemy trenches. They made sleep a liability. They made relaxation foolhardy. They spread stress and rumour and panic. They were the cause of men shooting at their own sentries and scout patrols. Altogether, trench raids were a big success, so much so that they were taken up by the Aussies and the New Zealanders and the Jocks. Eventually, even the English cottoned on to what an effective and economical tactic they represented.

By the time the Americans entered into the war, the trench raid was an established part of life at the front. And the farm boys from Kentucky and the boys from the swamps of Louisiana took to it like pigs to gravy. One junior officer in particular showed a real thirst for this bloody, guerrilla style of conflict. Interestingly, this fellow was not from the boonies. His name was Harry Spalding. He'd excelled both as a sportsman and a scholar at Yale. His people came from Rhode Island and he had been groomed for a banking career in New York. He was rich and clever and cultured, a lover of modern painting and poetry with a good command of the French and German languages. He had influential friends, or at least his father did. He had an easy charisma that made him a natural leader among the particular group of men chosen for the type of combat at which he proved to be so adept. And he was the bloodiest, most remorseless killer anyone on the staff of the American Third Army could remember ever having encountered.

One old colonel compared him to the Apache killers of the Indian Wars in which his own father had fought in the American West. But he came to believe that Harry Spalding was different from them, in the end. They had been skilled at killing. They were great hunters using their hunting prowess in the service of their own survival, faced with the threat of extinction. Spalding seemed to possess the same preternatural gift for tracking his prey. He had the same lethal savagery in combat. But it was not a matter of survival for him. The old colonel, who was forcibly retired on the basis of it, said in a report on the Jericho Crew that Spalding seemed to kill with a sort of glee. He was a man who revelled in killing. In a conflict where civilisation was at stake, the report concluded, to rely on such men for important results was more than a contradiction. It was an abject surrender to the standards and values espoused by our enemy, the Hun.

The Canucks invented the trench raid. The Americans refined it. And the Jericho Crew turned it from an art into a science. They did detailed surveillance work during their night patrols across no-man's-land. They carried out assassinations. They snatched intelligence personnel and interrogated them. They conducted acts of sabotage. They stole battle plans and brought back items of experimental ordnance for detailed examination. And they never lost a man.

'Come on,' I said, in the pub, as the bell tolled for last orders. 'They never lost a man? You're exaggerating, Suzy.'

'I'm not.'

'You had better explain.'

'At home. I'll explain at home. I'd kill at this moment, Martin, for a cigarette.'

'Now you are exaggerating.'

'Not by much, I'm not,' she said.

It was true to say that the Jericho Crew never lost a man in combat. But they did suffer one casualty. The bloody nature of their work meant that their number, which was fourteen, included a chaplain. He was a Baptist minister. His name was Derry Conway and he was a staunch patriot, an old-fashioned follower of what, a generation earlier, had been termed muscular Christianity. He had been an outstanding athlete at his college and his faith in God was thought unshakeable.

Conway was assigned because of the bloody and incessant nature of the missions charged to the Jericho Crew. By late 1917, quite a lot had been learned about shell shock and battle fatigue, the psychological problems nowadays referred to as combat trauma. If men were to survive these experiences mentally as well as physically intact, they needed spiritual succour. That, at least, was the theory. It was the Reverend Conway's role to provide this for Harry Spalding and his men.

But a month after being given the assignment, Conway was found hanged from a rope in the Béthune barn. His neck was cleanly broken. He had clambered on to a rafter with one end of the rope tied to it and the other forming a noose around his neck and he had jumped. There was a prayer book still clutched in his hand when he was found. Presumably he had taken it for comfort from a coat pocket before jumping. And despite the crude angle to which the fracture had forced his head, there was a smile on the face of Derry Conway's young corpse.

The death of their chaplain left the Jericho Crew with thirteen members. And none of them was killed or wounded by the war they fought with such bloody distinction. But Suzanne managed to find out what had happened to eleven of them after the armistice. And she discovered that the members of the crew had not been so very fortunate in their efforts to survive the peace. All of the thirteen were dead before their fortieth birthdays. Gubby Tench had enjoyed the longest life of any of them. Though she felt that where Gubby Tench was concerned, enjoyed was probably an incompatible word applied to life. At least at the end of his life, Tench had seemed to be living in a sort of hell.

She took the train to Dover and the ferry to Calais. As she approached the coast of France, the fine April weather England was enjoying ended as the ferry was enveloped in a grey and persistent rain, washing from an overcast sky. By the time she got to Calais itself, the rain was heavy and unremitting. She hired a car and studied her map. She had managed to contact the farmer whose family had owned for generations the land on which the barn still stood. He had not sounded overjoyed on the telephone about her proposed visit. But neither had he forbidden it. Suzanne spoke some French, but the farmer was content to communicate in rudimentary English.

'Tuesday,' he had said.

She tried to establish a time.

'Tuesday,' he repeated, sounding amused at this insistence on such precision. 'I will be here. Where else would I go?'

She tried to describe herself.

'I will know you,' he said. 'Do not worry, *madame*. This is not an English farm. You are not a candidate for my shotgun.' He laughed. She thought the joke a poor one.

The French countryside was flat and bleak and rain-defeated. The drive across it was monotonous. In an effort to distract herself from wanting to smoke, she switched on the car radio and tried to tune it. It was Suzanne's opinion that French pop music usually consisted of several competing tunes hammered out in parallel by lots and lots of fundamentally incompatible instruments. And the French language did not lend itself easily to pop lyrics. None of the words scanned in the convenient way English did. So she searched for a classical music station. But she stopped pushing the tuning button as soon as she heard something familiar and vaguely welcome to her ears that wasn't French.

It was the Prefab Sprout ballad 'When Love Breaks Down' sung plaintively by the failed priest. What had Martin said his name was? She knew it because it was a track from one of the wistful, whimsical albums Martin liked to listen to on the expensive audio equipment in the flat, equipment which he had bought and about which he could be so precious. She'd get the singer's name in a minute. Nothing stayed on the tip of her tongue for very long. It was one of her talents. She had an excellent memory for detail.

Just then, at that moment in her life, she felt her talents both taken for granted and somewhat abused. She had lost her staff job through a round of BBC cuts, which she felt had left all of the fat in her old department intact while removing most of the muscle. She had been offered the choice of a severance package or a freelance contract and had opted for the latter. But there was something subtly degrading, she felt, about her freelance status. Programme editors and producers treated her differently now that she no longer had the protection of the BBC as an employer. There was more rudeness. There was more pressure. There were shorter deadlines. And programme makers who found it an effort to fight their own sexism or inclination to bully stopped doing so in their encounters with her.

The Collins documentary series was a case in point. It was being billed as definitive and, over three forty-minute episodes, she was confident it would be. But the producer had wanted the Big Revelation. That was how he put it, in his memos to the department, in his capitals. And the Big Revelation he wanted was that Michael Collins was homosexual. His reasoning for this, laughable to Suzanne, was Collins' notorious fondness for wrestling colleagues and friends and his vanity over his appearance. She still had not decided whether the theory was a bigger insult to Collins or to the gay movement. But she had failed to find a single shred of evidence, physical, anecdotal or otherwise, to support it. And that was being interpreted as her failure, because the producer had a gut feeling about this and knew he could not be wrong. No matter that she had come up with hard facts about Michael Collins that the series would air for the first time. The atmosphere in the edit suite was poisonous. Three weeks before the transmission date, the sense of disappointment was almost palpable. Suzanne had done a brilliant job, she felt, that was being judged as somewhere between superficial and inept. And, as a freelance, she could ill afford a reputation for ineptitude.

'Paddy McAloon,' she said out loud at the wheel, remembering the name of the priestly novice turned rock star, startling herself, because the song was still playing and that couldn't be possible, could it? Unless there was a version of 'When Love Breaks Down' that played for ten minutes. That was unless, of course, the station was just playing the same song over and over.

She turned off the radio, glanced in the rear-view mirror

and saw that there was nothing else on the road. She brought the car to a halt with two wheels on the grass on the roadside and lowered the window and then switched the engine off. The wipers stopped and the windscreen blurred and blinded with rain. She could hear rain patter on the roof and the grass outside the open car window. Essentially, it was a reassuring sound, rhythmic and familiar. But it did not offer reassurance now. She felt alone and vulnerable in a raw way, at odds with the smudged landscape and soft, rainy light. She would smoke a cigarette, she decided. It was almost noon and it would be her first of the day. She reached across to the passenger seat, where she had put her bag. It was a myth, of course, that tobacco calmed you and helped you to relax. But it was a myth she felt she very much needed just at that moment to believe in and take comfort from.

At just after one o'clock, she reached the track leading to the farm, two deep grooves in thin gravel and the black soil underneath it, determined by years and decades of heavy tractor wheels. There was a hedge to either side of the track, high and impenetrable. It was so gloomy that she was obliged to switch on her lights. And the track was longer than she thought, so long that she wondered if she had taken the wrong turning. But there was no going back once she had started, because the way was too narrow. And when the hedge petered out she recognised the pattern of low, old farm buildings beyond from the aerial photos she had studied on her computer screen.

The barn was not among them. That was a solitary building a half-mile across fields from the farmyard, the fields divided by a ditch lined by poplars. You reached the barn by following the ditch. You did it in a tractor or a four-wheel drive over the rough, rain-soaked earth. Or you walked there. You walked across the fields of northern France to your destination. From somewhere not far away, Suzanne could hear the persistent bark of what sounded like a large dog. The bark did not bother her. Farm dogs were territorial, but they were not generally vicious. A vicious dog on a farm took too heavy a toll on the livestock and she knew that the farmer, Pierre Duval, kept geese and chickens and bred lambs here.

She went and knocked on the door of the building that looked most like a dwelling. It was old and brick-built with a porch, and there was smoke raising a thin stain into the rainy sky from a chimney. But there was no response. She walked round the side of the building and peered into a window. The interior was dark, dank even, ancient enamel appliances yellowing in its shadows. It was a kitchen, but it seemed cold and abandoned.

None of the other buildings were occupied either. Perhaps the farmer was just doing what farmers did, out in his fields. Suzanne looked around the farmyard once more, trying to persuade herself that there was something picturesque in the buildings with their half-timbered walls, their rust-coloured brickwork and sagging roof tiles. But in the rain, among the puddles, the place looked squalid. Rustic charm was absent from it. There was a damp and elderly smell of cow shit. Birds flapped in a ragged flock towards the poplars lining the ditch that led to the barn. Suzanne looked at her watch and decided to follow them. She wanted to be well on the way back to Calais and the bright ferry terminal lights by the time darkness descended here.

She walked for ten minutes before the barn started to look any closer. It was a trick of perspective, she decided. The building was both bigger and further away than she had first assumed. The aerial photograph had given an accurate impression of its rectangular outline, but not of its scale. As she got closer, she realised that the barn was of a really substantial size. And it was sturdily constructed, more than just solid, somehow formidable. It did not reflect the humble domestic architecture of the clustered farm buildings she had just left. They were simpler and more recent – built, she guessed, in the middle of the nineteenth century. The barn might be a barn now, in terms of its function. But despite its remote location, it surely must have been something grander at some stage in its past. It was a sombre building. Even in the flat, rainy absence of light, it seemed to cast a shadow bigger than itself.

It had originally possessed windows in what had once been an upper storey. They had been flat rectangles rather than arched. And they had been bricked in a great many years ago with blocks made of the same stone as the rest of the construction. They had weathered over time to the same grey as the walls. But the mortar between them had blackened and rotted and gave the old work away. Suzanne found herself wishing she had at least some working knowledge of architecture. But she possessed very little and what she did know she had learned incidentally. Because she had researched him for a documentary special, she knew quite a lot about the work and working methods of the Nazi architect, Albert Speer. But with a shiver, she realised that the building in front of her was calling to mind something far removed from Speer's grandiose classical plagiarism. It made her think, of all things, of the Whitechapel killer, Jack the Ripper.

She stopped dead in her own muddy footprints. It was an absurd subject to be entering her head, wasn't it, by a ditch at the edge of a muddy field in sheeting rain in France on an April afternoon? What did a Victorian serial killer have to do with Harry Spalding and the happy bloodlust of the Jericho Crew?

And then she had it. She had thought the barn looked a little like a Norman church deprived of its tower or its spire. But what it actually resembled, with those square windows it had once possessed, was a Masonic temple. There were tricks and puns and cul-de-sacs of architectural detail about the barn that she did not have the expertise to recognise. But the closer she got to it the more she could see they were there, just as they were perhaps the defining characteristic in Masonic temples. Some people had speculated that the Ripper was a Mason. There had never been any hard evidence to support this belief, because the Ripper had never been identified and convicted. But that had been the link in Suzanne's mind. And it gave her an even greater sense of uneasiness approaching the barn, thinking it perhaps a place that harboured more than just the chill inherent in buildings that were old and semi-derelict and standing in unhappy isolation.

Her feet were wet as well as muddy, now. The soil, black and clinging, had risen above her leather ankle boots and smeared her tights to the calf. She thought the boots probably ruined. They were from Russell and Bromley and not Millets and they had cost her a penny short of two hundred quid – and the credit card had done the buying, so they weren't even paid for yet. It was her own fault, of course. But who would think to pack wellingtons to take on a ferry? She looked around. The landscape was wet and desolate. She had thought the farmer would warm to her smile and politeness. She had thought rough-spoken but gallant Pierre Duval would give her a lift across the mire aboard something with a close gear ratio and chunky tyres. But she had got that part of the proceedings badly wrong.

Then, suddenly, she was there. The ground rose and hardened towards the building's walls. The incline was slight but the drainage effective and her feet approached the last few yards of distance on firm earth. She looked for the bedraggled squadron of birds that had led the way. She had thought they were starlings. But they had veered off on some other course. There were no birds. There were no rabbits or squirrels and the barking dog of the farmyard had long faded into silence. There was nothing living in proximity to Harry Spalding's old Jericho Crew hideaway. Even the poplars hereabouts seemed stunted and reluctant. But that was just her imagination, Suzanne knew. She looked at the walls, at rain-stained masonry, at the filled-in windows, like blind and baleful eyes looking darkly outwards at the featureless world of Pierre Duval's domain. She looked at the large oak double door, which did not appear locked. And she felt afraid and awfully alone and vulnerable wildly beyond what she had felt earlier, on the road, when she had stopped for the comfort of a smoke.

She forced her feet forward. What was the matter with her? She was a grown woman. She was here in broad daylight, for Christ's sake. She had wanted to come. She pulled one of the big doors open a fraction and slipped inside. And her first impression was of an almost sepulchral darkness and cathedral calm. She looked up, looking for the chinks in the building's fabric that would allow some meagre light for her eyes eventually to adjust to. The first thing that came into focus were the wooden beams from which she assumed Derry Conway had taken the last leap of his life. They were very thick and substantial and she could see no structural reason for them unless they had once supported a floor. That would make sense, too, of the height of the bricked-in windows.

Slowly, reluctantly, she brought her eyes down to the level of where she stood. And she saw that the barn did not stand empty. Crates of produce had been piled almost to the height of the ceiling along the entire length of the wall to her left. And there was, at the centre of the barn on the ground in front of her, a rough, high pyramid of beets. It reached almost to the beams. It was so big and high that it did not really look stable. She almost smiled. The prospect of being crushed by an avalanche of beets was an ignominious one. It would not be at all a dignified death.

The quiet in there was unnerving. And there was nothing very reassuring about the produce in the place. It should have given the building a workaday feel of farming domesticity. But it did not. Suzanne wondered precisely why. The quiet was one reason. Another was the fact that she could smell nothing in there, neither the earth from which the pyramid of root vegetables had been taken, nor whatever was stored in the crates. Perhaps it was not fruit or vegetables, but a hoard of wine, she thought. She would approach and recognise the musty, distinctive smell of corks stoppering old bottles.

She walked across to the crates. Her eyes were adjusted now to the lack of light. The crates were wooden and venerable. Some had dates in faded ink on the pale wood of their sides. Others had the year branded into them. They should have had bottles of wine in them, old and valuable vintages, she thought. None of the dates was more recent than 1915. But the crates were full of apples and plums and damsons and pears. The fruit was fresh, the burnish of red and russet and gold on firm flesh in the gloom. It was odd that nothing smelled. There was not the hint, not the ghost of the ripe and woody scent of an orchard from the fruit.

On the wall opposite the one against which the crates were piled, Suzanne saw something that almost caused her composure to abandon her. She was very frightened in the refuge of the Jericho Crew. Everything here was mundane. Nothing here had threatened her. And yet she was sure she had never been in a place that harboured so much pure and absolute menace. Before the far wall, she saw a uniform line of men standing perfectly still against the shadowy stone. They did not approach. They just waited and watched, motionless and poised. She almost screamed, before her mind was able to rationalise the sight as a line of coats on hooks, hanging there.

She could feel the muscles jump in her legs as she approached the coats. The weight of her body felt light in her ruined boots. They would be musty and rotten, the coats, and there would be thirteen of them. But there were only nine. And when she reached out and touched one, the nap of the fabric, where it was not mud-splashed, was firm and heavy and still soft. She turned the collar of the garment on its hook and could just make out the name, the letters forming it, *Waltrow S*, machine-stitched on to the pale name tag in red thread. Suzanne recoiled from the greatcoat as light and noise drifted into the building, and she cried out aloud and put her hands to her face.

'*Madame?*'

There was a figure at the door in a rain cape and a hat.

'*Madame?*'

The farmer Pierre Duval had a shotgun broken over his arm. He was tall in the bath of light at the door and wore a hat with a dripping brim and a heavy moustache and the rain cape was black and slick with moisture. He might keep his earlier promise and not shoot her, but he had brought the gun as a precaution. He frowned at her. In better English than he had displayed over the phone, he said, 'Have you discovered what you came for?'

She gestured vaguely at the crates, at the pyramid of beets. 'You use the place for storage?'

He looked around. He had not crossed the threshold. She sensed that he was reluctant to do so. She remembered what Martin had said about Frank Hadley's refusal ever to call Harry Spalding's boat by its name. He shifted on his heels and the twin barrels of his shotgun rose and descended again over the crook of his arm. 'I never come here,' he said. 'Nothing of this is work of mine.'

It was very quiet. Suzanne could hear rain splash on the step at the entrance as it dripped from the hem of Duval's rain cape. She did not understand. And then she thought that perhaps she did.

'Nothing rots in here?'

He just looked at her. The double shotgun barrel was thick and heavy-seeming, and it gleamed in the matt light from the sky as it rested over his forearm.

'Nothing perishes?'

'Not in my lifetime, *madame*. Nor in my father's. And nor in his. It is nature's joke.' The expression in his eyes told her plainly that Duval knew it was a joke played not by, but against nature.

She turned and looked back behind her at the still pyramid of beets rising from the floor at the building's centre. She tried to imagine song and camaraderie and the warmth of a campfire with a coffee pot or a bacon skillet rigged over the flames. But the image defeated her. She looked again to the ghostly company of coats in their line against the wall. Stillness and darkness were the only discoveries here. As it was a place where nothing perished, so it was a place where nothing lived. Derry Conway had managed to die here in the autumn of 1917. But Suzanne, having seen the place, having felt its raw malevolence, was pretty sure that Derry Conway had been assisted in achieving his death. She shivered again. What manner of man could ever have found comfort here?

'There is coffee inside,' said Pierre Duval, who had seen her shiver, gesturing in the direction of the farm. 'You were unwise to walk here. Come.'

He had parked his battered Land Rover behind the line of poplars. She thought it odd that she had not heard the approach of its labouring engine, because the engine did labour, when he started it. It chugged and then when he depressed the accelerator pedal, it roared and the vehicle vibrated on its high springs. But too much else was odd about the barn for the failure of sound to carry there to worry Suzanne unduly. She was grateful for the lift. With Duval's shotgun resting across the back seats, she was grateful also for the company.

He progressed beyond the farmyard, to another structure that the farmyard buildings themselves had obscured during her brief earlier exploration. And he parked outside it. This was a modern dwelling made of wood and designed to blend in with the earth and trees surrounding it. It looked more Scandinavian than typically French. She could see how she had missed it in her aerial search, looking for old stone and sagging clay tiles. Its steep roof was earth-coloured and made of some modern material. Its windows were tinted on the outside so that the building did not reflect light.

The impression that farming was a profitable business after all for Pierre Duval was strengthened when he unlocked the door and she was invited inside his home. He did not like clutter. But his furniture looked expensive. The kitchen was a hard, shining array of steel and granite. A large plasma television screen was mounted on one wall of his sitting room. There were logs in the open iron grate but the fire was unlit. He had a laptop on a small desk and a Bang & Olufsen stereo system in one corner with three immaculate rows of CDs stored on shelves above it. No one else lived here, she was certain. Pierre Duval did not share his life. She smiled inwardly at the thought that he had once lived amid the fading enamel and linoleum squalor apparently abandoned a few hundred metres behind them.

He took her coat and removed his and went to hang them where he said they would dry, and then he gestured for her to sit while he made the coffee. She had wiped her feet vigorously on the doormat outside. Now she saw that her muddy boots had trailed a few crumbs of wet earth across Duval's wooden floor. He would notice; the place was otherwise immaculate. But she did not think he would mind. She had picked a careful path between his scattered and expensive-looking rugs. And she sensed he had invited her in for a reason beyond her wish for something hot and sustaining to drink. She was here because he wanted to tell her something. He would tolerate a bit of mud to hear it told.

'In 1917 my grandfather was a boy,' he said, seated in the chair opposite hers when they both had their coffee. 'He was fourteen and he was very innocent. He liked the Americans. He liked the doughboys. They were generous with their chocolate and their chewing gum. They were cheerful. Many of them, whole battalions of their infantry, were coloured soldiers. Were you aware of that fact?'

'None of the Jericho Crew was black,' Suzanne said.

Duval did not answer her. He looked down at the contents of his cup. 'My grandfather was Pierre Duval also. And he was still a child. And the war was a great adventure. When the soldiers marched, they sang. Most of them sang. The Scots marched to the pipes, to their tunes of glory in their fighting kilts, with their battle standards raised. At night, in their camps, the coloured doughboys sang their slavish songs of devotion to God.'

'Spirituals,' Suzanne said.

Duval smiled, as though he himself were remembering. 'Their spirituals, yes, of course. They sang their spirituals in this land so far from home, in their canvas settlements, and their strong and ardent voices carried through the night. How marvellous and strange that must have sounded, here.'

He stopped. Suzanne felt no compulsion to interrupt the silence. He sipped coffee. 'It was all a great adventure to the boy who would become my grandfather. It must have seemed to him as an epic film in the cinema would. And then the Jericho Crew came here,' he said. 'And they did not sing, *madame*. They did not sing at all.'

Pierre Duval, who was fourteen and for whom the war was a great adventure, had seen none of the crew. They moved by night. And they moved with the stealth of ghosts. But he had seen the night glow sometimes of their fires. And knowing the friendliness of the Allied troops generally, and overcome with curiosity, he had approached the barn.

He had done so very quietly and carefully. He did not wish to be mistaken for an approaching enemy, nor to be mistaken for game and shot. His plan, such as it was, was simply to reveal himself in plain sight when the light of their encampment could illuminate him as a harmless, unarmed boy. Later, he was thankful for this cautious instinct because he was sure it saved his life. At the time, as he approached along the forgiving autumn earth between the poplars and the drainage ditch, he felt only a boy's excitement.

They were clustered in a group outside the rear of the barn. He saw the scene from a hundred feet away, from behind the screen of trees. And at first he could make no sense of it at all. This was because he knew that his father's land was flat. Every inch of it was flat. Yet they were sitting grouped around their fires on a hill. And then he saw its purpose, what it was they had constructed on their hill.

There were three wooden crosses. A uniformed man hung from each. The oldest and most senior-looking of the prisoners was at the centre. To his right and left, Pierre thought, perhaps the men flanking him were his aide-de-camp and his driver. Was the man at the centre a general? It did not matter. Other details imposed themselves with far greater and more shocking clarity on his young mind. They had been nailed to the crosses using bayonets. They were still, the pinioned men. Pierre thought that they were probably dead. And they had each of them been crucified upside down.

As he watched, rigid with the dread overwhelming him, one of the Americans, a man with a pale swatch of hair, rose from the ground and idled across to the victim at the centre of the tableau. He took a knife and sawed at the torso and Pierre was certain now that the German general suffering this mutilation was dead. The man tugged at the corpse and his free hand came away with something wet that glistened in the flames of their fires, and he lifted and dropped this human morsel into his mouth and started to chew.

And Pierre heard laughter and clapping. And then at the edge of the group, he saw a seated man lean over and vomit on the earth. This man was dressed in the same uniform as the other Americans, he saw. But his hands appeared to be bound at his back. And there was the glimmer of a clerical collar in the firelight around his neck.

'Derry Conway,' Suzanne said.

'They built their own Calvary,' Pierre, who was Pierre Duval's grandson, said. 'They constructed an abomination. They were an abomination themselves. After that, no one from the farm went near the place again. And, of course, the boy who was my grandfather revised his views concerning war.'

'Tell me about the building,' Suzanne said.

Duval stared down at his coffee mug. Suzanne thought that he looked not just sorrowful, but ashamed. He raised his head and looked her in the eyes. 'It has been there since the Great Terror that followed the Revolution. It was built by the *Société Jericho*. Such cults were tolerated, even encouraged, in those times so hostile to organised religion. My ancestors leased them the land on which to build their temple. They paid a toll for their access along the route through our land to get to it. We profited. We profited from them for a time. They were banned in the reign of the First Emperor. The building was gutted and made derelict. But my family has paid and gone on paying for the sin of our opportunism and greed concerning the Jericho Society.'

'Do you know why they are called that?'

Duval smiled. 'Jericho is the old Hebrew word for moon,' he said. 'They are called that because they are of the night. They are dedicated to the night and what flourishes under the mantle of darkness.'

Suzanne finished her coffee. Duval escorted her back through the rain to her rental car. Leaving his home, in a pen beside a stand of trees, she saw two Doberman dogs. One of them must have been the source of the earlier barking she had heard.

'Do you keep them for the company?'

He laughed, but it was bitter laughter. 'On the contrary, *madame*. The dogs are here not because I am alone. They are here because I have the suspicion that, sometimes, I am not.'

She thanked the farmer and, without another word passing between them, he walked her back to her car and saw her off his land.

She became aware of the vehicle in her rear-view mirror about twenty minutes after exiting the lane that led to the farm. It was a black van. It was quite large and, after a couple of miles, she was pretty sure that it was following her. This was because although she drove with the slow caution of a stranger to the area obliged to drive on the wrong side of the road, the van did not close the distance and attempt to overtake. It just sat in her rear-view mirror. She tried to dismiss her nervousness concerning the van as paranoia. But when, to ascertain the truth of the situation, she reduced her speed, the black bulk of it simply stayed, in relation to her, precisely where it was. She could not avoid the conclusion that it was waiting, deliberately lurking in her wake.

All Suzanne could do was continue to drive. Every kilometre she travelled brought the bright, commercial bustle of Calais and the ferry terminal incrementally closer. Brightness, though, was becoming a problem. More precisely, the lack of brightness was becoming a complication as a mist rose or a fog descended and the ribbon of road in front of her grew pale and spectral in the full, enfeebled beam of her headlights. She groaned. She tapped a tattoo with her fingers on the wheel. She switched off the wipers. She tried to comfort herself with the thought that at least the rain had finally stopped falling. But when she looked in the rear-view mirror, all she could see behind her was an opaque blanket of grey. Her squat black pursuer had slipped from sight altogether.

And then the van flashed past her. It was as sleek and sudden alongside as a shark beside a swimmer in the water. Except that this shark had steel flanks and something was etched and glittered on them in gold. In the dead lustre of the mist, the legend read, 'Martens & Degrue'. And Suzanne, who did not share her boyfriend's sometimes charitable belief in coincidence, wondered just how deeply, in what awful sort of trouble, Martin and his father were allowing themselves to become engulfed.

A kilometre or two on, the mist began to lift. She saw a sign at the roadside for Calais. Her numb fear receded enough for her to realise just how badly she was craving the comfort of normality. She looked at her watch and, having the time to do so, pulled in to a roadside café and went inside and ordered hot chocolate. The café was warm and light. Indifferent people with mundane routines sipped beverages around her. The Police played 'Every Little Thing She Does Is Magic' through wall-mounted speakers. The tables were

Formica-topped. There were the smells of roasting beans and toasting cheese and ham baguettes and the faint aniseed whiff of Ricard, served from a sticky optic behind the bar. If there was a smoking ban in the café, its patrons were ignoring it.

Sipping her drink, normality beckoned for Suzanne, and it was seductive. But it came only at the price of a sort of willing amnesia concerning the past few hours and their events and revelations. She could forget about them, which would be the painless route back to the certainties of yesterday. Or she could subject them to a clever, sceptical reinterpretation, which would take longer, but would eventually deliver the same comforting effect.

Comfortably numb. There was a song by someone, wasn't there, called 'Comfortably Numb'?

And there was a song called 'When Love Breaks Down' written by a failed priest called Paddy McAloon. She had heard it playing in a manner it very definitely should not have on the radio of the rental car as she journeyed to the farm near Béthune owned by the brave and cautious Frenchman, Pierre Duval.

Despite the temptation, Suzanne would not allow normality to settle its illusory claim on her. She had seen what she had seen and she had felt what she had felt and she had listened to what she had been told. Given time, she was sure that she could unravel the whole disquieting truth about Harry Spalding. But she hoped that it would not be necessary for her to have to do so. She hoped that what she had learned so far would be enough to deter Martin and more particularly his headstrong father from their planned voyage aboard Spalding's refurbished boat.

It was late by the time Suzanne wound up this account of her little journey to the old and bloody battleground of the Great War. And with the adventure of the *Andromeda* not yet a full day behind me, I was bone tired by the time she completed it. I felt pretty numb myself. And I felt pretty comfortably numb, to tell the truth. Nothing she had discovered seemed as bad as the hours-earlier prospect of being abandoned by Suzanne. That had been my fear at the outset of the night. And it had been terrible. In reality, I felt more flattered by her efforts on my behalf than disconcerted by their results.

The lurid atrocities of a conflict fought ninety years ago seemed very distant. The weirdness of the barn near Béthune seemed far more ominous for the stoical Frenchman farming the land around it than for my father or myself in contemplating a voyage aboard a vintage schooner.

Suzanne had gone behind my back, obviously, to discover what she had. Strictly speaking, as I've already acknowledged, she had deceived me. Relationships are built on intimacy and none of the ingredients that go to conjure intimacy is so important as trust. But Suzanne had acted with noble intentions. And my own sin, committed after her revelations that night, was simpler but considerably worse than hers. Mine was the sin, of course, of omission.

I know now what I should have done. The truth be told, I knew then. Regardless of my fatigue, regardless of hers, I should have told her about Straub's ghost. I should have told her that story and allowed the sharp mind behind that lovely face of hers to ponder on the place of it in the emerging pattern of things. But I did not. I dozed instead. She dozed next to me, the two of us close beside one another on our bed. And then, as the clock on the bedside table clicked towards one in the morning, I stirred and stroked the smooth flesh of her shoulder and, remembering, said, 'Tell me about Peitersen, Suzanne.'

Her eyes opened, dark and slightly bleary with sleep in the night gloom in our flat near the river. She went and made herself some tea, then came back to bed and sipped it as she lay down, alert again.

'Josiah Peitersen did indeed build the *Dark Echo*. By any measure, Spalding was still a youth when her keel was laid. So the boat was a tremendous indulgence on the part of his parents, regardless of their wealth. And they were prodigiously wealthy. She was a fabulous prize for someone barely out of his adolescence when she began her sea trials.'

'Unless she was something else,' I said, not really knowing why I said it, or where my thoughts were taking me. My mind was voyaging back to the dank waters of East Friesland, to Baltrum and the intrigue of Childers' *Riddle of the Sands*.

'What do you mean?'

'Only that she might not have been merely a gift. She might have been built with some purpose beyond the frivolity of regattas in mind. Perhaps Spalding was groomed to be her master for a reason we haven't discovered.'

Suzanne pondered. She twisted her neck to face me on the pillow. I could smell the scent of Earl Grey tea warm on her breath.

'From birth, you mean?'

'It's just a thought,' I said. And a terrifying one. 'What were they called? The debating society to which the Spaldings and the Peitersens and the rest of them belonged?'

'I haven't been able to find out,' she said. 'They referred to themselves as The Membership, but they were the membership of something, obviously. It must have been some clan or brotherhood or cabal. There was some secret, ritualistic name I haven't been able to discover. It's there in some FBI file compiled when the Feds went after them during Prohibition. But the file is classified or lost.'

'Or stolen,' I said. 'Filched by someone working for a Brussels-based firm called Martens and Degrue. Or lifted by the man masquerading as Peitersen, masquerading as someone else.'

'Josiah Peitersen and his wife had no offspring,' Suzanne said. 'That was an easy thing to discover. Both of them predeceased Harry Spalding. And they left no grieving son behind to carry on their bloodline.'

'Hadley said that Peitersen's references checked out.'

But that contradiction was an easy one, even for me. Peitersen was sent 'from above', so far as the beleaguered Hadley had been concerned in his storm-bound, curse-prone boatyard. Surrounded by his high-tech toys, with my father's baleful wreck lashed to the stanchions of the quay through his office window, he must have read the words in the airmail letter and thought Peitersen heaven-sent. Any check on the man's references would have been cursory at most, if it was ever carried out at all. In the circumstances, most people would have forgiven the desperate Frank Hadley a convenient lie. With the threat of ruin the alternative, he'd certainly have forgiven himself the telling of it.

My father was not usually easily fooled. He was a man only ever willingly gullible. But Jack Peitersen had been everything my father wanted and required of him. He was a part of the *Dark Echo*'s lineage. He looked and sounded right. His appearance and apparent pedigree would have appealed to my father's snobbery – a weakness his own childhood, bankrupt of pedigree of any sort, had made him prone to all his adult life. But all this begged the urgent question of who Peitersen was. What was the man's motive in coming to my father in this fictitious guise? The fact that he seemed only to have done good, his presence an almost miraculous benefit, somehow made the question even more compelling.

'I need to talk to Peitersen,' I said. 'Or whoever he is.'

'Good luck,' Suzanne said. 'I tried myself, this morning, after having what I'd found out about him confirmed in the

States late last night. I only saw the confirmation when I switched on the computer this morning. I called the yard at Lepe straight away. And then I called the hotel. But he was at neither place. He seems to have departed as abruptly as he arrived. Whoever he was, he's vanished.'

Six

I called my father as soon as I respectably could the following morning. My dad being by compulsive habit an early riser, that was just after 6 a.m. But he wasn't there. His housekeeper came to the phone after it had rung for a while and bade me a cheery good morning. She seemed reluctant to discuss my father's absence and then even more reluctant to discuss his whereabouts.

'Do you think he might be in Chichester, Mrs Simms?'

There was a charged silence on the line.

'Mrs Simms?'

'He might be, Marty. It's a fair assumption, since he did not discuss his destination on departure.'

She was an Irishwoman, was Mrs Simms. I'd known her since childhood. And I knew she liked a flutter.

'Mrs Simms?'

'Marty.'

'Would you bet money on Chichester?'

'Sure, I wouldn't bet my house. But I'd have a few bob on it, Marty, so I would.'

So it was a tryst with his new-old flame. I smiled to myself. Chichester would never again for me be just a quaint and prosperous town founded after the Roman invasion. The word had taken on a new significance. And it had become a verb. Forever on, Chichestering would be the euphemism for my father's energetic pursuit of sex. Or of romance. Or, most plausibly, his pursuit of romance through sex. He was an optimist, was my father, always reminding me of the fact through his outlook and behaviour. The glass for Magnus Stannard was never half-empty. With him, it was always full to brimming at the lip. The thought brought a fond, fearful surge of feeling for him. I felt, for the first time in my life, as though he really needed my love and protection. I realised in that moment, on the phone to Margaret Simms, that I had not had the remotest notion of how much I loved my dad before this sorry business began.

'Did he take his mobile phone?'

'He took the berry thing.'

'The BlackBerry.'

'The very item. He took that.'

'Thanks, Mrs Simms.'

'It won't necessarily be switched on.'

'What?'

'He told me it wouldn't necessarily be switched on. He said he might be off-message.'

I'll bet he did. 'Thanks, Mrs Simms.' I hung up. I made tea and took a cup in to Suzanne and pondered on what to do. There was no point in trying to find my dad in Chichester. I could hang about until he was back on-message and try to establish exactly how much, if anything, he knew about Peitersen's fraudulent identity and abrupt disappearance. That would have been the sensible thing to do. But I felt the need to do something more, the compulsion to do something immediate. I really couldn't stand to wait. So I decided to drive to Lepe and see what I could find out there for myself. I kissed Suzanne and told her not to tell anyone where I was going. What I meant was, don't tell my father, if he should call. Peitersen and my father were the only people to whom my arrival at the boatyard would be of any consequence. And Jack Peitersen had gone.

It was a lovely late April morning. I set off munching a piece of toast, sipping from a flask of coffee Suzanne had made me while I was in the shower. All the traffic was town-bound, coming in the opposite direction from the one in which I was travelling. I put on the radio and heard the opening bars of the Prefab Sprout song 'When Love Breaks Down' and almost scalded myself with coffee as the steel cup jumped in my hand against my lip. I switched off the radio. Maybe it had been sampled or something. That sort of thing happened now with old records all the time. Or it could have been used on the soundtrack of a hit movie or as the theme song for a hit TV series. It could have. And on the back of that, it could have been re-released as a single. Whatever, I made good time in the subsequent silence. But there should have been men working in the boatyard by the time I got there. I wasn't so early as to have beaten the morning shift. Yet there was no one, not even someone at the gate to guard against vandalism or the petty theft of on-board computer hardware or valuable boatbuilders' tools.

The breeze-block and corrugated-iron shed that had served Peitersen as an office offered no clues as to his whereabouts. There were some rough cost calculations for something or other on a desk blotter. Beside the columns of numbers there was a diagrammatic sketch of some kind of timber joint. It was exceptionally well drawn. But the quality of Peitersen's draughtsmanship was really neither here nor there. There was a filing cabinet, the one occupied drawer neatly filled with invoices and receipts pertaining to the job in hand. But there was no desktop computer there with files for me to ransack. There wasn't even a landline that I could see. Places like this always had a cheesy soft-porn calendar on the wall. It was an essential part of their fabric. But this one didn't. Instead, Blue-tacked to the concrete, there was a chart delineating the schedule of progressive works aboard my father's boat.

There wasn't an ashtray full of stale dog-ends or a bin of Peperami and Snickers wrappers or a single empty beer can.

He hadn't left a scarf or a winter sweater on the rack of coat hooks by the door. There were no work gloves or overboots. There was not one single personal item present there. People take pictures when they restore things. They take before and after pictures to amuse themselves with and take pride in and show off to people. It's human nature. They tack them up or leave them on their desks. But there were no pictures. He had done his job with the fastidiousness of a monk and then he had disappeared before its completion. And he had left no note. And the note, of course, had been principally what I'd been looking for in his office.

There was no sign of the *Dark Echo* on the dock. She had been pulled up on runners into the refuge from rough weather of the one big boathouse at the yard. That said, there was no weather just then to shelter her from. The day was benign, the water beyond the dock a smooth emerald shimmer of darkening sea stretching out towards the Isle of Wight and the harbour at Cowes. I breathed in. I was dismayed, often, at how stagnant the edge of the sea could smell, with all the rotting detritus burdened on an incoming tide. But the smell of the sea on this particular day had a cleaving freshness. And there was no ravaging wind or rain to slap at and sully the sheen worn by my father's precious acquisition. Nevertheless, in the boathouse she lay. It was as though Peitersen had finished his task on this quiet statement of neatness and precaution, I thought, approaching the building. He had signed off with the subdued flourish of a real craftsman.

She was a gorgeous sight when I unbolted and pulled open the double doors, revealing her to the bright spring light of morning. My father had said, when she was no more than a sullen wreck in the marine boneyard of Bullen and Clore, it was her lines that got to you. And I could see now what he'd already been so stricken by then. Even out of the water, the sweep of her hull made Captain Straub's *Andromeda* seem frumpy and staid. They were the same gender, but different generations; the plump Clyde dowager dressed in widow's weeds and the flapper heiress glittering at one of Gerald Murphy's Riviera parties.

Except that she did not so much glitter as gleam. The *Dark Echo* was svelte and sumptuous in the gloss of her paintwork and the lustre of her polished brass. I climbed aboard. It was quiet in the boathouse. I was dimly aware of the hiss of small waves breaking down on the shore. And faintly, there was the cry of gulls, ubiquitous in the sky above the water. But the boathouse and the boat it harboured were entirely silent. So perfectly grooved was the planking on her deck that the teak beneath my feet didn't so much as murmur under my weight. I ran my hand lightly along her rail on the port side close to the stern and sensed that the *Dark Echo* was poised, tensile, alive and awaiting her moment. It was not a forbidding feeling. There was nothing portentous or threatening about it. It was exhilaration, the promise of glamour and glory. It was, above all, a seductive sensation.

Amid the rusting and gigantic artefacts of marine engineering and salvage at Bullen and Clore, and again on those ramparts built against the storms of Hadley's dock, I had been made aware of the elemental depth and sometimes even the fury of the sea. The voyage to Baltrum, with its blast of Arctic wind and its high and persistent swell, had only increased my feeling of wariness at the thought of crossing an ocean. But the *Dark Echo* had substance, as well as abundant style. She had pedigree. She seemed not so much adequate to the beckoning task, in her grace and strength, as eager for it.

My father had insisted that there was no such thing as an unlucky boat. There were only unlucky owners, he said. Aboard his glittering prize, in that boathouse at Lepe on that benign and gentle April day, it was an easier argument to believe than you might imagine.

Whatever atrocities the Jericho Crew had cooked up and conjured seemed to have damned them all. Two of the men whose fate Suzanne had discovered had at some time owned the boat. At least one, perhaps as many as three men had died aboard her. But the others had all met their violent, early deaths on land. Spalding himself had perished stretched across the counterpane of a bed in a New York hotel room with his veins full of Cutty Sark whisky and a pistol barrel at his temple. The boat had been icebound in the harbour, miles away and surely blameless. The chaplain, among the Jericho Crew, had died first, in a French barn. Of the rest, only Tench and perhaps the Waltrows had met their fates aboard the *Dark Echo*. With what really happened to the Waltrows an abiding mystery, Tench was the only certain casualty of the boat.

It was the Jericho Crew that were cursed. They had done something, entered into some devilish pact to determine their own immunity in battle, and paid a heavy and gruesome price once peace was restored to the world. They had dabbled in dark magic learned by Spalding from his occultist parents in his youth. And they had indulged in dark atrocities. It was nothing to do with the boat. It was to do with the war and the diabolical part they had played in it. The accidents at Hadley's place had been unfortunate, but they had been just that. The washed-up dolphin, the gory omen of Hadley's fraught imagination, had been exactly what my father said it was. Lost and disorientated, it had encountered a propeller blade and had become an unfortunate casualty of the busiest waterway in the world.

Peitersen – the mystery of Peitersen and the hope of solving it – was, of course, the whole of the reason for my visit to the boatyard at Lepe. But I was naturally interested in seeing the *Dark Echo* again. She had impressed me as a work in spectacular progress when last I'd visited, with Suzanne. I was curious to see whether the refurbishment had reached a stage where it would entirely dispel the threat I'd felt when first aboard her. That malevolent, terrifying vision had dimmed a little with time, I'll admit. There was this natural temptation to place it in the Wagnerian winter endured by poor Frank Hadley. But Suzanne's story of the barn used as a base in France by the Jericho Crew had brought the terror of the moment back pretty vividly. And I wanted to find out how I felt aboard the *Dark Echo* after a voyage on a similar craft that was, according to its master, truly haunted.

I climbed down the companionway at the stern of the vessel. To the rear of its descending steps was the master cabin. I took a deep breath and studied the door of what would be my father's living quarters aboard. It was inlaid with a large central panel of polished walnut. It was possible to discern all kinds of fanciful patterns and themes in the rich and complex walnut burr. But wood was wood, however exactly carved and fashioned. It smelled like it had been lovingly oiled. It felt like velvet and glass combined in some clever alchemy under the caress of my fingertips.

I turned the burnished brass handle. The door was unlocked. I took another, deeper breath. I felt more nervous than on my last visit, the transformation of the *Dark Echo* no longer the happy novelty to me it had been then. And then, Suzanne had been at my side. Now, I was alone. I was aware of the blood pounding in my ears with my accelerated heart rate. I was not fearful exactly. I was nowhere near the state of hackle-raised fright I had been in on first setting foot aboard her. But I was apprehensive. It was easier to believe the curse on the owners rather than on the boat. It was much easier, now that the refurbishment had made the boat close to unrecognisable. But after all I had heard and experienced, after the disappearance of the fraudster masquerading as Jack Peitersen, I'd have been a fool not to feel a degree of trepidation.

The door opened on a magnificent room. I'd thought Captain Straub's master cabin cosy. My father's made it look squalid. He had paintings on the walls by Léger and Bonnard and Delaunay. There was a bookshelf, with first editions of Hemingway and Sinclair Lewis and Scott Fitzgerald and Gertrude Stein. There was the original of the photograph I'd seen of the *Dark Echo* winning its race in the Arthur Mee encyclopedia, framed on my father's magisterial oak desk among furled navigation charts and maps. There was a beautiful three-draw telescope and a teak humidor for his cigars. And there were his boxing trophies, those cheap and tarnished things of nickel and silver plate, mounted in a cabinet of glass that was subtly tinted, I suppose, to give the prizes within a lustre they had always lacked in the gritty impoverishment of life.

There was a gun cabinet, screwed to the rear wall. It was less a display case than a working rack for the placement of rifles and shotguns. My father was skilled in the use of both. Until the Dunblane tragedy and the ensuing legislation, he had also owned and practised with a variety of handguns. Firearms held a deadly glamour for him. Once, on my birthday, he had taken Suzanne and me to Las Vegas to see Ricky Hatton fight for a world title and we spent the morning after the fight at a desert shooting range. My dad got to blat off a few rounds with an M16 and a Kalashnikov, grinning like a kid as the brass jackets from the rounds chinked around his feet and a cardboard target in the shape of a man was obliterated in the near distance. Suzanne learned to load and fire a handgun and proved to be an excellent shot. I was hungover from the after-fight party and bored.

He had told me of his intention to bring a weapon or

weapons aboard. He had mentioned what had happened a few years ago to the great Australian yachtsman Peter Blake on the Amazon. We weren't going to the Amazon, but piracy had made a comeback in recent years on the Atlantic. Clearly, he had meant what he said. There were no guns in the cabinet yet. Looking at it, I was pretty certain that there would be by the time we embarked. It seemed fair enough. He had spent a fortune on the *Dark Echo*. When we left land, the vessel would be my father's domain. He clearly felt he had the right and obligation to defend it.

I head a noise, then, a scurry that was explosively loud in the silence of the boat's interior. It sounded furtive and aggressive at once, and it made me jump suddenly in my own skin. It had come from the galley, I decided. And, of course, it could only be a rat. The sound of it brought me back to myself, to the suspicion that the boat had been preternaturally quiet before the scurrying sound. Where the fuck was the yard security? Alright, it was a small yard leased for the commissioning of a single vessel. But this coastline was not immune to crime and the *Dark Echo* was a hell of a prize. An opportunistic thief could retire on the grey-market sale of the artwork alone on the boat I was aboard. And where the fuck was Peitersen? He'd overseen a lovely job. Had he even collected what he was owed for it, before he'd bolted?

I heard the rat again. It was large and scavenging and doing Christ knew what damage to the spotless wood and steelwork of the shining new galley. I was not afraid of rats. Nor, though, did I want to get bitten by one of the large seagoing examples. I looked for something to kill it with. There were knives displayed in a case on the wall of my father's cabin. Their present purpose was ornamental. They were beautiful objects with hilts fashioned from ivory and bone and blades of engraved steel. But they had been tools once and appeared sharp. That said, I didn't want to be swabbing rodent giblets from the galley floor. I swore under my breath and heard the bold and noisy fucker again, scrabbling a few feet beyond the master cabin door. I looked around. There was a polished mahogany billy club, clipped to the wall but not enclosed behind glass. It looked like the sort of evil weapon with which the Spice Island press gangs subdued reluctant sailors in the Pompey of the early nineteenth century. It was about twelve inches long and its grip was bound in twine, and it swelled at its business end to about the circumference of a tennis ball. I pulled the club free of its clips and hefted it. It was viciously well balanced. I felt a bite of pain, slapping the head of it into my palm, wondering that the pressed sailors ever came round after a blow from this thing. My antique weapon seemed ideal for dealing with vermin. I'd just have to make sure not to miss with it.

I stole out of the master cabin, ducked into the galley and shut the door behind me before snapping on the electric lights, grateful that the battery powering them was charged, grateful I'd remembered the location of the switches. I looked around the bright, polished surfaces. There was nothing there. I hefted the club and looked at the floor and work surfaces for telltale rat droppings. But the place was clean. It was also, once again, entirely silent. There wasn't even ambient noise now. Outside, the gulls had gone. The sea had receded. I hefted the club in my hand, dropped to my haunches and searched the cupboards and the oven and the refrigerator. But they were empty. Empty, too, were the head-height cupboards flanking the galley above the shiny racks of copper pans and steel utensils. It would have been a very sterile environment in which to discover a rat. There was not a crumb of food aboard the *Dark Echo* for a rat to eat. If any of the workers had left a half-eaten sandwich from their lunchbox in the galley, I would have seen the cling film or greaseproof paper used to wrap it. And I would have smelled its stale residue. All I could smell was wax polish and a faint, lemony hint of disinfectant. The place was spotless. But I had heard what I had heard.

I progressed through the length of the boat to my own cabin. It was modest compared to my dad's. But it was still better appointed than any living quarters I had ever spent time in aboard a boat. He'd had a picture of Suzanne and me, taken at one of his summer picnics, blown up and mounted in a rosewood frame and hung on the wall I'd be looking at if I ever used the desk he'd provided me with. My furniture was deeply upholstered in wine-coloured leather and I smiled, thinking I'd have to grow a moustache and wear a potent aftershave to achieve the necessary machismo to sit on any of it. I'd need one of his rifles across my lap. There was a combined radio and CD player and, beside this machine, a pile of CDs of the sort of music my father, or more likely Mrs Simms, knew I liked to listen to. There was the latest Apple laptop, dazzling in its whiteness at the centre of the desk. What there wasn't, was a scurrying rodent about to have its back broken by my borrowed billy club.

I thought about the sail store. But there was nothing in there for a rat to chew on yet. The sails were not due to arrive until mid-May, a full fortnight distant. There could be items of rigging. But ropes these days were nylon, not hemp, weren't they? Unless you were aboard the *Andromeda*. The only sort of rat I knew anything at all about was the sort you read about in tabloid newspapers. These cat-sized monsters would, allegedly, chew their way through anything. But I thought that even a tabloid rat would draw the line at rope spun out of some oil-based synthetic compound. There was no nourishment in nylon.

So I didn't check the sail store. I checked the shower stall and the lavatory, which flanked the short corridor between my cabin and the door through which you entered it. And I stood very still and listened very carefully for a full minute, standing in the corridor. But I did not check the sail store because there seemed no point. My rodent stowaway had avoided our confrontation by scurrying out of an open porthole, I decided. Several of them were open; I noticed this backtracking for a last check before climbing back up to the deck. On my way through, I closed them all. Doing so would not hinder a determined thief. But it might prevent an adventurous rat from getting aboard and nibbling at the canvas of my father's pictures. Lastly, before leaving, I slotted the billy club back into its brass display clips.

I vaulted down from the deck of the *Dark Echo* on to the boards of the boathouse, feeling really indignant about the way she seemed to have been abandoned. It was paradoxical, to say the least. She had been restored to the sort of specification demanded by an Arab sheikh. Yet here she was, at the mercy of any local vandal armed with a can of graffiti paint. It was more than paradoxical to abandon her like this. In fact, it was bloody odd.

There was a man at the gate when I walked out of the boathouse and back towards where I'd parked my car. He was wearing blue uniform trousers and a blue poly-cotton shirt with a flash above the breast pocket that read 'Security'. He put his hands on his hips and rocked on his heels when he saw me approach, narrowing his eyes. The effect would have been more impressive had he kept his cap and tunic on. But they'd been surrendered already to the rising heat of the late April sun and were draped across his seat next to the gatepost. He was Job Centre security, not the swaggering nightclub sort who supplement pay of five pounds an hour by dealing gear. I felt a bit sorry for him. He was out of shape and the wrong side of forty. His trousers were too tight and shiny with wear at the pockets and crotch. He was the sort of security lippy adolescents give the run around in big supermarkets.

'What are you doing here?'

Not thieving, obviously. I was carrying nothing, not even my mobile, which I'd left in the glove compartment of the car. He'd worked this out for himself, eventually. I saw it in the way his shoulders relaxed as I got closer to him.

'My old man owns the boat.' I looked at my watch. It was just before 10 a.m. 'Where have you been?'

He looked sheepish, embarrassed. But he said, 'I'm early. I'm not even properly on till ten.'

So I was overtime. Or I was undertime, if there were such a thing.

'Prendergast is supposed to be here,' he said.

'What's your name?'

'Chesney.'

'Where's Prendergast?'

But Chesney said nothing. He looked down at his cheap shoes where the hem of his polyester trousers broke over them.

'My father is a generous man, Mr Chesney. He appreciates a conscientious employee. Above all, though, my father values and rewards loyalty. Where's Prendergast?'

'He don't like doing nights.' The accent was very local. 'No one does. So we toss for it. Prendergast called wrong. Got a week of nights. Couldn't avoid it when Mr Peitersen was here all hours, he'd catch you out. But, well, with Peitersen gone, who wants to be here on his lonesome in the dark, eh?'

'So you'd have done the same?'

Chesney looked churlish, now. He ground the sole of a shoe into the gravel at the gate like a toddler nailed for some nursery crime. I felt less sorry for him than I had. Stupidity and petulance are an ugly combination.

'It's the noises, see, Mr Stallard.'

'Stannard.'

He nodded towards the boathouse.

'The rats?'

'The voices. The laughter. They carry, see. I tolerates it because I have a family to feed. But I don't like the nights any more than Mickey Prendergast does.'

I nodded. There didn't seem anything to say, not to Chesney, at least. But he had given me something to think about.

'Sardonic, the laughter? The tone of it?'

He looked at me like I'd just opened my mouth and spoken Martian to him. I took out my wallet. I always carried cash. It was a habit inculcated in me by my father, who always carried cash because he could never forget the time when he'd had none to carry. I peeled off three twenties and stuffed them into Chesney's pocket and walked past him through the gate to my car. I'd hinted at a reward when I'd asked him to tell me the truth. He'd done that. I meant to get him sacked and, as he'd said, he had a family to feed. Sixty quid did not seem overly generous compensation.

There were no messages on my mobile. I tried calling my father's BlackBerry with no success and tossed the phone over my shoulder on to the back seat in exasperation. I was no fonder of my less attractive traits than anyone else. Intellectual snobbery had always been prominent among my long list of obnoxious characteristics. I had dismissed Chesney the timid sentinel as pond life because I hadn't liked hearing what he said. But whether I liked it or I didn't, it needed to be considered. My next port of call was the country hotel where my father had put Peitersen up. He was gone from there, too, of course. But at the hotel he might have left the explanatory note he had not left in his boatyard office or aboard the *Dark Echo* either.

Sardonic laughter. I had heard it myself on my own first terrifying exploration of the boat, in Wagnerian weather on Frank Hadley's horribly luckless dock. But on the two visits since, at Lepe, I had felt entirely different. It wasn't so much as though the baleful threat had receded, though. It was more that I was seduced by the *Dark Echo* herself into ignoring any danger. Suzanne had been so disconcerted by her first exposure to the boat, my second, that she had lied to me and gone to France in a bid to uncover the secrets of the man who'd had her built. Yet I'd been reassured, relieved in the aftermath of the visit we shared.

On the visit just concluded to the *Dark Echo*, I'd been dazzled by her. I had heard that loud and furtive scurrying aboard and not just rationalised, but trivialised it. This despite the fact that I'd found no trace of the rodent sane thinking insisted was responsible for the sound. It was as though the boat herself lulled and stroked me into a sort of sedated glee. Aboard her, my senses were happily stupefied.

She did not lure me to her. The contamination did not spread that far. Away from her, I felt no great yearning for her. But once I set foot on the *Dark Echo*, I seemed to fall under her strong and sensual spell.

I had Chesney, in his shiny, pantomime sentry outfit, to thank for this belated insight. As I pulled up outside Peitersen's picturesque country hotel, it was not a comfortable thought.

Then I had another. What if I had looked in the sail store? I had a sudden and very confident intuition that I would have encountered not a rodent, but Spalding's pet bull mastiff Toby, stinking and wormy and dead. And panting and eager in its grotesque parody of canine life for the return of his long-lost master. The dog had lurked in the sail store, had gnawed rope there in the cool and the quiet when the weather and swell had made the deck unsafe. I knew it now. I knew it suddenly and with the same absolute certainty insisting that night follows day.

I had no trouble at all in accessing Pietersen's room. My driving licence established my surname. And there was no Chesneyesque confusion over it. The Stannard name had been the source of much guaranteed income for the duration of Peitersen's stay in the hotel, because my father had put him up in the best-appointed room in the place. His meals and his room had been paid for in advance until the end of June, the Easter and early summer premiums effortlessly accommodated by my father's happy largesse. So I was not surprised at the smiles and the opening doors and the all-round obsequiousness. In a microcosmic sort of way, they amounted to the story of my life.

The room, by contrast, offered me nothing. The windows were oppressively leaded and the walls punctuated by bucolic scenes of domestic country routine. The beamed ceiling was so low as to make the space seem cramped, despite its broad width and generous length. Logs sat in the grate of an authentic fire, but the bark was curling on them under a patina of dust. I patted the counterpane on the bed, sniffed at the plumped pillows. It was recently changed and made up, of course, but the bed had a cold, unslept-in look about it. Slowly, the details of the room revealed themselves. There was a TV and DVD combination, discreetly positioned and definitely not dating from the age of squires stretching before pewter jugs of porter after a hard day riding to hounds. There was a power shower in the adjoining bathroom. The bathroom was small. But its dove-white, downy towels were folded across heated rails. On a shelf under the mirror, there were little embossed bottles filled with creams and lotions, the sort hotel guests routinely steal to offset the pain of paying the bill.

Peitersen had paid no bill. And I was somehow sure he

had stolen nothing either. I felt a strong certainty that he had never unscrewed the top from one of the pampering bottles on the bathroom shelf. Just as he had never taken a DVD to view from the small library of them under his television. Neither had he enjoyed a drink from the minibar tucked against the wall beside the television. His first-floor window looked out on to the budding leaves of a stately chestnut tree and, beyond it, a lush sweep of descending lawn. I doubted Peitersen had ever so much as noticed the view. I had a strengthening suspicion that he had never slept in the bed.

The fastidiousness of a monk.

Again I searched for a note, but found none.

I sat among the vases of wild flowers and the horse brasses and heavily framed pictures in a window seat in the hotel's cluttered lobby to drink a cup of coffee. The sun warmed my back through the window. A Polish girl with pretty eyes fussed with her hair behind the reception desk. It was twelve o'clock. My mobile was still on the back seat of my car where I'd thrown it in exasperation earlier. I could hear the drone of a motor mower clipping the grass outside. Everything seemed perfectly normal but I knew that nothing was. I wondered if my father was still off-message in Chichester. I thought of the picture he had framed for me in my cabin aboard his blighted boat and felt like sinking to my knees and praying for his safety. Instead, I drained my cup and went over to where the Polish girl had been joined by a colleague similar enough to her for them to be sisters.

Yes, they had known the guest I described to them. The receptionist with the arresting eyes was called Magda. The other girl, her cousin Marjena, had given Mr Peitersen's room its daily turn. Marjena's English, while a hell of a lot better than my Polish, was nothing like as good as that spoken by Magda. I would ideally have liked to take Marjena for a walk in the hotel grounds for the sort of private chat that encourages people to recollect those careless details that can be significant. But Magda – who knew, of course, about the payment arrangements for Peitersen's stay – did not seem to inhibit her cousin from speaking at all. And, of course, I needed help with translation.

It seemed Peitersen had certain idiosyncracies. Middle-aged and well heeled, most of the guests were yachties or golfers or couples enjoying a romantic break from their regular routine. The hotel was famous for its kitchen. There were two other restaurants, one Italian and one that sounded to me like the Kundan on the Hamble, that the hotel was happy to recommend. Peitersen never ate at any of them. Nor did he ever go to the gastropub a mile down the road.

'And he did not eat in his room,' Marjena said.

'He must have eaten something.'

Marjena looked at the floor and said something incomprehensible.

I looked at Magda.

'My cousin says Mr Peitersen was starving himself.'

'Dieting?'

She shook her head. She narrowed her eyes, struggling for the English word. It came to her. 'Fasting,' she said.

When I got back to my car the message symbol was flashing on my phone.

'Martin. You've been trying to reach me. Since it isn't my birthday, and since I have not changed the terms of my will, I'm baffled by the attention. What can you possibly want?'

Under the humour, his voice was rich with contentment. Chichester agreed with him. Now I was going to deliver news that would ruin his day. I hesitated with my thumb over the redial button. How did I know that Peitersen had disappeared? I knew because Suzanne had told me the previous day. And how did I know that he wasn't really

Peitersen at all? I knew because Suzanne had done some digging, about which my father had never been consulted. What would I tell him? I would tell him the unvarnished truth. Killing the messenger was an injustice in which my father habitually indulged. And he might consider Suzanne's digging a sort of betrayal. But there was no point in lying to him. She had acted out of concern for me. I was motivated only by concern for him. He could be bad-tempered, vindictive, capricious and cruel. He could out-sulk a spoiled four-year-old and he was breathtakingly vain. But he wasn't stupid. I'd weather the verbal storm and wait for calm to return and, when it did, we would discuss the mysteries of the fraudulent boatbuilder and weigh their implications and try to solve them together.

Motive was the key to it, of course. I knew Suzanne's and I knew mine right enough. But Peitersen's motive was obscure and baffling. And my conversation with the Polish girls had thrown up as many questions about him as it had clues. I looked up through the Saab windscreen at the window of the room he had occupied. I could not see inside. Sunlight reflected back from the panes the dappled green of a chestnut tree against a pure blue sky. I took a deep breath and pushed the button on my phone.

He met me that evening in the West End of London at Sheekey's restaurant after a performance at Covent Garden. His metaphor concerning Hadley's yard and Wagner had been based on more than rhetoric. My father loved the opera and most particularly the leaden, myth-burdened Germanic stuff. He listened to it a lot at home on a hi-fi system that had cost roughly three times what I paid as the deposit on my Lambeth flat. But you couldn't really begrudge him the luxuries he'd earned.

He looked tired over dinner, as though some of the glitter had come off him. Maybe his new-old flame had worked him hard between the sheets. But I thought there was a bit more to it than that. Regardless, I didn't nurse him through what I had to say. I told him all of it. I told him last of all what I had learned from the Polish girls and from Marjena in particular.

'She should have knocked, but she didn't. He was almost never there. She doesn't believe he slept in the bed in his room, just rumpled it from time to time for appearance's sake. She should have knocked. Instead, she opened the door and surprised him.'

'And herself.'

'He was prostrate on the floor with a set of rosary beads in his hands. He was *incanting*, her cousin said. That was the translation.'

My father smiled at me. 'America is a nation with more than its share of pious Christians.'

'He was wearing a hair shirt, for Christ's sake.'

'And sometimes their piety knows no bounds.'

'Magda found his passport.'

'Disappointing. I thought the Poles were honest.'

'They were suspicious of him. They had a duty of care to their other guests. The night manager ordered her to do it. The passport was made out in the name of Cardoza. No more his real name than Peitersen was.'

I had told him about Cardoza Associates. I had told him about Martens and Degrue. He had looked mildly intrigued. His volcanic temper had not produced the expected eruption. I had not been able through any of what I told him to shake him out of what seemed to me like a strange sort of detachment. In the end, I lost my own temper.

'It would take more than Chris fucking Bonington to justify this stuff, Dad. And we haven't even fucking embarked.'

'I'd thank you not to use that language with me.'

'You use it with me. All the time.'

'Seniority, Martin. There's a protocol.'

'Aye, aye, Captain.'

I was frustrated and furious. I think he could tell I was. He raised his eyes for the bill and, as usual with him, that was all it took. A raising of eyebrows in the hurtle and hubbub of a crowded restaurant and the bill was on its way.

'I'll get this, Dad.'

He put his hand on mine. 'Don't be silly.'

I loved the touch of him. It was too rare between us. I felt my anger start to dissipate. I knew it would leak away from me in the grip of my father's unexpected tenderness. But I couldn't let it. The danger seemed too urgent and the portents too great.

'Tomorrow, Martin,' he said. He squeezed my hand under his. 'Tomorrow I shall let you in on a shameful secret. And I expect my doing so might put your troubled mind at rest.'

I picked my father up at 9 a.m. There was no wind and the sky, apart from its criss-cross pattern of vapour trails, was an unsullied blue. It was perfect helicopter weather. So wherever we were going, he felt he needed to be with me, in the seat next to mine, on the journey back. The mood is always lighter in the morning and so, waiting for him, I thought of making a joke about how I should start charging him by the mile, or about how Scandinavian cars were clearly growing on him. But when I saw his face, I decided against it. He looked like he'd been crying. In the bright morning, he looked raw with grief. And for the first time in my life, I thought my father looked older than his years.

He tossed a bag and a topcoat on to the back seat and got in. Then he closed the door on himself and sniffed and sighed. 'Sleep okay?'

'Surprisingly well.'

He fastened his seatbelt and took a long breath that caught in his chest.

'You alright, Dad?'

'I loved your mother very much.'

True as this statement was, I neither wanted nor needed to hear it. There were other, pressing imperatives. Any mention of my mother and her premature death was hard to take. I had indulged my father's lingering sense of loss at her passing for a long time, at the expense of my own feelings and unmet craving for comfort and consolation. But now was not the time, surely, for him to talk about the way that Mum was taken from us. Now was not the time.

He sniffed again. 'Can you find your way to Southend?'

I released the handbrake, eased off the clutch. 'If that's where you need to get to.'

He turned to me. 'Don't be callous, son. It's an effortless inclination in the young, I know. But please don't be callous. Today is going to be difficult enough.'

Callous. In his business life he'd behaved as though he had a monopoly on the word. 'Cutting the slack' had been his mantra. Ruining reputations and livelihoods had sometimes been the consequence. He thought I was soft-hearted, and maybe I was. He thought it an advantageous tendency in the priesthood but disastrous in the cut and thrust of commerce, and maybe he was right. But at that moment, pulling away from the kerb, I thought he had a fucking cheek to call me callous. And I thought his bringing up the subject of Mum a cheap and unforgivable tactic of avoidance.

My mother was killed by lung cancer. She filled my thoughts on the drive to Southend. I could not think about her in life without thinking about her death. This was because the manner of her dying made an abject mockery of everything of her that preceded it. Diagnosis came too late for meaningful treatment and she declined rapidly, stupefied by the morphine made necessary by intolerable physical pain. Gaunt and seldom conscious, she slipped away from us four weeks after entering the hospice. The disease had made a frail stranger of her by the time the moment of her death arrived. She had never smoked. She never developed a cough. Persistent fatigue had been the only really serious symptom before the cancer was discovered. She was a writer and occasional broadcaster on the radio who lost the energy to write and, in what became her final broadcasts, sometimes suffered a slight breathlessness.

My mother was a beautiful American woman from San Francisco who filled our lives with light and ended her own in a confused darkness. There was no time to settle her affairs, nor to reconcile herself or those around her. Everything about the illness happened with bewildering speed. When I think of her I think of her laughter and her kindness and her grace. And then I think of her death. She was forty-four years old when death arrived without a shred of dignity in its hurry to claim her.

The blue promise of the London morning disappeared on the A13, about twelve miles from our intended destination not of Southend but of Westcliff-on-Sea, the picturesque little town just to the west of its garish neighbour on the coast. The cloud came and lowered and then the rain began to fall in big drops, splashing audibly on the Saab's windscreen. My father had brooded throughout the whole journey. Neither of us had spoken much. He'd grunted that we actually wanted Westcliff, but that was it. The pleasantries were behind us. He seemed as lost in his own thoughts as I was in mine. The overcast sky and the rain suited the mood in the car better than the sunshine had. I thought about switching on the radio. But I did not particularly want to risk hearing Paddy McAloon singing about what happens when love breaks down.

He directed me through Westcliffe's pretty streets. We

stopped outside a vacant lot halfway along a row of suburban villas all with neat gardens dripping from precise hedgerows and pruned bushes in the persistent rain. It was odd, the empty space in the row of well-appointed little dwellings. It created an abrupt and somehow melancholy absence.

'Ever heard of Victor Draper, Martin?'

My father was staring at the breach of soil and rubble between the houses. There were puddles there and the unrelenting rain splashed into them.

'The name is vaguely familiar.'

'A medium. He was a medium, a man who claimed to have a clairvoyant gift. He was very successful at about the time of your mother's death. His column was syndicated in the middlebrow tabloids. He appeared sometimes on television. He wasn't one of those breakfast TV cranks. He was a cut above the pulp. He was persuasive and respectable. If I remember rightly, he was even the subject once of a BBC *Omnibus* programme.'

I did remember him. He had been a familiar name until a decade or so ago. He had been the respectable face and fluent public voice of the paranormal. His books had been advertised in the back pages of the Sunday supplements. His pull had been sufficient to fill theatres on public tours. Then he had disappeared. I suppose I had just assumed he had died himself.

My father cleared his throat. 'When your mother left us, I found it impossible to reconcile myself. My faith should have been strong enough to help me endure. But, God forgive me, it was not.'

'You went to Victor Draper?'

'He came to me. He was very convincing and I was half mad with the agony of my loss.'

Our loss, I thought. Her death did not just happen to my father. She was our loss. And she lost more than anyone.

In the seat next to me, in my car in the rain, my father was trembling. This was very difficult for him. He was exposing himself to his son as a fool. 'When did you realise?'

'After a couple of months. And around forty thousand pounds.'

'What gave him away?'

'Oh, he was very good. He had done his research. He had a formidable memory for trivia. And he was a most gifted mimic. He could modulate the tones of your mother's voice with uncanny conviction. I really thought it was her words coming out of his mouth when he simulated his trance.'

'But he made a mistake.'

'Yes,' my father said. 'He made a mistake.'

I'd turned the wipers off when he had begun to speak because their noise was intrusive. Now rain bleared the windscreen. There was no other traffic on the road. There were no pedestrians braving the downpour. I could hear rain drum on the roof of the car. I felt sad and fearful of what was about to be revealed to me.

'You were not an only child, Martin. You had a younger sister. She was born just before you reached your second birthday and she was very premature. She survived for only a few days.'

I nodded. I had not expected this. I was not prepared for a revelation of this sort. 'Why did you never tell me?'

'I've never possessed the strength to talk about your sister at all. And your mother kept silent on the subject, I think to spare me from the ordeal of being forced to do so.'

'What was my sister's name?'

'Catherine Ann. Ann for your mother.'

'And Victor Draper didn't know.'

'He lived there,' my father said, nodding at the empty space between the villas to his left. 'I had him exposed as a fraud by a team of private detectives. Ruined, I believe he skulked off to Australia. When he was forced to sell his house I bought it myself and had it razed to the ground.'

'Why have you told me this now?'

'I didn't stop with Draper, Martin. I tried to reach your mother through other mediums with reputations just as exalted as Draper's had been. All were charlatans. I'm telling you this because if it had been possible to contact your mother, I would have succeeded in doing so. There are no such things as ghosts. There is God—'

'Then there is Satan.'

'Perhaps. But there is no spectre of Harry Spalding to prowl the boat that used to belong to him. The dead do not mingle with the living. They don't communicate with us. They live as they did only in our memories, which is where I should have had the good sense and moral courage to allow your mother to rest.'

Catherine Ann. There had been four of us. 'It's why you always light four candles. After Mass.'

But he did not reply to that. He did not need to.

Catherine Ann. She would have been thirty or thirty-one now. Roughly the same age as Suzanne.

'What about Peitersen?'

My father smiled. It was a grim smile. Confession had exhausted him. 'A crank, which was my first instinct when Hadley showed me his letter. He's some boat enthusiast who read a stringer's report on the auction of the *Dark Echo*, probably on the internet. You'll remember I gave an interview to a press reporter at the sale. Working on a restoration project of that magnitude and pedigree was probably a dream come true for the man who called himself Jack Peitersen. It was just our good luck that he was competent as well as keen.'

'You really believe that?'

'I'm spending tonight aboard the boat, Martin. It's why I

packed an overnight bag. I'd be grateful now if you could take us on to Lepe. You can drive back to London afterwards if you wish. If Suzanne is amenable, you can stay on the boat with me. Or you can spend the night in a hotel. There's a comfortable room in a very well-appointed hotel of your recent acquaintance that's paid for until June.'

'I wish you'd told me about my sister before now.'

'I've arranged a little ceremony for tomorrow at the boatyard that it would be as well for you to attend. You can get down from London in time for it because it won't take place until about midday. But it would be less arduous for you, travelwise, to stay.'

'I wish you had told me about my sister, Dad.'

'I do, too, son. I wish it with all my heart.'

We stayed that night aboard the *Dark Echo*. We ate dinner first at Peitersen's hotel and I drank steadily throughout the meal. The kitchen there no doubt justified its excellent reputation. But the food I ate was ashes in my mouth after my father's earlier revelations. I was tired, too. It took almost three hours to drive the 160-odd miles from Westcliff to Lepe. Altogether that day I had been behind the wheel for a total of around five hours. I was in no fit state to drive after dinner and we had to leave the car and take a minicab back to the boatyard. I think that my father also drank too much. Alcohol is less than ideal as an anaesthetic. It leaves you with a sore head and a dry mouth and it depresses you. But it's easily accessible and doesn't harbour any nasty surprises. I'd had enough of nasty surprises for one day and craved and indulged, over dinner, the easy numbness of drink.

I couldn't have recalled what I ordered on surrendering the menu to our smiling waiter with the words just out of my mouth. And our conversation over dinner was a dim, inconsequential blur. My father prattled about navigation and communication systems and networks. He talked about patching through and piggybacking and other telecoms arcanery. I thought about the nursery my parents would have decorated and furnished for my lost sister, Catherine Ann. I thought about her painted crib. I pictured the toys they would have bought and the tiny items of clothing and the dreams for her they must have cherished together. I wondered how much the keeping of the secret of her death had contributed to the cancer that had grown and flourished in my mother's chest and killed her. In the poignant secrecy between my parents of Catherine Ann, I thought I understood something of what had driven my mother to an early death. And I thought I understood something, too, of what had driven my father through his subsequent life. But perhaps these insights were owed only to the illusory clarity of drink.

I did not dream that night in my cabin aboard my father's boat. Or if I did, I did not remember the dream. I slept soundly in a berth so comfortable it bordered on the luxurious. My quarters on the *Dark Echo* made a quaint joke of conditions aboard the *Andromeda*. I woke once in the night that I remember, just to take a swallow from the bottle of Hildon water by my bunk that I had scrounged from the hotel. We'd taken bottles of water and toothbrushes and fresh towels. The hotel treated my father in the way he was always treated; like some visiting potentate. And in the morning, when I knocked on his cabin door and he admitted me, that's what he looked like, too. He looked glamorous again and vibrant. He had recovered himself. With a fresh surge of grief for the sister I had never known, I knew then standing in his cabin aboard his boat, that my dad would never address the subject of his daughter willingly again.

We left the yard for breakfast at the hotel at about a quarter to eight. As we got into the car I saw a pair of transit vans pull up at the gate. One was blue and had the name of a security firm stencilled on its side in yellow capitals with a logo underneath of a portcullis wreathed in barbed wire. Three men got out of it, two from the cab and one from the rear with a German shepherd on a short chain lead. The three men were all well built and unsmiling and dressed in smart black tunics.

'Your Chesney anecdote alarmed me,' my father said. 'I've taken fresh precautions.'

The second van contained six men wearing a mixture of overalls or jeans with chambray shirts and puffa jackets. One among them, I assumed, was their foreman and showed some papers to the first group. They stood a little nervously while the dog was allowed to sniff at each man and learn his scent. Then the gate was opened and, carrying their boxes of tools, they approached the boatshed.

'We need to be back here by noon,' my father said. It gave us plenty of time. 'From now on, Martin, the only sardonic laughter you will be hearing around the *Dark Echo* will be mine.'

An item of mail was brought to our table at breakfast. It was carried on a silver salver by Marjena, who gave a little bow of her head on delivering it to my father. It was a sealed A3-sized Manila envelope and his name and the address of the hotel were written on it in a careful hand. The writing reminded me of the column of figures I'd seen on the desk blotter in Peitersen's office. Some of the letters had a similar character, as though described by the nib of the same ink pen. My father took the letter and thanked the girl and then held it out to me across the tabletop.

'Open it, Martin.'

I used the knife from my side plate. Before I did so I examined the postmark. It was a bit blurred and indistinct, but the letter had been sorted at the big central office at Mount Pleasant in London. When I slit the envelope, a small collection of banker's drafts slid out on to the tablecloth. I knew what they were. They were the monthly payments my father had been making to Peitersen. And they had remained uncashed. He had used the expenses account for the payment of other men and he had bought materials from that fund, too – I had seen the invoices at the yard. But he had taken nothing for himself. I opened the envelope with my thumb and saw that there was a note in it, still stuck at its edge to the gum that had closed the corner of the flap. I freed and unfolded the note and read it aloud.

> She's ready, Magnus. You could tinker and fret over her for ever, but she's ready. Rig the sails when they arrive. It's a job a vessel's master should oversee himself. Give her a week's sea trials off Scotland's Atlantic coast. Or take her across the Irish Sea to Dublin and back. It will take a voyage of that nature to determine whether you and the boy are ready for her. But she's ready for you, Magnus. And I wish you God Speed aboard her.

The note was not signed. My father raised his eyebrows and took it from me and read it himself. Then he folded it and put it in his pocket. He reached for the banker's drafts and aligned them in his hands with a shuffle, then tore them in half and dropped them on to the table. He dabbed at his mouth with his napkin and signalled by rising from his chair that it was time for us to leave.

His helicopter had arrived by the time we got back to the boatyard. It sat on the hard sand from which the early tide had retreated with Tom, my father's regular pilot, smoking one of his little brown cheroots and lounging in his aviator glasses at its side. I did not have long to wonder why they were there. Monsignor Delaunay stood at the edge of the sea in his Mass robes, his bright stole flapping in the breeze, his biretta secured to his head by the finger of a raised hand as he looked out over the Solent towards Cowes. It had been better than a decade since I'd seen my favourite seminary Jesuit last, but I recognised immediately the huge neck, the incongruous power in his Olympian shoulders and back. He must have sensed our arrival, because he turned and then saw and approached us. And I saw that God, or Providence, had been good to him in the intervening years. He was greyer at the temples, thicker about the jowls, perhaps. But he had not really aged very much.

'Martin!' he said, and he opened his arms and embraced me, lifting me clean off the sand. 'I've come to bless your father's boat,' he said.

But I had guessed that for myself.

'Have you seen her, Monsignor?'

'I have, Martin. And she is a work of art.'

'Speaking of which, there is one of your ancestor's paintings aboard her.'

He laughed. It was a real pleasure for me to see him. Much of my nineteen months in Northumberland had been purgatory. All the best bits, in my memory of that time, involved this formidable priest. 'My claim to kinship with that particular Delaunay is a mite tenuous,' he said.

He duly blessed the boat. This simple service passed without incident. He murmured the liturgy and sprayed the holy water with the flick of a brush. I assisted by holding the ornate silver vessel into which he dipped the bristles. He did it thoroughly. Even the sail store received a sprinkle. When I opened it, it contained no wormy canine odour, no trace of Spalding's phantom dog. Afterwards, he went to the building I still thought of as Peitersen's office and changed into the suit he must have worn on the outward journey from the seminary. He emerged with an old-fashioned canvas grip in his hand. It contained his vestments and his vial of holy water. It had been a long way to come and whatever my father's powers of persuasion, the trip had been made at very short notice. I was touched.

My father suggested a pub along the coast that did an excellent lunch. They also kept a comprehensive, even esoteric range of single malts. He had remembered that Monsignor Delaunay was partial to a whisky. We should set off in a few minutes, he said. It would be the perfect preparation for the Monsignor's return flight. Then he strode off across the sand to say something to Tom, whose own lunch lay in a refrigerated bag aboard the aircraft.

'It's very good to see you, Martin.'

'And marvellous to see you, Monsignor.'

He studied me. He still had a smile on his face. But he knew me, knew the workings of my mind and conscience. For a year and a half, he had been my confessor. I doubted there was a living soul apart from Suzanne and my father who knew me better. And my father's insight into my character was probably obscured somewhat by my almost constant efforts to impress him. Of all the men I'd met, perhaps Monsignor Delaunay knew my true nature best.

He gestured back towards the boathouse. 'When you return from this adventure, you might think about marriage and a family, my lad.'

I blushed. I was living in sin. Evidently he knew I was.

'It'll be the making of you. It will fulfil the woman you love. And it will provide your father with more pleasure than anything, once he gets this Conradian adventure accomplished and out of his system.'

I said nothing to that. I looked down at the drying sand as the wind gently scoured the pattern of tidal retreat from its surface. Then I looked back up again. The monsignor was still smiling. In the unforgiving light on the beach, his teeth were tea-stained. He would play the whisky priest for an hour in the pub for my father. But what he really drank was tea. And what he was really about was faith and penance and conversion. He had never in his life held a woman to him in the dark part of the night for consolation. And he never would.

'The boat is benign, Martin. She's a gorgeous toy, fashioned from wood and brass and steel. She's an extravagance, a rich man's indulgence. But your father is a great and compassionate giver to good causes. And a boat is only a boat. Retain sufficient of your faith to know that such constructions cannot be cursed. And now she is blessed. Enjoy your voyage. Delight in your father's company. I will pray you come home safe and sound.'

It was as much as he could say. We were going to try to cross the Atlantic in a vessel built ninety years ago. He could neither guarantee our success nor our safety. On the wilderness of the water, at the mercy of the tempest, that was God's responsibility and choice. He said he would pray for us. He promised it.

I wonder now was he ever telling me the truth about anything.

The sails duly arrived during the following week. They were Lee sails from Hong Kong and they were made from Japanese Dacron. We could have gone for the purist approach, done an *Andromeda* by rigging her with authentic canvas. But canvas tears in storms and, unless you have someone aboard with the skills to repair sails, it isn't worth the risk. The modern alternatives are easier to haul, altogether tougher, and they dry out quicker, too.

My father suffered no purist agonies over the Dacron sails in the way he had over the engine. But the sails were ordered after the engine and, I think, as the date of planned departure drew nearer, his natural pragmatism came more into play. He was a risk-taker, but not compulsively so. The demands and challenges of the voyage were daunting enough. There was no debate either over our auto-steer equipment.

It was electronic and dependent for its intelligence on computer chips. You plotted your course and the boat followed it. In the event of strong currents or shifts in wind direction, it was self-correcting. Essentially, it meant that we could both sleep at night, at least for a few overlapping hours. It meant that we could eat dinner together. The alternative was for one of us to be a permanent slave to the wheel. Captain Straub might frown at the employment of such technology. But when his schooner took to the seas, it did so with a crew numbering a minimum of six, not two.

I still worried about Peitersen. With the boat snug in the fitting-out berth, her head rigger was moved to abseil down from the top of the mainmast and say to me that she was as punctilious a restoration job as he had ever seen. I'd no grounds to argue with his expert judgement. But it nagged at me that Peitersen had taken no payment for the job. Regardless of his bogus identity, if the work was honestly carried out, surely he had deserved some kind of recompense for doing it so well? Jack Peitersen's taking no payment seemed to me to be every bit as symbolic as Frank Hadley's superstitious refusal to say out loud the *Dark Echo*'s name. I did not know the significance of it. But I had an uneasy feeling that I might one day find out.

Our voyage, intended to take us to Dublin and back, was little short of a triumph. We caught the Celtic Sea in a calm and gentle disposition. So uneventful was the voyage generally, that when we anchored in Dun Laoghaire Harbour, my father suggested an ambitious extra leg to the trip. At dawn the following morning we swung north out of the harbour and set a north-easterly course. We hugged the Irish coast as far as the North Channel and continued north until we passed Rathlin Island, taking us out into the Atlantic, into the storm latitudes. Once out far enough we turned west, for Erris Head. And then we sailed a southerly course all the way along the West Coast of Ireland, swinging homeward only when we reached Mizen Head and Cape Clear.

We were gone five days rather than the two originally intended. I called Suzanne to warn her about the change in plan. She sounded strange, different. It could have been an atmospheric thing affecting my mobile. But I don't think it was. I think it was frustration. I knew that she had come to loathe the whole *Dark Echo* enterprise.

The most noteworthy thing about that maiden voyage was a dream I had aboard. When we moored at Dun Laoghaire I went ashore and walked to Sandycove for a swim at the Forty Foot in the approaching twilight. My father stayed aboard. He and my mother had honeymooned in Dublin and I think going ashore would have reminded him too vividly and made him melancholy.

I dreamed of Harry Spalding and Michael Collins. They were both uniformed, resplendent in their respective uniforms, standing on the rocks at sun-up above the Forty Foot. Light, reflected off the water below the crag on which they stood, glimmered on their brass buttons and belt buckles and caressed the polished leather of their boots. Neither man had employed a second. And there was no arbiter there to officiate and no doctor with a black surgical bag. They were alone. But they were there, I knew, to fight a duel. I could see that the protocol was to be strictly observed. Collins whistled with nonchalant composure as he screwed the stock on to his Parabellum pistol. Spalding grinned at him as he loaded the big Colt pistol carried in the holster on his Sam Browne belt. Then they were ready. They cocked their respective weapons. I could see their breath on the frozen air as the pair of them stood in profile, facing one another. It was winter again in my dream of the Forty Foot. And ghosts breathed air like the living. The crash of their pistol reports woke me before I could see whose honour was satisfied, whose satisfaction gained in this strange, parodic conflict.

Suzanne turned down flat my suggestion of a romantic dinner at a good restaurant on the eve of my departure for America. She said that it was too formal a farewell altogether and might bring bad luck on the voyage. Better just to go to the Windmill for a drink after our usual supper, she said. And this surprised me. I had not appreciated that she had any serious faith in luck, good or bad. I had assumed she was not in the slightest superstitious. She always struck me as a black and white sort of person, drawn to certainty, repelled by any kind of ambiguity. But then, nobody really knows anyone as well as we like to think we do. It's one of our human failings to assume we know a person intimately. It gives us the confidence and security with them that we naturally crave. And the more we value their presence in our lives, the more inclined we are, I think, to this venal little sin of self-deception.

Anyway, to the Windmill we went, where the conversation was stilted and the silences charged. I think she wanted to say something to me, but whatever it was remained unsaid. We stuck with the reassurance of platitudes. I complimented her on the Collins series. The second episode had been shown by then. The critical reaction had been overwhelmingly positive. But maybe that was the wrong thing to mention, because her freelance contract at the BBC would be up in a few weeks and she had just been told it was not going to be renewed. The producer of the Collins series was an unforgiving man when it came to a grudge and his contribution to her regular three-monthly review had been a spiteful assessment that clinched the outcome.

What we mainly did that night was sit in silence, occasionally sip at our drinks and listen to Marvin Gaye, Billy Paul and the like sing their maudlin 1970s soul ballads while I searched for the inspiration of something consolatory to say and, I suppose, she longed for the consolation of a cigarette.

We did not make love that night. And this is something that I very bitterly regret. I was always aroused at the tremble of the mattress springs when Suzanne slipped her lithe, lovely body under the duvet. That night was no exception. But there seemed some obstacle between us and it seemed both complex and impenetrable. To my shame and eternal disappointment with myself, I feigned sleep until sleep finally came, leaving me with the convenient rush of the morning and barely time for a kiss before departure. And the thing was, I loved her so much. And the thing is, I still do and will die loving her.

We set out, my father and I, aboard the *Dark Echo* from Southampton Harbour. There was no fanfare. There was no weeping at the quayside, and no scarves fluttered as we hauled anchor and cast off. Plymouth might have been a more appropriate point of departure, it occurred to me, since my father had once compared himself to Drake. Plymouth was nearer our destination. But the comparison had not really been very serious. I watched the quay shrink in our wake with my father at the wheel and our efficient little engine propelling us through the thick maritime traffic towards open water. Then I thought I saw someone standing, as though watching us. It was a diminishing and solitary figure with a pale, still face under a head of wind-blown, strawberry curls. Frowning, with my father fully occupied at the wheel, I turned from the stern and went to his cabin and took the telescope from his desk. I clattered back up the companionway, drew the telescope and trained it on the still, small figure on the dock. And he raised his head as though looking straight back at me. It was the man we had called Peitersen, a priest's collar above the black of his soutane, his hair blowing, freed of its woolen watch cap, in the wind at the edge of the sea.

It's said that human beings have no memory for pain. I think it might be similarly true that we have no memory for fear. My fear of the *Dark Echo* had become remote from me by the time we embarked upon our transatlantic voyage. It had been to do with the winter, in my mind. And it was the summer by the time we finally cast off and left land behind. It was the time in the world of light and warmth. There had been signs still that things were not altogether right with the boat and with our ambitions aboard her. There had been Peitersen's enigma and Suzanne's suspicion and hostility. But, as I say, I think our memory for fear is like our memory for pain. We progress from timid to bold without thought for survival or sanity in our greed to live and enjoy sensation and adventure to the full.

Suzanne began her pursuit in earnest, on the trail of Harry Spalding, the day that Martin and his father set sail from Portsmouth Harbour. 'There's no room in my life for ghosts,' she had said to Martin, before her clandestine trip to the French farm way back in April. But even in the spring, that had been a lie. Suzanne had been obliged to make room in her life for a ghost. She had been forced to accommodate one. It was why she had come to believe in their existence. Martin was wrong about that. She believed before ever seeing the barn owned by Pierre Duval. It was why she had feared that the danger to Martin and his father was so real.

She had told Martin about her brief brush with the otherworldly in the room with the skylight at the Dublin safe house, on her return from the trip back in March. She had told him straight away. But that had been only the start of it. And what followed, she had kept to herself. Her own ghost had come to her in the seclusion of her small study in the Lambeth flat one damp evening a few nights later. Rain had wicked cosily against the panes of the window. But the window had, of course, been closed against the cold. So when she became aware of the mingled scents she was detecting, she knew they could not be penetrating from outside. Anyway, they smelled warm. They smelled as if they had been generated in warmth and, she also thought, in some warm and distant spirit of conviviality.

What Suzanne smelled was a mingling of Irish stout and sweet, strong tobacco. Sometimes there was a hint of boot and metal polish, too, about the smell, a whiff of leather and cologne. Sometimes there was the sharp odour of wet wool drying, as though in from the teeming Dublin streets before the heat of a fire or stove. But the scent seemed mostly composed of Guinness and Sweet Afton cigarettes on the breath and clothing of someone sitting not far away and perhaps studying her. It did not frighten her. But the ghostly scrutiny did make her feel somewhat self-conscious. It would arrive and then it would be gone. The presence would become faint and then vanish.

He came quite frequently after that first occasion. She never saw him. But she knew very well who it was. She did not know why he came and she never tried to converse with him. She felt in a curious way he had the right to come and study her. She had studied him. It occurred to her after his first visit that his famous life was soon once again to be held up to the glare of public scrutiny. And she had played an influential part in determining what details people would see and hear and learn about him. But she had developed a deep admiration for his character and achievements over the course of her research. So, although she did not know why he came to visit her, she did not fear his ghost. She felt no coldness or sense of menace from beyond the grave. She knew that this flawed, vain, sometimes ruthless man had been, in his generous heart, as good as Harry Spalding had been bad.

He came to her for the last time on the evening of the most miserable day of her professional life. It was the day after Martin's departure for America and she had cried herself to sleep before the presence awoke her. Her mouth felt gummy and dry from cigarettes and wine. Her eyes were raw. And she felt his still, patient presence watching, beside her.

She had been exposed at work. Someone from the Yale University alumni archive had returned a call she had made and left a message concerning Spalding. The producer of the Collins documentary had been told. She was being paid during her notice period out of the depleted balance of the Collins series budget. She was supposed to be fielding calls and emails from interested members of the public, academics and the press, concerning the claims made in the Collins series. Her brief was to verify those claims. She was not supposed to be working on anything else for the BBC. She was certainly not supposed to be doing private work on BBC time claiming BBC status and using the corporation's resources.

She was stripped of her passkeys and accreditation and hauled into the office of her boss. He closed the door and unleashed about three months' worth of bile, frustration and contempt. She did not have the protection of a chaperone from human resources. She was a freelance and therefore not entitled to that.

She was slipshod, he told her. She was lazy and stupid and amateurish and, since there would be no reference, she would be very lucky to find work again. She was also dishonest. Abuse of the resources that licence payers funded amounted to theft. In doing her private work on corporation time, she had stolen from the public. In acknowledgement of that fact and to punish her for it, she would forfeit her pay for the last month of her employment. And she should consider herself lucky to get away with that punishment. There were precedents in such cases in the new BBC regime, he said, for bringing in the police. After telling her this, he told her to leave the building, though the actual words he used were, 'Get out of my fucking sight.'

Her ghost shifted close to her side. She smelled the familiar, warm cocktail of scents he brought with him. And she heard his voice, for the first time, as he spoke to her.

He's picked his moment, she thought, lying still in the darkness. She could taste the charred tobacco and stale budget red on her own breath. She was broke and jobless and disgraced. Martin was in peril, she felt that with a gloomy certainty, and she had lost the means to help him. And her ghost was speaking to her at her bedside in the Lambeth flat in the soft, singsong lilt of County Cork.

'You were right, of course. You were right and the feller was entirely wrong. I was never queer.'

She had known who it was. But she had not *really* known. Now she did. And she knew that she would never again see the world in the same way. It was bigger and she could not imagine where its boundaries lay. It was swapping a small room for a vast hall walled in mirrors.

'Not that I ever had anything against them, mind. There've been some fierce brave and noble queers, you know. Casement, as an example. And Pearse.'

'Pearse was gay?'

'I didn't say he was gay. Patrick Pearse was the very opposite of gay. Men resigned to martyrdom are not by nature cheery. I never saw the feller crack a smile. But he was a very brave man. And I'd say he was queer, alright.'

She could hear the humour in his voice. She had not made enough of that. She could hear the humour and the humanity of him. But she could hear something else, too. It was an involuntary, background sound. 'This feller's been giving you all the trouble. Slime? Snot?'

'Smythe,' she said.

'Him. He shouldn't drink and drive a motor car. He should not submit inflated expenses. He should never have entertained that lady of the night.'

Someone should tell him, Suzanne thought.

'I have,' her ghost said. 'I told him myself not half an hour ago. Gave the man a terrible start. Report for work tomorrow morning, Suzanne. Trust me on this. You'll get no more trouble out of Smythe.'

She knew what the sound was. It was the drip on to the bedroom floor of blood from the bullet wound that had killed him. There was the faint, coppery taint of blood on the air. But there would be no bloodstain on the bedroom carpet in the morning.

'I can't help you any more after this, Suzanne,' her ghost said. 'Be careful over the Spalding fellow. You're putting your hand in a bucket of snakes. And all of them are vipers.'

'Why did you come to see me? I don't mean tonight, and I'm very grateful for the help. But why did you come, in the first place?'

Her ghost laughed, softly. 'Couldn't help myself. You're very easy on the eye, so you are, Suzanne. And in a manner of speaking, you came to visit me first. I thought I'd return the compliment. I thought I might pay my respects. And now, I have.'

And he was gone.

Gerald Smythe, *Michael Collins* series producer and all-round BBC hotshot, had a complexion the same colour as his office walls when he called her up from reception the following morning. Her laminated pass was restored to her. Her library card was returned. There was a note from IT saying that all her computer access codes had been restored. Smythe told her that she had been upped a pay band and should report to him, but need not do so for a month. Any travel expenses she expected to incur in her research work could be drawn in advance from petty cash. It would be helpful if she kept receipts, of course.

'Of course.'

She caught him staring at her intently as she put the pass and the cards into her bag. The look was an uneasy mingling of intense curiosity and draining fear. Then he excused himself to go and be sick in the lavatory. Then, she later heard, he went home.

She went and sat at the desk she had cleared the previous afternoon. She attracted a few curious glances from her neighbours on the floor. She was sure of three things. Nobody would ever know the level of personal and possibly even slanderous abuse to which Smythe had subjected her over a period of months. Nobody would ever know the true reason for her reinstatement. And she had heard the last ignoble word that Smythe would ever utter in her presence. Actually, when she thought about it, there was a fourth thing she was sure of. She was pretty confident that he had cheated on his expenses for the last time.

She switched on her computer. There was an email for her from the alumni archive at Yale. She read it. Harry Spalding had not graduated. He had been asked to leave towards the end of his second year. He had distinguished himself on the sports field and in the seminar room. But they had felt it necessary to banish him. The issue had been his membership of an organisation, 'the very existence of which is contrary to the ethos and guiding principles of this university and this great nation, besides being an affront to Almighty God'. The offending organisation was named as the Jericho Club. So now, almost by accident, she had learned a secret. She knew what the self-elected Membership back in Rhode Island had been members of. Their cabal had been the Jericho Club. It must have been a New World offshoot of the *Société Jericho*. It showed that not all of France's exports to the great and new republic of America had been so benign and beneficial as de Tocqueville, or Lafayette. And Spalding had taken its guiding principles to war with him, where she had to presume he had made converts of his men. Except for Derry Conway, of course. Spalding had not made a convert of him.

She wished the log of the *Dark Echo* had not been destroyed. Something compromising had been recorded there.

The log had contained some information it was considered necessary to conceal from the world. Given that Spalding's reputation was so insalubrious anyway, Suzanne could not imagine what it was he would wish to hide. He had seemed in his lifetime a man profoundly beyond shame or remorse. But there had been something in the log, some detail that could hurt him.

She would do an internet search for the Jericho Club. She was not optimistic about finding anything useful that way. She felt that you could divide followers of the occult into very serious and necessarily discreet practitioners on the one hand and a legion of cranks on the other. People who discussed the subject in cyberspace fell largely into the latter category. But she had to try. Before typing in the words, however, she took a pad from her bag and wrote down on it a list of the topics that she considered she needed most urgently to investigate. When she read back to herself what she had written on the pad, the word at the top of her list was *Peitersen*.

She knew from Martin about Peitersen's passport made out in the name of Cardoza. She had got nowhere in trying to find out anything about Cardoza Associates. Their motives in bidding for the boat remained a mystery. But Martin had told her about the blessing of the *Dark Echo*, too, on their last, miserable evening together in the Windmill. She wondered if the Jesuit Monsignor Delaunay would grant her an audience, just out of his obvious affection for the Stannard family. He might tell her nothing. He might let something slip. He might not know anything. But it was Suzanne's firm belief that Jesuits and secrecy went together like tarts and high heels or tea and biscuits. One was pretty much unthinkable without the other. It was worth a try, if only because she had no other immediate leads.

She looked at her watch. It was ten o'clock. She had glimpsed the red corner of the packet in her bag when she had taken out her notepad. And then she had thought of tea and biscuits. She did not want a biscuit. But she did want to get a cup of tea from the machine and take it outside and sip it while she smoked a cigarette. She stood up. And then she sat down again, because that was how addiction worked, wasn't it? Insinuating itself in sly increments. She did not allow herself her first smoke of the day until twelve o'clock and it was only just ten. She would be strong.

'Fuck it,' she said aloud, standing, gathering her bag. She would cut down when Martin and his father had safely returned. It wasn't twelve hours since she had spoken to the ghost of Michael Collins. She would give up altogether when she knew that the Stannard men were safe. But now was not the time to try to cut down on her cigarette consumption. Right now, it just wasn't a realistic ambition at all.

Delaunay was not at the seminary in Northumberland. He was at the Jesuit retreat in Barmouth with a mixed group of ordained priests and novices. She was told her request to see him would be passed on. The rules of the retreat were not strict unless that strictness was self-imposed, she was told. He might be out with a hiking party on Cader Idris. He might be swimming. He might be at prayer, but it was unlikely at this time of day. She was not offered the number of the mobile she was assured he was carrying with him. But she was assured that the monsignor would call her back, probably within the hour.

She did a computer search for the Jericho Club, with predictably useless results. Then she began to ponder on the words of warning spoken by her ghostly visitor of the previous night. He had known something of Spalding's character. But she could not see how there could be a connection between the two men. Collins had been dead by the late summer of 1922. Spalding had only a year or so later come to Europe from America and begun his splashy, playboy effort to squander his father's limitless cash.

She put her mind to the possibility of a connection. Spalding's family had accrued their wealth through banking in New York. By the end of the Great War, America was the wealthiest country in the world and the world's biggest lender. In 1919, Irish president Eamon de Valera had made Michael Collins Minister of Finance. The logic behind this had been two-fold. For a guerrilla fighter, Collins was surprisingly good at administration. And his impeccable rebel credentials made him just the man to try to raise loans to finance the birth of his new nation from America, a country ideologically opposed to imperialism and a natural friend and champion of any emerging democracy.

Excitedly, Suzanne tapped in the two disparate names and she did a web search. But she came up with nothing. Undeterred, she did an image search. She was twenty pages in and about to call it quits when an old photograph appeared. It was an interior shot. It showed a line of men in dark suits and stiff collars being presented to a solid and charismatic figure with whom she had, in recent months, grown very familiar. She knew the location. She recognised the stately decor of one of the reception rooms at the Mansion House in Dublin. One of the men in the line was slender and blond and noticeably tall. She knew, without reading the picture caption, who that was, too.

There was someone else in the photograph, someone who competed even with Collins for attention. And it was not because she was the only woman in the frame. She was seated at a large upright manual typewriter. The bankers were to the left of Collins. She was to his rear and to their right.

Collins was smiling genially at this gathering of American capital funds. The woman was looking straight at the camera. And the tall, blond man in the line of bankers was staring with a look of avarice at the typist.

Except that, for a typist, she wore an altogether disdainful look. Her dark hair was glossily bobbed. Under the fringe, her eyes had a feline, upward slant. She had sharp cheek-bones and a mouth struggling not to smile at some secret, mutinous amusement. My God, she really does look just like me, Suzanne thought, who knew that her looks had intimidated more men than they had attracted before Martin had turned up, shining in his armour, his sword clanking in its scabbard as he played the goodly knight in her moment of peril on the East London Line.

She read the caption. It began: *At the Mansion House in Dublin yesterday, Dáil Finance Minister Mr M. Collins meets New York Finance chiefs in a bid to drum up funds for the new Irish Free State.*

The caption went on to name everyone present. Harry was still called Henry Spalding Jr then. He had not yet imposed his playboy persona on the world. He was not the easy, glamorous, Lost Generation self-invention he later became. He was thin and tall and slightly awkward. This picture had been taken before the maturing of Harry on his crossing aboard the *Dark Echo* from America to the Riviera. In this picture he was the youthful representative of a New York banking dynasty, a business apprentice with a distinguished war record. He had successfully shed the vulpine look of the Jericho Crew. But he had not yet really grown into himself. He had yet to develop his tan. And there was nothing louche or bohemian about him. He was still, in modern parlance, what is disparagingly referred to as a suit.

What about the woman? What about the sepia mirror

image Suzanne had found herself staring at? She was an afterthought for the subeditor who had compiled the photo caption. But they were nothing if not punctilious, in those great days of hot metal in the print room and five or six editions a day rolling off the presses on to the streets.

Also pictured, extreme right, Miss Jane Boyte.

Jane wore a white, high-buttoned blouse with three-quarter sleeves that revealed a wristwatch. Suzanne thought it still unusual for a woman to wear a wristwatch in that period. It would be considered a rather masculine affectation. In the decade to come, the likes of Amelia Earhart might buckle one on. But she was an exception in the late 1920s. And this was still only 1919. Ladies were not expected to need to be accurate timekeepers then. And Jane was a lady. She was not some clerical skivvy. Her father was a prosperous boatbuilder with his own dock in Liverpool Harbour. Jane's status was obvious from her expensive and fashionable haircut, from the rope of black pearls around the high collar of her tailored blouse and from her general hauteur. It was gratifying to see the large ashtray on her desk, black glass with crenellations like the tower of a castle, Suzanne thought. Her own ashtray was a little pressed foil dish that sat on the study window sill. Hers was an apology. Jane's was a grand statement of intent. That too, though, challenged convention. Ladies smoked in 1919. But they rarely did so in public.

The biggest clue to Jane Boyte's position in the ruling mechanism of the Irish Free State was that she was in the photograph at all. Since she wasn't central to proceedings, was literally on the edge of the picture, it would be the logical thing for a picture editor to crop her out. A secretary would certainly have been cropped out. Jane had survived because of her status. Her presence here was the proof of that status. Her evident and brazenly public commitment to the Fenian cause made her later arrest in Liverpool much less of a mystery in Suzanne's mind, too. But the significant thing here was that she was the link between Harry Spalding and Michael Collins.

Suzanne was about to tap Jane Boyte's name into her search engine when the phone on the desk began to ring. It was Monsignor Delaunay, the Jesuit priest whom she had never met but of whom Martin had spoken fondly and often. Martin always described him as jocular, a sort of jolly giant of the priesthood. He did not sound jocular now, though. He sounded guarded, suspicious. But at least he had returned the call. She thanked him for doing so. She apologised for cold-calling him out of nowhere, for interrupting his hike on the slopes of the mountain, his dip in the Barmouth sea.

'It's quite alright,' he said, in a tone that suggested it was anything but. 'I was expecting you to call.'

'Really?

'I had resolved that, if you did, I would meet you and speak to you. You are concerned about the Peitersen business. You are worried about the deception. You believe the deception might place Martin and his father in jeopardy aboard the boat.'

'Does it?'

At the other end of the line, there was a pause. 'Not directly, it doesn't. But Magnus Stannard is owed an explanation concerning the Peitersen farrago. All three of you are, since all three of you were deceived.'

'I wasn't deceived for long,' Suzanne said.

'Nevertheless. You are owed an explanation. And I believe you are owed an apology. And I would prefer to offer both in person.'

After concluding her conversation with Delaunay, she did her search for Jane Boyte. She found nothing written. But she did find another photograph. This one was in an archive copyrighted by Sefton Metropolitan Borough Council and the sub-classification under which it was filed was Southport Tourism (Heritage). It showed two men wearing leather coats and gauntlets, standing next to a biplane on an expanse of hard sand. One of them wore a cap with goggles perched above the peak. The picture had been taken on a sunny, windy day. The detail in the shot was good, the contrast very sharp. Between the grinning flyers stood Jane Boyte. If anything she had grown into herself since the Dublin picture. Her precisely cut hair was raven black in strong, breeze-blown tresses. She wore a leather jacket, tightly cinched by a tied belt at the waist. The calf-length boots under her canvas jodhpurs buttoned all the way up the front. She was smiling, and her teeth were very white.

Suzanne whistled. It was a bit like discovering you had been a film star in a former life. The resemblance was so undeniably strong it almost made her laugh out loud. It did actually make her blush. The difference was the glamour. Jane Boyte was possessed of a swaggering sexual glamour that programme researchers employed on a freelance contract by the BBC in the early twenty-first century were generally and probably understandably denied. She felt a stab of something and, assuming it was hunger, looked at her watch. It was just after twelve thirty. But it wasn't a hunger pang at all, she realised. It was the feeling of envy.

The caption read: *The brothers Giroud pictured at their airstrip on Southport beach with Birkdale aviator Miss Jane Boyte. French Canadians and veterans of the late conflict on the Western Front, the Giroud brothers have assembled an impressive and varied collection of aircraft, all of which can be seen regularly flying over the North-West's premier resort.*

Suzanne considered it a bit unfair that the brothers Giroud

were denied Christian names in the caption. She thought it likely they had been discriminated against on the grounds that they were both French and Canadian. Miss Boyte was Birkdale's, so she was local. She did another web search. She tapped in *Dark Echo Boyte*. And this time, she got written information. And it was substantial. It came in the form of a story from an edition of the *Liverpool Daily Post* dated April 20, 1927. And it ran thus:

> Crack American yachtsman Harry Spalding brought his storm-damaged schooner *Dark Echo* into Liverpool Harbour early yesterday morning in a feat of seamanship that had veteran sailors raising their caps in admiration.
>
> Spalding was caught in a sudden and very severe storm off the Irish coast having left the harbour at Howth intending to sail to Scotland for a week of shooting and rod fishing. But his racing vessel was blown off course by a sea with waves cresting at close to fifty feet in an easterly wind meteorologists insist was gusting at its peak at between 80 and 90 miles an hour.
>
> Esteemed Mersey boat builder Patrick Boyte will undertake the challenge of trying to restore the damaged craft to the condition that has seen her triumph so often in regattas held off the coast of the United Kingdom and beyond.
>
> He describes the task as an honour and says he is confident that two months of works will see the *Dark Echo* restored to a level of seaworthiness and general reparation that will delight the dashing millionaire sportsman who has earned such seagoing distinction at her helm.

The story was written like a dictated telegram, Suzanne thought. But it wasn't just commas that were missing. There was no colour, no anecdotage. Spalding, crucially, had supplied no quotes. He was described as dashing. But the story had been written in a period when millionaires were dashing by definition. What had been omitted? Any mention of his crewmen had been omitted. Not even Harry Spalding could sail a schooner single-handedly through a storm like that described. The one thing the *Liverpool Daily Post* would be unlikely to exaggerate would be the severity of the storm. Its readers, many of them, would have been seafarers themselves in that period. Its shareholders would have also held shares in shipping lines. A port city prospered because of the sea. It was not in the interest of the major newspaper serving that city to exaggerate the sea's hazards. The storm would have been as bad as they said it was. Had Spalding aboard the *Dark Echo* lost crewmen to it? It was an intriguing question.

More intriguing was what he had done for the duration of the repairs being carried out to his boat.

Suzanne sighed to herself. She tapped the surface of her desk. Now she really did feel hungry. The thing was, intriguing didn't really cut it. She had felt at some nagging, intutive level that there must have been a connection between Collins and Spalding. And she had proved to herself that there was, through Jane Boyte. Jane had been present with both men at the Dáil in 1919. Eight years later, the *Dark Echo* had limped into a Mersey boatyard owned by her father, Patrick Boyte. This at a time when the successful businessmen of Liverpool built their expansive houses in the smart seaside town of Southport, eighteen miles away from the murk and spoil of the soot and steam-bound city from which they profited. Jane Boyte was a Southport girl, from the posh suburb of Birkdale. Harry Spalding had spent his Southport summer in the very places where Jane would naturally have socialised. And whatever her Fenian affiliations, Jane had been no drab political apparatchik. She was a pioneer aviator and drop-dead gorgeous to boot. This was a single woman with a social life. Encountering the playboy Spalding afresh at some party or reception somewhere would have been inevitable.

But so what? What did all that prove? It proved only that Suzanne had a knack for research. It reaffirmed her belief that she had a happy gift for what she did for a living. It did not help Martin and his father. It did not ease by one small fraction the danger her instinct told her they were in, aboard Spalding's boat, in the unkind vastness of the North Atlantic Ocean.

She should concentrate on Peitersen, her one real lead, and her meeting scheduled for tomorrow with Delaunay in Northumberland. The seminary was a hell of a long way away. But she felt she had no choice but to go and talk to the priest. The anxiety she had felt at Martin's departure had only increased in the time since then. He and his father had made themselves into competent sailors. They had all sorts of high-tech gizmos on board to attract help should they get into any kind of trouble. And the boat was incredibly substantial and completely seaworthy. Modern racing vessels, with their obsession with weight and drag, were absurdly flimsy by comparison. Despite all this, though, she was still worried and the worry was increasing. So she should go and see Delaunay and see whether he could offer some help or peace of mind.

She went to lunch. In the afternoon, because she did not want to go home and bite her nails and pace the carpet, she tried to find out more about the storm that had hit in the Irish Sea in the early hours of April 16, 1927. Trawlers putting out from Holyhead and Dublin had foundered in it. A warship had beached in it near Douglas on the Isle of Man. There was coastal damage as far north as Bangor and Carrickfergus on the Irish coast and Whitehaven in England. It was estimated that twenty-one sailors had perished. The storm had been huge and very violent and had lasted for three days. And Harry Spalding had survived it in a boat built for recreation. That fact alone said something for the *Dark Echo*. But it was not reassuring. The bad presentiments had begun for Suzanne in the barn in France that had not looked very much like a barn at all. They had been worsening ever since.

She used a BBC account to pay the nominal amount that enabled full access to the archive of the *Liverpool Daily Post*. She searched for stories concerning Spalding in the weeks after the storm. And from the issue dated May 2 she discovered this:

> Following a disturbance at the Adelphi Hotel in Liverpool described by management as a practical joke that got out of hand, American yachtsman Mr Harry Spalding has been asked to vacate his suite there forthwith.
>
> Mr Spalding is expected to relocate to the Palace Hotel in Southport to be nearer to the Birkdale links course where this keen golfer regularly plays off an impressively low handicap. He is also believed to be interested in chartering an aircraft from the aviation club owned by the Giroud brothers at the resort, and seeing from the sky something of the area where he plans to spend the summer.
>
> 'The incident was a storm in a teacup,' Mr Spalding told the *Post*. 'And I'm an authority on storms. I'm looking forward to Southport. I'm looking forward to spending some money on Lord Street.'
>
> An Adelphi chambermaid was treated for burns at Speke infirmary following the failed prank. She was kept in overnight but allowed home the following day. A detective from the Liverpool constabulary took statements both from the injured woman and from Mr Terence Sealey, night manager of the hotel. He is also believed to have interviewed Mr Spalding, but the *Post* is told no charges are likely as a consequence of the incident.

So Spalding had possessed a sense of humour, or at least a sense of irony. The incident itself must have been very serious back in those cap-doffing, forelock-tugging days for the police to have been called and for a millionaire guest to have been told to pack his bags. The clear implication was that the maid had been paid off. Suzanne assumed her injuries had been quite serious. In 1927, twenty-one years before the National Health Service was introduced, a hotel chambermaid did not qualify for hospital treatment unless it was a medical necessity.

Suzanne had wondered about Harry Spalding's attitude towards what was then called the fairer sex. She knew that he had been dumped by a girlfriend in Marseilles or Rimini or somewhere on arriving in Europe. Now she wondered if he had dumped *her* in the harbour. All she had to go on was the feral look he was giving Jane Boyte in the photograph she'd seen earlier of the US bankers invited to Ireland by de Valera's government. Had that been the source of some friction between Spalding and Collins? Had Spalding made a crude pass at Jane, or made her the victim of one of his practical jokes? Collins was notably chivalrous and quick to defend any woman he considered insulted. There were five or six recorded incidences of him leaping to a woman's defence, the most famous being when he came close to punching Lord Birkenhead at dinner in London during the treaty negotiations in 1922 over a perceived insult to his hostess, Hazel Lavery.

But it didn't matter, did it? It was neither here nor there in helping Martin and his father if they were in peril on the sea. Suzanne thought that she was making progress on the subject of Harry Spalding. Detail was accruing, a picture emerging. But she felt that she would have to wait until late the following afternoon and her audience with the Jesuit in Northumberland before there would be any real further enlightenment.

Her search revealed only one other mention of Spalding in the *Post*. It was a page-two filler. It said:

> American playboy Harry Spalding has rented a mansion for the summer in Birkdale's prestigious Rotten Row. Flamboyant millionaire Mr Spalding had previously been resident at a luxury suite in the nearby Palace Hotel.

It was interesting that in just a few weeks, he had gone from being a heroic yachtsman fabled for his sporting prowess, to a mere playboy. Was his behaviour so degenerate? The disdain of the press virtually dripped off the page. The impression was of a man barely in control of himself.

Lastly, she sourced the piece in the *Post* she had first seen and shown to Martin months earlier, detailing Jane Boyte's release from arrest. She printed it off and compared the photograph there to the picture of Jane, the aviator, on the beach between the brothers Giroud. One picture had been taken willingly in benign and jolly circumstances. The other seemed by comparison a stolen moment in a blighted life. Jane was still glamorous in the second picture. She was perfectly tailored and fiercely beautiful. But the joy had vanished from her face. And Suzanne sensed that this absence of mischief, of the defiance that characterised her expression elsewhere, had to do with more than just the ordeal of her arrest. A woman who had moved in Michael Collins' political orbit was not a woman to be traumatised by twenty-four hours in a Liverpool police cell. Jane had been much tougher than that. She had been resilient, steely. But something had happened to her. The carefree adventuress pictured on the sands in her flying outfit had endured some dreadful ordeal. And the outcome had been a bleak and dispiriting one.

Aboard Dark Echo

We made good time on that first day out from Southampton. By sunset we were well west of the coast of Ireland, the last land we would see before America a receding smudge on the glittering sea to our rear. I was at the wheel. My father was seated on the deck beside me, studying a chart in the fading light. He had anchored the chart with coins, a penknife and a brass pocket compass, and was quite unaware of himself. I was anything but. The luminescent glow of the descending sun played like Klieg bulbs on his ageing film star features. In his seaman's sweater, with his wind-whipped hair, with his eyes the same bright emerald as the stole Delaunay had worn for the boat blessing, my father looked magnificent.

His appearance was a little short of the truth. Perhaps that was why I studied him with such care. We had both been obliged to take a medical in the prelude to our voyage. Mine had been a fusspot formality, I think. My father's had been a necessity. Rich men can take risks. But risks, when self-inflicted and physical, are only taken reluctantly with rich men by their insurers. I came out okay, probably having my father to thank. If you box and you allow yourself to get out of shape, you make a beating in the ring pretty much inevitable. I never wanted to take that beating. I did not box any more and hadn't for a long time, but the cautionary habit of keeping in shape had stayed with me and I still trained fairly hard and pretty regularly. I was healthy and fit.

Dad did not come off quite so well. Why would he? He was fifty-five to my thirty-two. He had toiled to build an empire, accrue a fortune. He had suffered the grief of his wife's premature death and the disappointment of a son who was, simply, a disappointment. As I had also very recently discovered, he had endured the loss of a baby daughter. And he had kept that loss a secret to himself. And all this had inflicted high blood pressure on my father. And there were, too, incipient signs of diabetes. He was a long way from being an invalid. But without treatment, he would tire easily and he was at moderate risk of a stroke.

Since the medical and the diagnosis, he had obediently taken the blood pressure pills prescribed. He had cut down on his whisky and port consumption and he had even, to an extent, laid off the cigars. His health was okay. But though he was reminiscent of some cinematic god, there in the lambent ocean dusk, what he really was, despite all of his looks and charisma, was a fallible and fast-ageing man facing a formidable and unfamiliar challenge.

'What's on your mind, Martin?' he said, without looking up. 'Wondering how long the old man's got? Wondering when you will finally inherit?'

I laughed. He wasn't that far off in a way, though money had been the last thing on my mind. 'I was thinking about Chichester, Dad. I'm baffled as to why you find the place so . . . seductive.'

He got to his feet, gathering his chart. His face was flushed now in the last of the descending sun. But it was only the light, I was sure. He was too shameless to blush. 'It's a nice place. It's very picturesque.'

'I'd have thought it a bit staid and old-fashioned for you, Dad.'

'It's not staid and old-fashioned at all. It's very handsome.'

'All a bit antique and parochial, though, isn't it, Chichester? All a bit chinzy and, well . . . drab?'

He rolled his chart and looked at me through narrowed eyes. 'Beauty is in the eye of the beholder, Martin. I happen to think the charms of Chichester utterly delightful. I'm also fond of Edinburgh and find Bath quite ravishing.'

'Now you're just boasting.'

'I'm in retirement. I have to occupy my time. If you were to marry that gorgeous girl so inexplicably devoted to you and start a family, I could do what respectable men of my age do.'

'And what's that?'

'Dote on my grandchildren.'

He turned and walked to the hatch and went below. He had never mentioned the possibility of my starting a family before. Perhaps his revelation about Catherine Ann had brought it to the forefront of his mind. He was serious, though. It was why he had gone where I could no longer see and study him. Just as he was shameless about his Chichester trysts, so he was genuinely embarrassed about his sudden confession that he wished for a grandchild to spoil and love.

I engaged the auto-steer and followed him below, a bit stunned by the implications of what he had said. And I thought I heard a low growl coming from the direction of the sail store. It sounded like a large and antagonised dog. Remembering Spalding's dog, I listened hard, still for a moment. Toby, it had been called. It was a bull mastiff and had a vicious temper. With a shiver, I remembered the odd experience in the Lepe boatshed. I paused and listened. But all I heard was the churn of water under the hull, the slap against the prow of small waves, the pull and sigh of rigging above. I smiled to myself. Dogs did not live to the age of ninety. It must have been a snarl unkinking in the anchor chain, something like that. Old sailing boats were noisy at sea by definition.

I paused outside the door of my father's cabin. I wanted to continue our conversation. I felt flattered by the idea that he wanted me to extend the family, by the notion that there was a fund of love in him waiting to be spent, lavished, on a son or daughter of mine. It meant that he was finally and completely over the disappointment of my failed vocation. And he wanted Suzanne to be the mother of his grandchild. I had known he liked her. I realised then that he probably loved her. She was kind and clever and amusing and independent and she made his only son happy. It occurred to me, too, that she was the same age as the daughter he lost would have been. I wondered how often, looking at Suzanne, that thought had occurred to him.

I could hear opera music from behind his cabin door – the Germanic stuff, of course – a *Heldentenor* wailing sonorously about a water nymph or some such, no doubt with a spear in his hand and a helmet with horns on his head. His sturdy torso would be clad in burlap sacking, cinched by a sword belt. I shook my own head, grinning, and lowered the fist I was about to knock with, deciding to leave him to it. There would be plenty of opportunity for us to discuss personal matters, the important, intimate stuff of life. There was no hurry. It was not as though we could escape one another's company aboard the boat for very long. Perhaps that had been my father's motive in inviting me, or among his motives. We were close. I was close to him, because I chose not to compete with him. But in his business life, generous with everything else, he had been a miser with his time. Now we were to spend a fair bit of it together and I was pleased at the thought. But there was no rush, so I left him to his Wagner in his cabin and went back on deck.

It was almost fully dark. The weather was very clear. I could see the lights of no other vessels but, looking up, could make out the faint twinkling of the first stars. In practical terms, crossing open sea was much less demanding of seamanship than sailing around the coast of Ireland had been. Along a coastline there were currents, riptides, sandbanks and submerged rocks. Fog was a hazard and the seagoing traffic heavier. There were trawlers to avoid as they turned for their home ports after a night's fishing in the dawn murk. But traversing an ocean, out of sight or reach of the safety of land, aware of the profound depths beneath you and your isolation, brought psychological pressures that vastly outweighed practicalities.

Awed at that moment, as full darkness descended, I was also aware of just what freedom a boat represented. It was a very exclusive sort of freedom, of course. It helped to have a wealthy father to endow you with the privilege. Ironically or not, that was something I had in common with Harry Spalding. In having this boat built, Spalding had engineered his freedom, his licence to sail the oceans, to roam the world unaccountably, a rich stranger in its remotest ports and harbours. You had to wonder what his motive had been. Because it had not very likely been a simple love of the sea, had it? What had Spalding done with all that freedom?

I shivered. It was cold without the sun. And the answer to the question I had just asked myself was that we would never know. The *Dark Echo*'s log had been destroyed. And with it had perished any hope of uncovering Spalding's secrets. I shivered again, and it was not just the wind off the dark sea and its chill that made me do so. I did not want to discover Spalding's secrets. What I knew already suggested they were sadistic and insane. The boat was a better legacy than her first master had deserved. My father and I would surely put the freedom she gave us to more innocent use than he had. If we had not already earned our berths aboard her, then over the coming days we would surely do so.

I heard a noise again then, a kind of keening howl that sounded like a dog. I tried to tell myself it was a whale. There were whales in these waters. There were other marine mammals capable of barks and cries that would carry on the wind, distorting, for miles. There were porpoises and seals. But it seemed to have been coming from the direction, under the deck, of the sail store.

I engaged the auto-steer and went below. There was a sheath knife in my cabin and I ducked in there to grab it. I had not heard a rat. But what I had heard had not sounded friendly or well disposed. So I opened the hatch to the sail store with the knife in the grip of my right hand. I switched on the row of wire-bracketed lights that lit the long, low space. I could see no dog. I could see no movement. All I could see was pale folds of Dacron and loops of neatly coiled ropes and block tackles depending from hooks screwed into that section of the bulkhead. But there was a smell. It was sour and feral. And to me it smelled canine. It put me in mind of the wolf enclosure at the zoo in Regent's Park, near the football pitches, before they got rid of it. That same smell had drifted over the pitches from the wolf enclosure, when the wind was right. I looked again. A big dog would have left hair and strings of drool, wouldn't it? There was nothing. I turned out the lights and relatched the hatch. It was my imagination.

But I was slightly spooked. So after putting the knife back, I went and knocked on my father's cabin door. Supper would be my pretext. I'd offer to cook something, ask him what it was he wanted to eat before retiring to his berth.

The opera was very loud. He had poured himself a large measure of whisky. A cigar smouldered in an ashtray and the air in the cabin was yellow with the fug of smoke. He had the guns out of the cabinet. They were on his desk. He was cleaning and loading them. One, a semi-automatic rifle, had been disassembled and the action lay in pieces on a swatch of oily cloth. The ammunition – the shells and cartridges – was coiled in thick bandoliers and spilling from white cardboard boxes of bullets. My father eyed me down the sights of a carbine held one-handed and took a drag on his Havana. He did not look very grandfatherly.

'Readying yourself for World War Three, Dad?'

'You need to be prepared, Martin,' he said. 'We are in an environment that could turn hostile.'

'Way to go,' I said. It seemed to me a life raft might prove more useful.

'Sit down, son.'

There were high splotches of colour on his cheeks and forehead.

'Have you taken your medication, Dad?'

He waved the question away and the smoke from his cigar piroutetted lazily. Someone in the chorus in the opera hit a long, lamentable note. Unless the sound was the ghost of Spalding's dog, keening for its master. A substantial wave hit us then and the boat juddered and I had to steady myself by gripping the edge of my father's desk. One of his ammunition boxes toppled and brass-jacketed bullets spilled out on to the desktop, somc rolling from the desktop on to the floor.

'I said sit down.'

I pulled a chair across obediently and sat.

'All that talk earlier, about Chichester.'

'A joke, Dad. Just a bit of innuendo. It wasn't meant sarcastically. You seemed to take it well enough.'

'You need to know something.'

He was going to make a confession. I really did not want to hear it. The Catherine Ann revelation had been bad enough. I had not really recovered properly from the shock of that and wanted nothing more just then from my father's stash of family secrets.

'I was never unfaithful to your mother. Never. Never once. Neither in thought nor in deed did I ever stray from or betray her.'

There were tears in his eyes. He looked at the burning tip of his cigar, as though the bright glow of that could give him consolation. Then he sniffed and ground it out in the glass ashtray beside the guns. 'My romantic life might seem like some sort of adult infantilism to you, as sometimes I'll admit it does to me. But I never played around while your mother was alive and I think it important that you know that.'

My dad, who had never seemed infantile to me but only ever truly admirable, was crying. I got up and walked around the desk, around its murderous litter of armaments, and pulled him to his feet and hugged him. And he shook with grief for his lost wife and his dead daughter in my embrace.

Eight

The seminary was a vast neo-Gothic pile built from granite on the crags topping cliffs at the edge of the sea. Approaching it in her hire car along a road that twisted as it rose, Suzanne thought the place utterly forbidding. The weather did not help. It was late afternoon, but gloomy enough for her lights. Her headlamps picked out white and spectral bits of scrub and scree in a desolate landscape. Everything seemed contrived to diminish the scale of the merely human. The sky above the turrets of the building was wide and angry with cloud. She thought that Martin's short-lived vocation must have been very powerful at its outset. This was the least inviting place to which she had ever come. You would need to be resolute in your choice of a life serving God to think of living here.

Cars were directed to an area at the left flank of the seminary, overlooking the sea. The ground here was flattened and surfaced with cinders. She got out and walked to the cliff edge. The sea was turbulent, wind-whipped, its white caps ominous as they shivered into being and then slid away to nothing again on the surface of the black water. There were no ordinary cars parked alongside hers. The three other vehicles in the car park were all of a utilitarian character. There was an old Jeep and two Land Rovers. They had seen a lot of mileage. One of the Land Rovers had a trailer attached with a tarpaulin over it.

Lights dotted the building as she approached. But most of its windows were dark in the gloom. Some of the lights flickered, as though from candle flames. Most of them were yellow. But the effect was remote rather than cosy, lights in narrow arches and window slits doing nothing to illuminate or brighten generally the huge warren of stone. Suzanne glanced at her watch. It was still only just before five. She was punctual. The calendar was approaching the longest day. It would not get dark for almost five more hours. But it felt like dusk. As she got to the main entrance, rain began to splash from the sky in cold and heavy drops.

Delaunay received her in his office. It was far less austere a place than she had expected, passing though the grim corridors and along the enclosed stone staircases that led to it. And she herself was led. She would never have got there if she'd been merely directed to where she was eventually taken. The seminary was a labyrinth. In its chilly vaults, she thought she understood better one or two of the aspects of Martin's character that had remained locked away throughout their relationship. This place would have appealed to the side of him given to melancholy and silence. And his secrecy, too. The part of Martin that was closed to her would find something attractive about this great Catholic tomb hewn for the living.

But Delaunay's room was panelled in wood and enjoyed plush upholstery. There were paintings on his walls far too handsomely framed to be mere reproductions. There was a rich smell of leather from the bindings of the many books on his shelves. There was a laptop computer at the centre of his desk and he had a laser printer and a hands-free phone there, too. But the impression was still overwhelmingly of the past. Images of Christ crucified and dying under his crown of thorns had once been common throughout the Christian world. In the early twenty-first century, that was no longer the case. But there were several such stark reminders of God's sacrifice of his son for mankind in Delaunay's place of work and, Suzanne supposed, his place of prayer and contemplation. Altogether, it looked like a chamber from a more august and pious time.

He thanked the pale novice who had brought her there and then shook her formally by the hand. He was, as Martin had said, enormous. Her hand was completely enveloped in the grip of his, and his arms inside his soutane were as broad and dense-looking as those of a shot-putter or a power-lifter. He had not acquired muscles like these in the gym. She was certain of that. He was one of those men born strong, his future muscular power determined even as he grew from something tiny in his mother's womb. The word for what he possessed physically was almost archaic, Suzanne thought. But it was accurate. And it was 'might'. Monsignor Delaunay was mighty. His handshake, though, was gentle. And in his demeanour he seemed almost abashed.

There was a leather sofa at the opposite end of his room from where his desk was placed, and it was to this that he guided her. He took her coat and hung it on a corner stand. He gestured for her to sit. But he did not sit himself. He offered to have tea or coffee fetched, but she declined both. He offered water and, when she nodded acceptance, poured her a glass from a carafe on a small circular table. Then he stood before her with his hands clasped behind his back. She sipped from her glass. The water was very cold. She wondered was it drawn from a well – they might have their own. It had not come from a bottle left to stagnate for a month under fluorescents.

'Thank you for agreeing to see me.'

'When I tell you what I have to tell you, you'll agree it was the very least I could do.'

She sipped water, wondering how bad this could be. She had left her cigarettes in the glove compartment of the car.

Then again, you weren't allowed to smoke in church. And she was unacquainted with the protocol. Everything here might be a church, the way that embassies shared the status of sovereign states.

'May I call you Suzanne?'

'Of course you may, Monsignor Delaunay. I'd like you to. And I'd like you to tell me the truth about the man who masqueraded as Peitersen.'

'He is one of us, Suzanne.'

'A representative of the Catholic Church?'

'A priest.'

'He did not seem very much like a priest.'

'Nor was he meant to.'

'For example, he really does know about boats.'

'Yes, he does.'

'I might take that cup of coffee off you.'

'You must feel free to smoke.'

'Damn. I mean, darn. I left them in the car.'

Delaunay smiled. 'It may shock you to learn that there are priests who indulge that vice, Suzanne. What I mean is, I can probably cadge you a pack of Marlboro Lights.'

Peitersen, whose real name was Sean McIntyre, was a Boston Irishman who never knowingly entertained a religious thought until he was forty-five years old. His family business was building fishing boats. The business went back five generations. He broke with tradition and began building racing yachts after racing them himself as a teenager and realising that his own makeshift improvements to the basic design made any yacht he raced both significantly faster and easier to handle, too.

McIntyre Marine prospered. Sean celebrated two decades of business success by buying a cruiser as a fortieth birthday present for himself. When the cruiser foundered a week later on a reef off the Bahamas, Sean's wife and fourteen-year-old son were aboard and Sean, piloting, had drunk the best part of a pint of white rum. His wife and boy drowned. Sean was picked up alive. He'd been in the water eighteen hours and was delirious but, by that time, sober. He began his training for the priesthood a month later.

'Why did he pretend to be Peitersen?' Suzanne said.

'Because we told him he should,' Delaunay said, who was still meeting her eyes, she thought, only from supreme effort of will.

'Because we told him he should. As penance.'

'I think you had better explain, Monsignor.'

Delaunay was at the window. Its shape was arched and its glass heavily leaded. It did not let in much light. It was one of a row of four that embellished the exterior wall of the chamber. Even collectively they did not admit much light. But then the weather outside was foul. Though the windows were all tightly closed against it, Suzanne could hear the rain hurled against the panes.

'Early in the winter of 1918 an infantry captain called Harry Spalding looted something very valuable from Rouen cathedral. We know this because one of the men charged to protect this object survived the raid.'

'What did he take?'

'Something brought out of Palestine in the First Crusade. An item taken to France lest it be sold by Rome for influence with kings during the great Papal Schism. This artefact is among the most important relics in the entire history of the Church. And Spalding was successful in stealing it.'

'For profit?'

'For power. For the power its desecration would give him with the great adversary we have faced since the Fall. That was why he stole it.'

'And you thought McIntyre, masquerading as Peitersen, might find it aboard the *Dark Echo*?'

Delaunay smiled. 'You're very bright, Suzanne.'

'No, I'm not. Because actually, I'm very confused. If it was that valuable to you, Cardoza Associates would have won their pissing contest at Bullen and Clore with Magnus Stannard.'

Delaunay turned to the window and the rain.

'I'm sorry, Monsignor. I'm sorry for the profanity.'

He spoke with his back to her. His voice was grave. 'We did win the pissing contest. With respect to Magnus Stannard, the Vatican has very deep pockets. But the auctioneer was incompetent, or he was drunk. And the gavel came down early.'

'Who are Martens and Degrue?'

'You've heard of the Jericho Club?'

'Recently, yes.'

'They are the continuation of the Jericho Club by other means. Or, perhaps more accurately, under another name, because the means remain the same.'

'Why are you choosing to tell me all this now?'

He turned back to her. 'None of this was known to me until a few days ago. None of it. Martin told me about Peitersen over lunch on the day that I blessed the *Dark Echo* at Magnus Stannard's request. Magnus was convinced he was merely some kind of crank. Then Martin mentioned Spalding and I remembered only that the name had vague, uncomfortable associations. I made some enquiries of my own among knowledgeable people in Rome. And I was told what I have told you.'

'Weren't you sworn to secrecy?' Suzanne had considered that the sort of question she would never have asked without her tongue firmly in her cheek. She had been wrong.

'I was pledged to silence on the subject. I have chosen to break that pledge.'

'Why?'

'Father McIntyre did not find what he was looking for aboard Harry Spalding's boat. He is convinced it is not there. But Martens and Degrue may think it is. These people are not beyond an act of piracy.'

Suzanne thought about what she was hearing. 'When you blessed the boat, Monsignor, did you think it benign?'

Delaunay smiled, looking at the floor. Then he looked at her. He raised an arm and tapped at the window with his knuckles. His fist was enormous. The impact thudded dully in the silence of his chamber. 'The sea down on the shore outside our refuge here is sometimes benign. And sometimes it rages. Its power waxes and wanes. At the time I was aboard her, at least, the *Dark Echo* was no threat to anyone.'

'I cannot believe you let them go.'

'I knew about none of this until after their departure. I had not set eyes on Martin for a decade. Magnus called me out of the blue.'

Suzanne smiled. 'Come, Monsignor. Does anybody ever really do anything entirely out of the blue?'

'Now is not the time for theological debate,' Delaunay said. 'We are not here to discuss predestination. I have broken a vow in order to tell you what I have.'

'Because I called you. Out of the blue.'

'I was concerned for them on their departure. My concern for them has only increased since learning what I have since then. I would have called you, Suzanne. I was resolved to. I would have called you, had you not called me first.'

And this, she believed.

She did the calculation in her mind. They would be three, perhaps four hundred miles beyond the West Coast of Ireland. And they would be heading directly west, if they were on their charted course. And Delaunay had told her nothing that would make Magnus Stannard turn back. Quite the opposite, since McIntyre had established that Spalding's desecrated relic was not aboard the *Dark Echo*. Good luck to them, she thought Magnus might remark, warned of Martens and Degrue's potential piracy. He had guns aboard, Martin had told her. And he was expert in their use. He was a man capable of such hard-headed belligerence that he would probably relish the action if pirates tried to board.

She rose to go.

'I don't think it wise for you to leave here tonight.'

'You have facilities for female guests?'

'We have facilities for any guest of our choosing.'

Suzanne looked at her watch. It was just after seven in the evening. Outside, the rain fell unrelentingly from a sky sullen with cloud. She had booked a room at an inn just outside the village of Holburn. It was a drive of around eight miles. It had looked very cosy in the pictures on the website. She had travelled most of the day to get here and was tired. She wanted an early night and an early start.

'Why don't you think it wise for me to leave?'

'An intuition,' Delaunay said. 'It might be more circumspect to wait until morning. You will be comfortable here.'

'I'll take my chances,' she said.

'As you please.' He got her coat from the stand and helped her into it. Then he guided her out the way she had come. They were both silent on the walk back through the dim, stone-flagged corridors and staircases of the seminary. But, to Suzanne's mind at least, the silence was a comfortable one. Everything necessary had been said between them. She found herself liking Monsignor Delaunay despite the disturbing implications of the things he had told her. He had broken a vow in order to impart the information. He had chosen to sin out of friendship and loyalty and the instinct to protect. She suspected that he loved Martin. She thought that if it were not for his vocation, he would have made a very different kind of father than the one Magnus Stannard was. His strength, his might, was the key to him. He was mighty, so he could express his tenderness without fear of being considered weak. As a priest, of course, he should not have cared about whether or not his character impressed people. But she suspected that he did. He was possessed of enormous strength. His great weakness was his vanity.

She ran from the shelter of the seminary doorway, using her coat above her head as a hood. The rain sang a shrill note through the cinders under her feet in the car park. It felt more like October than June on the cliff top, in the exposure to the sea. She shivered, unlocking the car door, reminded of the capricious nature of the sea by its fury now, boiling on the rocks beneath her. And she wondered, as she kept on wondering, how Martin and his father were doing aboard the boat. She did not think the *Dark Echo* intrinsically evil. But her first master had been. Harry Spalding had been evil and corrupt and had practised dark magic since his boyhood. Was evil contagious? Could malevolence seep into the timbers of an old racing vessel?

Despite knowing what she did about the Waltrow brothers' mystery and the death of Gubby Tench, Suzanne did not think that it could. But there was danger. She'd felt it in the barn in France. She had been warned about it by her ghost. With her car door unlocked, staring at tussocks of grass on the cliff edge at the brink of the void, she realised where her logic led. The baleful influence of Harry Spalding persisted because the stolen relic remained an object of desecration.

It made her wonder if Spalding had ever really died.

It was 7.20 p.m. when she turned the key in the ignition.

That was still early in England on a June evening. But the weather on the Northumberland coast was so bleak and gloomy that she felt obliged out of caution to switch on her lights. She drove carefully, but saw no oncoming traffic on the road that led to the village and to her hot date with a lamb casserole and a decent glass of Cabernet Sauvignon. At some point, as it travelled inland, the road became tree-lined. A gust of wind soughed through branches and leaves and dumped rain from trees on the windscreen. Reflexively, Suzanne switched on the wipers. And switched on the radio.

The volume was so great that Paddy McAloon's croon was a bellowing roar as 'When Love Breaks Down' burst out of the speakers. She leant forward against the restraint of her seatbelt to switch it off and the windscreen imploded in stinging fragments of shatterproof glass as the car halted and the roof bulged inward. Suzanne looked up at the thick shape of the fallen trunk in the thin steel above her. She heard the rasping strain of metal and knew she would be crushed and die here.

She snapped the seatbelt off and slithered down to the footwell to try to hide and make herself small and safe as the interior of the car continued to diminish under the weight of the tree trunk crushing it. Suddenly she heard the rent of metal on the passenger side. She glanced over and saw two huge hands pulling at the jammed door through foliage over the lower edge of the window. Blood spilled blackly down the door interior from the palms as glass still embedded in the sill bit into them. The thick fingers whitened with strain and the door was torn from its hinges and lock as Delaunay's head intruded, wide-eyed. He reached for her and she was jerked like a strung puppet out of the car as it folded in on itself like something deflating under the burden of the fallen tree.

Delaunay half dragged and half carried Suzanne through the pelting rain back along the road. He lifted her into the passenger seat of his Land Rover as she tried to regain her breath and composure. He unscrewed the lid from a spirits flask and offered it to her. She was alert enough to notice that he held the flask by the tips of his fingers so the blood from his palms would not smear it. She took the flask and drank. It was whisky and its warmth and strength were very welcome.

'You followed me.'

'A precaution.' His eyes were looking down the road, where the cabin of her hire car was now flat to its axle with the weight of the fallen tree. One of the rear tyres had punctured. Oil or petrol was leaking out of the vehicle in a rainbow stain on the road. The colours were subdued in the absence of real summer light.

'You tried to warn me.'

'An intuition.'

'I think that Harry Spalding never died.'

Delaunay stopped. After offering her the drink, he had torn a cloth fetched from the back of the Land Rover into strips and was bandaging his hands with them. He leaned forward, plucked the flask from her grip and took a couple of hefty swallows before giving it back. He was wearing a cagoule over his soutane. The hood was down. His hair was plastered to his dripping head. When he had thrust that head through the branches and leaves of the fallen tree at the car window, he had reminded her of one of those pagan pub signs depicting the Green Man. She had thought he was a demon, not a priest.

'I owe you my life.'

She was saying everything, she knew. And she knew it was the shock making her do so. Delaunay merely nodded and blinked. He got behind the wheel of the Land Rover and turned it, spraying through the surface water on the road, back towards the seminary.

Because she was trying to avoid the implications of what had just occurred, Suzanne spent the short journey back wondering what the seminary's facilities to suit every guest were going to be like. The women's were bound to be different from the men's. She imagined a bed chamber built for one of those wan Pre-Raphaelite beauties from the paintings of Millais and Arthur Hughes. There would be tapestries and stained glass and the bed would be heavily canopied. Her well water would reside in a silver chalice. Should she require the diversion of music, she would have to learn the harp and play the one standing in the corner. Or she could take the lute down from the wall.

The shock and the giddiness it provoked did not subside in Suzanne until she had eaten the really excellent beef stew they provided her with in what amounted to a comfortably furnished, self-contained flat. There was wine with the food, along with bread so good she assumed it had been baked in the seminary kitchens that morning. Her sitting room was equipped with satellite TV and a desktop computer with internet access. There was only one clue as to her actual location. A large crucifix hung on the sitting-room wall. A bronze Christ writhed, nailed through his hands and feet to a hardwood cross.

But she was glad of that. As calm and normality returned to her, she was glad of the fact of where she was and the potent reminder of it up there on the wall. When she went to bed and turned out the lights, she knew she would be grateful for the reassurance of the holy fortress surrounding her.

'You'll lose nothing by leaving in the morning, in the daylight,' Delaunay had said.

'I owe you my life,' she repeated.

'It's to God you owe your life,' he said. 'But thank you anyway, Suzanne. I'm a vain enough man to accept any compliment going.'

She laughed. But she had known that about him.

'Where do you intend to go? You're going after Spalding, aren't you? You're undeterred.'

Suzanne nodded.

'I tried telephoning them. I wanted to appeal to their good sense and urge them to return.'

'They won't,' she said.

'I couldn't get through. We've a satellite phone, but I could not get through on that either.'

'I'm going to Southport, Monsignor Delaunay. He settled there for a while. He must have had a reason. Like you, I sometimes have intuitions. You're right. I'm going after him. I can't just do nothing. I'd go mad.'

'Then for God's sake take the train.'

She laughed. 'I've no choice. My hire care isn't up to the journey.'

Delaunay waved an imaginary irritant away. His hands were still bandaged, blood in dried clots and stains on the fabric. 'I'll talk to the hire car people. They'll believe a priest. They might call you for confirmation and send you papers to sign, but I'll deal with it here. And I'll have one of the lads drive you to the station in the morning.'

'My travel bag is still in the boot. My laptop's in the bag.'

'I'll have one of the lads go and fetch it now. Novices live for the opportunity to do someone a good turn.' He winked.

She hugged him. She had not known she was going to do it until it was done. 'There,' she said.

He held her head between his hands and kissed her forehead. 'There,' he said.

In the flat in the seminary, Suzanne turned the computer

on in the drowsy preamble to going to bed. She logged on to the web and accessed the BBC news homepage and saw an item about storms raging across the North-East of England. It was only then, with a start, that she realised neither she nor Delaunay had even for a moment indulged the notion that what had happened to her earlier had been an accident. But trees fell in tempests, didn't they? And some of them fell on cars. She, of course, had heard the song on the radio immediately prior to the impact. But he had not. She had switched off the radio in the fraction of time before it occurred.

She went to her email. There were no messages for her she had not read. She pulled up Martin's email address. And she tapped in the sentence: *I've been researching Harry Spalding.*

Aboard Dark Echo

We were three full days out. We had made about nine hundred miles at an average of twelve knots since departing Southampton. We were in the middle of the North Atlantic and the sea was running high and the wind was gusting at around thirty knots. Every fourth or fifth wave was breaking over the bow. The sun was going down and the ocean was a lurid, foaming crimson where the last of it glimmered and sank. I was cold and wet and needed a break and something hot to drink and there was no sign above deck of my father. I had not seen him for what seemed like hours.

He had taken to spending more time in his cabin over the past couple of days. I thought this reasonable enough. Sailing becomes a chore when there is nothing to look at except an endless expanse of churning sea. His cabin was warm and dry and handsomely appointed, and if he chose to take refuge there when he wasn't at the wheel or the galley stove, that was a captain's privilege. But I had a suspicion that he locked the door. And when I listened outside his door, I could hear something beyond the groan of the hull beneath me and the sound of straining rigging and the whip in the wind of the sails above. The opera was played, when it was played at all, very quietly, as a backdrop. Above it, I could hear my father conversing quietly and earnestly with himself.

Wet through and more than slightly pissed off, I engaged the auto-steer and went below, stripped off my wet weather gear, towelled down and then went to make myself a cup of cocoa. I took it into my cabin. And I saw that I had new email and the source of the message was Suzanne.

Sometimes the email connection on the little white laptop worked and sometimes it didn't. It was supposed to function wherever you were in the world but in the middle of the ocean there seemed to be voids or black spots that stopped it from doing so. Maybe it was something to do with electromagnetic fields or something. Possibly it was a consequence of atmospheric conditions. Maybe it was deliberate interference, jamming from a submarine or a warship somewhere in our proximity. The Cold War was long over, of course. But beyond their own borders, it was no secret to anyone that the superpowers still played out their hostile psychological games.

I sat down at my desk and sipped cocoa. She had only just sent the email. She should be online right now, I thought. I opened the message, which comprised a single line.

I've been researching Harry Spalding.

My fingers hovered over the keyboard. Outside, I heard the wind shriek and caterwaul. It was going to be a testing night, our roughest yet by far.

Oh? What have you found out?

I pressed 'Send' and waited for a moment. My cocoa was not as good as I'd imagined it would be in the half-hour I'd deliberated about leaving the wheel and making it. A drink is never that good when you have to prepare it yourself. It's never as good as when someone else makes it for you.

He spent the summer of 1927 in England. He rented a mansion on Rotten Row in Southport while his boat was laid up for repair in Liverpool. He joined the flying club run by a pilot war veteran on Southport sands. He played golf at Birkdale. And he partied hard.

Suzanne was very skilled at her occupation. She was clever and tenacious. But nobody was going to pay her for this particular job of research. I wondered why she was wasting her time with it.

Sounds like an Anglophile Jay Gatsby.

I pressed 'Send'. A moment later, a reply came back.

Not really. Gatsby was only a bootlegger. Harry Spalding was the Devil himself.

And then the screen on my laptop froze. I switched off the power button and drained my cup. What the hell was my father doing? I went and stood outside his cabin door with my knuckles raised to knock. And I hesitated. I thought I could hear music, very faintly, from within. And I felt incredulous and cold when I thought I recognised the tune as 'When Love Breaks Down'.

'Come in.'

But I had not knocked. My knuckles were still poised an inch from the walnut burr of his door.

'I said, come in, Martin.'

He was seated at his desk with his back to me. The room smelled curious. It smelled of smoke. It was not the plump whiff of one of my father's Havanas, though. It was the thin, strong odour of Turkish tobacco. The music had stopped.

There was some effect in the cabin, some dulling of the acoustic that made the rising sea outside distant and numb. And in the haze of smoke, objects seemed to ripple slightly before settling, subtly out of focus. The barrels seemed bloated, swollen and belligerent on the shotguns and rifles where they gleamed in his gun cabinet. The handles of the knives in their case on the opposite wall of the cabin looked yellowy. The pale bone and ivory hilts seemed tainted and nicotined. I did not want my father to turn round. I felt very strongly for a moment that I did not want to see the expression on his face. Then this sensation of dread passed and he did turn round. He looked frayed, distracted, as though dragged reluctantly from some refuge of the mind where he vastly preferred to be.

'What do you want, Martin?'

'What are you doing, Dad?'

'I'm composing a letter I'll never write and shall never send, Martin.'

'To my mother?'

'Not on this occasion to your mother, no. This one is to your sister. To Catherine Ann.'

I nodded. I was not surprised. His mood was that of a man dwelling among the dead. I turned and closed the door behind me and, in my own cabin, climbed back into my foul weather gear and went up on the deck to take my place at the wheel in the gathering fury of the night storm.

For nine straight hours, I battled the sea. The sun was well up by the time the cloud cleared and calm returned the following morning. I took a bearing. We were twelve hundred miles from home. The storm had propelled us further into the wilderness of the Atlantic. I stayed at the wheel, dazed with fatigue, as the salt dried in crystals in my beard stubble and my eyes began to play the tricks they will when everything they try to fix on is in turbulent motion. I retched, not with seasickness but with exhaustion. There was nothing by then in my stomach for me to part company with but bile. I thought about Suzanne, wondering what she had meant by what she had said in our cut-short email conversation. In my mind I saw Harry Spalding in his golden, Southport summer. The only thing I knew about Southport was the story of the long-demolished Palace Hotel. A huge neo-Gothic pile built near the sands at Birkdale, it had been haunted, so it was said. The men who demolished it had heard the lifts ascending and coming down again long after the electricity that powered them had been cut. Had Spalding dined at the Palace Hotel? Had he sipped cocktails on one of the sun-drenched terraces there? He had probably danced in the great ballroom at the Palace in his white tie, charming the local beauties with his murderous smile. Almost certainly, in his Southport summer, he would have done that.

I woke with a start over the wheel. I was dozing, which was dangerous. Where was my father? Was he still grieving and remembering below, wreathed in old tunes and bitter tobacco smoke? I engaged the auto-steer. I was desperate for sleep, close to hallucinating with tiredness. What had awoken me? Of all things, I had been brought back to full alertness by what had sounded like a baby crying. It must have been a gull, I thought. But the sky when I glanced about was empty. And there were no gulls perched on the rail or the rigging of the boat. Below deck, I paused outside my father's cabin door. He was talking to himself again. It sounded like a grim and antagonistic monologue. His tone lacked any tenderness. He was no longer communicating, I thought, with his lost, precious daughter. I was beyond tired. I limped to my cabin. My mind engaged in a numb debate over which was more disturbing – the howl of a phantom dog or the crying of a ghostly baby. It was the baby, I decided. It was the distressed, invisible child. I was no great lover of dogs, and I thought the crying baby might be my little sister, conjured back to be among us. It was a sinister and disturbing thought. I wrestled my way out of my clothes and took to my berth and oblivion.

Nine

She arrived in Southport at four in the afternoon of the following day. She left the apocalyptic weather in the wake of the express as it rattled south-west across the country. By mid-morning there were fields golden with wheat and vivid with rapeseed to remind her again that it was June. She had to change twice. Southport was not the resort it had been in Victorian times, when trains full of excursionists in their masses made the summer rail journey faithfully there each holiday from Scotland or the Lancashire and Yorkshire mill towns and the Black Country of the Midlands. Nor was it the gaudy seaside tribute to wealth it had been in the 1920s. The great Art Deco outdoor pool had gone now, replaced by a windblown retail park full of discount names. The grand, and some said haunted, Palace Hotel was long demolished. Even Lord Street, the great tree-lined boulevard of exclusive shops, was in decline. Panes were missing from many of the cast-iron pillared awnings that covered the pavement for most of a mile. And there were security guards outside a couple of the splashier jeweller's shops.

Suzanne knew all this before seeing the evidence herself. She had been able to print off information about Southport in her guest quarters at the seminary. The most openly critical assessments of the town's aesthetic and economic decline had come from its own tourism department. The town had been beautifully planned and maintained and then systematically vandalised from the early 1970s onwards, when Southport ceased to be an independent borough and came under the authority of Sefton Metropolitan Council. Sefton's rule seemed to be typified by spite, envy, indifference and greed. If ever there was a goose to lay a golden egg, in Southport, Sefton killed it. The first big decision was symptomatic of what followed. Southport's buses, attired in a splendid yellow and red livery and proudly adorned with the town's crest, were painted over in Sefton's drab, utilitarian green. It was the imposition of a grim visual austerity entirely out of keeping with the gaiety visitors expected. Subsequent decisions were just as crass and much more damaging. Sefton's decision to sell sand from the beach to the building trade had destroyed the dunes on which generations of families had picnicked and played. The yellow, rolling hills of sand had vanished from the end of Weld Road in Birkdale, all the way south to the nature reserve at Formby. Sefton had been obliged to leave the nature reserve intact. That was Formby's reprieve. Southport had not been treated so mercifully.

But the Southport Harry Spalding had known had been a splendid place; handsome, sun-drenched and dedicated to pleasure. It was a cut above Blackpool and Morecambe to the north, and knew it. There were casinos and luxury cinemas and theatres and concert halls. There was marble and terrazzo and parquet and there was money. The thoroughbreds ridden at Aintree were trained on the shore. Birkdale was considered the best links golf course in the whole of England. The Giroud brothers ran their aviation club on a hard, smooth strip between the sand hills and the sea. Star entertainers were lured in the season to the Floral Hall and the summer flower show held in Victoria Park was at least the rival of the show held annually at Chelsea. Then, Lord Street had boasted an array of shops to compete with anything in Paris or Milan.

Suzanne walked through the station approach to Chapel Street. She had booked her accommodation the previous evening by email, after choosing a small private hotel in Birkdale that had looked nice without being massively overpriced. The fact that she had found somewhere so easily was indicative, she supposed, of the decline of the resort. Once its hotels and guesthouses would have been full to capacity from the end of May until the beginning of September. But it was no longer the case. It was made plain in her reading that the town saw its future appeal more as a conference location than a place where people sought to spend a holiday.

She was aware that she was spending the BBC's money on something that was nothing at all to do with the corporation. But in her five years there, she had seen a great deal of money squandered.

Chapel Street was pedestrianised. Late afternoon shoppers browsed the windows of generic stores or sipped coffee at the tables in Café Nero. A pair of middle-aged buskers stood with electric guitars in the middle of the street and played an old hit by Dire Straits. She felt a stab of disappointment. It wasn't that the town looked any drearier than anywhere else did. It was just that she could have been anywhere in England. Then she sniffed and looked up at the sky. And she smelled ozone and salt on the fresh summer breeze from the sea and saw the shimmering, layered cobalt light that only skies on the coast possess when the sun is shining on them and reflecting back the sea.

Chapel Street ran parallel with Lord Street. Or rather, with part of Lord Street, which was much longer than Chapel Street. She walked through a covered arcade that connected the two and found herself on a wide avenue with high trees and fountains. To her left, she knew, she would find the town's main library. And opposite the main entrance to the library, on the same stretch of wide pavement, she would find the Tourist Information Office. She hefted the single bag comprising her luggage. Unpacking her bag could wait. There were mysteries here to be solved.

But she solved none of those mysteries on her first visit to Southport's main public library. The Atkinson Library was situated in a grand building paid for by the philanthropist after whom it was named. Other parts of the building housed an arts centre and the Atkinson Art Gallery. In Spalding's era, the arts centre had been a theatre given to glittering premiers and productions hailed for their extravagance. But Suzanne was aware that she lived in a more practical age. And the reference library there was excellent, she discovered, once she had completed the formality of taking out a temporary membership. There was a rich and vivid archive charting the history and development of the town. There was lots of information on the great maritime disaster that occurred when the crew of the Southport lifeboat went to the aid of the stricken vessel *Mexico*. There was nothing whatsoever in the library about Jane Boyte.

After an hour and a half of searching without result, Suzanne decided that she would go for coffee. She crossed the road from the library to the west side of Lord Street, where the shops were arrayed, then turned right and after a block came to a Costa coffee house. Costa roasted their beans at a plant in Old Paradise Street, around the corner from the Lambeth flat she shared with Martin. When the wind was blowing in the right direction, it was a familiar, homely smell. She was a fair way from home. When she ordered her drink, there was even a photograph of the Old Paradise Street street sign in sepia as part of a montage on the wall. And, of course, that was fondly familiar, too. But as the June shadows began their slow lengthening towards dusk, she felt a very long way from home indeed.

What if Martin never came back? It was a desolate thought,

and one she had tried to avoid consciously thinking, while thinking it all the while at some deeper and less disciplined level of her mind. What if they never sat down again at their corner table in the Windmill for a drink to a soundtrack of the landlord's tearful soul? There would be no more impromptu picnics in Archbishop's Park, no more games on balmy evenings on the tennis courts, no more shopping amid the fruit and bric-a-brac stalls of Lower Marsh, and no more browsing in the book and record shops there. What if they had shared a bed for the last time, exchanged their final intimacy? She looked around her, trying to dismiss the thought, at the young girls in their northern gaggles wearing too much make-up for the daytime and wearing generally far too few clothes. What if she never heard the familiar sound of his key in the lock ever again? If his clothes just hung, limp in the wardrobe, and the scent of him faded altogether from the pillow? It was why she was here, wasn't it? It was why she was in this unfamiliar place. She would do everything she could to bring about his safe return. She would do anything.

She sipped coffee. She looked along the still-handsome avenue she sat in, trying to imagine Harry Spalding here. He had said he was looking forward to shopping on Lord Street. She imagined him rigged out in a summer suit and hat. It would not be seersucker and straw boater for him, though. He was Europeanised. He had drunk cocktails with Scott and sparred with Hemingway in Paris. Maybe he had been granted an audience with Gertrude Stein or the scholar madman Ezra Pound. Certainly he had been on nodding terms with the dark magician, Aleister Crowley. No; it would not have been straw and seersucker for him. It would have been slubbed silk and a pale fedora and a malacca cane to twirl in his louche search along Lord Street's glittering windows for a diamond tiepin or an engraved silver case for his cigarettes. She could imagine him fairly well, pretty vividly. There was no absence of detail. But when she saw him walk, he did not stroll. Instead Harry Spalding moved with the lope of a predator along the pavement.

The following morning, because it was all she knew to do, Suzanne went back to the library. Her Birkdale hotel room had been comfortable enough. She had thought over breakfast about exploring the locality. It looked encouragingly unchanged. She had Jane's old address. But she knew that she would not knock on the door and discover Jane's daughter there, cogent at eighty and happy to reminisce. Jane Boyte had died in 1971. There had been no descendents. The internet and the fashion for the subject on television made genealogy a very easy subject to research. She had researched the descendants of a northern comic from this very region for just such a programme herself two years earlier. She was familiar from that study with the old Southport surnames. The salient facts had taken Suzanne fifteen minutes to discover. Jane's life ended in a cul-de-sac. She had encountered in her life a great man in Michael Collins and a bad one by the name of Harry Spalding. How well she had known either of them remained to be established. But her own life seemed to have ended with a whimper rather than a bang. Such was the lot of most people. Glamour was not a quality that sustained itself, unless you were Marlene Dietrich. Unless you were Pablo Picasso.

Again, she came up with nothing at the library in Southport. After two hours of musty, futile digging she went and got her cup of coffee and sat in the shade of an umbrella at a pavement table on sun-drenched Lord Street and pondered on what to do next. Maybe she ought to go to Liverpool and examine the maritime archive at the library there. What if, as she supposed, *Dark Echo* had been as accident-prone in Patrick Boyte's boatyard as it had in that owned by poor Frank Hadley? There might be something.

She sighed. She sipped cappuccino. She watched traffic for a bit, the cars predominantly that silver metallic they were everywhere nowadays, and she toyed with her Marlboro packet without opening it and lighting one. What would an accident-prone boatyard in the Liverpool of eighty years ago prove? She knew that Martin and his father were in danger. She did not need a catalogue of old accidents to prove that to her. She knew it already. What she needed was the something indefinable that her instinct had impelled her to Southport in search of. It was not a coincidence in all of this that she did what she did for a living. It was her duty and her solitary hope. And sipping coffee, and resisting the craving for nicotine, she had to do what she could now to prevent a deep and powerful hopelessness from engulfing her like the tide.

'Mind if I sit here, love?'

Suzanne smiled into the light against which the voice was silhouetted. The honest answer was that she did, of course. In the proximity of old people, you risked conversation. And this was particularly true in the north, where she knew that complete strangers often inflicted chat on you in the way that only care in the community victims ever did back in London. Age wasn't even a consideration. Young people here did it, too. It was an indiscriminate vice.

Martin had warned her about it, years ago. But he had not done so deliberately. Magnus Stannard did it. Magnus was from Manchester. He talked to strangers all the time. He actually engaged people he did not know and had never met in conversation. Suzanne was there on a couple of occasions when he was blatantly guilty of it.

'What is it with your dad?'

'What?'

'The compulsive attention seeking.'

'He's an attention seeker. But it's not compulsive.'

'He'll talk to anyone.'

And Martin had laughed. 'He's from Manchester, Suzanne. And he might be a terrible show-off. Christ knows he's got his faults. But my dad's never had any side.'

'Any what?'

'Never mind.'

Eventually, she had understood. It was why she smiled in a manner she hoped might be warm and welcoming to the old lady who had invited herself to share her table outside Costa on Lord Street in Southport in the north of England where people spoke habitually to strangers and had no side. She swivelled her eyes, surreptitiously, to right and left.

'All taken, love.'

Which they were. Every other table was occupied by families, by shop girls on their break, by fat men sweating in suits and dragging furiously on their outlawed choice of smoke.

'I'm truly sorry,' Suzanne said. And she was. She stood slightly and held out her hand. 'My name is Suzanne. I'm very pleased to make your acquaintance.'

The old woman smiled. A waiter from somewhere in Eastern Europe delivered her iced coffee. So she was a regular. Of course she was. Suzanne had felt surprised at the choice of beverage and now cursed herself for her snobbery. It was a kind of bigotry. What it was, was *parochial.*

Harry Spalding had not been parochial.

'You look a bit lost, love. If you don't mind me saying so.'

Her hair had been blonde a lifetime ago. Now it was grey and tied back above the patina of tiny creases on her forehead. It was fine and thick and still abundant on her head. She wore Ray-Ban sunglasses, which she took off and put on the table. They had those old-fashioned green lenses. They had tortoiseshell frames. She put her elbows on the table and clasped her hands together and Suzanne saw that she wore a Cartier Tank wristwatch and a huge ruby eternity ring. So much for care in the community.

'My name is Alice Daunt. I'm tempted to ask why someone so beautiful looks so crestfallen. And you are beautiful, you know, dear. You are exquisitely beautiful.'

'Thank you.'

'But I won't ask.'

Suzanne nodded.

Alice Daunt winked. 'I'll just let you tell me. If, and only if, you choose to do so.'

Suzanne sighed. 'I'm researching a woman from Southport. Specifically, she was from Birkdale. Her name was Jane Boyte.'

'I knew her.' Alice Daunt raised and sipped her drink. There was condensation beading on the glass. Her hand was steady as she brought it to her lips. 'Well, I say I knew her. I didn't really. But my mother did.'

'I'm trying to research her life.'

'Oh? How?'

'Over at the library there.' Suzanne gestured.

Alice Daunt snorted into her drink. 'Jane Boyte was a Birkdale girl.'

'I know. I know that was where she lived.'

'There was a Birkdale library, love. Gone now, like everything that was great about this town. Destroyed, the land sold on, by Sefton. Flats. Offices. Desecration.'

'What was she like?'

Alice Daunt smiled. The smile was sly, concealing. 'She looked uncannily like you do, Suzanne. It might be why I stopped. I was walking along Lord Street and I was transposed these eighty years. I thought for a moment I'd seen a ghost.'

Suzanne smiled back, or tried to. 'Aren't you afraid of ghosts, Alice?'

Alice Daunt sipped from her glass. 'Of course I am. But a man whose opinion I respected very much told me a long time ago that we should confront our fears.'

The use of the past tense was not lost on Suzanne. 'Your husband?'

'My son,' Alice Daunt said.

'I'm so sorry.'

'And you're very nice.' She put down her iced coffee and picked up her sunglasses from the tabletop. 'I could have only been seven or eight. But if you would like to meet me here at the same time tomorrow, Suzanne, I'll tell you what I remember about the rather unfortunate person you so resemble.'

Suzanne sat for a while after Alice Daunt's departure and watched the ice slip and subside in the June warmth at the bottom of her coffee glass. Southport had a lot of elderly residents and they had lived here all their lives. It was a demographic oddity. But it was a fact. There was a sprinkling of nonagenarians and even centurians among their frail number. But how many of them had known Jane Boyte? Had her meeting with Alice Daunt just now been a matter of coincidence or fate? Suddenly, she missed Monsignor Delaunay. His strength and certainty had been a reassuring comfort to her. She felt very alone and isolated, doing this. She shivered in the warmth and decided she would spend the afternoon exploring parts of the town relevant to her stalled investigation.

She walked south towards Birkdale and Weld Road. The shops petered out and eventually the road became lined instead with huge gardens and enormous, grand houses. Many of the houses had been turned into rest homes or dental clinics or bases for genteel professionals like chartered accountants, architects, solicitors and surveyors. She saw the signs on the grass and the brass plates on the gateposts saying so. Some had been divided into flats, their expansive lawns pulled up and paved over to accommodate residents' cars. But many more of these grand houses were still still exactly that. Merchants made wealthy by businesses in Lancashire and Merseyside had come to live here in their opulent droves. That had been the Southport of Harry Spalding's golden summer here.

Eventually she reached Birkdale and turned right on to Weld Road. The road rose into a gentle hill at its conclusion half a mile away, beyond which she knew the beach lay. To right and left, if anything the houses were even grander here. No two were exactly alike. But they shared characteristics beyond their enormity. Many had turrets and towers and crenellations. She smiled, reminded of her preconceptions concerning the women's guest quarters at the seminary in Northumberland. Here, there was a great deal of Victorian Gothic. It was easy to imagine dark drawing rooms filled with William Morris furniture beyond those high front doors of studded oak and stained-glass panelling. The theme had been continued and exaggerated at the Palace Hotel, which had sprawled across the area approaching now to her left as she neared the rise that would take her to the sea. What a self-styled modernist like Harry Spalding had made of it was anyone's guess. The Palace had been much more Tennyson than T.S. Eliot. Then again, it had been haunted. And that might have amused and even delighted its sardonic American guest.

There was only one place left in the locality of the Palace now to serve as a public amenity, and that was the Weld Road pub called the Fisherman's Rest. It had originally been built as a coach house for the hotel and was later converted into a non-residents' bar. It was here that the fourteen lifeboatmen who drowned attempting to reach the *Mexico* had been brought on a December night in 1886. The bar became a makeshift mortuary as the corpses were laid out for identification.

It was at the neighbouring hotel that a coroner's enquiry was hastily convened. Suzanne ordered her half of Guinness and fingered one of the fourteen small brass mermaids holding the handrail of the bar in place. They were cast and fitted as a tribute to the lost lifeboatmen. She shuddered, thinking of death at sea, of brine-filled lungs and being washed up drowned, the tide lapping at grey, indifferent flesh. And she took her drink outside to sip in the sunshine at one of the bench seats attached to the tables there.

The Palace was opened in November of 1866, built by the Manchester-based architects Cuffley, Horton and Bridgeford. At its peak it boasted 1,000 rooms and had its own railway station on the Cheshire Lines to link it directly, for the convenience of guests, to the racecourse at Aintree. But there never were enough guests. And in 1881 a health hydro was added to the building to enhance its appeal to the ailing victims of northern industry. By Spalding's time, the hotel was even equipped with its own runway. Famous guests in its latter years included Clark Gable and Frank Sinatra. But rumours of paranormal activity plagued the hotel almost from its opening. Two sisters died there in a suicide pact. The last and saddest event in its grisly history occurred when the body of an abducted child was found under a bed there in 1961. She had been taken and assaulted by a kitchen porter later hanged for the crime. The hotel never really recovered from this damaging scandal. In 1969 it was demolished. And the demolition men were unnerved and eventually terrified by lifts that groaned into life without power and wouldn't stop the steady, clanking habit of their work.

But there was nothing of Harry Spalding for her to find

there on the spot where the Palace Hotel had been. Suzanne finished her drink and decided to recross Weld Road and walk north along Rotten Row back into the centre of the town. Spalding had left the hotel and rented a house on Rotten Row. You could not see the houses here, though. They lay at the top of a steep grassy slope above a drystone wall to her right as she walked, with the flower beds and high hedgerows of Victoria Park on the other side of the road to her left.

'Sod it,' Suzanne said. There were summer pedestrians on Rotten Row. There were gardeners tending the flower beds beyond the park boundary and there were cars in a bright procession on the road itself. But she had to see. She had to have a look. She scaled the wall and climbed the embankment to the fences protecting the mansions of Rotten Row from prying eyes. The slope was steep, the ground too hard for purchase and the manicured grass covering it dry and glassy under her feet. Once again, she was wearing shoes inappropriate to the task. But she had not planned this. This was spontaneous. She had lost a pair of boots to bad planning in France. Here, all she might lose was her balance and her dignity if she slithered on her leather soles on to her backside and tumbled down the hill.

She knew which of them had been Harry Spalding's house as soon as she saw it. She knew because as she saw its clusters of ivy and black, sightless windows staring back, a chill gathered in her chest and gripped her heart. There was a stillness about the long lawn and the grouping of stunted ornamental trees providing shade by the path that wound from the front porch to the summer house. Thirty feet along the rise from where she stood, steps had been cut into the earth to give the owner access through a latched gate. She looked at the old brick and terracotta and knew that Harry Spalding had ascended those steps with his lupine stride and his cane gripped in his fist on his grinning journey home. She started, her eyes reclaimed by the house itself as she sensed a shape, just for a sly instant, at one of the upper-floor windows. A cleaner, she thought. Even in Southport, the Poles and the Filipinos would come to polish and scour. An address as prestigious as this had not sat empty for eighty years awaiting a spectre's return. He had rented it for a summer only. He was here for a solitary season. He was not here now. But by God, Suzanne thought, shuddering with cold in the high June heat, he had left his baleful mark on the place.

Because she did not know what else to do, Suzanne went back to Lord Street and Southport Library. And then in the late afternoon, because she was facing a dead end, she left the library and walked up Nevill Street and found the promenade and the pier. Nevill Street embodied everything that was wrong with Southport as a modern tourist destination. Fat clouds of fish batter and beefburger grease scented the pavement. There was rock in stripy midget walking sticks, and toffee apples and pink candyfloss swollen in the breeze in bags of cellophane pinned and flapping against wooden racks. Men peered over pints with long-suffering wives from inside the picture windows of sad, modernised bars.

She walked the length of the pier, over the Marine Lake, over the start of the flat wastes of Southport beach and finally over the water as the sluggish wavelets of the Irish Sea began their shallow approach. The tram passed her on its path to the pier head. It was full of smiling day trippers. She waved back at a toddler waving at her though the rear window. She squinted over the railing to her right. She could see Blackpool Tower faintly through the heat shimmer over the salt marsh, rising on the peninsula thirty miles away.

At the end of the pier, she went into a modern and, to her mind, absurdly incongruous glass and steel visitors' centre with a big display devoted to the wild birdlife of the Fylde Coast. To her left there was a café area with views out over the featureless wilderness of sea and sand. To her right, there was a cluster of antique machines she assumed had been salvaged from old amusement arcades in the resort. You could change modern pounds into old-fashioned copper pennies to use them. You got ten old pennies to the pound, which Suzanne knew was more robbery than exchange rate. But she thought she might have fun here, or at least lighten her prevailing mood. So she changed a couple of pounds.

After spending about half of them, she shuffled through her remaining pennies, looking at the dates. She got to the last one, King George V's bearded profile stoical and aristocratic and resembling rather the slaughtered Romanov tsar to whom, of course, he'd been related, on one side. She flipped the coin. And the date underneath Britannia, sitting with her spear and shield on the reverse face of the penny, read 1927.

As she had known it would. She jumped. A child had put a penny in the slot for the laughing sailor and, inside his glass case, this sinister relic was swaying and wheezing in a show of mirth in his fusty, mottled blues. Next to him, there was a fortune-telling machine. You fed it money and your character and fate emerged neatly printed in tiny letters on a little rectangle of board. Suzanne fingered the flat, worn-smooth edges of her penny. She raised it to her nose and smelled its acrid, copper smell. Had Spalding handled it? Had he flung it bright and new among others across the Palace bar as a careless tip? She slipped the penny into her pocket. She did not want to know her fortune. She thought her fate predetermined. She knew who it involved, even if she was unsure of the what and precisely of the when.

Further to her right, beyond the old machines, a film about the history of Southport was showing on a projection screen mounted up on the wall. Images, grey and sunny at the same time, showed the great days of the outdoor pool and the flower show and the bandstand next to the town's large cenotaph of dignified Portland stone. Water shimmered and roses bloomed in this monochrome world of long ago. She stiffened as she saw a scene from the 1920s. Black sedans prowled the length of Lord Street, sleek as panthers. Women in furs and cloche hats walked arm in arm and discussed the intrusion of the camera, smiling at it. She did not see Harry Spalding. She did not recognise any of the women as Jane Boyte. Fingering the old penny in her pocket, unaware that she was doing so, Suzanne sat down on the chairs before the screen and waited for the film to reach its conclusion and loop back again to its beginning.

Aboard Dark Echo

Night had fallen again by the time I awoke. I looked at my watch. The date wheel told me I had been asleep for a full twenty-four hours. I dressed in an incredulous rush and climbed to the deck. A fog had descended and under it the sea wore the still torpor of a lily pond. I had been forced to reduce to nothing the amount of sail we were carrying in the squall of the previous evening. Everything had been hauled in. Now I saw to my irritation and disappointment that nothing had been done to raise sail since. There was no wind. Every inch we carried should have been up in a bid to keep us moving, however sluggishly, on our course. Then I became aware that we were moving. The engine was not being used. But we were in motion, the *Dark Echo* travelling as though being tugged through the water, at a speed sufficient to leave a wake churning under the fog at our stern. We felt to be doing about ten knots. I walked to the wheel. The auto-steer was on, of course. I took a bearing from the binnacle compass next to the wheel. It was impossible. With no wind and no power and under no sail, we were doing about ten knots on a south-easterly course. We seemed to be in the grip of a current. And still more than a thousand miles off the coast of America, we were coursing swiftly back in the direction we had come.

My father must have done something to the auto-steer, I thought. But even if he had, I couldn't understand from where the *Dark Echo* was deriving this propulsion. She weighed seventy tons. What freak force under the covering of the fog could be urging her on at such a rate? I needed to gather my thoughts. Nothing in my recent maritime schooling had prepared me for something so odd as this. The auto-steer had suffered a malfunction. That was clear. It might or might not be repairable, but for now there was no option. I had to switch it off. I had to take the wheel. I had to turn us swiftly about and raise sail and sit out the fog and, if necessary, the night. The North Atlantic was a very large expanse of ocean. We had plentiful supplies of food and water aboard. But we could not afford to lose our momentum. We had to keep going. It was what vessels under sail were obliged to do. If you failed to do that you became not just becalmed but helpless and you risked disaster and tragedy.

I realised then how hungry I was. I had not eaten anything substantial for well over twenty-four hours. Where was my father? What was he doing? I felt as though I faced this sinister crisis entirely alone. I was hungry and thirsty, too. And I was close to clueless about what was going on with the boat, still slipping urgently through the fogbound sea in the wrong direction under my feet. With a loud curse, I locked the wheel. I had to eat. I had to rouse my father. I would wrestle with the boat's steering but could not do it without sustenance. He could make me a mug of soup. It was the very least he could do.

There were voices coming from his cabin. I knew he was the only person in there. But he was reading and reciting stuff and doing it in character. I stood outside his door and listened. There were snatches of Imagist and Vorticist poetry. There was some Wyndham Lewis and fragments of T.S. Eliot and what I thought I recognised as E.E. Cummings and part of a story by Ford Madox Ford. It was all of a piece, really, all from the same decade and most of it having originated among the expatriates in Paris. He began to recite that line from the Hemingway short story, the one that begins: *In the fall the war was always there, but we did not go to it any more.*

I knew it as the first line of the story 'In Another Country'. It was familiar to me as the first line of what my father had often said he thought was the most beautiful paragraph of prose fiction written in English in the twentieth century. And I wouldn't have argued with him. It was vivid and it had this melancholy cadence and it really was very beautiful. But he was reciting it over and over, behind his cabin door, like a mantra. And like a mantra, with repetition the words seemed to lose their sense of meaning altogether and become an abstract, inconsequential jumble of sounds.

In the fall the war was always there, but we did not go to it any more.

And behind his door he laughed and the laugh was sardonic, almost a chuckle. And it was delivered in a high, viperish register that did not sound at all like the rumble of my father's familiar laughter. And I thought that perhaps Harry Spalding was behind the door, sharing his desk and a joke with my dad, perusing the contents of my father's gun cabinet with judicious expertise and the hole still jagged and dripping in his head from his self-murder.

I almost slapped myself, then. It seemed as if my father was losing his mind. If I followed, then both of us were lost.

I was very afraid, listening to what I was hearing from behind that door, the snatches of nonsense, the weird logic of its period somehow dictating it was not, any of it, entirely random. In his mind, he was in the 1920s. He was in the decade of Lindbergh and Dempsey and Carpentier and Bricktop and Al Capone.

And Harry Spalding, of course. Who Suzanne had insisted was the Devil himself.

If I succumbed to panic now, then I would not be able to save my father. Both of us would be lost. Under me, I thought I could feel the boat gathering speed and impetus. I stole away from the cabin door towards the galley. I would have to get my own food. I had to eat or I felt I would faint. Though now, of course, I found my appetite was entirely gone.

'Martin?'

I did not reply.

'Martin? Why don't you join our little salon? We're devoting ourselves to a cultural evening.' More laughter, this time muffled, as though the mirth were contained by a stifling hand. 'It's all very intimate and not at all formal. You're more than welcome.'

Was this how people sounded when they went mad? Was I sharing this wilful, disobedient boat in the middle of an ocean with a madman? When I got to the galley I realised I was sobbing. Tears dripped from my face on to surfaces still with the showroom sheen of newness on them. We had been at sea less than a week and were victims of catastrophe. The situation was hopeless. It was hopeless. But it was not terror that made me weep, and it was not self-pity either. It was grief for my father, believing him lost.

I ate a bowl of chicken and lentil broth in the fog at the wheel with a chunk of defrosted bread. And I drank with my meal a large measure of rum. I had brought the rum aboard myself as a sort of ironic joke, played against the traditions of the sea. But I badly needed a drink and it was warm in my belly and a comfort as the *Dark Echo* continued with smooth relentlessness through the water on its rogue course. The booze emboldened me, I think. I realised that I would have to confront my father. There were guns in his cabin. In his present, irrational mood, he was a danger to himself and a liability to both of us. Maybe I would be obliged to restrain him. Perhaps I would have to do that and then dump the various weapons over the side. But I could not just ignore what was going on. It was a reversal of our normal roles, but I had a duty of care to my dad. And there was an urgent practical imperative. If I could shake him out of the delusional fugue he was in, he could help me with the boat. His seamanship was more than the equal of mine. Maybe he had tampered with the auto-steer and maybe he had not. Whatever, the graveness of the situation and the rum told me that I had no choice but to confront him.

I knocked.

'Enter.'

His cabin looked normal. There was no harsh smell of tobacco and the lamps lit the space with unambiguous clarity. I stole a glance at the guns in their cabinet. But there was no belligerence about them now. They looked like the lethal tools they undoubtedly were. But there was a neutrality about them that had been troublingly absent earlier. My father looked groomed, composed. He must have eaten, too, I thought. Certainly he had discovered the presence of mind from somewhere to shower and shave. Under us, I could feel the *Dark Echo* smooth on its mutinous path. If anything, the vessel was getting faster in the fog. It was inexplicable.

'We're on a homeward heading, Dad.'

'I know.'

'Why?

'You're a good sailor, Martin. I've watched you. You're punctilious and possess no shortage of endurance.' He smiled, but it was a flawed, conflicted smile. 'I've been delighted with you. I've been proud of you, truth be told. But I'm no part of what the *Dark Echo* is doing, in answer to your unasked question. She's doing what she's doing. It's no doing of mine.'

I dumped myself in the chair at his desk in front of him.

'All our communications systems are out. Cellular, satellite phone, wireless. We don't have sonar and email is so sporadic it's virtually useless. The engine is completely dead. The binnacle compass is the only instrument still working consistently. That, and the emergency beacon, which no one can see anyway in the fog. We know which direction we're going in, but we can't pinpoint our own position. Even if we could, we can't get on to the emergency frequencies to put out a Mayday call. We're on our own.'

'Do you think this fog is some sort of experimental thing we've blundered into?'

He smiled. 'Are you asking me if it has a military application? I don't think so, Martin. And neither do you. It's a long time since the character who conjured this fog had anything to do with the military.' He reached for the framed picture of the boat, the one he had seen originally as a child. He held it between his hands. 'I remember very vividly the time I first saw this photograph. The volume containing it lay open on the page. It lay in a pool of sunlight on the bedside locker at which I would sit to do my homework. My mother swore she hadn't put it there. We did not run in those days to domestic staff, Martin. And I did not take it from the shelf and put it there myself. Was it destiny, do you think? Or was it some omnipotent design, dictating my ambitions, shaping the fabric of my dreams.'

He put the picture back down. He lifted his hands to his

face and rubbed at his eyes with his fingers. 'It gets hard, after the age of forty or so.'

'What does?'

'You lose the resilience. You lose the dynamism. There are all sorts of ways of continuing the illusion of youth. But that's what it becomes, son. It becomes an illusion. And it turns itself, regardless of your will, into a memory. You become tired. And fatigue makes a man vulnerable.'

I didn't much care about what he was saying, to be honest. I was just relieved that he was sounding like my father again. It was that happy mixture of portentousness and self-pity and good sense I fondly recognised as him. But we had still the problem to confront of our ungovernable boat. I'd have called her delinquent, but she was ninety years old. There were forces aboard her, I felt, far more profound and troubling than delinquency. She felt possessed.

It was then that I noticed the mirror. The small brass-bound mirror in which I had caught Spalding's reflection on my first terrible visit to the boat was back were I had seen it then. It had been mounted in its original place on my father's cabin wall.

'I need you on the deck, now, Dad. We've got to try to turn her about. We have to assert control over her. Either you're the master of this vessel or you're not. I believe you are.'

'So I am, by God,' he said. He thumped the table. His jaw jutted. He held my eyes steadily. He sounded as though he meant it. Had I succeeded in rekindling the pride that remained in him? It was his cherished dream, after all, that had descended into this waking nightmare. Perhaps he had remembered Monsignor Delaunay's blessing. Whatever, with what seemed like fresh hope and newly summoned defiance, we went above.

The fog had thickened. And it seemed the *Dark Echo* had

gathered speed. I wrestled with the wheel, but she kept heading back to the same slyly insistent course. We raised our sails to try to put about by harnessing the wind. It was what you did aboard a sailing boat. But there was no wind to harness. The sails sagged in the windless mist like shrouds. We dropped a dragging anchor, just in an attempt to slow her down, to arrest the impetus of the vessel. The anchor chain merely strained and groaned against the capstan as her speed through the still water further increased.

'It's as though we're only provoking her,' I said.

'It's him we're provoking,' my father said. He was standing beside the deck compass. 'If we continue on this heading, in four or five days we shall reach the Irish coastline. There we will founder. Unless we can stop her, on her present course, she will either run aground or break up on the rocks off the coast of County Clare.'

I could see the boat in my mind, dashed to pieces in the boiling surf under the great, indifferent ramparts of the Cliffs of Moher. Was that to be our fate?

We stood there beside one another on the deck, mist prickling our skin, salt in our lungs, all silence except for the water trailing the stern of the seventy tons of wood and metal aboard which we were now no more than hostages. Or prisoners. Despite my father's cryptic mention of Spalding, I did not feel that his ghost shared our voyage. I felt rather that my father and myself were the only people left in the world. And the sense of isolation and our helplessness in it was terrible.

'I'm going below, Martin. I can do nothing here.'

'You can do nothing there.'

'I can get drunk,' my father said.

I did not answer him.

'I'm going below.'

I went below myself. I turned on the computer, but my

email would neither send nor receive. So I started to write – which had become almost a compulsion with me – and, I thought, might provide more comfort for the moment than the bottle in which my father would be seeking his consolation.

I began writing this account on the evening of the day all those months ago at Bullen and Clore that my father bought the boat. I have kept at it faithfully over the days and weeks and months since then. I brought it aboard the *Dark Echo* on a disc. And I transferred the file to my little white laptop. Writing it, as the account grew, I'd often wondered what it was for. It seemed part diary, part chronicle and part confession. Reading it back, sometimes the tone of it seemed to me a bit pompous or hysterical. Its singular virtue was truth. Every word of what I'd written – and now continued to write – was a true account of what had taken place. And now I did at last know what its function was to be, always assuming that little bit of luck or providence required. I was not confident about this part. Luck seemed an element in desperately short supply aboard the *Dark Echo*.

I was interrupted by a roar from my father's cabin. It could have been a cry equally of pain or triumph. But whatever it was, it was inspired, I was sure, by more than just whatever it was he was choosing to drink. I got up from my chair, walked towards the stern and knocked loudly on his door.

'Come in, Martin.'

There was a sea chest sitting at the centre of his desk. It was old and iron-bound and water-stained. And my father was breathless from the exertion of putting it there. I looked around the cabin. He had removed a wall panel from about waist height on the starboard side. I could make out the struts and rivets strengthening the bulkhead in the shadowy gloom of the gap.

'I heard a rattling,' he said. 'I decided to investigate. This must have belonged to Harry Spalding.'

Or the Waltrow brothers, I thought. I swallowed. Or Gubby Tench. But it couldn't have belonged to any of them, could it? The man who called himself Jack Peitersen would surely have found it during the refit. And that had been only the boat's most recent overhaul. Surely this box could not have lain there undiscovered for eighty years? My father clearly thought it had. Just as he thought he had heard it rattling in its snug cavity, with the boat on a straight course over water as smooth as glass.

'There's a toolbox in the sail store, Martin.'

I nodded. I knew there was.

'Go and fetch a crowbar or a jemmy.' The padlock on the trunk was made of brass. It had tarnished, of course. But it had not corroded. I went and got the jemmy and came back and forced the lock. I lifted the lid of the trunk. It opened on a foul stench of marine decay. This long-dead odour could not have accrued over a matter of weeks. It was years, decades, since the interior of the trunk had been exposed to light and air.

I had to stand away to let the stink dissipate for fear that I might gag and vomit. The smell was nauseatingly strong. When it had weakened a little, diluted to pervade the cabin, I took a step forward again and looked into the trunk. It contained a badly tarnished rectangular wooden case. There had been padding put around the case and it had rotted to a putrid black paste. That was the source of the awful smell.

'What is it?'

'It's an old-fashioned sewing machine,' I said. I had seen them in antique shops, even in the houses of people who liked their homes stuffed with chintz and curios.

But I was mistaken. When I lifted the heavy box free of the trunk and set it down on my father's desk and took off the lid, it was not a sewing machine at all. It was a record player. It was one of those primitive machines that plays recordings cut into wax cylinders. And there were three such cylinders in the box with the machine, carefully laid into a velvet bed grooved to house them. I realised that the cylinders were also to blame in part for the foul smell rising to pervade my father's cabin. The wax had corrupted somehow and had a clinging, fetid reek.

'Put one on,' my father said. 'Let's hear what we have, Martin.' His voice sounded sane and calm. He was quite serious. He had stumbled upon a mystery. And now he wanted to explore it.

'They won't play,' I said. 'The wax has become unstable, you can smell it decomposing. What do you think that vile stink is?'

'Put one on.'

'The machine will have long seized up, Dad. You can't possibly expect it to play.'

'Then I'll put one on myself,' he said. He shouldered me out of the way. His hand hovered over the cylinders and he selected one. The lights in the cabin flickered, then, dimming. I looked up at one of the portholes. The fog was bruise-coloured. You could not tell if it was night or day. He put the recording in its cradle at the top of the machine and dropped the needle and began to turn the handle. I knew what would happen, before the handle turned, when he dropped the needle on to the wax. It slotted down as smoothly as if the machine had been routinely cleaned and lubricated only yesterday.

The static of eighty years ago filled the cabin. And then the voice came, keen and high and cruel. 'Magnus, old sport. Wanted to welcome you aboard. And your son, of course. Wanted to welcome Martin, too. Hope you're both having a fine old time.' There was laughter, then. And it was sardonic down the decades, reaching us. The hair on the back of my neck prickled at the sound of it. It was a sound neither sane, nor human.

'Thought I'd tell you about the Jericho Crew, Magnus. But make yourself comfortable, sport. Take a seat. Occupy a pew, why don't you. Please don't worry about the machine. It will continue to function quite capably.' My father nodded. He took his hand off the handle. He went and sat down and reached absently for his whisky glass. His face was rapt. I had lost him.

'Took me weeks to find twelve apostles with just the right combination of qualities, Magnus. I needed the sly and the insubordinate, the savage and the self-interested. It helped enormously to have men who were both cunning and stupid at the same time. And that's an unusual blend of attributes. A dash of cowardice was an advantage, too. I needed men prepared to do pretty much anything to guarantee their own survival in the fray. They had to be willing to submit to the necessary ceremonies, you see. There were, too, what might be termed certain contractual obligations. It helped if, above all else, they valued their own skins. It smoothed things along.

'It was terrible at first, Magnus. They lined up the brave and the noble for me. There was lots of bravery and nobility among the American forces in France in the fall of 1917.' On the cylinder, he laughed. 'Those qualities were as common in the line as chocolate and chewing gum. And they were all very fine in their way. But they were no good to me in the way I intended to fight the war. Bravery and nobility would have been . . . how shall I put it? Help me out here, Magnus. You've been a leader of men.'

'They would have been impractical,' my father said.

'Precisely,' Spalding said. 'Knew you'd understand, sport. Took me weeks to select my band of faithful acolytes. One of them was plucked from the cell of a makeshift military prison. Always a mistake to rape a civilian from the side you're supposed to be fighting for. Positively dumb when they're under age. Another two were deserters, snatched from in front of firing squads with the blindfolds already tied. And, of course, I was only starting out myself. I was pretty green, Magnus, a raw tenderfoot in the business of killing. But I had leadership quality, I think, as history proved. And I had an appetite for the work.'

My father nodded. He was no more enjoying this than he could escape it.

'Still do, Magnus. Still possess that appetite, don't you know. And, if anything, I'd say it's grown.'

My father had his head in his hands.

'We'll enjoy being shipmates,' Spalding said. 'You'll have to accept a subordinate role, of course. But you'll be keeping the boy in line, so you won't be on the bottom of the heap.' The voice turned to steel. 'And I will want the boy kept in line, Magnus. I run a tight ship. I will not tolerate insubordination. The Waltrow brothers discovered that, to their cost. So have other crewmen over the years. There is no escape on the high seas from the need for discipline.'

The voice had risen to a high, angry screech.

'Why the Jericho Crew?' I said.

There was a pause. 'You'll refer to me as captain, boy.'

'Why the Jericho Crew, Captain?'

'The name derives from the Jericho Society, into which I initiated my men. We completed an important mission in the cathedral city of Rouen. We arrived aboard a barge, berthing in the port there in the fog. We became a crew aboard that barge. It was a joke made by Corporal Tench. But the name stuck. We became the Jericho Crew.'

'Rouen was always in Allied hands.'

Laughter snickered. 'Student of conflict, are you, boy?

I'll teach you about war. I'm looking forward to you, Martin.'

The voice had subsided, become lower and more intimate again. 'Let me tell you about our base in France, Magnus. Indulge the reminiscences of a proud old soldier. Let me tell you about how we came to build our own Calvary by a barn on a farm near the town of Béthune.'

But I knew already about their Calvary. I knew from Suzanne, who knew from Pierre Duval. And I had no wish to listen to the voice of Harry Spalding any longer as it smirked and bragged. I turned and walked out of my father's cabin and closed the door behind me and went back to my own. I had my writing to conclude.

Passing through the galley I saw a rat. It saw me first and tried to slither into a cupboard it had prised partially open. But my hands were fast when I boxed and I have retained that speed of reflex and I was too quick for it. I grabbed it by the tail and raised and smashed it with a vicious downward swing against the sink edge. Blood flecked the metal. I unscrewed the butterfly nuts locking a porthole, opened it and dropped the dead rodent out of it into the sea. It had been a large rat. Its tail was as thick and coarse in my fist as an abseil rope. It was large enough for me to hear the splash as it hit the water. I cleaned the stain off the sink with some wadded kitchen roll and dropped that out of the porthole, too.

And now, a momentary change of tenses, as I sit for the last time and tap out the letters forming each painstaking word of this account, in what will be my last contribution to it.

All this has happened before. I knew it in my heart back as long ago as the winter, when clever Suzanne found that news page from the archive of the *Liverpool Daily Post*. I was distracted by the resemblance then between Jane Boyte, the beautiful criminal suspect in the picture, and Suzanne herself. Who wouldn't have been? The likeness was uncanny. But it wasn't the point. The point was the worry and fatigue worn on the face of her father, Patrick Boyte. I had seen it in life on the face of Frank Hadley with the *Dark Echo* lashed to his dock and tragedy afflicting the men in his boatyard. Spalding just now, his disembodied voice, had referred to contractual obligations. It seems to me that sacrifices were required, also. And I think that thought occurred both to Patrick Boyte and Frank Hadley in the period when their men were the ones being sacrificed. Suzanne said as much at the time. It has all happened before, she said. Jesus, I wish I had listened. In a moment, I will write to her. It may be the last opportunity I will get and she may never get the message. But I will do it anyway. She is owed that.

Earlier I called this part diary, part chronicle and part confession. And one of those words has given me my clue as to whom I shall send it to. It is likely to be the last of me, I think. And as such I value it. In doing so, do I commit the sin of pride? I suppose I do. But it is a small sin to be guilty of in the scheme of things. And I want this story to be a warning. Because I really do believe all this has happened before. And I do not want what is happening to my father and me now ever to happen to anyone again.

Are you reading, Monsignor Delaunay? I very much hope that you are. And I'm equally very sorry to have burdened you with this. But you are almost at the end of the account, now. I must break off to write my goodbye to Suzanne. I hope, with all my heart, this reaches you. You will know what to do. You called the *Dark Echo* benign. You called her a beautiful toy. In that judgement you were woefully wrong. But Spalding has been at this game of his a long time. The boat has gone under different guises and its master many aliases, I am sure. But it has always been essentially the same vessel, the same game, the same nightmarish voyage.

I can hear the crying of an infant child again. It is no gull. It is coming from outside my cabin door and is my lost sister, Catherine Ann, I fear. Spalding has brought the torment of her back to us.

God bless you, Monsignor Delaunay.

And God help us all.

Martin.

She was hungover the following morning, waiting for Alice Daunt at a pavement table outside the coffee shop. She had drunk too much wine the previous evening, seeking the numbness of drink because she felt lonely and frustrated with her lack of progress and fearful for Martin. She had a reasonable head for alcohol. But she was slightly built. There was only so much of her. And this morning, most of that felt full of last night's Merlot. The furled umbrellas of Costa's lurid purple livery made her wince. In the hard sunlight, they were as bright and poisonous as pirate sails. Everything on the street shared the same vivid, sinister cast. The shadows were black on the pavement and capered when people innocently passed.

Alice Daunt sat down, punctual to the minute. Suzanne looked up at her and tried to conceal a yawn she could not stifle. Alice smiled over her at the waiter from Poland. She took off her Ray-Bans and put her handbag on the table. It was crocodile skin and very glossy with a clasp that wore the dull sheen of gold. 'One over the eight, dear?'

Suzanne smiled. The smile was rueful. 'I don't know, Alice. I lost count at six.' And most of a pack of Marlboro. She could have done with Jane Boyte's Dublin ashtray. She could have filled it.

'The woman you're researching was a very rebellious creature,' Alice Daunt said. 'She was a supporter of the suffragettes from the age when she began to be able to read. She didn't understand the politics, but she could appreciate the gestures. Flinging bricks through windows. Hunger strikes. Sitting down in Whitehall to stop the traffic. That sort of thing excited her.'

Suzanne nodded.

'This isn't my opinion, by the way. It's received opinion. But I received it from my mother, who was a good woman and an impartial judge.'

'Go on.'

'Jane Boyte became disillusioned with the suffragette movement when Christabel Pankhurst started making patriotic speeches at the outbreak of the Great War.'

'She could only have been an adolescent.'

'A disillusioned adolescent. But her next big cause wasn't far away. In 1916, the Easter Rising destroyed a large section of the centre of Dublin. I might add that it did so much to the disgust of the vast majority of the Dublin public. But Miss Boyte had another banner to brandish.'

'She became a Fenian,' Suzanne said.

'Indeed she did. When she was nineteen or twenty, she met Michael Collins. I believe she worked for him. There was talk of an affair, but there always was with that fellow where any woman in his proximity was concerned.'

Suzanne nodded.

'Overcompensating in my view,' Alice Daunt said. 'He was probably trying to cover up his incipient attraction to men.'

'I don't think so,' Suzanne said.

'Oh?'

'Only received opinion, Alice. But received from an impeccable source. He really did prefer girls.'

'Well. Jane Boyte was certainly one of those. I'll give you no argument in that department.'

'Was this allegiance embarrassing for her family?'

'Not really. Certainly not after the conclusion of the war, when it became public knowledge. The Fenian cause would always have had support in and around Liverpool once it gained ground in Dublin. Lot of Catholics of Irish extraction in Liverpool in those days. Even more than now. And Patrick Boyte, Jane's father, was one of those. And Collins always enjoyed personal popularity in England. When his train pulled into London for the treaty negotiations with Churchill, he was practically mobbed.'

Suzanne knew about that. 'What else can you tell me about her, Alice?'

Alice Daunt toyed with her coffee glass. 'Nothing. After Collins' death, after the fratricidal bloodbath of the Irish Civil War, she became disillusioned with all that, too.'

'You hinted yesterday that there was more.'

The old lady shifted in her seat. 'Did I?'

'Yes.'

For a moment, Suzanne did not think that she was going to add to her account. Then she said, almost imperceptibly, 'Don't imagine it can hurt, can it? Not after eighty years, it can't.'

She was talking to herself. It was herself she was trying to convince. She looked at Suzanne and Suzanne knew that her internal effort had succeeded. 'There was some trouble with the police. Jane Boyte made a very serious allegation against a prominent and wealthy foreigner.'

'Harry Spalding.'

Did Alice Daunt shudder at the mention of the name?

'Him. Yes. She made the allegation against him.'

'Do you know the nature of the allegation?'

'I do not. I was a little girl at the time. I was never told. You will have to find that out for yourself.'

'I've tried,' Suzanne said. She gestured back in the direction of the library. 'I've discovered nothing. It all went under the bulldozer, as you said yourself yesterday, when Birkdale library was demolished.'

Alice Daunt drained the last of her coffee. Ice slipped and clacked against her dentures. She lowered the glass. 'There is one other place you might try. There is a museum in Southport, at the Botanic Gardens in Churchtown. If Jane Boyte had things to say, and I'm sure she did, she might have deposited the relevant papers there. It would be worth a try.'

'What happened to her, Alice?'

'She was broken,' Alice said, simply. 'The business with the American broke her completely.'

'You won't say his name, will you?'

And Alice Daunt smiled, tightly. She put on her sunglasses and she picked up her bag. 'I never have, dear. And I shan't as long as I live.'

'We should confront our fears,' Suzanne said.

'My son's name was David. He was a wonderful boy and a wonderful man. And he was wise, despite the effects of the tumour, almost to the very last. But when he said that, my dear, I believe he was referring to our earthly fears.'

Alice smiled a final time and turned and walked away through the flitting sunlight and the shadows of the trees and the shop awnings lining either side of the street. Suzanne watched her stiff, stately progress until her pale coat disappeared in the throng of shoppers and trippers indistinct in the distance. Then she got up and crossed the road and asked about the opening hours of the Botanic Gardens Museum in the tourist office. The tourist office looked like someone's giant conservatory plonked on an empty patch of pavement. But they were very helpful. The girl behind the counter did not know the museum opening hours without having to look, which suggested to Suzanne that it was possibly one of the resort's more obscure attractions. She thought that a good thing. She thought the new, interactive, user-friendly breed of museum both terrible and virtually useless. A repository of the past should be just that, was her opinion. She was provided with a map. The route was north along Lord Street and then east along a lengthy road called Roe Lane. She asked if it was walking distance. The girl screwed her face up, debating this with herself. It was three or four miles. Suzanne decided that she would walk. The exercise would punish her for drinking too much and might cure her hangover at the same time.

Walking to Churchtown, she did not think about Jane Boyte and what she might discover there. She did not think much either about Harry Spalding, or not consciously. She thought about Martin and his love and tenderness and the courage that he had displayed before she had even known him. His bravery she thought remarkable and deeply impressive. She did not think it was a quality of which his father was aware at all.

She had been on an East London Line underground train. She had been to see Brunel's tunnel under the Thames. She had been researching the great engineer for a series about Victorian technologies. She had her laptop with her. Three hoodies burst into the carriage. One of them had been brandishing a knife. It was a large, open-bladed weapon, somewhere between a bowie knife and a machete. It was meant to terrify. It was also meant to hurt. When the thug with the knife made a grab for her laptop, she had stupidly tried to hang on to it. And he had brought the knife down to slash her face.

Martin took the blow. He came out of nowhere and held out his arm to protect her from disfigurement, and the blade was embedded with the force of the blow deep in his forearm. And the thug lost his grip on the weapon as Martin wrenched his arm away and jerked the knife out of the meat of him and sent it skittering along the carriage floor. And then he grinned and inflicted a few blows of his own. He delivered a series of savage punches with incredible accuracy and speed.

He just beat the three of them senseless while the rest of the carriage looked away and pretended that none of this was actually going on.

He saved her from disfigurement. He did it purely on instinct, oblivious to the pain it would cause him or the further physical consequences. When he was released from arrest afterwards and treated, it was discovered that he had severed a tendon. Fighting with a severed tendon in his arm had made the damage worse. It took an operation and four months of physiotherapy to enable full recovery. The scars, from the knife blow and the op, he would always carry.

When she tried to thank him, it was obvious from his reaction that he thought he had done nothing at all remarkable. He thought that everyone, in those circumstances, would behave exactly as he had done. There was a right way and a wrong way to do things and he had done the right thing because, well, that was what you did. It was one of the things she loved about him. It was not the thing about him she loved most, but courage nobly used was a very attractive quality. She had made a joke about it, they both had, knights in armour, damsels in distress and so on. But it was an attractive quality for a man to possess. And she also thought it rare.

Churchtown announced itself in a cluster of tiny cottages, some of them thatched. They were plain as well as small and Suzanne knew that they dated from the early nineteenth century. This was the oldest part of the whole settlement of Southport. Neighbouring places like the hamlet of Hundred End and the village of Ormskirk were much older. They dated back to the first Viking invasion. But Churchtown was as old as anywhere in Southport and so a fitting location for the town's museum. Some of the cottages had been turned into shops of an artsy-craftsy variety. They sold hand-painted children's toys and embroidery kits and watercolours and antiques. The roads were very narrow and the shops were very quaint. But the effect was somewhat spoiled by the huge lorries trundling through in a procession of stinking diesel in the heat. Churchtown seemed to be a traffic rat run.

The Botanic Gardens themselves were quiet and secluded, well away from the sound and smell of traffic. But they did not look spry. Everything seemed mossy and mildewed. There was a lake, green with silt and clogged with floating lily pads, a few ducks besieged on its surface. A wooden bridge arched over the lake. Its paint was peeling and its planks sodden and Suzanne would barely have trusted it to take her weight. The museum was off to the left, occupying a building with a classical portico next to an old conservatory that had been converted into a souvenir gift shop and café. She took in the scene, thinking that nothing she was looking at would have been incongruous fifty years ago or, for that matter, eighty years ago, in 1927. She climbed the steps to the entrance and walked inside.

Most of the ground floor was occupied by a shrimper's cart with its nets extended and a full-sized figure of a shrimper in oilskins staring through sightless glass eyes at a point where the sea and his catch under it would have scurried. There was a Victorian fire appliance and a vintage motorcycle. There was a faithfully reproduced High Victorian parlour. It was all very picturesque and interesting. But there were no books. Suzanne was not encouraged. And there were no staff, either. She could hear a transistor radio very faintly somewhere. But there seemed to be no one about.

She climbed the stairs. The first-floor display comprised two large rooms. One of them was pretty much dedicated to the *Mexico* disaster and its aftermath. The other was full of stuffed wildlife from the Fylde Coast. The taxidermist had done an excellent job. The animals were as lifelike as any dead beast was ever going to be. But Suzanne was starting to feel that Alice Daunt had surely misdirected her to this haphazard assemblage of local relics and curios. She wanted books. Or she wanted microfiche or an easily accessed computer database. She wanted facts and revelations, not dust and elderly pictures.

She followed the tinny sound of the radio. It was playing 'When Love Breaks Down'. Suzanne thought that she had never disliked a song more. But she listened carefully, trying to track its source. It was coming from down below her, from the ground floor. She descended the stairs. The music barely increased in volume. It was being listened to surreptitiously, in a sly near-silence. Gaining the ground floor, she looked around. There was something in the gloom to the right of the Victorian parlour. It was darkness on darkness, an added dimension, the suggestion of a shadow or opening. She walked towards it. The song grew louder without gaining body. It was shrill, exactly the sort of sound reproduced by a pocket radio from the 1960s or 1970s. Suzanne thought that no pleasure could be gained from listening to this starved melody. With a song you liked, it would be even worse.

It was a sort of cupboard without a door. Her eyes adjusted and she saw a figure sitting there. He looked up at her and jumped. He was wearing a liveried sweater, uniform trousers. He was the museum staff. And if he wasn't on his break, he was skiving. He switched off the radio.

'Can I help you?' He stood, finger-combing his hair, clearly caught out and embarrassed.

'I'm researching a Southport resident called Jayne Boyte.' Suzanne took out her BBC accreditation and showed it to the man.

'People generally make an appointment. I mean, they email us or telephone ahead, unless they're just casual visitors.'

'I'm not a casual visitor, as you can see. But I'm not from

Southport, obviously. I wasn't previously aware of the existence of this museum, of this resource.'

The man had recovered from her ambush. He seemed to like the flattery implicit in his place of work being termed a resource by someone with a laminated pass. Work avoidance, Suzanne thought, looking down at the radio where it sat on his bench. It was silver and rectangular and held together in one corner by adhesive tape.

'Essentially, we have two separate archives,' the man said. 'The photographic archive is catalogued both by date and by subject matter. The written archive is not catalogued at all. We did have an archivist scheduled to put it all in some kind of order about three and a half years ago. But budget cuts put paid to that.'

Suzanne nodded. It was a familiar complaint.

'You're more than welcome to have a look. It's all on shelves, roughly alphabetically listed by author, in a room in our basement.' He began to search for a key from a bunch attached to a key ring on his belt. 'You have to come with me around to the back of the building to gain access to it. It's through a door at the rear and down a set of steps. Do you have a mobile phone?'

'Yes.'

'Then put my number in it. I will have to lock the door behind you. It's nothing personal, but we have to do it as a security measure. It's one of our rules.'

'Fine,' Suzanne said.

He shuffled past her and began to lead the way. 'I hope you don't have any allergies.'

'What?'

'Specifically, I hope you're not allergic to dust.'

Suzanne expected mildew. She expected splotched pages and books with gummy spines. But there was a dehumidifier purring away in the corner when the museum worker switched on the overhead lights in the subterranean room. Everything looked dry and comparatively clean and well ordered. The shelves were neatly stacked. The lights cast a brilliant flare of white brightness. They revealed her guide's glasses as bifocals and gave his eyes an avaricious gleam. She realised that the remark about dust had been his little joke.

'Good luck.'

'Thank you.'

'We close at five. Appreciate it if you could summon me to come and get you by a quarter to, at the latest.'

Suzanne looked at her watch. It was just approaching one. She had not eaten breakfast, but this was one day when lunch could wait. The walk along Roe Lane to Churchtown had been just the thing, she realised now, for her hangover. All trace of it was gone. She felt alert and fresh. And she was excited at the nature of the archive that clearly resided here, well maintained but scarcely ever used. There might be secrets here, committed to paper by Jane Boyte before her rebel instinct was destroyed. As she heard the key turning to lock the basement door, Suzanne had Jane pictured in her mind on the sand in the sunshine, wearing her flying leathers, feline and gorgeous with her bobbed hair raven black and her smile full of life and mischief between the brothers Giroud.

She found what she was looking for within fifteen minutes. The Dáil delegation press picture had led her to expect something typed rather than handwritten. And it was typed, double-spaced across eighty pages which had then been professionally bound. The binding was blue canvas-backed board and it had faded with the years from what Suzanne had imagined was cobalt to something much paler. There was nothing on the cover to tell you what you were reading. But on the volume's slim spine were printed the words: *Jane Elizabeth Boyte. My Deposition. August 12, 1927.*

There was a desk in the corner of the museum basement.

Suzanne went over to it and pulled up its chair and sat. She had no protective gloves with her to shield the pages of the deposition from damaging secretions. But she had the strong instinct that she was the first person in eighty years to open what she held between her hands. And she thought that it would survive the experience. She opened the volume and flicked through the leaves with her thumb. They were thicker than flimsy, thicker than foolscap. They were somewhere between foolscap and cartridge paper and would have been stiff in the roller of Jane's Royal or Remington machine. The letters forming the words were even in their depth of ink and the impression left by the individual keys on the page. Jane Boyte had been an expert typist, fast and confident and clean. There were no mistakes at all. Her deposition was, Suzanne could see from the dates at the top of each entry, strictly speaking, a diary. At least, it was a chronological account. It ran from May 10 to August 8. And it concerned itself only with the days and weeks and months in between those two dates during the single year of 1927.

Jane's entire deposition had been written during Harry Spalding's Southport summer.

There was an introduction. Jane had signed it with a fountain pen, writing her full name. There was a curious, sombre formality about the whole vintage exercise. There were secrets here, Suzanne was sure. She lifted the document and held it to her nose. It smelled very faintly of ancient tobacco and expensive scent. Suzanne was pretty sure the perfume Jane had worn at that time was Shalimar. She had been a proto-feminist, a privileged revolutionary who flew an aeroplane and smoked cigarettes in public. She had been bright. She had been a celebrated beauty. When she was nineteen or twenty, she might have shared Michael Collins' bed.

Suzanne read the introduction.

Every word of what is written here was written in sincerity. You, reader, can draw your own conclusions as to its veracity. But there was no revision, no tinkering or retrospective editing of the account. I have described events as they occurred. My conclusions have been based on compelling evidence. That evidence is circumstantial, but when you have read what is contained here, you might agree that this unfortunate fact was not for the want of me trying to effect its reversal. And I really did try. But wealth is a more compelling imperative than truth, even in our modern times. And the weight of a woman's opinion and justified suspicions are still not accorded that of a man's. I am given to wonder if they ever will be.

When you have read this, you might justifiably wonder about the writer. What can I honestly tell you? I am impressionable and impulsive. My morals might not sit very easily with you. I am comfortably off. I possess independence of spirit and was, until recently, generally a stranger to fear. I have known real and thrilling greatness in a human being. And I knew that human intimately and the knowledge did not impair or diminish in any way the impression of that greatness.

But, reader, I have also known the Devil himself. And it is with this encounter that the following account is concerned.

Suzanne rang the number given her by the skiving museum staff member. She did not want to read Jane's deposition in that barren, white-lit, book-infested room. She had followed her intuition to Southport in the absence of hard information about Harry Spalding and his blighted boat. She felt vindicated now. But she wanted to read what she had discovered in the space and at the time of her choosing. There was urgency here. But she felt she would glean more from the deposition away from where she had discovered it. She would take it, if she was permitted to, and read it at one of the tables outside the Fisherman's Rest. There was no doubt in her mind about the identity of the devil to whom Jane referred. The Fisherman's Rest had been an adjunct to the long-demolished Palace Hotel. And it was only a few hundred yards from the mansion hidden on Rotten Row where Jane's devil had lived. She would read her deposition there, as afternoon turned to evening, as close to the memory and spoor of Harry Spalding as she was able to get.

'Hello?'

'I've found what I came here for.'

His radio was on again. Coldplay were feeble, almost anorexic in the background. He was hiding in his cupboard. 'Congratulations.'

'Could I take it away with me?'

There was a pause. 'Absolutely not.'

'Why?'

'Intrinsic value.' The Southport accent had a flat quality. It wasn't nasal, like Mancunian. And it was slower and more deliberate than Liverpudlian. Words delivered in it had a finality about them. But Suzanne was not intimidated. 'This isn't Magna Carta we're talking about here.'

'Then photocopy it.'

'Not the same. Twenty-four hours?'

But the museum skiver was entrenched. 'No.'

'I'll leave you a deposit. Fifty quid. Non-returnable. Twenty-four hours.'

There was a pause. 'More than my job's worth.'

Suzanne thought the pause significant. 'A hundred?'

'Done.'

She left the Botanic Gardens museum with Jane Boyte's deposition in her bag. On her way back to Roe Lane through Churchtown she stopped at a picturesque pub with tables outside called the Hesketh Arms. She did not read. She ate. It was after two thirty now and she was very hungry. The sun was warm on the weathered surface of the table she sat at. Ivy grew green and verdant on the white walls of the pub. Flowers in window boxes filled with freshly watered soil smelled sweet and fragrant. She ordered a cheese salad and it was very good: fresh, crusty bread and crumbly Lancashire cheese and plump tomatoes freshly picked from the greenhouses outside the town at one of the farms on the South Lancashire plain. The scene would have been idyllic, were it not for the lorries trundling by, their emissions rippling in the summer light, distorting the view.

Suzanne walked back the way she had come. They did not have taxis you could hail in Southport. They had mini-cabs. And there were plenty of those, but none stopped for her when Suzanne had tried in the preceding days to hail them. They stopped at designated ranks to pick up fares, she supposed. But she did not know where any of the ranks were located. Or you could ring them. But she did not know the numbers. They would have put her right on that score in the Hesketh Arms, of course. But the weather was lovely and the unfamiliar streets were picturesque and totally different from what she was used to. Southport was largely Victorian and very largely, in terms of its domestic architecture, still intact. She was enjoying the exercise. She was enjoying the anticipation. And so she walked.

It was almost four when she reached the point on Rotten Row where she knew Spalding's mansion lurked above the rise. She looked at her bag. Jane's deposition wore the protection of a large padded envelope. The fellow in the museum had provided it, to keep the covers of the volume from the sun. It was his overdue bid at professionalism and conscientiousness, his tardy attempt to be seen as competent. Suzanne was very keen to examine the contents of the envelope. But the lure of the house over the steep grass slope was inexplicably strong. She wanted another look. She wanted just a peek at the place. She did not see how, in the bright sunshine, with schoolgirls passing on the way to the cement courts in Victoria Park with their tennis rackets swinging from their hands, it could hurt just to sneak another look.

This time she was more brazen about it. She climbed the stone steps with their smooth inlay of terracotta tiles. She unlatched the wooden gate at the top, took a breath and walked through into the garden. And it hit her immediately. It hit her like an arctic shift in the weather or a solid punch to the gut. Everything was different here and none of it was right. She began to shiver and sweat at the same time, chilled but clammy at the forehead and temples. The feeling got worse with every footstep she extended towards the house. She was surrounded by a silence that her deep foreboding insisted would be torn asunder any moment by a scream she knew she would share. And she recognised this feeling. She remembered it. It was the selfsame instinct of terror she had felt in Duval's barn, before she reached the barn door and Duval himself confronted her, comforting in his surly rudeness, safe wielding his shotgun, after the other-worldly hazards of the barn interior.

What had he done here? She turned round. She had to. She could not will herself to take another step. The ground felt corrupt under her feet. The taint of death hung like a pallor above the earth. She ran for the gate and escape, and descended the brick steps back to sanity, back to smiling pedestrians, a clopping bunch of riders, back to cars in the sunshine driving slowly along Rotten Row, giving the horses a wide berth as they edged past them in the safe and pleasant hope and colour of a lovely June afternoon.

Aboard Dark Echo

It seems that the writing habit is a hard one to lose. Though I am writing this in longhand in one of the handsome morocco-bound volumes my father intended to have serve aboard the vessel as his log. My laptop battery has failed. Since we have no electrical power aboard any more, I write by the light of a paraffin lamp. And the instrument in my hand is my father's fountain pen. The master of the *Andromeda* himself could not better me at this moment for simplicity or tradition. But Captain Straub would not be proud of me. He passed on a warning that I should have heeded but chose to ignore. I was no longer strictly under his command when he delivered the warning. But I should have listened to him. He would be disappointed to know my predicament now. And he would be right in thinking that I have only myself to blame for it.

I am in my cabin, writing this seated at my desk behind the locked cabin door. My father lies unconscious on my bunk. Occasionally, things slither past along the gangway outside. Or at least, they sound as if they do. There is the growl of a dog or the whimper of a child. More rarely, and the more shocking for it, there is the sudden loud scream of a woman hysterical with terror. That sound comes from my father's cabin, which is really Spalding's cabin, of course. There is often laughter, but it is dark. There is whispered pleading, which is met by silence. And there are scents. These are more varied than the noises. Sometimes they are pungent and sometimes subtle. Sometimes it is a hint of perfume, Arpège or Mitsouko, florid and heavy. Sometimes it is the whiff of strong tobacco. Sometimes the treacle aroma of rum is in the air. On occasion I've smelled cordite, sharp and strong as though from the barrel or firing chamber of a gun just discharged in close proximity. There is often the coppery odour of blood, freshly spilled. There is the sour secretion of fear. Worst of all, there is now and then the overwhelming stench of mortal decay that radiates from the self-murdered corpse of Gubby Tench as his remains stew in the heat of Havana Bay.

They are the boat's memories, these various and randomly occurring sounds and smells. And they are growing in strength and vividness as we approach our meeting with its one true master. Harry Spalding haunts the boat. But he does this in a paradoxical way. For I believe Spalding haunts the *Dark Echo* without really being a ghost at all.

Suzanne encountered a ghost, I remember, in Dublin back in January. Her ghost was benign. I suspect she encountered him again and never let on to me about the fact. Her ghost, in life, had an eye for the ladies. She was looking pretty hard at him, back then. He probably considered he had the justification to take a look right back at her. Whether she sensed him again or not, he meant no harm. And being dead, he could do no harm, either. I don't believe a dead man can physically hurt the living.

Nothing about Spalding was ever benign. I had pondered on this after my efforts to send my account of events to Monsignor Delaunay, as my father got steadily drunker and the boat shifted under me as it continues to do now on its own relentless course. He had used his occult knowledge to keep death at bay in the war. He had practised barbaric and blasphemous rituals to guarantee his survival. He had sacrificed and kept on sacrificing. I suspected that the woman who supposedly dumped him on the quay at Rimini had been the first of his peacetime offerings. But Tench and the Waltrow brothers had been sacrifices, too, hadn't they? Another had been made only recently, in the man who bled to death following that impossible accident in Frank Hadley's yard. Between Gubby Tench and Hadley's man, I suspected that the lost log of the *Dark Echo* would have documented a lot more deaths down the years and decades. But Spalding had ended his own life in 1929. Why did a man, long since deceased, need to go on paying the Devil the price of immortality? There was no reason. He did not need to do so. So what was the obvious conclusion? My own logic impelled me to believe that Spalding had never died at all.

The 'Send' light was still flashing feebly on my computer screen. Providence would determine whether Delaunay ever got my emailed testament. It was beyond my fingertips now, in cyberspace, out of my hands. I got up and went to confront my father. I wanted to ask him about the log. He once said he had read it. I'd thought the claim blithely made and untrue, just something said to shut me up when, at Hadley's yard, the *Dark Echo* really had seemed cursed. But it was possible he had actually read it. He was a voracious reader and an intellectually curious man and the boat had been his coveted prize.

But when I got to him he was beyond interrogation. He was stretched unconscious on the floor. At first, I feared he had suffered a stroke. But his features wore their familiar symmetry and there was nothing rigid in his posture, lying there. His breathing was ponderous but steady. I bent to listen to his heart and it was regular and strong. The sounds aboard of infant crying had tormented him, as perhaps they were supposed to do. I knew with dull certainty in my own heart it was not my sister but some infant victim of the boat's bloody history. My father, though, had believed it was Catherine Ann, come back to chastise him for some sin he had never committed.

My father had now taken to the refuge aboard the *Dark*

Echo of deep shock. I was on my own. I gathered him in my arms and carried him to my cabin and put him in my bunk. I kissed him on the cheek and brought the blanket snugly to his chin. I smoothed down his dishevelled hair to restore some dignity to my dad. I said a prayer for him. Locking the door behind me, I returned to the master cabin. The machine that played the wax cylinders looked like it had when I'd brought it out of its rotting box. It looked like it would never play again. I took the cylinder we had listened to from the cradle bevelled for it and put another in. It stank and slipped between my fingers with greasy decay.

'Why did you fake your suicide?'

The needle dropped on to the cylinder and the cylinder began to turn.

'You'll call me captain,' Spalding's voice commanded, 'or you'll call me sir. I will not suffer insubordination, sport. You will learn this to your cost.'

'Why, sir, did you fake your suicide?'

There was a long silence. I could hear the sludgy moan of the needle on the wax. What I was hearing defied the laws of physics. But Harry Spalding had engineered his own bleak path through the rational world. He had harnessed magic to do it.

'My parents followed a faith frowned upon by the land of the brave and the home of the free. Our faith was persecuted, outlawed. A Federal Bureau man called Grey oversaw the destruction of our place of worship. My parents prayed for revenge.'

To whom, I wondered. But I knew the answer.

'Grey had a daughter. She had aspirations to be a dancer. I courted her. I wooed her, Martin, old chum. I took her to Europe cherishing dreams of the stage and ovations and garlands. And I butchered her with a boning knife and dropped her corpse in weighted pieces in the harbour at Rimini.'

'And her father found out.'

'Her father was dead by then. But he had buddied up for years with a loyal and dogged partner in the Bureau by the name of Gianfranco Genelli. Genelli's entire family were Sicilian hoods. He was the white sheep of the flock. But he kept on good terms with people on both sides of the law. Things became a little hot for old Harry Spalding in the years after Rimini. Harry moved around, but Genelli's people were only ever a step behind. It rather cramped my style. Eventually and somewhat flamboyantly, Harry was obliged to say adieu.'

Which was not a hard thing to accomplish, I supposed, in the New York of 1929. Not for a man as stupendously wealthy as Spalding had been. Not after the Crash, when it must have seemed as though the Great Depression would just go on deepening for ever.

'So you got away with it.'

'With what?'

'With her murder.'

'I get away with everything.'

'Where are you now, Spalding?'

'You'll find out soon enough, sport. And you will call me captain or you will call me sir. I sparred with Hemingway, you know. And I bested Hem. I drank Scott Fitzgerald under the table.'

'And you offered Bricktop a hundred grand to sleep with you and she turned you down, you fucking creep.'

There was a groaning, smudgy silence. Then, 'I'll see you soon, shipmate. I'm looking forward to it.'

My bravado was exactly that. I retreated to the dim, troubled refuge of my cabin and my ailing dad. Nothing will happen aboard the boat. Nothing will happen until we reach land. We are in no real danger until then. When we reach land, we will be in the proximity of Harry Spalding, who has never died. He will come aboard and take command. We will embark upon our real voyage. The *Dark Echo* will begin to fulfil its real purpose. And what will happen then does not bear further speculation.

Eleven

Southport, May 10th, 1927

I am to meet him after all. The Rimmers are holding a garden party and I accepted my invitation ages ago, and this morning I discovered that the man everyone refers to as Jane's obnoxious American is also on the list of invited guests. Tommy Rimmer, who was very apologetic on the telephone this morning about it all, does not think that he will attend. He has, apparently, a reputation for not turning up to things. It's something he probably cultivates, a kind of unpredictability designed to make him appear interesting rather than merely uncouth. But I think he will turn up. I have thought a meeting with him inevitable ever since his battered racing schooner limped into Liverpool Harbour and my father's yard. He does not know about me. It was a ghastly coincidence, the fact that his boat fetched up for repair where it did. My father has had no reason, I'm sure, to mention me to him and I have every reason for never mentioning him to my father.

I will have to go to the Rimmers. It would be rude, now, not to go. And I will not have my life dictated to me by any man. This one in particular I will not allow to force me to act out of fear. Do I fear him? I suppose I do. Even after eight years of added experience and maturity and the resilience those elements bring to a person's character, I still do fear Harry Spalding. But it would be absurd for me to miss the Rimmers' party on his account.

Perhaps he will not remember me. I will not remind him if my face and name have slipped from his memory. I have always confronted my terrors, but this one is different. Where he is concerned, if he has forgotten me, I will be pragmatic. In the words of a saying expressing a sentiment I would ordinarily loathe, I will, just this once, let discretion be the better part of valour.

But he won't have forgotten me. What would be the point of us meeting if he had? I've already said I believe this confrontation has the inevitability of fate about it. Of course he will remember me. I just hope he has matured enough to feel the shame and remorse that seemed to elude him in the aftermath back then.

Harry Spalding tried to rape me. He forced the door of my room at the Shelbourne Hotel and attempted to take me by force. I fought back, but he was enormously strong for so slightly built a man. He seemed inconceivably strong. Perhaps it was the strength of a madman. I was changing for dinner when he burst in. He tore my dress off and flung me across the bed and pinned my arms. I bit him hard enough to draw blood. But he seemed encouraged by that. I must have been screaming. Boland came into the room with a pistol. He put the point of the pistol under Spalding's chin and told him very calmly that he would blow his head off if he did not release me. I swear the grin never left Spalding's face. It was a rictus, death's head grin that stretched his features grotesquely. He moved back from the bed, but Boland kept the gun on him. He did not look safe. As I have said already, he did not look sane.

Mick Collins came in. He must have heard the commotion. He took off his coat and put it over me and asked me was I alright. He asked Boland to take me to his room and to book me another. You can't stay in this one, he said. I heard the first blows land as Boland closed the door on the room. Mick Collins was a powerful figure in the peak of condition then and every ounce of his reputation as a fighting man had been earned. I thought he would beat Spalding to a pulp. I hoped he would. But he did not. After I had been brought brandy in Mick's room by Boland, Mick himself came in. He went into the bathroom and ran the tap until the water could only have been scalding and I heard him wash scrupulously. When he emerged, his hands were bruised, the knuckles visibly swelling. And one of his eyes was marked.

I caught a glimpse of Spalding later, leaving the hotel between two of Mick's men. And his lip was cut and his face was swollen and carried contusions. But they were healing already. A half-smile played under the congealing gash on his upper lip.

I'd easier have beaten Lucifer himself, Mick said, helping himself to a brandy from the bottle Boland had fetched. Maybe I should just have him shot, he said.

You'll shoot no one on my account, I said.

Cause a stink with the rest of the Yanks, Boland said.

The rest of them are decent men, Mick said.

You will shoot no one on my account, I repeated.

Then we'll have that scum on the first boat out of Dublin. Boland here will make the call. Mick put down his glass and came over to me. I still wore his coat, the smell of him on the collar a comfort as I tried to stop trembling. He smiled and stroked my cheek. The touch of his sore hand was infinitely tender.

And that was the end of it. And I did not really think about Harry Spalding again. I did not think about him until his boat struggled listing up the Mersey and I read the story of the storm in the newspapers.

May 12th, 1927

The Rimmers host their party tonight. Their house is one of the grandest on Westbourne Road. It overlooks the golf links, which is where Tommy and my obnoxious American met. I am slightly surprised that the party is going ahead as planned. But this is nothing to do with Spalding. A chambermaid has vanished from the Palace Hotel. The same girl worked for the Rimmers for a while, helping Nora Rimmer look after their youngest daughter until Bonnie started school. She left because she wanted the variety, she said, of hotel work. And her departure was cordial enough. But she worked for the Rimmers for almost a year. And the police say in the papers that they suspect foul play. And Bonnie was really very fond of her. It seems slightly callous to hold the party until there's word of the girl turning up safe. But maybe that's just me and what Tommy Rimmer would call my Fabian pretensions. Fabian or Socialist. I don't think men like Tommy are aware of any distinction. When a man lives only to see his handicap get down to scratch, his mind can't help but suffer from the consequent neglect.

May 13th, 1927

The party passed without incident. At least, it did so far as the obnoxious American was concerned. Spalding had greatly changed. He is no longer the scrawny fellow in pinstripes of Dublin in 1919. He is the international playboy and yacht-racing sportsman now. He is very tanned and has filled out physically. There is no fat on him. But he is muscular, I suppose from all that raising of sail and hauling of anchor. His blond hair has been so bleached by exposure to the sun and salt water it is almost white. He was dressed impeccably, with pearl studs embellishing his collar and cuffs. I do not think I have ever been in the proximity of a more deeply unattractive man.

He did not recognise me. Or if he did, he did not successfully place me in his mind. No one is that accomplished an actor and his manner was relaxed and expansive throughout the evening. He held forth about the Paris scene before an audience of Southport's self-styled bohemians. I could hear enough on its periphery. He has this harsh tone to his voice and New England vowels that carry on the summer air through the hubbub, whether in a room or outside. He knows Hemingway and Scott Fitzgerald. He knows Braque and Picasso and Delaunay. Anyway, he says he does. His world when on dry land seems to be the world of Bricktop's nightclub and the racetrack at Auteuil and ringside seats at Montparnasse for the boxing matches fought by Georges Carpentier. It all begs the question, what is he doing here? But of course, he is here more by accident than design. And with the aero club and the golf at Birkdale and racing at Aintree there is enough to keep him temporarily entertained while my father's men toil to fix his boat by that rash deadline Father gave the press.

He likes Dublin, too. He speaks fondly of Ireland. I would have thought his treatment at the hands of Mick Collins and Harry Boland at the Shelbourne Hotel would have ended any nascent love affair with the ould sod, as he calls it. But Mick and Boland are long dead now, distinguished footnotes both in the bloody saga of Irish political history. But only footnotes, when you subtract the sentiment. So perhaps Spalding has had the last laugh and can afford a bit of magnanimity where Ireland generally and Dublin in particular are concerned.

I don't think my estimation of Spalding as repulsive is widely shared. He is rich and strange and athletic and worldly. And that is enough of a cocktail of attractions for many women. It was not only the bohemian crowd surrounding him in the hope of titbits of gossip from the table of the artistic greats. Several of the unattached women drifted into his orbit during the course of the party. But despite his presence, it was generally all very pleasant. The weather was glorious, the food wonderful and Tommy Rimmer on outrageous form. Spalding was only one among over a hundred guests at the Rimmers' place. There was a jazz band. Orchid and rose petals had been strewn like a glorious carpet over the surface of the swimming pool. Iced bowls were piled on the tables with gleaming mounds of caviar, and two professionals from London played an exhibition game on the tennis court and then coached any of the more competitive guests on how to improve their strokes. Though there was one unfortunate incident I shall recount that spoiled things slightly for myself, at least.

Tommy Rimmer has a happy knack for making money. He discovered this during the war, in which he served as a lowly second-lieutenant. They put him in supplies, because he has a flair for detail and a slight congenital weakness of the heart. He was invalided out, after a German bombardment that must have gone astray. Instead of hitting front-line troop positions, the shells detonated in Tommy's supply dump. He recovered. But in his time in the field hospital and then the proper French hospital to which they sent him for convelescence, he worked out in his mind a more efficient approach to the logistics of war supply than the chaotic model he had been obliged to follow.

He was not so stupid as to try to apply this to the conflict that had almost cost him his life. But, decommissioned after the armistice, he was able to persuade a War Ministry panel to listen to his conclusions. They were impressed enough to take him on as an adviser on the procurement of war material. Tommy's reward was to be a shilling for every pound he was proved to have saved. The contract signed, he set about making himself a very wealthy man.

Tommy Rimmer's politics are a mystery to me. I think they are to him. And I'm sure they are to Nora, the wife whom he adores. But the one area in which he has been very liberal is the raising of his children. They have the run of the house. The doctrine of children being seen but not heard seems anathema to the Rimmers.

Or it did until today.

It was a garden party. So, of course, the children were there. But darkness comes late to Southport in May. It was still light at nine o'clock, when the three Rimmer children were all ushered up to their various cots and cribs and beds. By then they were exhausted, I think. Parents, mindful of their own children, make a sentimental fuss of the children of their friends. It's a cherished instinct. It is one of the things that makes us human. In my guise of Auntie Jane, I gave each of them a kiss myself before they trooped off, tired and obedient, to the land of nod.

Except that Bonnie came back. I heard rather than saw her return at first, as the conversation subsided with her unsteady progress through the Rimmers' garden. Then I saw her. Everybody did. The entire gathering turned with their drinks and cigarettes and cigars in hand and, much less than sober, saw this small child sway on unsteady feet through the throng. All was silent. Bonnie raised an arm and turned. Except that she did not so much turn, as *swivel*. And she pointed. And she let out a scream that would have curdled sleeping blood.

She swooned afterwards. And her father scooped her into his loving arms and took her off to bed. And such was the momentum of the party that it continued on, despite the poor child's sleepwalking fit. But my appetite for revelling, poor already because of Spalding's presence, was killed entirely by the moment. I tried to talk to one of the brothers Giroud, excited about the great oval lido about to open on the Southport foreshore. Having overflown the last of the workings, the placement of the plunge slide and the high diving boards, he described it as *magnifique*. But my enthusiasm for gossip and sensation was entirely gone. I said my goodbyes and gained the happy refuge of the car Father had provided for my journey home. I was not drunk. I could have driven my own car. I could have walked, the Rimmers' house being only a mile or so from my flat. But it would have been foolhardy to plan to walk home from the party without first knowing how Harry Spalding would react to my presence.

When Bonnie screamed, I looked at Spalding. And I saw that he was looking back at me. His expression was impossible to read. There was nothing obvious, no salaciousness or overt curiosity about the look. But it was as though he were blind and deaf to the odd distress of the little girl. And then a woman in a brightly feathered stole approached him and he was all smiles and solicitous charm with her and seemed to forget entirely about me.

It was very foolish of me to mention to anyone that I had ever met this man. I did so casually, after reading of the storm and his survival in the newspaper. I did not explain the circumstances, merely saying that we had shared an unpleasant encounter in Dublin. But I should have kept the matter a secret to myself. Under the urbane talk of Hemingway and Picasso, I think Harry Spalding is a cold and dangerous man. Polishing enhances the facets of the stone, brings a bright glitter to its surface. It does not reduce its hardness or change its fundamental nature. What I wish is that I had let Mick Collins have him shot. What I really wish is that I had taken Boland's pistol and blown his brains out myself.

Suzanne looked up from the pages she was reading and blinked at the sky. The light was fading. The evening would be long, but the heat and intensity had gone out of the day. It was six o'clock. Already, she liked Jane Boyte very much. And she felt very sorry for her. She had not even had the consolation of seeing Michael Collins' reputation restored, his achievement recognised. They had been relatively recent developments. Self-serving Irish politicians resentful of their place in his shadow had undermined Collins' character and deeds for decades after his death. In 1971, when Jane Boyte had died, he had still been the footnote in Irish history she had described him as in 1927. There had been no consolation in her grief.

Suzanne slid the deposition across the table, opened her bag and took out her Marlboro pack and lit a cigarette. She was too fastidious to breathe smoke over the precious pages. She would wait to read on until she had finished. She sipped her drink. She was the only customer outside the haunted pub. There were but three or four inside. Off across the tarmac to her right, there was a concrete barbecue pit veined by rust stains. Clearly it rained here sometimes. But she had been very lucky with the weather. She looked out over the area where the Palace Hotel had been, vast and imperious in its high gables and princely turrets. There was nothing of it now, no sense that it had ever been there at all, with its ghostly lifts and glittering guests and sad little litany of deaths still awaiting proper explanation.

To her rear, a hundred yards or so away on the other side of Weld Road, Rotten Row began. And the sense of Spalding's house and lurking presence there was contrastingly strong, a cold prickle of the flesh between her shoulder blades, an itch she could not scratch. She ground out her cigarette in the ashtray and exhaled at the sky, slightly dismayed at how wonderful the tobacco had tasted.

May 26th, 1927

A group of us went to the open-air bathing pool for the first time today. The queue for the twin turnstiles stretched and wound in a gaudy, excited procession. I thought it would take ages to clear, but it did not and we were in after a wait of only ten minutes or so. The pool really is immense, a great oval lake of seawater surrounded by landscaped rocks and seats rising as they would in an ampitheatre. On the side to seaward there is a huge domed cafeteria with a great glass globe of the world at its summit. I saw it from the air, overflying it a week ago. But the whole place is much grander and more spectacular from the ground. The changing suites, at either end, are pillared and gabled like temples. It made me proud of the town. Civic pride is a novelty to me, something I would have dismissed as a bourgeois conceit a decade ago. But I have grown up somewhat since then. And this magnificent amenity is open to anyone who can pay the modest entry fee. With its high diving boards and steepling metal slide, it is a wonderful place. People deserve it.

Even seeing Harry Spalding there could not much diminish my enthusiasm. I saw him on his haunches in his bathing costume, rubbing oil into the back of a companion I recognised as the woman in the feather stole from the Rimmers' party. He was wearing sunglasses and his tan has deepened even further. He is extraordinarily muscular and, in the harsh sunshine, his dark body reminded me with a shudder of the carapace of some large and deadly creature. There is something of the crab or the praying mantis about him.

I went to the pool with Helen Sykes and Vera Chadwick. Helen vaguely knows the Ormskirk girl who went missing a week ago. Vera is courting a police inspector who works with the murder squad in Liverpool. As if having a romantic liaison with a police officer isn't bad enough in itself, Vera is full of the phraseology of crime and investigation. She told Helen, with me a reluctant audience, that the police are linking this latest disappearance with that of the Palace Hotel girl. I suppose it was fair enough for them to discuss this subject, since Helen has an interest and Vera seems to have the inside line. But it did seem grim stuff in the circumstances, surrounded by languid sunbathers and with the squeal of delighted children splashing down the water slide shrill in our ears.

I smoked a cigarette and tried not to listen. I watched the divers in their acrobatic grace, gathering for a leap and then launching from the springboard, showing off to their sweethearts. Then I saw Spalding in the line in a blue rubber cap the same sudden colour as his eyes. He executed a perfect jackknife and entered the water so cleanly he left barely a ripple on the surface. And I thought that the man should by rights be dead at the bottom of a Dublin dock and not sullying our bright little town with his dark presence.

The town doesn't mind him, of course. The town has welcomed him and his style and extravagance with open arms. It is only my spirits that his presence here darkens.

You can bet there are more than two, Vera was telling Helen. That is what her detective has told her. If two disappearances have been reported, there will be others that people have tried to explain away without raising public alarm.

What does he think the motive is, Helen asked her.

Sexual, Vera said, flatly. But she had lowered her voice.

I was contemplating a swim. Instead, I lit another cigarette. The girl who worked for the Rimmers was far from beautiful. And the picture in the paper of the Ormskirk girl showed her to be bland-looking and overweight. They did not seem to me the sort of women a sexual predator would obviously seek out. I looked around me. My immediate conclusion was that attractive and shapely would-be abduction victims are plentiful in this part of the country. It wasn't a charitable thought and there would have been a time when I would have regarded even thinking it as a betrayal of the sisterhood. But contemplation of lethal acts of crime requires clear thinking, not blind loyalty to one's gender. There are many more tempting targets than those two would have been. Perhaps the Palace chambermaid simply upped sticks and spent her savings on a ticket aboard a steamer to America. Women are capable of independent thought. She was a somewhat restless girl with an impulse for action and change.

That still leaves the Ormskirk girl, of course.

I went for a swim. The depths of the pool were deliciously cold in the heat of the day. I swam five lengths. It is only yet spring, but we are in the grip of a heatwave. After my lengths I floated with my eyes closed against the sun and my hair floating in fronds like seaweed as the water lapped about my head. I hope that the missing girls are safe. I hope that Vera's detective is given to lurid exaggeration in the cause only of impressing her. But I doubt it.

Afterwards we walked back and along the promenade to the end of the pier. I am always amazed at the number of crippled men and amputees one sees out when the weather is warm. Almost ten years after its conclusion, the casualties of the war are still very much among us, living their diminished lives in pain and poverty in the land they were promised would be fit for heroes on their return. I stopped to give a man with a begging bowl half a crown. Blinded by gas, the sign around his neck said, and he wore a ragged, filthy blindfold to hide the disfigurement of his eyes. He was genuine, too. Some scoundrels beg, but I heard the wheeze and rattle of his liquefied lungs when I bent to put the money in his bowl. My half-crown joined a tarnished threepenny bit. I paused and took a guinea from my purse and pressed it into his grateful palm and he blessed me for the gift and then raised a salute.

He'll spend it on drink, Vera Chadwick said. Her courtship with the murder detective has made her hard, I think, bled out of her the compassion that originally made her so attractive to me as a friend.

I hope he does, I said.

And Helen Sykes laughed.

I hope he finds happy oblivion for a night at my expense, I said. We should be humbled at the bravery and sacrifice of men like him.

I thought you were a Fenian, Vera said. But I did not reply to that. Perhaps she has discussed her Fenian friend with her policeman sweetheart. I want no trouble to embarrass my father. My heart went out of rebel politics when Mick Collins was killed. Before that, to tell the truth, with the senseless killing of the civil war even before it claimed his life.

At the end of the pier, there was a Punch and Judy show. It is the one seaside and fairground entertainment I detest. The violence of a man against a woman, even caricatured, is not to my mind a fit subject for humour. Nothing is funny about Punch cudgelling his shrew of a wife. It is comedy from a more robust time, I suppose. But it is crude and cruel. Punch beats Judy because she is ugly. I watched him do so, feeling a pang of guilt about my own thoughts earlier regarding the looks of the missing women.

There was a Pierrot show. And there was a brass band sweltering in their thick serge uniforms as they blew through the mouthpieces of their burnished instruments. Some of the players were very young, a couple no more than fourteen or fifteen years old. At the interval, Vera Chadwick bought ices for the band's child players and congratulated them on their musical prowess. And I liked her again, recognising my friend happily returned in her pretty smile and thoughtfulness.

Afterwards we went for cocktails at the Prince of Wales Hotel. We were not really dressed for the restaurant, but took a balcony table in the cocktail bar and had sandwiches and fruit served there. We were all three of us famished after the swim and long exposure to the sun. I have a strong head for drink but was quite light-headed after two pink gins.

Ballast is what you need, girl, Helen Sykes said, ordering a bowl of pistachio nuts and some salted crackers.

Mention of ballast made me uneasy. And then I realised why. Her image of things nautical brought thoughts of my father's boatyard and his race to have Spalding's schooner repaired by his own impossible deadline. That deadline seems more than ever impossible now. Two men were seriously injured aboard the *Dark Echo* yesterday. They were proofing a section of the keel with some sort of varnish or protective paint that should not be used in confined spaces. They were doing so under an open hatch that slammed shut and somehow jammed. The heat apparently made the toxic effects of the stuff they were using worse. Father said it was sweltering on the dock, ninety degrees in the open air and more in the vessel's hold. The more fortunate of the two has badly blistered skin. He is burned and scarred. The other man is unconscious in a bed in Liverpool infirmary and is not expected to recover.

Helen and Vera tried to tease me about the money I gave my war hero, asking had the impulse cleaned me out, speculating on whether I would honour my share when the bill was presented, asking was I prepared for washing dishes in a hotel kitchen. But the sombre mood had descended and would not lift.

Tommy Rimmer told me the other day that his new golf friend Harry Spalding is a war hero on his own account. Apparently he led a special unit called the Jericho Crew. They were charged with particularly dangerous missions carried out behind enemy lines. They were very successful and greatly feared by the enemy. And I was not greatly surprised to hear this. Courage comes in many forms. It can be noble and reckless, as Mick's brand of it certainly was. And it can be a function of savagery. Who can say a snake lacks a certain primeval courage, locked in a battle to the death against a mongoose? Spalding is a killer. I've known it in my heart since the night it took Boland's gun to discourage him from raping me. He would not have stopped with the violation. The evening would have ended in my death. How he must have loved the war and the killing spree to which it would have treated him.

June 10th, 1927

A farm girl from Burscough has gone. Vera Chadwick telephoned and told me this morning. Tonight there is a grand ball at the Palace Hotel. I do not feel like going, with the intimation of death about the region. Vera says her detective beau has told her confidentially that no woman in the area is safe. Three makes five, he said. He is an experienced catcher of killers, so I suppose his opinion has to be respected. Three makes five. His theory is that if the police know about three, there are likely to be at least two other victims whose disappearance has gone unreported.

Vera asked him why. And I asked Vera.

Shame, he said, is the reason. Families think their little girl has absconded. They do not want the attentions of the police. Even less do they want the attentions of the press. What would their neighbours think? How would the dismaying news be received by the congregation at their church? Perhaps they had given their daughter just cause to bolt the family home. The police would press them on this and the police were expert and relentless in their questioning.

Three makes five, Vera's detective says. And I am apt to think him right. And I am impressed with his psychological insight. But there is no suspect yet identified for the crimes he believes he is investigating. And he has told Vera that the best thing she and her friends can do is to be escorted or stay off the streets altogether and double-lock our doors. I am less impressed with that. We pay for the police through our taxes. We are entitled to their protection. The notion of being confined to my home is an unattractive one. My home is a spacious and comfortable Birkdale Village flat. I have good furniture and a marble bathroom and a painting by Bonnard on the wall. But I do not want the place I live in to be my prison.

And it won't be. The one advantage I possess that those poor girls did not, is a gun. I have a Mauser pistol given me as a keepsake years ago by Mick Collins. It has existed more as a treasured memento than as a weapon all this time. But I have had it serviced regularly if only out of respect for its proper function. I like mechanical things. I like them to work, whether at the joystick of a Tiger Moth or the wheel of a Morgan roadster. And, of course, the Mauser is, before it is anything else, a functioning tool. It is a potent weapon. Mick, also, was of a practical turn of mind. The Mauser was a keepsake. But it was intended to protect me should the need for it to do so ever arise.

My gun is oiled and loaded with eight soft-point nine millimetre bullets. I was never the best shot on the range at Parbold when I taught myself how to use it, but I was far from being the worst. My marksmanship was good enough to make some of the men embarrassed. And I remember well the advice given me by Boland on firing a pistol. Aim for the centre of the target, he said. And keep on squeezing the trigger until the gun is empty. Never trust to accuracy. Trust to the percentages. Blow the life out of what you wish to kill. Never stop until you're out of ammunition.

I liked Harry Boland. He was a good and spirited man. I liked him even before his intervention saved my life. Mick was wrong over their falling out and the breach depressed Mick afterwards, I knew. Anyway, Boland taught me something that might save my life. If it does, I'll walk to Saint Theresa's Church in Birkdale and light a candle and say a prayer for the safe delivery of his soul. Do I need to? I imagine both their souls were safely delivered. They were good men. They were the best of men, says she, having re-encountered the worst.

I feel weary and defeated after Vera's call. I have never felt less like a party in my life. But I will go. It's what we do. It's the modern way. In a sense, I suspect that in this modern age, it's what we're all of us for. There is a painting in one of the rooms at the Atkinson Gallery. It portrays this mad whirligig. The passengers aboard are frenzied, their grins crazed and their knuckles white with the insane strain of hanging on to the ride. I cannot remember the name of the painter. It is someone from the Modernist school. But it is us he has portrayed in this painted metaphor. It is us, in our hysteria and hurtle and addiction to novelty and the future.

Suzanne groaned. She was in the gloaming, now, outside the Fisherman's Rest. She was amid the creeping shadows of the night. And she had in her hands a document that had told her in an evening more about the character of Michael Collins than she had learned from the known sources in a year. And Collins wasn't even the point of what she'd been reading. Her glass was empty. She wanted another drink. She had about a third of Jane Boyte's deposition to go.

'God, you were wonderful,' she surprised herself by saying out loud. 'You were really something, Jane.' Suzanne wiped at a tear she could not suppress or contain. 'You were brave and true.' She sniffed. She bent over the typed pages and continued to read.

June 15th, 1927

The ball was a spectacular success. The ballroom at the Palace was decked out in balloons and taffeta and silk ribbon of every shade and two bands shared a swivel stage. There was a full orchestra for half of the evening. And that alternated with a jazz band playing the wild and frenzied music of New Orleans. It was sweltering in the heatwave. Someone at the hotel had come up with the clever idea of ice sculptures to cool the dancing throng. They decorated the ballroom on two opposing sides, depicting a four-funnelled ocean liner running almost the full length of one and a great, streamlined steam locomotive on the other. Someone told me that the steam engine fashioned from ice was modelled on the prototype of one being built at York to break the world rail speed record. By the end of the evening, there were puddles on the parquet from these perishable masterpieces adorning the room. But they were very finely wrought and kept the air cool and breathable for the crowd in the cigar smoke under the bright, burning electric globes of the ballroom's giant chandeliers.

I went with my father, who looked fraught and sad. There has been another mishap at the yard and the men are whispering that Spalding's boat is cursed. Work is not so plentiful in Liverpool Harbour as to make them boycott the job. Not yet, at least. But men involved with the sea are always superstitious. And the project is taking its toll on my father's mood and perhaps also his health. I don't think he is sleeping well. I don't think he is sleeping much at all. He usually teases me about the way I wear my hair and my choice of clothes and my insistence on smoking in public. He does it good-naturedly. It has become a sort of humorous ritual between us. But on this occasion I think my appearance barely registered with my father.

There does not seem to me to be very much wrong with Harry Spalding's luck. He did not attend the ball. But he was at the hotel. He is no longer resident there, of course, but can often be found in the evening in the gaming room. On the night of the ball he won five thousand pounds at the blackjack table. It is a colossal sum of money. A streak like that at cards does not come to a man who sails an unlucky boat. If his boat really was unlucky, it would not have survived the worst storm in living memory. It would have sunk under him. Though I have heard an ugly rumour about the fate of his crew during the storm. Spalding says he was sailing alone. The Dublin harbour master insists there were two French crewmen aboard. The log should settle the matter. But so far, Spalding has been reluctant to produce the log. There might be an enquiry and there might not. Probably there will not. Whose jurisdiction covers the fate of two French deckhands aboard an American-registered vessel in the Irish Sea? Perhaps Spalding is telling the truth and he was sailing the *Dark Echo* alone. He is a very considerable yachtsman. The only thing I know with certainty is that my father will be well rid of the boat when the repairs to her are finally completed. I may not believe her cursed. But I think that he does.

Pierre Giroud sent a bottle of champagne to our table. It was a nice gesture from a sweet man who would be distraught to hear himself described as such. I don't mean to sound patronising. He is a sweet man. He is also an accomplished flier and tall and good-looking in his Gallic way. But the shadow cast by Mick Collins is a long one. The affairs I have had in the years since my return from Ireland have been tepid. My heart was not in any of them. It will not always be like this and I am fully aware that fast cars and aeroplanes are my compensation for those sensations most people enjoy between their sheets. It will not always be like this, but poor sweet Pierre Giroud is wasting his time and squandering his money buying Moët & Chandon in the hope of winning over this particular girl.

July 13th, 1927

I have deliberately stayed away from this journal for a full four weeks, concerned on rereading it that Harry Spalding was becoming an unhealthy obsession with me. But something occurred this afternoon that has left me badly shaken. It has also confirmed some of my worst suspicions about that monster walking the streets of Southport in the urbane and civilised guise of a man. It happened on Lord Street, near the junction with Nevill Street, as I was crossing from west to east after collecting my wristwatch from the jeweller's shop where it was being repaired. I almost collided with him. I was fastening the strap of my watch and not really paying attention to what was in front of me when I gained the pavement. I stopped at the sight of Spalding's broad back and pale trilby hat. He was switching his cane against the heel of his shoe and staring at the cenotaph. I saw him stiffen as he became aware of me. He took off his hat slowly with his free hand. But he did not turn and I did not move an inch from where I stood. He chuckled. And he spoke.

Great days, Jane, this monument celebrates. I do believe they were the making of me.

I did not move. The sun was very bright above us. The white stone of the memorial was quite dazzling and Spalding was pale and almost insubstantial in his linen suit and cream leather brogues. He was mistaken, of course. The cenotaph celebrated nothing. It acknowledged sacrifice. It commemorated loss.

Sacrifice, he said, as though reading my mind. But there's no point in dwelling on the past, is there? He switched his cane, idly. A man must live in the present, he said. And a wise man must secure his future.

The riddles in which he spoke seemed to carry the chill of

foreboding through the warm air. Everything about him felt and sounded threatening. I shivered.

Shame about poor Mick Collins, he said. He still had not turned to face me. He could fight, could Collins, Spalding said. It would be churlish not to concede the fact. He could fight. But could he love, Janey? That's the question.

Janey. It was what Mick had called me only in our tender moments together.

It was then I saw Harry Spalding cast no shadow on the pavement.

I hurried away from him. But he had one more trick. He had stopped my watch. Later in the day I took it back to Connards and their man took the back off it and could find nothing wrong with it at all. He blew on the movement and it started again. He was mystified. I was relieved that the trick was only temporary, the magic simply mischievous and not permanent. But I know now that Spalding really is a monster. He has known who I was all the time and toyed with me. He is evil and powerful and deranged. Can it be a coincidence that three women from the vicinity have gone missing while he is in our midst?

I think a clue was presented and ignored by all of us at Tommy and Nora's party back in May. Little Bonnie came down and raised her arm and pointed at something and screamed. Tommy has long recovered from the shock of it, of course. And Bonnie, thankfully, has no conscious memory of the event. Tommy even jokes about it, saying that Bonnie was pointing in the direction of Blackpool Tower. It's a vulgar eyesore, Tommy says. It has earned his daughter's scorn. And he's right that she was pointing in that direction. But I think she may have been pointing at something a lot closer than the tower across the bay at Blackpool. I overfly the town and know the lay of it. I can close my eyes and see a map of it painted accurately on my mind. And I know that Bonnie pointed that evening precisely in the direction of the house rented for the summer by Harry Spalding on Rotten Row. You could draw a line from Bonnie's pointing finger to the tower and it would pass through Spalding's garden. What secrets does he harbour there? I wonder. What summoned that little girl's unconscious accusation and her scream?

July 16th, 1927

I have rowed bitterly with Vera Chadwick. She does not think my evidence compelling enough to take to the police. She thinks her Liverpool detective would laugh in my face presented with my accusations. I'm not making accusations, I told Vera. I am merely raising suspicions. Surely the police need to follow all lines of enquiry if they are to solve the mystery of the disappearance of the three missing girls?

You cannot make accusations against a rich and popular visitor to the town, Vera says. The evidence simply is not there. You will look like a bigoted fool, taking against a stranger simply because he is a stranger and not a Southport man born and bred. And the culprit is likely to be a local man, her fiancé says. Only someone who knows the ground could stalk the victims and evade capture without leaving witnesses or clues. He's from Ainsdale or Crossens. He is not a stranger to the terrain. He is likely to be someone inconspicuous, superficially unremarkable. And this is all well and good and makes perfect sense, of course. But Spalding was able to ghost through enemy lines on the Western Front not a decade ago, wreaking havoc and eluding capture. The taking of three women would be child's play to a man with his deadly predatory skills.

I should have kept my own counsel. I had hoped for an ally in Vera's detective, or a least a sympathetic hearing for one of the closest friends of his intended. I fear that the real problem for Vera is less the subject of Harry Spalding than my own past Fenian connection. She is loyal enough to stay my friend despite that. But she doesn't want our friendship known about by her police detective. Perhaps she fears it would compromise him. As I said, I wish I had kept my own counsel. But there is something concrete I can do myself. And I intend to do it tomorrow. Vera is right in one regard. I have no hard evidence. Tomorrow I believe I might be able to provide myself with some.

I made the preparations earlier today, shortly after my angry exchange with Vera. I motored down to the Giroud hangar where Pierre was in his overalls stripping the turbine yet again on the troublesome Sopwith they bought. The Sopwith is supposed to be an easily maintained aircraft. It has a reputation for being relatively trouble-free. But theirs isn't.

Did you come to thank me for the champagne, Pierre said. He looks more handsome in his blue overalls with grease smeared across his face than he does in black tie and tails. He looks more the man of action, which of course he is. He and his brother both.

I want to fly early tomorrow, I told him.

Of course. How early is early?

Dawn.

He did something French with his mouth, a sort of shrug of the lips, and nodded. The Tiger Moth?

I shook my head. The Hawker Siddeley, I told him. And I need it fully equipped.

He smiled at that. You want us to mount the machine gun?

Almost all of their aircraft once belonged to the Royal Flying Corps. The brothers Giroud made a killing on military surplus when it was still cheap. I'm quite surprised they did not buy a tank just to tow their aeroplanes through the soft sand on the beach to the landing strip.

Not armed, Pierre, I said. But fully equipped.

Of course, he said. I will see you here tomorrow at dawn. And the Siddeley will be ready for you.

July 28th, 1927

I am just returned from Liverpool. I do not think I have ever felt more exhausted in my life. Detective Chief Inspector Bell of the

Liverpool Constabulary had finally acceded to my request for an audience. Perhaps it was the newspaper headlines that persuaded him to grant me half an hour of his precious time. Three days ago Helen Sykes became the fourth woman from our little corner of South Lancashire to disappear. The other women were not worth a splash in print on their own account. Too poor and too plain, I expect. But Helen is both well-off and beautiful. I use the present tense in the hope that she still lives. But each day that passes makes that less likely, as even DCI Bell was moved to agree. Helen has no motive for orchestrating her own vanishing act. And she has no reason for ignoring the appeals to allay concern by coming forward made in every edition of the *Post* and the *Echo* and the *Visitor* sold by those bellowing urchins from the hoardings on the streets.

Bell is senior to Vera's policeman in rank. And he showed no sign whatsoever of recognising my name when I was ushered into his office. He made me wait. But I waited in an anteroom rather than in the general waiting area, with its green linoleum and scatter of flattened cigarette ends and stink of sweaty desperation. The anteroom was bad enough. It had a large brass lock on a door which whooshed on its steel frame, flush with the floor and the top of the lintel it hung so heavily in. The green canvas chairs and heavy brown varnish and silence of the anteroom could not have symbolised confinement more solidly without bars and handcuffs. The only way out was when they came to escort me to Bell.

The Detective Chief Inspector's office was replete with the shields and rosettes of achievement on all four walls. Liverpool is a port city and a town as rough as they come and he looked as hard as granite. He was slender and cold-eyed where I had expected him to be stout and bellicose. But there was steel in his handshake as he rose from behind his desk to greet me and offered me a seat. Please, he said, gesturing to the stiff-backed chair. The one word carried the thick, adenoidal character of unschooled Scouse. I know it from my father's yard. Mr Bell, I knew instantly, had come up on merit earned on the streets through the police ranks. I noticed then a glass case on the wall with a truncheon and a constable's helmet displayed inside it. And I had no doubt they had belonged to him at the outset of his career. I could see him on Scotland Road under the street lights at closing time, putting violent drunks to punishing rights at the business end of that hardwood club.

He asked did I want tea or coffee and I declined. He poured a glass of water for each of us from the carafe on his desk. He held his hands out in a gesture of expansiveness and said, I'm naturally intrigued by your claim to have information regarding the missing women.

Helen Sykes is a friend of mine, I said.

And our colleagues in Southport are doing everything they can to try to find her, he said.

But they lack your expertise and resources, I said. They do not possess your rank. And though two of the missing women are from Southport, two are from elsewhere in the region. It all falls under your general jurisdiction, does it not?

He did not answer that question. He just looked at me over his steepled fingers and said, tell me what you think you know, Miss Boyte.

It was sweltering in his office. There was a fan on a filing cabinet, the curved blades of it like a Sopwith propeller in miniature. But he had not turned it on. His one window was open to the hot blast of our relentless heatwave. It displayed the thrilling vista of the building opposite, soot-blackened over decades of belching Liverpool industry. He did not seem discomforted by the heat at all. He had on a suit with a coat of heavy gabardine wool, and a tie was knotted firmly at his throat. These were distinctions he had earned, the plain-clothes trappings of rank, and a spot of seasonal sunshine was not about to oblige him to shed them.

I told him about my encounter at the Shelbourne with Harry Spalding seven years ago. I did not mention Mick or Boland. I did not seek to explain what I was doing then in Dublin.

He never took his eyes off me. When I had finished, he said, seven years is a long time.

I opened the briefcase I had brought with me and took out the print I had brought for him to see.

What's this?

It is an aerial photograph of the garden of the house Spalding has taken for the summer on Rotten Row, I said. It was taken a week ago. There is clear and substantial visual evidence of excavation. He is burying the bodies, Chief Inspector. He is burying the women in his backyard.

Bell looked at the photograph. But he did not touch it. I was not encouraged by this.

How did you obtain this picture?

I fly, Chief Inspector. I leased an aircraft used in the war for aerial reconnaissance. I overflew Spalding's house. There is a camera in the fuselage.

His eyes were still on the print. It is not a crime to have your garden dug, he said.

He's a monster.

DCI Bell finally looked at me. It was not a pleasant look. He smiled and it was not an encouraging smile. Some weeks ago Mr Spalding won five thousand pounds at blackjack, he said. He gave every penny of the money to local charities. An orphanage near here received the gift sum of a thousand pounds. It will transform lives, that money. It will enable them to repair the building's roof. It will buy clothing and pay for books. Coke for their fires in the cold of winter, you see. Solid food for fatherless kids deprived of nourishment all of their young lives.

I wondered if Bell himself had been an orphan.

Please listen to me, Chief Inspector.

His only stipulation was that his generosity go unrecorded publicly.

Please, Chief Inspector. Listen to me.

No, Miss Boyte. You listen to me. You are a Fenian. You have been an associate of assassins and traitors. Some would cloak you in the romanticism of independence and rebellion. Others might point to your treachery and the timing of it and argue compellingly that you were bloody lucky not to hang.

He was shaking with rage. I have never been sworn at before. The Liverpool police are known to recruit sometimes at the Orange Lodge. All was abundantly clear. Bell's spirit lay in Ulster, regardless of where his career resided.

Scum rises, I said, rising myself. And you, sir, are the proof.

He grinned and tore my photograph in two and tossed the pieces across his desk at me.

I don't know your motive in maligning a generous and distinguished man, he said. But you should go home, Miss Boyte, and investigate more wholesome pursuits than snooping on innocent people from the skies.

I walked the route from the police headquarters to the harbour. I was numb. I walked through Liverpool's dark and sweltering streets, over her greasy cobbles, until I came to the cranes and gantries and the proud hurtle and industrious filth of the Mersey river. I saw the great funnels of the ships in dock, heard the wail of tugboat horns and saw the hemp sacks of unknown cargoes hauled on straining ropes. I smelled the steaming shit, rich from the drays tethered to horsecarts, and had the rumble of petrol engines fill my ears from lorries in patient, throbbing convoys. All my life this stuff has raised my spirits in a soaring, living cocktail of sensation and excitement. All my life, I have felt privileged in the access to all this given me by my father's status and profession. But not today. Today I found a public bench behind a row of iron bollards and took my precious torn photograph and sat and tried to reassemble it between clumsy fingers, certain that Helen is dead. She is dead. The monster Spalding, the sneering beast I saw at the cenotaph in Southport, has killed her. I wondered how much of his recent largesse had gone to the Liverpool Police Benevolent Fund. It would not have mattered, though, to Chief Inspector Bell. My Fenian past had undone me with him before we ever met.

Disconsolate in the heat, I wiped a tear away. Frustration rather than self-pity or grief for poor Helen had prompted it, I think. But it was all the same. It was all the same. I latched the pieces of my precious evidence back into my briefcase and stood. And I found the way as a somnambulist would towards my father's yard.

My father wasn't there. He was away doing business with a lumber cutter, his clerk said, buying a consignment of hardwood. But the *Dark Echo* was there. She was in the dry dock, her hull supported on a great wooden brace, her new rudder fitted and her masts erect. She looked like someone's gigantic toy, which is what she was, I suppose, the Devil's handsome plaything. Her brass gleamed under the high sun and her paintwork and varnish were immaculate. She was almost ready to sail. Any day they would flood the dock and float her into the gentle waters of the estuary and see how she balanced and manoeuvred and performed generally. I had no doubt she would handle well. My father knows his craft.

I stole up the gangway aboard her. There was no one else aboard. She really was as good as finished, only awaiting the rigger for the final task Spalding would no doubt wish to supervise himself. She was quiet and serene in the light and heat of the day. Inside all was turmoil with me from my interview with the Orangeman and bigot detective, Bell. Without, all was teak splendour and seductive curves and the faint smells of metal polish and beeswax. There was no threat on the deck of Spalding's boat, no sense of menace whatsoever. The stars and stripes lay furled in brightly coloured coils on the short mast at her stern. She really was almost ready.

I went below. I sneaked into the master cabin. Everything had been taken from the storage shed and put back there at the service of the vessel's master. There were first editions on his bookshelves of Eliot and Ford Madox Ford and Michael Arlen and Pound. I saw a copy of Hemingway's novel *The Sun Also Rises*.

There was a copy of Scott Fitzerald's *The Great Gatsby* and one of *Ulysses*, the banned novel by James Joyce. The Pound and the Eliot, though, were well-thumbed. He had a taste for poetry.

There was a cabinet filled with his trophies from the war. Displayed there were several Luger pistols and saw-edged bayonets and a couple of the stick grenades the German infantry used. There were some barbaric-looking knives and clubs I supposed had been improvised by his Jericho Crew. They did not look like war material from the Krupp factory. They looked like relics from a medieval battlefield. Oddly, there was a crucifix. Even more oddly, it had been positioned upside down. It lay anchored like this in a little hill of black-painted putty, surrounded by a circle of rusty trench wire I thought might be a tasteless visual pun on Christ's crown of thorns. I hoped it had some other than this blasphemous significance. But then I forgot about this puzzling composition of keepsakes altogether, because I became aware of the smell in Spalding's cabin.

It was faint, but growing curiously stronger. It was the bitter odour of Turkish tobacco mingled with a perfume I half recognised, the two scents competing over something altogether cruder and more primitive. It was more a secretion than a manufactured smell, I thought. Was it sweat? It was more urgent than sweat, somehow more pungent. It was something similar to the musk of a large animal distressed.

There was a recording machine on Spalding's desk. The wax cylinders on to the surface of which the sound is cut by a vibrating needle lay next to it in a velvet-lined display. It almost made me smile. The machine was a symbol of his preening vanity. He would love the sound of his own high, harsh-vowelled voice, of course. I could imagine him reciting Pound's unfathomable stanzas to himself. Another symbol of his vanity was the brass-bound mirror fixed to the cabin wall. I went over and looked into it. Was the glass dirty? No. The reflection was lazy with tobacco smoke. It cleared. And behind me, I saw the face of Helen Sykes, her mouth fixed in the rictus of terror, her eyes bulging in her pale head with it. I turned. And there was no one there. And I fled the vessel and the boatyard, too, aware of what the smell had been in the master cabin aboard her. It was the stink of dying in mortal fear. It was the scent of poor Helen's last moments of life.

I ran along the cobbles, desperate to hail a taxi. And when I found one and told the driver to take me on to Southport I had to formulate a plan to fight my own shock and panic. I could barely control my breathing. I was dripping perspiration. The briefcase handle felt greasy in my grip and I was cold and shivering as the heat-drenched streets thrummed under me against the hard suspension of the cab. I would talk to Seamus Devlin in London. I would get explosives. I would buy dynamite and rig a bomb and blow Harry Spalding and his boat to kingdom come. If I could not use the law I would become the law. I did not possess a bomb-maker's skills. But Devlin did. I would pay him to assemble one. I would pay whatever it cost.

August 4th, 1927

With Devlin's lethal construction in my bag I went to the yard at dawn today after a sleepless night spent at the Adelphi Hotel. Of course, I arrived unannounced. My father was there, dishevelled and distracted, his collar soiled and askance and his whiskers unshaven. He looked stale and rattled. He was surprised to see me, but he showed no pleasure at the sight of me. Nor did he show any sign of suspicion. He is resigned to me and my unpredictability, I suppose. In his defeated way, I know my father loves me.

Spalding's boat had gone. I had missed him by but half an hour. I asked my father, as casually as I could, what his destination was.

I've no idea, he said. And then he mumbled something.

What?

I said I expect he's gone back to Hell, my father said. That's where he came from and that's where he damn well belongs.

I stood on the dock with my deadly cargo redundant in my carpet bag, nodding my head and knowing in my heart two things. The first was that my father spoke the truth. The second was that I had failed in the most vital task I had attempted in my life. It was not for the want of trying. But I had failed.

Twelve

It was almost dark when Suzanne reached the last page of Jane's deposition. She went inside the pub, because she felt cold despite the gentle warmth of the summer night. She got a drink from the bar, found an interior table and called the seminary in Northumberland and asked for the Jesuit, Delaunay.

'I think I know where to find your desecrated relic, Monsignor,' she said to him.

He was silent for so long that she thought the connection broken. Then he spoke. 'I'm relieved to hear you're safe,' he said. 'Has there been any further attempt to harm you?'

'No. When I return your relic, Monsignor, you must straight away bless or re-sanctify or exorcise the thing. You must do whatever it is you have the power to do to nullify the effects of the desecration.'

'That would be the sacred duty of any priest,' Delaunay said.

There had been no further attempt to harm her, it was true. There had been no spiteful, spectral attempt to impede her. And that was puzzling to her. But it was a mystery that solved itself in Suzanne's mind when she was awoken early the following morning in her hotel room by a return call from Northumberland.

'Half an hour after I spoke to you last night, I received an email sent from aboard the *Dark Echo*,' Delaunay said. 'It had a lengthy written attachment. I've only just finished reading it now. The last dozen or so pages of it deal with the voyage. You need to see those, I think.'

'Magnus is keeping a log?'

'It's Martin's account. It's Martin's log. I'll send you the pages now.'

She read the log in her hotel room, sitting by the open window. When she had finished, she switched on her computer. He had sent her a message at the same time as he had sent his testament to the priest. The laptop came to life. Hers was a much briefer missive.

I loved you. I did not love you for long enough, but I loved you as well as I could. I will die loving you.

Martin.

She looked at her watch. The Botanical Gardens Museum would be open in an hour. She ordered a minicab at reception, thinking that Martin was not going to die if there was anything humanly possible that she could do to prevent it from happening. She loved him back, and he was right. They had not had anything like long enough with one another.

'Boyce, you say?'

'Boyte.' And she smiled at her museum skiver. She had returned the borrowed document meeting her own twenty-four-hour deadline. She was comfortably within it. Now she wanted to know if anything else had been deposited here all those years ago by poor, desperate Jane. She felt very strongly that something had.

'There's a box,' he said, looking up from the written ledger he was perusing. 'Contents not inventoried.'

'Can I see it?'

'You can see it, certainly. But you cannot look inside it.

Not until a member of the staff here has inventoried the contents and signed and dated the inventory. It's the rules.'

Suzanne took fifty pounds in tens from her wallet and spread the notes on the desk between them. 'Ten minutes,' she said.

He stared at the money. 'Five,' he said.

He just had to have the last word.

'Done.'

He swept up the cash like a croupier. 'I'll find you the key.'

She took what she needed from the strongbox Jane had left at the museum. She did so swiftly and without sentiment. In other circumstances, she would have lingered over the legacy of someone she had come so greatly to like and respect. She would have opened the box on eighty years of darkness and history and carried out the necessary violation with gentleness and decorum and perhaps even a touch of ceremony. But there was not time. If the speed of the *Dark Echo* were consistent, the vessel would arrive in a couple of days. Magnus Stannard had been wrong. Her destination was not the West Coast of Ireland. She would alter course and skirt the Irish coast and not founder and break up on the reefs there at all. She was headed for the coast of Lancashire. She would beach somewhere between Formby Point and the pier at Southport. And she would float off again for ever on the next high tide. Here was where the thing that had once been Harry Spalding would board her and become her master again, where Magnus and Martin both would be enslaved as her crewmen. And Spalding did not have the best of reputations, did he, when it came to the treatment of his regular crews.

Spalding was here. She had seen him behind the windows of his old house, just fleetingly. Out of cowardice she had fooled herself into thinking it was the figure of some domestic helper there. She had felt his presence and could feel it still. He could not hurt her, she did not think. The attempt to crush the life out of her on the road in Northumberland had been the first and last he had been able to make. He could not hurt her because all his power was consumed at present by his efforts to lure back his boat. He was subduing and bewildering Martin and his father. He was somehow blocking the vessel's bristling array of instruments. He was shifting, by some demonic sorcery, seventy tons of wood and steel with some urgency through the silent ocean. But when he got aboard the *Dark Echo*, with Magnus and Martin in thrall to him, she felt that he would be powerful again. He would flex the insectile muscles Jane had spoken of with such distaste. And then, at his leisure, she supposed that he would take delight and relish in dealing finally with her.

She walked the short distance from the museum to the Hesketh Arms. She sat at a table and used her mobile phone to get the number for the police at Southport from directory enquiries. She asked if there was an officer designated to handle cold crimes and closed her eyes and prayed that there was.

'How cold?' said a jocular voice.

'Eighty years.'

There was a pause. 'Goodness, that is chilly. That's not so much felony, madam, as history.'

'It's murder, is what it is,' Suzanne said. Her tone must have conveyed some of the seriousness and anger she was feeling.

'Wait a moment,' the voice said. 'I'll patch you through to Mr Hodge.'

She had been hoping for a Wright or a Rimmer or a Halsall. She knew the names from her genealogy work on the northern comic. She had said a short prayer to herself in the hope of a really local man to listen to what she had to say. Hodge was about as good as she could have wished for, though. And now she silently thanked God for that. There were Hodges from around here in the Domesday Book. They had cultivated the land at Hundred End and Ormskirk a thousand years ago. The word itself was the Viking word for farmer. It helped to know the land, Suzanne thought, if you were going to be excavating it. Her appointment with Mr Hodge of the Southport Division of the Merseyside Cold Crimes Squad was made for nine thirty the following morning.

She went to the library and used her laptop in the reference section. The Paddy McAloon ballad 'When Love Breaks Down' had entered the chart in September of 1985. That was when it was current, when it was getting its airplay, when it would likely enter whatever passed for the conscious mind of Harry Spalding. She went over and asked to see the microfiche files. It seemed a remote time, 1985, when she saw the page layouts and the photographs. She found what she was looking for in an issue of the *Southport Visitor* from October of that year.

Two friends had disappeared fishing off Formby Point. They were assumed drowned, but their bodies had not washed up. They were both seventeen. They had been at school together. Their fishing hobby had progressed from freshwater brooks and ponds and the Leeds and Liverpool Canal to the bigger catches to be had sea fishing from the end of Southport Pier. This was only the second time their parents had permitted them to fish by night from a boat. The weather had been calm. The forecast had been clear. And they and their dinghy had vanished. The families had provided the paper with portrait shots. Fashionable lads, in their quiffs and overcoats, they looked in these photographs a little like rock stars of the period themselves. They did not look like Paddy McAloon. They had that look of the period more defined by bands like Echo and the Bunnymen, or The Smiths. Suzanne did not think they had drowned. But she thought she knew what had been playing on their radio or tape machine when the prow of the *Dark Echo* loomed in the night over their little craft.

'How did the picture get torn?' Hodge asked. He was scrutinising Jane's aerial photograph, recovered from the strongbox left at the museum. He was doing so in bifocals, seated at his desk, the picture tilted into the bright sunshine coming in through his window. Suzanne guessed he was in his mid-fifties. He was unremarkable-looking. His hair was turning from blond to grey and was close-cropped and thick. There were lines around his blue eyes. His worsted suit seemed a bit warm for June and, like his plaid flannel shirt, looked straight off a rack at Marks & Spencer. His rank had been Detective Inspector at the time of his retirement. Perhaps he was bored in retirement. Perhaps his pension had not stretched as far as it needed to. It could just be that he needed something to keep him from the temptation of the lounge bar of his local pub. But he did not look like a drinker. He looked alert and competent and, though he was polite, seemed rather distrustful. She could hardly blame him, in the circumstances, for that.

Suzanne had given Mr Hodge some of the background. She had told him about the missing girls. She had told him about Jane's suspicion of Harry Spalding. She had told him about the Dublin encounter between Spalding and Jane and how the picture came to be taken. Now she told him about the meeting in Liverpool between Jane and DCI Bell.

Hodge nodded, without comment. He had not commented so far on anything that Suzanne had said. He had restricted himself to a couple of questions just to establish chronology and fact. Now, he did comment.

'I remember my granddad telling me something about these disappearances.'

'Was he a police officer?'

'No. He wasn't. He was head barman at the Palace Hotel. He knew the chambermaid.' Hodge put the separate pieces of Jane's photograph down on his desk. 'He knew Helen Sykes and her circle. Miss Sykes was a lavish tipper. My grandfather remembered that. Could I get you some tea or coffee, miss? Have you been offered anything?'

'Please, call me Suzanne. Coffee would be great.' And a cigarette would be even greater. But that comfort would have to be forgone.

'I have to go to our computer room for a few minutes,' Hodge said. He closed the notebook he had been filling during Suzanne's monologue and slipped it into the pocket of his jacket. 'You are welcome to drink your coffee in our canteen. Or I can have it brought to you in the yard to the rear of the station where you are welcome to smoke.'

'The yard, please,' she said.

Hodge smiled at her. The smile seemed warm enough but the eyes above it stayed alert. Suzanne did not think he was doing this to prevent himself from downing too much beer or to pay off stubborn credit card bills. They had brought him back only because he was so bloody good at it.

It was thirty-five minutes before he returned to his office and he did so with a sheaf of documents under his arm. 'Much easier, now everything is computerised,' he said. She nodded. Without computers, her own job would be near impossible. Not that she really had a job any more. With a shock, she realised that the struggle to deliver Martin from the spectre of Harry Spalding had taken over her entire life.

He sat down and gestured for her to sit, then he lowered the open blind so that the light was not dazzling through his window. It was still bright in his office through the chinks of the blind. He tapped his fingers in a tattoo on his desk and sucked his teeth. Then he sifted amid the pile of print-outs his computer time had delivered him. 'Do you believe in reincarnation, Suzanne?'

'No.'

There was a silence.

'Do you?'

'I didn't,' he said. He slid a black and white picture of a woman seated at a café table across the desk. Suzanne looked at it and coloured. It was like seeing a snapshot she hadn't known existed of herself.

'Surveillance picture. Taken by the Special Branch on Lord Street in 1925. Miss Boyte was a known associate in Dublin of a bomb-maker by the name of Devlin. It isn't surprising that Bell gave her short shrift. He wasn't an Orangeman, either, by the way. He was a Freemason. That's probably neither here nor there. Lots of police officers were and are Freemasons. What is more significant is that his brother was killed in Tipperary serving with the Black and Tans. Corporal David Bell was blown to pieces in a Republican ambush.'

Suzanne didn't say anything.

'Not everyone was so enamoured of Michael Collins as Jane Boyte so clearly was.'

'So she was kept under supervision.'

'There's quite a comprehensive file on her. She was pulled in from time to time. Did you know that she gave birth to a daughter?'

'I suspected it. She wrote something in her journal about children and one's feelings towards them. It struck me at the time as something only a mother would have written, an insight only a mother would have had. Is her daughter's married name Daunt?'

'Was. It was. Alice Emmeline Daunt. She died three years ago. She was eighty-four.'

Suzanne swallowed. 'And she was born in 1921. She was the daughter of Jane Boyte, and her father was Michael Collins.'

'Do you have a more sensible pair of shoes than the ones you're wearing, Suzanne?'

'Why?'

'Because even in clement weather, digging is a very dirty business.'

'You're going to start digging today?'

'Not personally. But I'll have a team there by this afternoon. SOCOs, forensics, a mechanical digger, men with spades. You, if you so wish.'

'You can move that fast?'

'Spalding was either very unsavoury or incredibly accident-prone where propriety was concerned. That picture Jane Boyte took is highly suspicious. I don't believe very much in coincidence. And if those women are there, I think they've waited long enough to be laid decently to rest. Don't you?'

Suzanne turned the two pieces of the picture around, put them together and looked at the image there, at the grainy reality of turf torn and earth disturbed. 'What's particularly suspicious about it, Detective Inspector?'

'The timing. The fact that it is there at all. Playboys like Spalding didn't dig holes big enough to be seen from the air for fun or as a hobby. Unless he was nostalgic for the war and was digging himself a trench.'

'What about the occupants of the house? Won't the people living there object?'

'There aren't any people living there,' Hodge said. 'The house is Grade II listed and empty. It's never really been successfully occupied. People don't feel comfortable there. They say it is haunted.'

Suzanne stood. She was momentarily at a loss. 'What should I do now?'

'We're close to Lord Street. You could do some window-shopping and then grab an early lunch. Then you should go back to your hotel and change out of that smart outfit you so courteously assembled for our appointment. Put on some practical clothes. Meet me at the site at two o'clock. Bring something to wear on your head. The sun is hot in June. And bring something to drink. We are in for a long day.'

Suzanne left the police station and walked along Lord Street. She felt that in a few days she had come to know Southport very well. The past kept breaking through into the present, but in a peculiar way it was that kind of place and the intrusion was only fitting. Once, she thought she glimpsed Jane Boyte staring at her from inside a chic department store. But when she looked again, it was just her own reflection, with her hair groomed, in the grey pencil skirt and tailored black jacket she had worn for her appointment with the old policeman.

She stopped at the Costa coffee shop. It was eleven o'clock, a busy coffee time, and there was a queue. She saw again the street sign in the Costa montage that reminded her of the home she shared in Lambeth with Martin Stannard. She wondered if she had seen Martin for the last time. She remembered their last awkward night together. She had been remote from him, cold with disapproval of the intended voyage. That disapproval had been fully vindicated. But she regretted her coldness deeply now. The invitation to share one another had been offered by neither of them. She hoped now with all her ardent heart to be given the chance to compensate for that.

She took her coffee to one of the tables on the pavement outside. Through the line of old trees on the kerb, she could see the pale splendour of the cenotaph. It was magnificent from here in its scale and simplicity, the seamless blocks of Portland stone shaped in two great, white edifices flanking a tall obelisk. She thought of Spalding standing in linen, switching his cane and paying mock homage to the dead while he teased Jane Boyte on the flagstones behind him. There was no one there now. The flagstones shifted in patterns of light and shade wrought by the canopy of trees and the sun through their summer leaves. Suzanne sighed and sipped coffee and shifted her attention to her own side of Lord Street. It was very crowded and bright with people in their summer attire. She realised that she was looking for Alice Daunt. But she knew she had seen the last of Alice, as she knew she had seen the last of her father, too.

There were five bodies, when they had done their digging. The remains were skeletal. It was dusk by the time they were done and the bones were bleached white by the big search-lights fighting the encroaching night and illuminating the scene. They were positioned sideways on in the attitude of jackknifing divers, the dead women, with their spines at the apex and their hands touching the feet of their neighbour. The significance of this human geometry was plain to see. The remains formed a gruesome pattern. It was the five-sided star, the pentagram. The killing had been a ritual. The purpose had been sacrificial. Suzanne wondered how the women had died.

'Not well,' Hodge told her. He looked a full decade older than he had in the bright sunshine of his office that morning. He was sipping coffee poured from a steel flask. 'We won't know the specifics until forensics have a proper look and we won't get the full picture until the pathologist's report. But judging from the abrasions plain on their neck bones, I would say that the women had their throats cut. My guess is that it was done with a saw-edged weapon, perhaps a German infantry bayonet Spalding kept as a memento from the war. My belief is that they bled to death where they lay and were arranged like this afterwards. But I've got no context for this kind of killing, to be honest with you. I've never seen anything like this in my entire professional life. And I hope to God I never do again.'

The women had been buried deep. The pentagram was twelve feet below the surface. It was why the police digging had taken so long. The circular pit they had gouged from the earth had needed to be shored up by poles and scaffolding planks banked behind the poles on their edges. Even with this revetting, the soil tried to bulge and break through. It was unstable, like a living organism trying to conceal itself. Little avalanches trickled through breaches and cracks in the planks down to the pit.

'It was dug by hand, by shovel and pick, we can tell that much,' Hodge said. 'If it was dug by one man alone, then he had colossal strength. Carrying the women here would have been no burden to him. A man possessed of that kind of strength could have carried these poor wretches here two at a time.'

From the centre of the star formed by the dead women, they had retrieved a brass cylinder about three and a half feet long. It had been buried bound in oilcloth. The oilcloth had been very carefully removed. The cylinder was barely tarnished by its time under the earth. Suzanne had at first assumed it was a telescope. But its sides were parallel and it was not sectioned and it had a cap, on close inspection, that screwed on to protect and secure whatever it contained.

Everyone at the scene crowded round when the cap was unscrewed and the contents of the tube revealed. Suzanne watched in some anxiety. The whole operation was conducted with incredible delicacy but she was concerned anyway because by now she knew what the object was and she was afraid that it would simply crumble to nothing in the exposure to the white, halogen-lit air. The thought terrified her.

This was sea air, harsh with ozone and salt. She clenched her fists and closed her eyes and murmured a prayer. But when she opened her eyes again what emerged, emerged intact.

She could imagine no more unprepossessing an object. It looked like a piece of broom handle. Except that it was almost petrified with age and, in the brilliance of the lights, you could see the faint indentations where the twine or rawhide of its grip had once been tightly wound.

'Some kind of staff,' Hodge said.

'Not a staff, Detective Inspector. A shaft,' Suzanne said.

He turned to her. The suspicion and hostility had gone from his gaze during the course of the afternoon and evening. Suzanne suspected she had vindicated herself. She could not really imagine any vindication more terrible and sad.

'Call me Bernard,' Hodge said. He held out his hand. She realised that he had held off from this gesture from their outset until this moment. She shook hands with him.

'What will happen now?'

'There are all sorts of protocols. Not least, the American Embassy will have to be notified. We won't have a forensic report for a while and it might be useless when we get it, unless we exhume Spalding and recover DNA. But the circumstantial evidence is too compelling to ignore.'

'It always was.'

'Yes, Suzanne. Jane Boyte was quite right in that. It always was.'

And anyway, Suzanne thought, Spalding's casket in his cemetery in New York lies empty. Because Harry Spalding never died.

'You know what that object is, don't you, Suzanne? That modest little bit of wood uncovered just now.'

'What do you think it is?'

'I'm a stranger to demonic ritual. At least, I was until

today,' Hodge said. He sipped coffee from his steel cup. He was speaking softly, so that his voice would not carry beyond his audience of one. 'I'd say it is a holy relic. And it was the subject here of an awful desecration. But that's just an old copper's intuition. It doesn't look much.'

'It's priceless,' Suzanne said.

'It's just a stick to me.'

'I know a Jesuit priest who would be very relieved to get it back on behalf of the Church from which it was looted.'

'Then he'd best give me a call. On my mobile number.'

'It isn't evidence?'

'It isn't the murder weapon, if that's what you mean. I'd be as keen as anyone to see as much of what was done here undone as can be. My keeping that piece of wood won't bring back the women killed here. Have your priest give me a call.'

'Fingerprints?'

'Good ones on the brass of the case. And I think we both know whose they are. We don't need that stick.'

'Won't people see it's missing?'

'It won't be missing. I'll replace it myself with one similar from the dead wood in the park over the way.' He was almost whispering. 'Materially, it doesn't matter to this investigation. Whatever properties you think it possesses, it isn't bringing those poor lasses back.'

Suzanne nodded. He was right about that. 'If you release it into my charge, I'll take it to the priest myself, Bernard,' she said.

He looked at her. 'At some stage, you are going to need to make a statement. I'm going to trust you to come back and see me over the next few days to do that.'

She nodded again.

'Call yourself a taxi. I'll meet you outside the front in five minutes. Goodbye, Suzanne. And God go with you.'

She risked her first real look at Spalding's house. The windows stared back blackly at her. She was fearful of the face that might be gazing out from behind the glass. But he wasn't there. The house was empty. She had no sense of him at all. He was elsewhere, in one of his other places. He was deliberately elusive, as Jane had remarked of him. And Harry Spalding must have known many places on the travels of his long and awful life, the affliction of him spreading like disease.

She drove all night to get to Northumberland, having taken a taxi from Southport to Liverpool Airport to hire a car. She had to go south to go north-east. But she thought it was worth it as she pulled up at 5 a.m. outside Delaunay's Gothic keep and saw him waiting there for her amid a deputation of grim and eminent-looking Catholic clergy. She wondered for how long they had maintained their vigil. And she saw that it did not matter to them in their relief and joy when she took the holy relic from its bed of screwed-up newspaper pages in the boot of her rental car.

She had a mind to turn round immediately and press on. But Delaunay leaned into the open driver's window and the look of concern on his face persuaded her that this was foolish. The window was open because she had nearly nodded off at the wheel once already. She had been awake too long. She had never in her life needed greater alertness, sharper clarity of thought and instinct for danger. She had time. She had done the calculation. At ten to twelve knots, it would be another couple of days before the *Dark Echo* reached its destination. At Delaunay's invitation, at his insistence, she ate a bowl of soup and slept for two oblivious hours in their guest quarters before setting out again.

Delaunay was waiting for her at the door.

'Re-consecrate what I gave you, Monsignor.'

'It's done,' he said, simply.

She drove to Dover in five hours, crashing every speed camera on the route. She prayed she would not be stopped for speeding and she wasn't. Others were praying on her behalf, she knew. And she thought she might need every intercession made for her, every flicker of flaming brightness from every candle lit, if she was going to succeed. The weather was good and the traffic, as far as the London orbital at least, was light. She was forced to slow down in Kent. But she made the 11 a.m. ferry with five minutes to spare. And this time she did not need to slow for directions. She knew where she was going. She did not turn on the radio, of course. But one thing was the same. The sky grew sullen and bruised and, still a dozen miles from her destination, the rain began to steeple down from the clouds.

She drove over Duval's fields to his barn along the track beside his ditch, hoping that the rain was a recent thing and that her wheels would not be claimed by a quagmire of French mud. It was muddy, but the ground had been cindered. She could hear the crunch and squeal of the cinders wedging in the tread of her tyres. The barn grew in her windscreen from a monument incongruous and remote to one ever closer and more disturbing. She felt the tiny hairs prick on the backs of her hands with the sheer, out-of-kilter strangeness of it. All her instinct, just as on the first occasion, was to flee this odd and morbid place. But she could not.

She slammed on her brakes with a final, cindery crunch and sat in the silence before her destination. Rain pattered on the car roof. The stopped engine ticked, cooling. And she saw that the high door of the barn was slightly ajar. It opened on a void of pure blackness. And as she got out of the car she felt her legs buckle and her resolve weaken, engulfed by the pure terror flooding through her. She watched the rain dance on summer puddles. She felt drops of it plaster her hair to her head. And she was undone. And she thought then of Martin with his arm cleaved open in an underground carriage and she battled with her quavering will and she gathered her strength.

She took the spade she had borrowed from the seminary out of the car boot. She walked into the barn and heard a collusive whisper from the spectral army of coats that hung, shivering, under a draught that wasn't there, over on the far wall. She heard a distinct and undeniable whistling. The tune was 'Camptown Races'. And it was distorted and faint with some last, scornful vestige of remembered humanity. There was a bark of laughter, a short explosion of mirth. And there was accordion music, heard as if through a dim green sea, 'Roses of Picardy', the notes distorted, drowning on the air.

'Fuck this,' Suzanne said. 'Fuck you all, you crew of fucking butchers. And fuck you in particular, Harry Spalding.' And she gathered the spade in the grip of both hands and began to shovel away the beets at the base of the high pyramid of them. And all around her, they tumbled and they fell. Rolling down from the pinnacle, they ricocheted and bounced and ran. And she heard what she thought sounded like explosive gunfire, twice, in her ears and ignored it, teeth clenched with such ferocious resolve that she brought forth the blood from her own gums and swallowed it bitterly down.

She booted away beets from the centre of the flattened pyramid and revealed the earth and began to dig. And only a foot beneath the surface, she encountered bone. It was a skull. It was long with bleak-shaped eye sockets and a narrow jaw and she knew it had been the head of a goat. And what she was looking for had been used, she thought, to kill the goat, skewering the brain of this animal sacrifice in some baleful ceremony from which the other remnants, revealing themselves now, included a burned Bible and a votive candle, a smashed statue of the Virgin and a chamber pot, amid the old encrusted filth of which had been placed a set of rosary beads. Shit had been daubed on the crucifix. Blasphemy was a puerile art. But it was the blade embedded in the skull of the goat, only, that concerned her. It was the tip of the ancient spear to which she had already recovered the shaft.

She thought she heard another noise outside. She disregarded it. It would wait. Outside would wait. There was business here. There was no more important business in the world. Knowing what it was, she felt reluctance to touch the spear tip with her hands. This was not squeamishness. Suzanne was not a squeamish woman. This was awe. She had been told the significance, symbolic and actual, too, of the glimmering, ancient shard of hammered and honed iron she retrieved from inside the skull of the goat and held between her own soiled fingertips. On her knees, she kissed the metal, as Delaunay had told her to. As Delaunay had told her to, she crossed herself with the metal in the grip of her right hand.

The assault of corruption hit her then. From the crates heaped high over against the wall of the barn, she could hear the fizz and burst of decay and smell the blister of erupting, rotten fruit. All around where she knelt, the beets steamed and flattened with decomposition, gaseous, foul, an affront to nature exposed finally to nature's immutable laws. Suzanne coughed and retched and rose to her feet and looked over at the ragged army of Jericho Crew greatcoats and saw that they were becoming thin and threadbare, pale shrouds descending to dust as they should have done decades ago. She gave out a grunt of satisfaction. It was not triumph, though. Some sly instinct told her that pride in such a situation would be a dangerous, perhaps even deadly indulgence. Cradling what she had recovered, she made for the door.

Duval, the farmer who owned the land, was there outside, with his shotgun over his arm. He was waiting for her. Trespass on his domain was not a thing that went unnoticed. She knew that from her last visit here. But this time, the gun was not broken. Rain dripped from the brim of his hat and his mouth was set under the bristles of his moustache. Rain dripped, too, from the twin barrels of the gun. And smoke drifted lazily upward from them. There was a van, Suzanne saw, beside her car. And she thought with a shock that she recognised the livery. She approached the van. She saw the legend, *Martens & Degrue*, etched on the black body of the van in gold. She walked around to the front of the vehicle. There were two men inside. They wore pale-brown overalls. The windscreen of the van was punched with twin holes in front of where they sat. And they were dead. Each wore the fatal blossom of a shotgun blast, florid across his chest.

'They would have killed you,' Duval said. He said it flatly. It was a simple truth.

Suzanne looked at the ground. She looked up at the sky. 'Does it always rain here?'

Duval shrugged. 'It suits the crops.'

Suzanne nodded. She tried to smile. In the face of death, in the presence of its immediacy, she could not.

'I must compliment you on your courage, *madame*. You are resolute. You have laid the curse.'

'Could you not have done it?'

'My father tried. It destroyed him.'

She gestured to the van. 'And them?'

'Food for the pigs,' he said. 'My crime. My sin to reconcile, not yours. As much as they deserve.'

So he was reconciled already. 'Thank you, Pierre Duval,' she said. 'Thank you for saving my life.'

He looked at her for a long moment in the dripping rain. 'It is the least that you deserve.'

She turned back to the barn. It was a strange building, still. But it was a curiosity now of site and architecture and no longer a threat, she knew, at all.

'*Bonne chance!*' Duval said, as she drove away. The spear tip was in a velvet bag on the seat beside her. Delaunay had begged her not to consign it to the boot. It was an easy request to grant. She did not feel inclined to be careless or cavalier with what she had recovered. She had never endured a more difficult ordeal in her life. And then there was the artefact itself. She could feel the sacred nature of the metal radiating off it as plainly as intense cold or vibrant heat.

It was Suzanne's belief that the thing that had once been Harry Spalding waxed and waned in its power and grip on life. The suicide in Manhattan in 1929 had been it testing its claim to immortality. By then it had been very strong. And by then, it was no longer really human. It was not the Devil, as Jane Boyte had supposed. But it had bargained with the Devil. It had gained a sort of reckless invulnerability as reward for the desecration enacted in the barn. Then, back in 1917, the black mantle of safety from harm had extended to the rest of the Jericho Crew. It was still working, to some extent, for their leader after the war. But Suzanne thought the effect had weakened by that time. Mick Collins had not really been able to hurt Harry Spalding at the Shelbourne Hotel with his cudgelling brawler's fists. But by 1919 the barrel of Boland's revolver had given Spalding pause for thought with the tip of it shoved under his chin.

Later, in Southport, he had carried out the second blasphemous ceremony. The sacrifice had been greater, the desecration all the worse. And Jane had seen Spalding's subsequent transformation into something more diabolical than strictly human. His strength had increased. His appearance and even the dimensions of him had shifted and altered.

But there was no harder or more demanding striker of a bargain than the Devil. Eventually, each and every one of the Jericho Crew had needed to be sacrificed. It was the fate of the Waltrow brothers. It was the fate of the gambler Gubby Tench, who rode Spalding's demonic luck at the tables until the debt to his old commander was called in. They were all in thrall to Spalding. And Spalding was in thrall to Satan. And when Satan realised Spalding's sacrilegious offerings no longer held, when he realised Spalding's pledges were no longer honoured, he would be human again and fallible, and no longer able to cheat a mortal death himself. He was strong, now, though. Wasn't he? He would be strong until it came to the Devil's attention that there was nothing left worth having any more in Harry Spalding's depleted account.

This was Suzanne's logic. This was her rationale, arrived at driving a rental car towards Calais through the French rain. And it made her laugh out loud. With the covered relic on the seat beside her, with the blood from the bodies of the men sent to kill her by Martens and Degrue still fresh in her nostrils, she had to laugh. She thought she might cry, otherwise. Her logic was the logic of nightmare. And the nightmare was not over yet.

When she got back to Northumberland and Delaunay, he wept as she handed over the thing she had recovered. 'Why is it so important, Monsignor?'

'It was the spear used to kill Christ.'

She knew that. She knew the story. The Romans had crucified Christ. And as he hung on the cross in the long agony of dying, a Roman soldier took the spear and pierced his side with it, draining the last of the life from him in a brutal act of mercy. But Christians did not believe in mercy killing. The Roman, Longinus, had repented, had converted to Christianity after the death himself. But she could not see that as the significant fact in the story either.

'The spear thrust marked the moment of God's sacrifice

of his son for the sake of man,' Delaunay said. 'It is the only thing physical we have of our Redeemer. It pierced His flesh. It was bathed in the blood of Christ.'

'Aren't there nails somewhere from the crucifixion? Aren't there supposed to be wood fragments in existence from the true cross?'

Delaunay smiled. He shook his head. 'Medieval forgeries,' he said. 'They are objects with no provenance, manufactured for the profit of unscrupulous men at the expense of those desperate to believe. But this . . .' He kissed the metal.

Whatever endowed the spear with its significance, she had no doubt concerning its power. There were other relics claiming to be the Spear of Longinus. There was one in the museum at Cracow. There was one Hitler had taken to Germany from Austria after the Anschluss. General Patton had been most keen to recover that after the fall of Berlin. But this was the genuine article. The fact of Spalding's continuing existence and baleful influence was surely proof of that. She remembered the thing of Jane's she had taken from the strongbox in Southport and left hidden in the guest quarters at the seminary the previous night. She went with Delaunay to retrieve it.

'I need you to bless this, Monsignor.'

He frowned. 'I cannot.'

'You must.'

'I blessed the boat, Suzanne. To what avail?'

'Just do it, please. Matters are different now. The circumstances have changed. I myself have altered them. Do it with the spear point held in your hand. Do it for Magnus and Martin's sake.'

He hesitated. Then he nodded, relenting. And when it was done, Suzanne slept eight hours of wretched, troubled sleep, dreaming of women writhing as they bled to death under the ground.

* * *

Suzanne knew the boat would beach by night. Spalding liked to think himself the sun god, the bright, Jazz Age boulevardier who quoted poetry and possessed an incandescent sophistication and dazzled with the white innocence of his smile. He was dapper and wealthy and well connected and generous. But he was a creature of the night. He was a thing of the Devil. And all his most distinguished work had been done in darkness. The Jericho Crew, which had first given him his name and status in the world, was a nocturnal entity. The crew slouched out from their hides in the earth and killed and maimed after the sun had gone down and before it rose again. It was his preference and his habit. He had done his digging above Rotten Row in the darkness, she was certain. He played by day and worked by night. His days had been in Southport for golf with Tommy Rimmer and the track at Aintree. His nights had been for murder and ritual. Muffled to silence in its shroud of mist, the boat would beach with the sun shining on the other side of the world.

She stood and waited on the night beach at Birkdale. She had the beach to herself. Off to her right, she could see pricks of light delineating the outline of the pier. She fingered her penny from 1927, still the talisman carried everywhere in her pocket. It seemed a long time since she had first come across her lucky coin. It had come from the pier, her penny. It seemed she had possessed it for eternity. In fact she had owned it only for a couple of days. Out over the hard-packed sand and the distant water, she could see the lights of an oil or gas rig twinkle. The structure was tiny and vague from here, miles out on the brink of a horizon she could only sense and guess at. The lights aboard it would be fierce, bright orbs, gigantic electric lamps. But from here, they were scarcely visible.

She suffered a moment, then, when the futility of what

she was attempting came close to overwhelming her. The boat would not come. The boat had sunk in the fathomless, indifferent depths of the North Atlantic, its hapless crew of two lost in some shared, hopeless delusion at the moment they perished. And she could not fight Harry Spalding. He was a phantom and a monster and she had not the means to confront and beat him. She had not the power or the knowledge. Her legs buckled and dumped her on the sand. She did not try to get up. The sand was soft here and still warm from the heat of the long summer day. It was a small, radiant comfort through her clothes against her skin. She let it sift through her fingers in tiny, countless grains. They were very fine, the grains of sand. And she could no more fight Harry Spalding than she could guess at their number.

Suzanne began to cry. She looked up, blinking out at the sea, and the tears blurred and clouded her vision. She wiped at her eyes with the back of her hand. And the cloud was still there. But it was not a cloud. It was a rolling patch of mist. It was tumbling over itself, growing or seeming to, as it neared the shore. Steadily and in eerie silence, it was approaching the land. Suzanne climbed wearily back to her feet. She sniffed. She brushed sand from her fingers. She felt for her lucky penny and clutched the strap of the bag on her shoulder. She looked around, but she sensed that she was entirely, profoundly alone. She began to walk towards where the mist approached. The sand firmed under her feet until it was packed hard in dry rivulets baked by the sun after the going-out of the last tide. The tide was coming in again though, wasn't it? And the *Dark Echo* was coming ashore on the flood.

She heard footsteps then. She heard a rhythmic plucking of feet out of the mud sucking at them. She remembered there was quicksand here. In the past, it had swallowed the wheels of their cars, those fools who sometimes tried to drive to Blackpool over the treacherous illusion of solid ground. She steeled herself for the onslaught of the beast and turned and looked. But it was not Spalding. It was a woman in a fur stole and a cloche hat, struggling through slime and seaweed in a pair of buttoned boots.

'Jane?'

'I'm not Jane.'

The woman came closer. She peered. Her kohled eyes were bloodshot and her face was pale. Her lipstick looked black in the darkness and she was dead. 'Do you know who I am?'

'You're Vera Chadwick.'

'And I've come to say I'm sorry, Jane. I wish I'd listened to you. If I'd listened to you, we might have saved poor Helen's life.'

Suzanne nodded. She had seen Helen lying in the ground. They had known it was the wealthy woman from the jewellery her bones still wore. There had been a bracelet, earrings. Helen had been taller than the other victims, a tall and slender woman. And, as Bernard Hodge had observed, she had not died well.

Vera Chadwick sighed. In the freshness of the night beach, her breath was the cold odour of the crypt. 'It was nothing to do with you being a Fenian, of course, Jane. I only said that. Philip's family were Bootle Catholics. He'd probably have approved.'

Suzanne said nothing.

'I discouraged you from meeting him because I thought he'd be taken with you. Everyone was, you know. You're very beautiful, Jane. You always were. It was never fair, really. It wasn't.'

'Nothing is fair,' Suzanne said.

'Anyway,' the ghost of Vera Chadwick said, 'I'm very sorry. I really am so very sorry.' She took gloves from the pocket of her coat and struggled to pull them on to pale, flapping hands. Then she wandered into the darkness with that sucking noise her feet made and was gone.

Suzanne turned back to the sea, to the direction from which the boat had been approaching. Tendrils of mist were snaking now around her ankles on the sand. She could make out the bulk of the *Dark Echo*, at rest and canted slightly to one side on its hull, aground and huge in front of her, wrapped in its cloak of fog.

A rope ladder hung from the stern when she reached it. She walked from the bow, the length of the hull, unable to believe how weathered and barnacled the boat had become over the course of a single voyage. The wood was scarred and scraped. In places it looked soft and spongy with incipient rot. Patches of her timber smelled waterlogged. She dripped and oozed from a dozen small breaches in her superstructure. Whatever magic had been used to bring her here had taken a terrible toll on the integrity of the vessel. It was as though immense strain had been put on her. She had not travelled willingly. She had been aged and wearied by her perverse trail through a thousand miles of reluctant ocean.

Suzanne climbed the rungs of the ladder carefully to the deck. There was no one there to greet her. She climbed into the open hatch at the stern, down the steps that led to Magnus Stannard's master cabin. There was a dim, yellowy sort of illumination below, the light cast by oil or paraffin lamps. There was a smell of paraffin. And she saw that the master cabin door was open. She walked into it. And she saw that the rot afflicting the *Dark Echo* was not confined to her hull.

The cabin walls were hung with mildewed pictures. They were photographs. They were framed black and white prints. Many were so rotted that the image they portrayed had been completely spoiled. But others retained some detail as her eyes adjusted to the gloom. They were everywhere on the walls. She thought there must have been close to a hundred of them. She felt compelled to look more closely.

There was a shot of Spalding sharing a boxing ring with a grinning, hirsute Ernest Hemingway. A sign behind them on the gymnasium wall advertised Caporal cigarettes. There was a shot of Spalding in harsh sunlight holding up a trophy against the backdrop of a brilliant, billowing sail. In black tie and tails, he chatted to a strong-featured woman in a feather boa in front of the wheels of a giant locomotive hewn from ice. Elsewhere he was poised on his toes in a bathing costume, darkly tanned and muscular at the end of a diving board. There was a formal portrait of Gubby Tench, grinning under the ragged rim of hair and bone where the top of his skull had been. His teeth were stained and his eyes were open and he still held in his lap the Very pistol that had ended his life. One photograph showed a headless, limbless female torso puddled in congealing gore on a rubber sheet. A blood-soaked linen towel had been folded neatly beside the corpse. The victim was young and possessed a slender waist and high, pert breasts. The handle of a boning knife protruded from the area just below her sternum. In a landscape shot, three crosses illuminated by the light of burning torches had men in uniforms nailed to them with bayonets, upside down. The bayonets had been hammered to the hilt through their ankles and wrists. The left hand of each man had been hacked off and stuffed in his mouth. Fingers protruded like the scrambling limbs of pale spiders. The expressions on their faces told Suzanne that this work had been done to the men while they were still living.

She began to back away from this image of obscene atrocity, recoiling instinctively, stumbling slightly. Then she stopped. There was a sort of rustling noise over by the bookcase to her right. She did not look towards it.

'Don't leave us so soon, Jane,' a high, harsh voice from over by the bookcase said. And she knew it was the voice of Harry Spalding. He was aboard already.

Suzanne risked a look across the cabin. Spalding wasn't there. She heard his laughter, a dry and penetrating chuckle devoid of mirth. It was the recording machine. She saw the waxed cylinder on its spindle, saw the handle that had no right to do so on its own, revolving slowly to crank out the words. She heard Spalding's disembodied laughter again. It was an awful sound.

'See you soon, Jane. Can't begin to tell you how much I'm looking forward to it.'

'Where are you?'

There was a pause. 'I've a suite at the Palace Hotel.'

'It isn't there any more. It was pulled down. It was demolished forty years ago.'

'It's there, Jane,' Spalding said. 'It's there if you know where to look.'

He slipped between worlds, voyaged through the past in the periods of the boat's dereliction. After what she had accomplished, she did not think he would be doing it any more after tonight.

She turned towards the door. There was a small brass mirror screwed to the wall to the right of the doorframe. The metal was tarnished and the glass was cracked. But the reflection it showed was rich with glamour and detail.

In the waxy illumination of a dozen or more large candles, Spalding was fastidious in spectacles and cotton gloves and a buttoned, chalk stripe three-piece suit. His hair had been carefully combed and gleamed almost a tortoiseshell colour, groomed with cream or oil. He was standing at his cabin desk unstrapping the fastenings of a circular box made from rich, embossed leather. Its buckles were silver in the candle flames. He undid the last of them. He lifted the lid and smiled. There was no sound. It had happened, Suzanne was sure. But she knew it wasn't happening now, to her rear. It wasn't happening now because behind her, the cabin was entirely silent. But she had no doubt it had happened. What she was seeing had occurred.

He placed the lid delicately on the desktop and put a hand into the box. It emerged again, gripping a human head by the hair. Suzanne recognised the heavy-featured woman who had chatted to Spalding wearing a feather boa before the frozen locomotive in one of the photographs on the walls. She no longer had need of her feathers. Her hair was auburn and abundant and her neck ended in a ragged absence. Spalding smiled and turned the head slowly by the hair in the grip of his fist. In candlelight, it still wore the creamy pallor of life. Then he closed his eyes and brought the head close and kissed it passionately on the mouth.

Suzanne dragged her eyes away. She turned round. She saw only the gloom of the cabin. One of the pictures fell from the wall with a decayed thump when it hit the floor.

The mirror seemed to blink, bright and sudden like a camera flash. She looked back into it. She did not possess the will to look away. The scene had changed. Spalding was in evening wear. The cabin was bright under a glittering chandelier. A woman Suzanne thought might be Helen Sykes reclined with a drink on a leather sofa. Yes, it was Helen Sykes. Suzanne recognised the jewellery that had glittered in the soil under the hard lights of the police excavation, adorning Helen's remains.

Suzanne groaned. Helen faced the mirror in an ivory satin gown. She was blonde and quite stunningly beautiful. No wonder Vera Chadwick had felt insecure, with friends like Jane and Helen around. Her long legs were crossed at the knee. She was laughing at something Spalding was saying, standing to her rear, busying himself with a cocktail shaker. She seemed relaxed and amused, having a good time.

And then he turned and made a remark. And Helen paled and stiffened as though petrified at whatever it was he had said. And in two strides he crossed to her and bent and drew a knife smoothly across her bare throat and just as swiftly recoiled again. He had moved with the speed of a striking snake. Helen's drink slipped from her fingers. There was a pause when nothing else happened. And then blood engulfed her dress in a purple tide and she brought her hands hopelessly to her throat and her feet thrummed on the cabin floor.

Spalding strolled around to the front of the sofa. He moved more deliberately now. He had taken off his coat. There was a cocktail glass in his hand. There was a towel over his shoulder. He dropped it to the floor and used his foot to move it, mopping the blood. Helen's legs jerked behind him in spasm. Spalding mopped with the towel under his shoe. He was calmly dealing with the aftermath of the murder before the life had fully drained from his victim. He sipped almost absently from his cocktail glass as he dealt with the mess.

The mirror went dark. It was reflecting the present again, the dank gloom of what lay behind Suzanne. She lowered her eyes and shivered. She heard the wet stab of a needle into a cylinder of corrupt wax and the silence groaned into sound. There was the crump of artillery fire and the screams and imploring of men. There was a snatch of marching song. There was the hard stride of a jazz piano and low conversation and wind thrumming against canvas and some sonorous recitation of verse and more screams, female this time. There was the judder of a springboard and the spinning ball of a roulette wheel and a pistol hammer being cocked and high, bitter laughter. She heard more moans, anguished, infant. Water lapped idly as though against tiled sides of a pool in sunlight. Cloth tore raggedly and beads unravelled from their string and danced on a floor of stone, and there was the saw of a knife though something yielding and wet. Ice tinkled in a glass and matches struck and flared and there was the low murmur of seductive conversation. She was hearing the soundtrack of Spalding's long and destructive life and bleak music it made, she thought, but it played with a churning glee.

'What a time I've had,' his voice whispered to her. 'What a time, Jane!'

And now it's over, she thought, clutching her bag under her arm, fingering the copper talisman of her lucky penny deep in her pocket. You're human again. You don't know it yet, but you are. And you can die like anyone else. And by God, you will.

She walked out, towards the door of Martin's cabin. His door was unlocked. She tested the handle and it moved freely. She opened the door a chink. Everything inside was darkness and silence. There was a smell of decomposition that was sour and sweet at the same time. She did not think it was human decomposition, though. It was not the smell of a rotting corpse. It smelled like food, as though rations had been hoarded here and then allowed to go bad. She entered the room and felt her way about it in darkness. She became aware of the shape of a sleeping figure in a chair. There was another in the bunk. She could tell from the silvery outline of his head that this was Magnus. The figure in the chair stirred. And Martin awoke and saw her with eyes that must have grown entirely accustomed in there to the prevailing absence of light.

'Suzanne?' His voice was a whisper, hoarse, incredulous and fearful.

She rushed to him and gathered him in her arms.

'How did you get aboard?'

'We're aground.'

'You've got to get away. Spalding is coming. You have to get away, Suzanne. You should not have come aboard. He's real and alive and he's coming.' Martin had stood. He was half pulling and half dragging her out of the cabin towards the companionway. She stopped and shook off his grip. She slapped him as hard as she could, realising as the heel of her palm hit his jaw that he was bearded. Something slithered against her leg.

'What was that?'

'A rat,' Martin said, dully.

'Nice.'

'Rats aren't the half of it. He's coming, Suzanne.'

'I got the log you sent Delaunay, Martin. I read it. I found you. I came here deliberately and I won't leave without you.'

'He can't get you, too. Oh, God, he can't.'

She slapped him again. She was very frightened and she loved him very much, but there were times when he was too noble for his own good. She was not running away. Not by herself, she wasn't. They were all getting out of this. 'What's wrong with your father?'

Magnus Stannard was a light sleeper, she knew. He had not stirred.

'Has he had a stroke?'

'I don't think so. I think it's shock. He has stirred, sort of, once. But he lapsed back again, deeper, afterwards. I've been feeding him, chewing his food. He throws a lot of it up.' He looked with concern and tenderness at his unconscious father.

'Can we get any light in here?'

He gripped her shoulders. 'There's no time. Spalding is coming.'

'Matches, candles – think, Martin. I want him to come. I want him to see the light burning all over the boat and come here in a rush. His haste will be our advantage.'

Martin smiled. She thought that he looked beaten. She hoped for all their sakes he wasn't. 'Not much of an advantage,' he said. He found candles and lit one. Suzanne's eyes, too, had by now become accustomed to the cabin gloom. The candlelight seemed very bright, dispelling it. She looked at Magnus, who looked grey-complexioned under his grey hair. But his breathing did not sound laboured in his sleeping retreat from the world. She saw a framed picture on the wall. She took in its detail. She knew it from Martin's description, a black and white picture of the two of them taken at some garden party. Magnus had had it done as a surprise. Except that now it showed Jane Boyte sharing a picnic on what Suzanne thought looked like College Green in Dublin with Michael Collins.

Martin had his head in his hands.

'Marty?'

'Yes?'

She thought he looked very handsome in his beard. 'Do you remember what I said to you? When I was leaving for my trip to Dublin that wasn't to Dublin at all?'

'Yes. You said there is no room in your life for ghosts.'

'It wasn't true when I said it. It was more in the way of a wish than a fact. I'd like, more than anything, to make it true.'

'Then wish it harder.'

But Suzanne knew that wishing would never be enough.

'He's coming,' Martin said.

'Can you carry your father?'

'He's my dad. Of course I can.'

'Then put him over your shoulder and follow me. We're leaving.'

Martin had to knot a rope around his father's chest and lower him down from the deck to the sand where Suzanne waited. As he tied the knot and looped the rope through a block and tackle in the rigging, she looked to see if there was any thinning of the fog around the boat. But there was not. It was dense, enveloping.

Their feet were wet, sloshing around the hull. The tide was coming in to bear the *Dark Echo* away. Spalding would be here soon, on his way to board her. Her master would want to set her course and take her helm when she floated off the sand. Martin's tread was heavy under the burden of his father. He was strong, but his ordeal had weakened him. She hoped with all her heart he had some fight still left to offer.

Suzanne heard something large slither or scuttle, crablike, through the folds of mist. Martin must have heard it, too, because he stopped.

'Jane!' a voice said.

Martin put his father down carefully on a dry bar of sand amid the swelling rivulets of incoming tide. The scuttling sound clattered through the mist again.

'Oh, it's good to see you, Jane! You've no idea of the fun we're going to have.' Spalding's voice rattled and brayed through the foggy air. Martin Stannard took off his shirt and dropped it on the sand and raised his fists. Suzanne saw with a sinking heart that the old knife wound on his arm had opened up again. It was deep and suppurating. The flesh was raw and the bruising around it a livid yellow. A blow exploded from the fog and caught him flush on the jaw. Martin staggered, but he did not go down. His adversary scuttled, on the edge of sight, poised for another assault.

'We'll conclude that tender business begun at the Shelbourne, Jane. I can promise you I've matured since then.

We'll linger over our embraces. You'll enjoy me. I'll enjoy you. I know now how to take my time. I know how to pleasure a woman.'

A kick, no more than a vicious blur of a blow, followed the punch, doubling Martin up with its force. He groaned and gathered himself and resumed his guard.

'Necessary chastisement,' the voice said. 'You've been intolerably insubordinate.'

'Come and chastise me, then.'

'You can't beat me,' Spalding crooned from somewhere close.

'You're old,' Martin said. 'It's a young man's game.' He spat a tooth on to the sand.

Suzanne could see the hatred and contempt in him, giving him strength, feeding him endurance. He had suffered aboard the boat. She thought that his arm looked gangrenous. She could have wept for him. She could have wept for all three of them in the fearful proximity of Harry Spalding. But she needed to wait. She was obliged to bide her time.

A punch pistoned out of mist and hit Martin squarely in the face and broke his nose with a sharp snap of bone. And he staggered and reeled. And Suzanne saw a hulking, agile shape come on to him. But he did not go down. And somehow, Martin slipped the follow-up blow. And in the blur of fog she heard him land the first measured and precise punches of his own. They landed solidly in a hard and rapid cluster. Suzanne could hear their impact more than see them hit home. Spalding was still just an indistinct, dangerous, imposing shape. But Martin could hit, Suzanne knew. She'd seen how destructively he could fight up close in the bright glare of a tube carriage. Through the dark unseeing air, she heard Martin's fists beat a spiteful tattoo of retaliation. And she was sure Spalding could not now avoid becoming human again. She had done what was needed to make him so.

Spalding countered then with a huge blow of his own and Martin staggered under its impact back out of the mist. The mist was thinning, shrinking. He took another clubbing punch and this time, he did go down, sinking to his knees on the swift-flooding sand. He was hurt, stunned. And he was damaged. The side of his face looked punctured like a balloon, to Suzanne, his handsome features spoiled, his cheekbone smashed. Spalding stole into sight, the first of him a rotting canvas boat shoe under the flapping hem of ragged whites, as he tipped Martin with a toe at the temple and then pressed his head down hard into the ooze of the tide. Martin's head and shoulder sank in a drowning fizz of bubbles and blood. Scum on the water lapped at his floating hair. Suzanne watched and thought that it did not matter. It did not matter to her that he had lost the fight. He had possessed the strength to accomplish this. He had antagonised Harry Spalding into her sight. That was Martin's victory. That was all that signified for any of them, now.

Suzanne took Jane Boyte's pistol out of her bag. She took the pistol she had retrieved from the museum strongbox and that Delaunay had devoutly blessed. She flicked off the safety catch and she raised and steadied and aimed the weapon, entirely mindful of Boland's considered advice about shooting people. And Harry Spalding turned and grinned at her, because he did not know. She had time to see that the decades of bloodlust had turned his eyes from the bright blue Jane had described to a dark crimson, and that the teeth in his grinning skull were almost black. And then she emptied the full eight-bullet magazine into his body.

She dropped the pistol on to the sand. She pulled Martin

from under the tide. When his eyes opened, alertness had returned to them. In the aftermath of the shots, the fog began more rapidly to clear. But no corpse was revealed to them on the shore. There were just rags and bones there when they looked, the bones mired and sinking and the rags washing away in flurries on urgent water.

'Pick up your father, Martin,' Suzanne said. 'We're going home.'

Martin pawed at his face where the cheekbone was depressed. There was raw agony in his expression. He was trying to control himself, to accommodate the pain. But he was very badly hurt. When he spoke, his voice was shaky and the words slurred with shock. 'My dad knew that Spalding kept coming back to the boat.'

'Hush.'

'He half came round last night, told me as much.'

'Hush, Martin.'

'He hoped Spalding might return once more. He thought he would be charming, like Jay Gatsby.'

'It's hurting you to talk.'

'I need to tell you this.'

She nodded. Martin's voice was an urgent slur in the damage done to him.

'My dad thought Spalding might share the secret with him of communicating with the dead. He never reconciled himself. Not to the loss of his wife. Not to the loss of his daughter. He never gave up on that hope.'

'It's overrated,' Suzanne said.

'What is?'

'Communicating with the dead.'

Martin looked at her. 'He thought you were Jane Boyte.'

'I've got to know Jane.'

'What was she like?'

'Brave and beautiful.'

'Sounds like someone I know.' He smiled. He looked terrible. His jaw was swollen and his cheekbone was fractured. He was missing a tooth and his broken nose was dripping blood down from his chin on to his chest. He was slurring his words like a drunk.

'How is your arm?'

'Oh, you know. Getting better already.'

Suzanne saw a burnished flicker on the water beneath her and wondered if the sun was coming up. But when she turned, she saw that the light was coming from the wrong direction for the dawn. And it was not the sun at all. It was still much too early for the sun. The candles they had lit to lure her master had caught aboard the boat. And the paraffin she had smelled must have caught from the candle flames. And the *Dark Echo* was ablaze now, a listing pyre drifting off on the tug of the tide, orange and burning fiercely and finally, fittingly she thought, doomed.

No one would mourn her. But her belated fate was one that others should have witnessed and enjoyed. It was a pity they could not. A strong part of Suzanne wished that Frank Hadley and Jack Peitersen and Patrick Boyte and Bernard Hodge and Monsignor Delaunay could be watching this. And maybe, too, the brave and taciturn farmer, Duval. And Captain Straub of the proud and bedraggled *Andromeda*. And Magnus Stannard, of course. Magnus was missing it, in his therapeutic slumber on the shore. There were others, people long dead, she thought might enjoy the spectacle. In being dead, without the strictures of the living, perhaps they were. Actually, she was sure they were. But she had given up on ghosts. And she sincerely hoped that ghosts had altogether given up on her.

Suzanne crossed the distance between them to Martin, bloodied and filthy as he was, and she embraced him. 'I love you,' she said.

'Thank God you do,' he said.

'Pick your father up and carry him,' she said. 'Gather your dad gently, Marty. Gather him gently, now. We're all of us going home.'

Epilogue

I almost lost the arm. It was touch and go for while, but the surgeon was skilful and persistent and he saved it. The physiotherapy was even more painful and boring than the first time I managed to hurt it. But the muscle recovered and the skin grafts took and eventually I healed. The arm would never punch with the speed and impact it had once possessed. But I hoped and prayed my punching days were over and could be forgotten.

I thought my father's recovery would be trickier. I had not known until we got aboard the boat how debilitated grief had made him. His spirit had been damaged and diminished even at the outset of the voyage. Retirement gave him the time to dwell, I think, on the people he had loved and cherished in his life and lost. His latest marriage had disintegrated. Chichester was only a superficial thing, a diversion that did not really divert him at all from the pain and solitude that he felt. He bet everything on the boat providing him not just with a challenge but with a new way of living. He bet everything. And, of course, he lost.

I thought that a return to business, even a partial return, might be beneficial for him. Or I thought that he might take a more active role in a charity. He has always been a generous giver to the needy. He could have taken on a more structured role in representing one of these good causes. It would have been a positive thing to do. Virtue is its own reward, as the saying goes. But it did not work out like that, because he found a new vocation. He still Chichesters off on his libidinous trips to Bath, or Edinburgh, or even Chichester itself, from time to time. I'm pretty sure he does. His housekeeper finds the first-class rail travel tickets in his suits when she searches the pockets before they go to be cleaned and pressed. But this pursuit no longer has the importance in his life for him that it did.

It's coming up for two years since Suzanne and I were married by Monsignor Delaunay. We married as soon as my arm had properly healed and my face had stopped looking like something had stampeded over it. She fell pregnant almost straight away. Our son is called Michael. I like the name. I like simple, traditional names. And Suzanne, who has given up on ghosts, nevertheless feels that some debts have to be acknowledged and properly honoured.

Magnus Stannard is a grandfather. That's his new vocation. He has taken to the role with energy and infinite joy. His grandson is the reason for his recovery. Delaunay was right in predicting that, what seems like a lifetime ago. It would be stretching a point to say that good has come from bad. But we have survived something very bad and have gained something better than merely good. It is all anyone can hope for. It is our truest and most enduring hope. We all endeavour, in our lives, to emerge from darkness into light.